A Game of

Starlight

and Secrets

GRACE MARTIN

PART ONE

Tethia woke up as the stretcher was being pushed into the back of a van. She kept her eyes closed so the people murmuring around her didn't realise that she'd woken up. She didn't know why she was on a stretcher. She had no medical conditions – at least, none she was aware of. She had no recollection of being in an accident. There was a pain in her temple – that was new. She listened, eyes closed, to the hushed voices.

'Everything will be better in the morning.' It could be a man. It could just as easily be an unTied person. Given the professional tone, it was unlikely to be a woman. The motion of the stretcher stopped.

'Checkpoint.' Tethia recognised the bored voice of the guard. She passed that checkpoint every day. They were at the gates of the Special Services division of the Imperial Military Services. She listened closely. After a moment she heard what she'd been listening for: the double thump of the stretcher wheels going over the security grid. Were they taking her back to her quarters? Did that make sense?

'Wait – I think she might be waking up.' That was a different voice. A familiar voice. Tethia carefully kept her features lax but inside she was seething. The next time she saw Tannep she was going to castrate him.

'She won't wake up.' The androgynous voice was soothing. 'I assure you, we're very good at what we do.'

Not good enough, Tethia thought smugly.

Tannep spoke again. 'What if someone tells her she's been Re-Educated?'

The stretcher stopped. Tethia's blood ran cold. Keeping her face still and relaxed, she frantically searched her mind. Why would they have taken her to Re-Ed? She'd done nothing wrong. She spent most of her life not only following the rules but making sure others followed them, too. She hadn't done a single thing to earn her a visit from an Auditor.

Well, she amended privately, not for the last fifteen years anyway. She'd paid the price for that infraction with her silence. There was only one person who knew. No one else knew about her daughter. There was no way, *no way* anyone could know about Sheya.

But if she'd been to Re-Ed, maybe she'd broken her conditions for some reason? What could possibly have made her do such a stupid thing? Now her memories had been tampered with. Re-Educators were probably specialists, but that didn't mean that Tethia wanted her brain taken apart and put back together again.

She was so busy searching her mind she didn't notice that the talkers had fallen quiet. In the silence, there was the sound of an odd little beep. 'Another dose, I think.'

'But she'll remember!'

'She won't remember.' The androgynous voice was calm. 'The medication only makes her sleep. The memory reorganisation is carried out by skilled professionals. How else do you think we could get someone to forget specific people and events and not become a vegetable? She's already finished the Re-Education process. Those troublesome memories are forgotten and we have a nice obedient Lieutenant on our hands again.'

'But what if she finds out she's been Re-Educated?'

'So what if she does? She'd be a fool to break the Laws again. As long as she keeps the Laws, I personally don't care *what* she remembers.'

Tethia told herself later she'd felt the drug go into her vein, but it was hard to be sure as was suddenly so very, very sleepy.

#

Tethia woke, bleary eyed and heavy with dreams. She looked around her room in the barracks and noticed with growing horror that the dawning lights near the ceiling were already on. She turned the other way to look through the protectively-tinted window. The nebula had already set and the sky was completely dark. Her heart pounded a frenzied rhythm from her dream, and more important than any dream – she was late!

She dressed quickly, with an efficiency born of thirteen years of military service. She didn't hurry – that would be unseemly. As she closed the door behind her, she realised that she'd forgotten something. In sheer desperation, she pressed her forehead against the cool metal of the door. She'd forgotten the damn bird.

She hurried back inside the room – seemliness be

4

damned! – and leaned over the table to get the bowl of feed from the windowsill. She paused.

The window was shut. Locked.

She never locked her window. She was on the fifth floor. It wasn't as though anyone would ever come in unannounced via a fifth-floor window. And, here in New Rome, the dome protected the atmosphere from both the dangerous exposure to the nebula and from the vagaries of the weather. It was neither too hot nor too cold, so windows were more ornamental than anything. She never locked her window. If she did that, then the falcon might get trapped and as much as she loved the bird, it was still a wild thing. She loved it for its wildness, its strength and independence.

Her foot bumped something under the table. She went very still. Her heart still pounding a tattoo from her dream and her race out the door, she stepped back slowly. The falcon was on the floor, underneath the desk. She knelt, stretched out a hand. The feathers she had never dared touch before seemed almost rough. The flesh beneath them was cold and still.

Tethia snatched her hand back, a cry of disgust escaping her. She rose to her feet and shot open the window. She picked up the dead, magnificent thing and flung it out the window into the dark morning, then turned and ran from the room.

There were three separate checkpoints between the Officer's Barracks and Tethia's office in the Imperial Military Special Services building and at every single one she had to slow down to a respectable speed, cast her eyes down like a respectable woman and allow them to search her briefcase. At every single one she had to make a statement, as she did six times a day, every day of her working life, that the computer she carried was used solely for the purpose of work.

'In accordance with conservation and wastage laws,' she repeated each time, thinking irreverently that detaining her this way when she was clearly running late – look at the time! –should be against some kind of law. Wasting time was surely as bad as wasting resources? But there was no point, so she kept her eyes down and said what she was supposed to say.

The sentries looked at her closely in the amber light of the checkpoints, the lightsticks set so close that each pool of light overlapped into the next, ironically known as lovers-light. Out in the suburbs the lights were spaced further apart. Where the pools of light did not meet, they were known as stranger-light. While Tethia's foot ached to tap impatiently where the lovers-light overlapped, she didn't feel much like a lover, more like a vengeful ex.

And then, when she *finally* reached the Special Services offices, she couldn't even get in. There was a crowd being held back by Servicemen dressed in distinctive black uniforms. Tethia wasn't tall enough to catch a glimpse of what was happening over the shoulders of the grey-garbed Servicemen in front of her, all waiting patiently to be let into the building.

There was the sound of people making an undignified commotion – shouting and yelling, grunting from others who were probably trying to restrain the shouters. Finally, irritated beyond bearing with shifting from foot to foot waiting in the street, Tethia tapped the shoulder of the Serviceman in front of her.

'How much longer is this going to take?' she demanded, raising her voice so it could be heard above the hubbub.

The Serviceman turned, a look of irritation on his face that was swiftly changed to deference when he saw in the white light that surrounded the offices that she outranked him. Tethia smirked – but only on the inside because she wasn't an idiot. Since she outranked him, she didn't have to keep her eyes downcast and she could eyeball him properly.

'I said, how much longer is this going to take, Corporal?'

'Salve, sir! I can't say for sure, sir! It only started a few minutes ago, sir.'

'Well, what's going on then?' She kept her voice sharp. It made her easier to hear.

'Deviants, sir! Audited and found to be committing infractions against the Laws, sir.'

Tethia ground her teeth together. Deviants were the province of the Auditors and the Re-Educators. They had nothing to do with her and therefore there was nothing she could do to influence the situation.

The corporal went on. 'I don't know which Laws they broke, sir.'

'Did I *ask* you which Laws they broke?' Tethia snapped. 'What do I care what a bunch of Deviants do? I just want to get to work like a good little Lieutenant. Now clear me a path to the front. If I'm not the first person through those doors, even an Auditor won't be able to help you!'

'Sir!' He saluted smartly, if awkwardly, to avoid hitting another Serviceman in the crush around them. He turned and grabbed the man next to him, muttering frantically. In a moment, the two of them were shoving their way to the front, Tethia trailing behind. It took a few minutes but, by the time the doors were re-opened, Tethia was among the first to shove her way through. She didn't cast another look at the two corporals who had cleared her way.

She hurried – respectably – into her office then drew a deep breath in, solely for the joy of letting it out. Her heart still pounded, and the rapid breathing fostered by sheer panic hadn't helped.

'Kela,' she whispered to the woman sitting at one of the desks, 'did I make it on time?'

Kela looked up sharply, her blue eyes serious. 'No one could get in, Lu. They were removing the Deviants. No one would hold being late against you today.'

'I'm never late.'

'No, you're never late.' Kela's voice made Tethia look up. She wasn't sure if her assistant was trying to be soothing or sarcastic.

'How did you get here on time?' Tethia asked.

'I have no life outside this place,' Kela said drily. 'Come on. Get to your desk. You'll draw attention standing like that.'

Kela was right. Tethia sat down and spent a few minutes rifling through the papers on her desk to gain control of herself. She drew the computer out of her briefcase.

'Is there anything interesting out there today?'

Kela quirked an eyebrow but didn't pause in her typing. 'On your desk, Lu. My handwriting.'

'One day someone's going to hear you call me that,' Tethia warned, finding the envelope with Kela's obsessively tidy writing on it. 'They'll haul you away for being too familiar with your superior.'

'And I'll tell them I meant to say "Lieutenant" only I've got this awful frog in my throat.' Kela finally stopped typing, looked up and grinned. She coughed a few times, experimentally. 'It's your fault. Here I am a dusty old maid and it's your fault.'

'UnTied is not the same as an old maid. Being unTied is a choice and a privilege.'

'It wasn't my choice... *Lu.* I've been working for you for the last five years, watching the best years of my youth slip away, all because you won't introduce me to your brother.' She smoothed a strand of short, pale hair past her ear and looked haughty.

Tethia laughed. Kela had been her assistant for five years and by now it was an old joke. 'He's not your type. You have a sense of humour and the capacity for independent thought. He has neither of those.'

'But he's the best boxer in New Rome.'

'So I hear. I don't much like sports, but people keep telling me about them. I've never understood what was so amazing about two men bludgeoning one another.'

'He *is* amazing, Lu. I saw him in the arena the other day. He took his shirt off in front of the crowd before the match and I swear the whole arena sighed.' Kela rested her head on her hand dreamily. 'I don't want much. Just let him wrap me in those big muscular arms just once and I'll die happy.'

'You would die, so be sure you've made out a will. You'd smother. He's got an awful stink after a match.'

Kela wrinkled her nose. 'You know that's disgusting, right?'

'He's my brother. Of course I know he's disgusting.'

The door of the office was safely closed, protecting the quiet giggles of the two unTied people. It also muffled Tethia's gasp when she opened the envelope.

#

Half an hour later, Tethia and Kela were in the main

11

conference room. Tethia was seated at the large metal table, its surface polished to a shine that revealed every set of fingerprints, so she sat back a little to avoid smirching it. She kept the trembling of her hands in her lap, sitting upright in what would otherwise be a comfortable chair. The subtle golden lighting from the centre of the table and near the ceiling illuminated the formal, yet frugal room. Even the decoration of a conference room fell under wastage Laws.

She kept her eyes downcast. The General would arrive soon, and any impropriety would be a gross impertinence. Kela stood behind her chair, her hands clasped and eyes downcast. They were the only unTied people in the room.

A few quiet words were uttered when each one came in. A word of greeting here and there. Tethia had learned to recognise nearly everyone without seeing their faces, so she murmured her greetings with the rest. She was deferential, polite. They all outranked her. Even their assistants – male, so they could look around but were still required to be silent – nearly equalled her in rank.

One of the officers near Tethia knocked on the table once when the General entered, to let Tethia know it was time to rise to her feet. That was something they'd only

introduced in the last fifteen years, since unTied women
had been admitted to membership in the Special Services.
Until Caesar had proclaimed the Edict of Caracalla, unTied
people hadn't existed under the law and women hadn't
even been full Citizens, so the question of admitting them
to the military had been redundant. Now they had to make
room in military ceremonial for the presence of unTied
people. The assumption that everyone in the room could at
least *see* what was going on was an assumption the military
could no longer afford.

Fifteen years and they're still not ready for a
woman to look up yet, Tethia thought bitterly.

She sat, polite and civil as assignments were handed
around, receiving hers obediently with hands that trembled.
She'd got it! Kela had been right! The trouble was that she
had to endure the rest of the meeting before she could go
somewhere private and whoop for joy. She straightened the
file in front of her, aligning the manila cover so it was
perpendicular to the edge of the table. She kept her eyes
down, as was appropriate for a woman, even a woman who
was unTied and an officer and therefore a Citizen and not a
woman at all.

The General droned on.

Tethia struggled to stay awake. The manila folder,

its contents hidden, was not nearly exciting enough to keep her mind off her dreams. Her head had been reeling with them this morning, so close and real that it was hard to tell them from reality. It all seemed so jumbled! Running along dark streets, chased by shadowy foes. A face from the past, mixed in with a crowd of faces both half familiar and fully foreign. There were whispered messages, lost in the shock of sudden waking and under it all was Sheya.

Her daughter.

No one could know. She hadn't been married, not even betrothed and even after Caracalla, an unQualified mother was no mother at all. Tethia had given Sheya up for a quiet adoption when she was born fifteen years ago and promised the Auditors faithfully that she would never breathe a word about her infraction.

She'd only seen her once, a strange coloured jumble of sticky skin and hair, who cried out in language that even an unQualified mother understood. She wasn't allowed to hold her, nor to feed her or to kiss her. Tethia had laid back on the birthing couch and watched her daughter from a distance.

An alarm went off in a ward nearby and the midwives rushed from the room. One of them hesitated, holding Sheya, looking at her fleeing colleagues, then to

Tethia and back again.

'Hold her until I get back,' she said sternly. 'And don't you drop her.'

So Tethia held her baby after all. She'd adjusted the blanket, rocked the infant to silence. Sheya, only minutes old, had turned her head, seeking the breast. One eye on the door, Tethia pulled down the neckline of her gown and allowed her baby to feed.

She'd gotten into terrible trouble for that. They'd threatened to Re-Educate her, but she'd promised to be good, eighteen years old with tears in her eyes. Since then, Tethia tried not to think of her and often didn't. It was only in dreams that Sheya appeared, growing to young womanhood in every dream Tethia ever had.

There was nothing else in the meeting that required Tethia's attention. She watched the manila folder until she nearly fell back into dreams again. Her head nodded for one dreadful moment, jerking back up to the sudden thump of her heart. She cast surreptitious eyes to left and right, but no one seemed to have noticed. Her heart continued its heavy thumping, keeping time with the rhythm of pounding feet remembered from her dream.

Tannep Baen, General, knocked his knuckles against the polished metal tabletop to signal the end of the meeting before Tethia's heart rate had returned to normal.

'Stay behind, Tethia, Lieutenant,' Tannep Baen, General ordered as the others saluted and filed out. 'Uh, you may go, Corporal.'

'Yes, sir,' Kela murmured, a wealth of meaning in her tone that Tannep Baen, General wouldn't notice even if she put it in an Intra-Office memo.

Tethia stayed at her place, eyes downcast until she heard the door close. She looked up surreptitiously just as the General – Tannep as he'd said she was to call him when they were in private – laid a broad, square hand softly over hers, the thick, white fingers tangling intimately with her own. Most people of the New Roman Empire were albino-fair, their skin adapted to the dark sky lit by only the stars by day and the nebula by night. She stayed utterly still.

'I hope you know what a lucky girl you are,' he murmured.

Tethia raised her eyes to look at him. He was a big man, tall and solidly built, with broad shoulders and a square jaw, just like they advertised when the recruiters came around the schools. This is what you can be, they said, and it was true… if you were a boy. And every day now there was some new freedom for unTied people that made it all worth giving up being a woman.

Sure, there were still those who thought the idea of women in the military was preposterous, even if they were only allowed in the auxiliary arms of the Imperial Military Services. Tethia would never have been permitted to serve Caesar before Caracalla. To be eligible for full Citizenship, a man had to prove his ability to make a living, maintain a debt free lifestyle for five years, manage his household slaves without any infractions recorded by the Indenture Auditors – in addition to this, he had to serve Caesar for two years in military service. Since, before Caracalla, women were forbidden to join the Imperial Military Services, they had been automatically ineligible for Citizenship.

As it was, even now, women could only be full Citizens if they were respectably married to a Citizen; if they were the respectable, unmarried daughter of a Citizen; or if they were an unmarried woman who had jumped through the bureaucratic hoops required to be declared unTied. As an unTied person Tethia would never be permitted to contract a legal marriage, but at least she could be a legal Citizen. Anything better than being Tied to a slave or a Freedman. Then she would have had no hope of advancement. Marriage would be no compensation for the loss of the privileges she currently enjoyed as a Citizen.

That was what made the General's propositions so difficult. The thought of allowing his thick fingers to touch her made her skin crawl, but Tethia had spent her whole life in the Empire. She should do whatever was necessary to stay safe.

'Yes, you're a lucky girl.' His voice was slower now, thicker, as his fingers stroked hers.

She should have said, "Yes, sir." She should have murmured it. Instead she snapped, 'I think you mean 'Lieutenant,' sir!' and the look she flashed at him was anything but femininely submissive.

He took his hand away. Tethia sneaked another glance at him. He looked angry – well, she should have expected that.

'I apologise, sir!' she said, before he had a chance to say anything else. 'Women are known to be emotional and prone to responding poorly in times of stress, sir!'

To her surprise he laughed. 'You don't even know how right you are, you little smartarse.'

'No, sir!'

He leaned closer. 'You have just been given the best assignment to ever cross my desk and you have the nerve to be impertinent while the folder is still in your hands?' He flung himself away from her. 'You ungrateful little bitch!'

He came back in a rush, as she'd known he would. He plucked her easily out of her chair and threw her across the room. She fell hard against the wall and scrambled to her feet, keeping her eyes downcast. Plenty of people would have heard the impact. No one would come.

'I'm sorry, sir,' she whispered hoarsely, the breath knocked out of her.

'You damn well ought to be sorry and by Caesar's Mask you *will* be.' He was in front of her now, his hands on her shoulders shoving her into the wall. 'I'll have you know that Caesar – *Caesar!* – requested *you* specifically, you little piece of garbage! If it wasn't for that then so help me, I'd-'

He shoved himself away from her so suddenly that she fell. The manila folder's contents were all over the floor. She didn't dare pick them up. Slowly, she got back to her feet.

'Ala Freeo is the niece of Caesar himself,' the General said. 'She needs to be Qualified to give birth to Caesar's child. She spent most of her life in exile on Capreae so she will need your services as a linguist while she is Audited. As it happens, you are our *only* female linguist and the *only* linguist fluent in the Imperial tongue, which is the *only* reason you are on this assignment. All of this is classified information. All the rest of the world needs to know is that you're doing more translations of ancient materials at the Imperial Library. If the newsspeakers get a hold of this story, I will know it was from you. I'll *start* with an Audit and once you're declared a Deviant, you're mine.'

Tethia stayed very still, pressed flat up against the wall. 'Yes, sir.'

There was a long pause while the General walked around the large table. He came back around to her side and leaned one hip against the polished metal.

'I wonder what a piece of trash like you would have done if the Edict wasn't passed to allow women to become Servicemen?'

The question surprised her but not so much she let her guard down. 'What does any woman do?' Her tone was offhand, but the answer was deliberately evasive.

'Is your father still alive?'

'If my father were alive then I would be at home, performing the duties proper to the daughter of a Citizen.'

'How did he die?'

Tethia looked away. Being caught in a lie was a serious infraction and might result in being Audited. 'It was before I came here.'

'Do you ever think that you would have been a disappointment to him?'

Tethia straightened away from the wall but didn't look up. 'Every day, General.'

He made an irritated sound. 'You're dismissed. Keep that smart mouth of yours to yourself next time.'

'Yes, sir.'

She gathered up the fallen papers and fitted them back into the manila folder. Her hands shook and she despised herself for it. She'd been through worse, and probably would again. He was her superior officer. He had the right to do anything he wanted. And in a way he was right. She really ought to learn to keep her smart mouth to herself.

Kela was waiting outside the door. She stood to attention and saluted when Tethia reappeared and led the way to their office.

'Anything need medical attention?' she asked matter-of-factly after Tethia closed the door.

'Just bruises,' Tethia said, dropping the manila folder onto her desk. She sank into her chair, her legs suddenly weak. Out of everything he'd said to her, it was the threat of being Audited that was the worst. 'I wonder what it was like for them,' she wondered aloud.

'Who?'

'The Deviants, this morning. I wonder what it was like, realising they were going to be Audited? I think I'd lay down and die if I ever found a yellow card at my desk.'

'You wouldn't be Audited,' Kela said, going to sit at her own desk. 'Not if you hadn't done anything wrong.'

'No, of course not,' Tethia said.

Kela was discreet. She played the part of the helpful assistant to perfection, although Tethia knew that Kela was pushing herself hard, every day, to become more and more fluent in the languages of the New Roman Empire so that she could pass the test to become a linguist and join Tethia as an equal. She went to prepare refreshments for them before they went out on their business into the city. So discreet. Tethia took the time to gain control of herself again.

#

A first level Auditor accompanied them to their first appointment, meeting them at the underground train station that departed from within the Special Services compound. He was pacing up and down the platform, his black cloak billowing around his black and silver uniform, listening to a newsspeaker give the Daily Review. The newsspeaker's blank eyes stared right past the Auditor as he paced. The only people who didn't have to worry about Auditors were the newsspeakers, for whom the worst had already happened. Once convicted of a serious crime, their minds were wiped and filled with the daily news for dissemination to the public. The Re-Educators programmed the newsspeakers every day, but it was the Auditors who took them to Re-Ed in the first place.

The Auditor saw them coming and stopped pacing.

'Salve,' he said in greeting. 'My name is Berisus.'

'Salve,' Tethia replied, bowing her head. It was always jarring to hear someone introduce himself without giving his family names, but as an Auditor, his family connections were irrelevant. 'I am Tethia of Valdennes, Lieutenant, daughter of Meropius, General. I am the Serviceman who will be translating for you in this Audit, as well as serving as a witness. This is my assistant, Kela Sirron, Corporal, who will serve as the second witness.'

'Pleased to meet you,' Beris said cheerfully. He was much younger than Tethia, barely even old enough to be an Auditor. He was only pledged to accompany them to the Audit in Gatheron. A first level Auditor wouldn't be allowed to even speak to Caesar's niece.

The train arrived. Beris stood back and gestured the women forward with unnecessary politeness.

'It's my first Audit,' he admitted when the train pulled out of the underground station and headed towards the outskirts of the city. He flashed each of them an engaging grin. 'Be gentle with me then, eh?' He opened up a manila folder similar to the one Tethia had received that morning. 'We've got a woman in Gatheron who needs Qualification for childbearing, but it should all be done well before lunchtime. Have you been translating long?' he asked Tethia.

Tethia shifted uncomfortably. Auditors didn't chat. The whole world feared them. One wrong word in an idle conversation with an Auditor could lead to Re-Education. 'Thirteen years,' she said.

'Unlucky thirteen, eh?' he joked. 'Do you enjoy it?'

'It is my work,' she said.

'It mustn't have taken you long to gain your certification. Caracalla was only, what, ten years ago?'

Tethia was aware that Kela was staring at her. 'Fifteen,' she corrected. 'And yes, I passed my certificate as soon as I attained my majority. I had been studying ever since Caracalla.'

'You must be very good,' Beris said warmly.

Tethia refused to be charmed. He was still an Auditor. She bowed her head in acknowledgement of the compliment but only said, 'I do my work to the best of my ability, sir, and I hope my assistant and I will live up to your expectations.'

Beris seemed to get the point and didn't chat any further until the train pulled into Gatheron station.

Gatheron was a poorer quarter of New Rome, where large buildings clustered together as though afraid that the dome would fail and the slow poison of starlight would fall on unprotected skin. The three of them walked along the sidewalk from the train station, looking out of place in their immaculate grey uniforms and black and white braid.

Beris looked particularly uncomfortable.

'Is it all like this?' he asked in a low voice.

'Like what?' Tethia asked. She looked around.

'All the people on the streets,' he said. 'And so many children? They can't possibly all be Counted.'

'I couldn't say, sir.' But he was right. In Gatheron there always seemed to be more people on the streets than in other areas and exponentially more children. In areas like Gatheron, many children as well as adults were unCounted, illegal residents who appeared on no census. Tethia didn't like to draw Beris's attention to it. He could destroy countless lives by an incautious word. Many residents in this area were from distant parts of the Empire, so Tethia found herself in that part of the city at least once or twice a week to translate for an Audit, a childbearing or professional Qualification or for legal and civil matters.

'Are we far away from Galalla's house?' he asked, looking nervously at a group of small children dancing in the street. They formed themselves into a circle and held hands while one of them stood in the centre, singing a song that Tethia could tell that Beris had forgotten. He must have known it as a child. Every child in the New Roman Empire knew the song.

"Starlight, starlight, underneath her skin!
From the other side of the globe
Skin burned like a tattered robe,
And her hair on the ground behind her.
Don't let her give you the starlight!"

The children broke apart and ran away, squealing as the child in the centre chased at them with her hands held out as though they were indeed infected with starsickness.

'Disgusting disease,' Beris muttered, a shudder moving up his spine. 'Did you ever know anyone who was affected?'

Tethia couldn't avoid answering a direct question,

not from an Auditor. 'I'm told that my mother had a brother. He died.'

'My father and my mother,' Kela murmured. Tethia shot her a glance. She hadn't known.

Beris shook his head. 'Disgusting. I hear they're very close to a cure now. Caesar has been very generous to the Starlight Project.'

'I couldn't say, sir,' Tethia replied.

'No, you wouldn't, would you?' he snapped. Tethia almost felt sorry for him. He didn't seem to understand his position as an Auditor. She wondered how long he'd been doing this job. 'Look, we're here now, anyway. Let's get it over with.' He turned away.

A rangy dog slipped past them as they went into Galalla's building. He bounded up to Tethia and fawned around her feet. Tethia frowned and batted at him. 'Go away!' she cried.

'He's only being friendly.' Beris reached down to pat the dog. 'He's a good boy. Are you a good boy?'

Tethia looked on, one eyebrow raised, as the Auditor made a fool of himself. Kela turned away. This was the sort of situation that could result in a yellow card.

Irritated beyond bearing, Tethia snapped. 'I said, *go away*!'

The hound stopped frisking at once. He turned to face Tethia for a moment longer than was normal. Then he turned away from Beris's caressing hands and ran back to the door. He sat down and waited patiently. Tethia followed and opened the door for him to exit the building.

Beris rose to his feet. 'That was interesting.'

Tethia froze. For a moment, she couldn't breathe for fear. She wasn't going to get a yellow card because of a damned dog. 'As you said, he's a good boy.'

Galalla lived in a small room on the fifteenth floor. The slow, rattling elevator that took the three Servicemen to the fifteenth floor was cramped. They had to stand so close together that they each breathed in the others' breath. Tethia felt Beris's eyes on her. For once she was glad she was expected to keep her eyes downcast.

A tiny woman met them at the door, her pale eyes darting around the dim corridor behind them. She only opened the door a crack, standing in the aperture so they couldn't see past her.

'Salve,' Beris said, bowing a little. That surprised Tethia. There was absolutely no need for someone of Beris's rank to bow to someone like Galalla. 'May I speak with Galalla, please?' Tethia repeated his words in Galalla's Chiaune dialect.

'I am Galalla.' The words were thickly accented, spoken more awkwardly than a child. She looked at them suspiciously, examining each of their faces closely.

Beris bowed again and gave his name as well as Tethia and Kela's. 'We are here to conduct a Qualification Audit. I believe you put in an application to bear a child?'

Galalla's tense fingers relaxed on the door frame when Tethia repeated Beris's words. She nodded and opened the door wider.

Inside the room there didn't seem to be anything that she might need to hide. Poverty wasn't yet a crime, Tethia mused. If anything, the frugality of Galalla's surroundings was a testament to the wastage and conservation laws that she herself testified to six times a day at the checkpoints. The room was clean and tidy, everything in it well cared for and arranged in an attractive manner. Galalla closed the door behind them and turned around.

Beris drew in a sharp breath and Tethia could see why. Galalla must have been at least eight months pregnant, the swollen curve of her belly showing clearly beneath her white chiton.

'You should have made this application months ago!' he said sharply.

Galalla merely stood where she was and folded her hands across her belly as Tethia translated.

'Will you sit?' Galalla offered in her own language. Beris looked around for a chair and found none. Pitying him more and more, knowing how this interview would end, Tethia sat down first, arranging her legs so she was cross-legged on the floor between Galalla and Beris and prepared herself to translate as inconspicuously as possible between the two. The others followed suit.

'Why didn't you put in an application before this?' Beris asked.

Galalla looked down at the hands she'd spread once more across her belly. The thin fingers moved in a caress against flesh that ululated beneath her touch. Beris's wide eyes followed the movement compulsively.

'My child is a part of me,' she said, her voice soft and tender. 'He is as close to me as my own heart. I love him already. I will love him more when he is born and more when he grows day by day to become a man. What need do I have of a Qualification, a man in a golden mask to tell me that I will be a good mother? I am a mother already.'

Beris went very still. 'Galalla, I must tell you – given your circumstances – you will not be allowed to bear a second child if you already have a first.'

Galalla shook her head, but her smile was luminous. 'This is my first baby. But I am a mother. See? This is my baby.' She smoothed the thin cloth of her chiton close against her belly and made the same caressing motion as before. The movement beneath her skin was visible through the fabric. 'He always does that.' She looked up at Beris, her eyes warm with humour and love for her child. 'He is clearly a baby – a woman cannot conceive and give birth to a thing that is not a baby. A baby must have a mother – that is only common sense. If he is a baby, then I am a mother.'

Beris sighed. 'Galalla, I cannot overstate the importance of this interview. I need you to speak clearly and answer my questions as honestly as you can.'

Galalla nodded.

'What is your husband's name?'

Tethia realised then that Beris was doing his best to get Galalla off the hook. All Auditors, even brand-new Auditors on their first job, knew to ask open ended questions. Their job was to allow people to incriminate themselves. They got people to talk about themselves in their own words, describe their situations and allow them to say the words that put them into Re-Education or separated mother from baby or classed what had previously been a person as unCounted.

Galalla gave a name. Beris asked her husband's profession. She replied that he worked as a janitor at the Ambience Department, where the lights that automatically came on to signify day and night were regulated.

Beris stood up. 'Thank you, Galalla, that will be all,' he said.

Kela rose to her feet but Tethia stayed seated on the carpet. She felt as though she were as heavy as lead, as though she couldn't rise to her feet if she tried. She had once been in the very same position Galalla was in. The Auditor handling her case had not been as kind as Beris. She wished with all her heart that she could allow him to be so kind.

But still... what if it wasn't kindness? What if it was a test? What if Beris had a dual purpose here today?

'Galalla,' she said heavily, 'do you have documents to prove that any of this is true?'

A vein throbbed in Galalla's temple. 'Of course,' she said softly, and rose to her feet.

Beris and Kela looked at Tethia questioningly as she stood up. She glanced up at them.

'She has to show her husband's papers,' she said heavily. 'It's p-proper procedure.' Her tongue tripped over the words, knowing what she'd done.

Galalla went to a table near the window and started shuffling through papers. 'It's so stuffy in here. Four people breathe so much bad air in a small room.' She went around the table to open the window. 'Do you have children?' Galalla didn't look at any of them in particular, her hands busy in a drawer beneath the table.

'No,' Tethia said shortly and translated her words for the others.

'Not yet,' Kela replied, her voice softer.

Beris smiled at Kela. 'Not yet for me, either.' Tethia translated back to Galalla, who looked away.

In a sudden rush, Galalla threw herself out the window.

Tethia lunged forward and caught at Galalla's hand with a sudden desperate grasp. The weight of the tiny woman wrenched her flush up against the wall and halfway out the window. Sudden fear overcame Galalla's hasty suicide attempt and now she writhed dangerously against Tethia's grip. Both her hands held onto both of Tethia's, but neither of them had a sure grip on the other.

Acting quickly, Beris grabbed Tethia around the waist to stop her following Galalla. Kela wedged herself in between them and took hold of Tethia so that Beris was free to reach down to Galalla. He caught the woman's arm, then her belt, crossed between and beneath her breasts. He heaved her upwards while she screamed and kicked. The tendons strained in his neck, his knuckles white where they held onto her. Heavy hands pounded on the locked door of the apartment, responding to her screams. Voices shouted in Galalla's dialect.

Galalla was still screaming when he raked her over the windowsill and back onto the floor of the small room. He slammed the window shut and locked it. Galalla didn't stop screaming. Not when Beris tried to comfort her, not when the ambulance came to take her to hospital. Her chiton clung wetly to her legs.

After Galalla was loaded into the secure ambulance, Beris turned to Tethia. She'd been watching the play of emotion on his face and was caught with her eyes up.

'Apologies,' she muttered, casting her eyes down.

'An apology won't fix it,' Beris snapped. 'You just ruined that woman's life – deliberately! And her child, too. She will never even touch her baby! Don't you care? No, wait,' he said, before she had a chance to speak. 'You couldn't say, is that right? What do you think will happen to her child now? Her precious boy will be sent to the Starlight Project and-' He clamped his lips together.

Tethia pounced. 'Is that where unCounted children go?'

'I shouldn't have said anything. If you had any manners, you'd let it go.'

'I thought the unCounted were adopted – by childless couples.'

'What childless couple would take an unCounted child? You can't be so naïve. The newsspeakers tell stories every day about the tainted blood in those born to unQualified mothers. Who would risk taking a tainted child into their home?'

'So, what *is* the Starlight Project?' She kept her voice light, but her heart was pounding even faster than it had when she'd made that desperate lunge to stop Galalla going out the window, even faster than it had when she'd woken from a nightmarish dream that morning.

Beris looked away from her, his eyes scanning the tall, dingy buildings around them, the stars in the dark sky above it all invisible beyond the glare of the streetlights. 'It's science,' he said finally. 'That's all. They're trying to find a cure for starsickness.'

The heavy, rhythmic pounding of Tethia's heart skipped a beat. 'With children?' she asked, trying to keep the horror out of her voice.

'They're unCounted.' Beris's voice was harsh and dismissive. 'Given what you just did, I'm astonished you even thought twice about it. Look, let's go. You've got to get to your next appointment.' He stood to the side and gestured Tethia and Kela forward. They started walking back to the train station. Beris went on, 'The trains to the Palatine always take forever this time of day.'

Tethia's feet stuttered to a stop and for a moment she feared her heart would do the same. 'How do you know where our next appointment is?' she asked, her voice thin with fear. If the General found out that even a first-day Auditor knew her business, he'd finish her off for sure. She looked up to meet Beris's eyes. She saw him hesitate, deliberately leaving her waiting. She looked down again, but she heard the pity in his voice when he answered. She wondered again why he had ever become an Auditor when he was plainly unsuited to it.

'My father is the Consul of Capreae,' he said. 'I have known Ala all my life. She told me it was you who would be coming to translate for her.'

Very briefly, in a moment of raw horror, Tethia's jaw went slack. She'd offended a Consul's son, a man who was important enough to be friends with the woman who would bear Caesar's child. Her career was over. She only had time to think it before Beris spoke again.

'Don't worry,' he said. 'I won't get you into trouble.' He sighed and started walking towards the train station. 'You were only doing your job. I suppose after a while they're all alike to you.'

They travelled in silence once they were on the train to the Palatine Hill. That was more usual with an Auditor, but with Beris it now felt uncomfortable. Most Auditors were glad not to talk. What they didn't know they didn't have to report. Tethia supposed that Beris was in such a position that he could choose to report – or not report – anything he chose.

The train was full when they got on at Gatheron Station, the people pressed close together in one heaving mass braced against the movement of the train. Beris's black cloaked figure was highly visible among the thin white chitons of the women and the serviceable brown shirts and trousers of the Tiedmen. The silver braid on his upright collar caught the light in the enclosed carriage.

A group of women seated near them rose to their feet to make a place for the Servicemen, pushing against the crush when they saw the three in uniform. Beris gestured for them to stay where they were.

'Please, sisters,' he said, raising his gentle voice to

be heard. 'Please, stay seated. We don't mind standing.' He turned to Tethia and Kela. 'Do we?'

So, of course, they had to agree. The women subsided back onto the benches, but kept casting glances at Beris. They drew their veils close around their faces and whispered, assuming no one could understand them.

Tethia tried not to listen. She looked down at her own grey uniform and mentally compared herself to the three women in chitons so close nearby, their blue belts proclaiming that they were Citizen's daughters. A Citizen's wife would have worn the same chiton, belt and brooch, but it would be hidden under a calf length mantle.

Tethia had once worn the same every day of her life until Caracalla. I'm not a woman, she thought. I'm a Serviceman. A woman wears a chiton, not trousers and a tunic. A woman wears a veil and long hair, not a peaked cap and a short haircut that is easy to maintain. She looked away, out the window at the passing city lights. Not that it made any difference. She might as well be a man. She wasn't sure why the thought unsettled her. That was the point of being unTied, to have the same rights as a Citizen.

As they came closer to the Palatine, the crowd thinned as more and more people got off. The three women left the train, gesturing to Beris, Tethia and Kela to sit.

Tethia caught another fragment of their language, spoken in the half-tamed land of Chiau where there was a revolution against the Empire at least once a month. It was the same language Galalla had spoken.

#

By the time they reached the Palatine Station, the only people left on the train were in uniform. No one went this close to Caesar unless they had a good reason. They disembarked in an orderly manner, moving efficiently on paths that were apparently familiar. In moments, the platform was deserted. Tethia would have followed them, but Beris seemed to be waiting for something, so she folded her hands and settled in with pretended patience.

'Oh, are you waiting for me?' Beris asked after what had to have been at least several long minutes. 'No, don't wait for me. I don't have to go through the public gates. My slaves will be here shortly.' He paused and looked from Tethia to Kela and back again. 'Unless… you could come with me… if you wanted to?'

'I wouldn't dream of imposing on your hospitality,' Tethia said, her lips pursed and prim. She hoped she'd never see the man again.

'I'd hoped,' he said with a nasty look, 'to hear from you – at least once before we parted – to hear one word from your mouth that wasn't a lie. I see I am to be disappointed.'

A lie! A *lie?* Before she even thought about it, Tethia's hand flew up and she slapped him across the face. Hard. He stared at her and she stared straight back at the red mark forming fast on his cheek. She drew in a deep, fast breath into a chest tight with shock. She couldn't look away from his face. It struck her that this was the first moment that they'd honestly looked, really looked at each other.

A shout drew her attention. She and Beris both turned to look at the same time. It was his slaves, coming with the litter. And with them, running now, were his bodyguards.

'Don't be a damned fool for once!' Beris muttered roughly, catching Tethia's attention. She swung back to face him, just in time to see him lunge forward. He caught her face in both his hands and pressed his lips against hers.

Tethia was too shocked to respond. The kiss, if it had even been a kiss, lasted only a few moments and she was nearly as shocked when he pulled away as when he'd first touched her. His hands were still cupping her face. Her hands were on his forearms, catching gently at his wrists. Dimly, she realised that the bodyguards had slowed to a walk.

Beris slipped his hands from her face, catching one of her hands to hold it tight by his side. He turned to face the guards, who were positively dawdling now. He put up his free hand to cover the mark on his cheek and gave the guards a rueful grin.

'Sorry,' he said when the guards reached them. 'It was my own fault.' He glanced at Tethia, then at Kela whose attention was so firmly fixed on the pavement that she might as well have been back at the office. 'I looked twice at her assistant,' he said. 'I should have known better.'

And the guards laughed.

Beris gestured for Tethia to precede him into the litter. The slaves lifted it off the ground with the practiced smoothness of expensive slaves and carried them through the first gate of the Palatine. Kela walked behind them.

With the curtains of the litter drawn and a soft golden light coming from the roof of the litter, it felt like they were in their own private world, but Tethia was acutely aware that both the slaves and the guards outside could hear every word they spoke. So, she whispered.

'You saved my life. They would have killed me,' she went on when he shook his head, apparently as aware of their lack of privacy as she was.

'Call me crazy,' he whispered, 'but I make a point of not being the reason people die. Call it my motto.'

'How, in Caesar's name, did someone like you become an Auditor?'

'Six-week training program.'

Tethia put her hand up to her face to muffle the giggle at the irreverent response. She should have guessed he was the son of a Consul. No ordinary man would get away with such behaviour. 'How long is it since you came here from Capreae?' she asked, guessing the answer and waiting for it with a smile, laughing when it came.

'Six weeks.' He relaxed enough to grin at her.

The litter was set down. Tethia looked around as though the closed curtains could give her an answer. 'Are we there already? When I come here to translate at the Palatine Library it takes me ages to get there – and there are three separate gates to go through.'

'There are still three gates.' Beris told her. 'This is the second gate.'

'Is it all offices and administration, like the part I travel through?' she asked, curious about the world beyond the curtains.

Beris shook his head and leaned forward. The litter rose as the slaves picked it up again. 'Look outside now,' he invited.

Tethia drew back the curtain. Beris hooked it behind a special fastening to hold it open. Her first impression was that it was dark outside. 'Why is it dark?' she asked, drawing back.

Beris laughed. 'You're so impatient. Give your eyes a moment to adjust.'

Tethia looked outside again. A small light caught her eye, low down on the ground, half concealed by a plant with dark green leaves. 'Oh, look at the colour!' she exclaimed involuntarily. 'They're so green!'

'They react to the special lights in the garden here,' Beris said. 'It darkens the colour of the leaves and makes the plants grow shorter and thicker.'

'It's so unusual,' she said.

She'd heard about the Palatine gardens – who hadn't? – but she'd never seen them. Except for one ungroomed tree in the inner courtyard of the villa in Valdennes, the only trees she'd ever seen in her life were the clipped beauties in the more expensive plazas in the heart of New Rome. She'd never seen them like this, placed close together like a forest, underplanted by tiny flowers of blue and white on drooping stems, illuminated by cunning lights that peeked out from between leaves and above branches. Even the darkness beyond the leaves was lovely; richer, deeper than she'd seen anywhere else.

'Would you like to walk with me?' Beris asked.

'But aren't these gardens only for Caesar?' She looked up and pointed to a place at the top of the hill, barely visible through the garden, where a flag proclaimed that Caesar was in residence. That in itself was rare enough, the current Caesar preferring to spend most of his time on Capreae in a palace by the sea – ironically enough, where he also sent exiled members of his family, although it was death to even whisper why he was believed to spend so much time there. All the same, it was well known that he and his sister had always been… very close.

'Don't worry. You won't meet him here.' Beris suddenly reached out and laid his hand over hers, 'Listen, Tethia, there are things I need to tell you.'

Tethia drew slow even breaths and tried not to blush. 'All right,' she said, suddenly shy. She hadn't been blushed like this since she was a girl – not since before she was a mother. Beris was at least ten years younger than she was and would be soon married to a girl from his own class. A kiss she had never even expected was making her silly.

Beris called for the litter to stop. He got out first and gave her his hand to help her rise from the litter. His hand was broader than she'd expected, stronger, more masculine. She'd expected that the son of a Consul would have feminine hands.

He kept hold of her hand. They walked a little way apart from the others, far enough for privacy, but close enough to still be in sight of his guards.

'I've never seen anything like it,' she said softly. She turned to Beris and looked up at him. 'There,' she said. 'That wasn't a lie.'

To her surprise, he flushed. 'I'm sorry about that,' she said, looking down at her. 'But in my defence, I was provoked.'

'So was I.'

'So, we're square then?'

'I suppose we are. My father was General Meropius of Valdennes,' she added, apropos of nothing.

'Believe it or not, I was actually aware of that.'

'You were? How?'

'Six-week training program or not, I'm still an Auditor. They trained me, Tethia, and I learned. I did my research on you, and on your assistant. There is nothing about either of you that isn't in your files.'

Tethia stayed very still. His hold on her hand was loose; she slipped her hand free. She didn't want to touch him anymore. 'I adhered to my conditions,' she whispered. 'I did everything they asked of me. I have nothing that can be proclaimed against me. I am a Law-abiding Citizen!' She realised that she'd raised her voice and drew in a sharp breath.

'I had no intention of proclaiming against you,' Beris answered in a low voice with a glance out the dark garden around them, lit by cunning lights from above and below to nurture the fragile, exotic plants. 'I didn't become an Auditor for you,' he said. 'I never thought I'd meet anyone quite like you. You drive me insane and we see the world very differently, but somehow once I looked at you, I couldn't look away.'

Tethia glanced up at his face and looked back down at the little flowers that bloomed among the grass, suddenly shy. Beris's hand came up under her chin to raise her face. Once he'd caught her eyes she couldn't look away, either.

Tethia wished she could just look at him and keep her stupid mouth shut. Having him look at her like that made her wonder for the first time if being unTied was worth it. She felt like she would pay any price to keep him looking at her like that. But the words came tripping out.

'Who *did* you become an Auditor for?' she asked.

Beris's hand dropped away from her face. He looked away, looking back at the group of patient slaves and guards. Tethia waited, and even though she hardly knew the man, she grieved a little for the loss of the easiness between them. He drew in a deep breath and slowly sighed it out again.

'It was for Ala,' he said at last.

'Ala?' For a moment she couldn't even remember where she'd heard the name. Then it came to her: Ala was Caesar's niece, the woman who was to be Qualified today to bear Caesar's child.

'We grew up together. When she came here from Capreae we all knew what would be expected of her. We knew that she would need to be Qualified. There are things that... things that could not be told. Caesar knew this as well as we did. I entered the training program and I will conduct the Audit.'

'But Audits are supposed to be independent! How can someone, even the niece of Caesar, request special treatment in an Audit?'

'You're right. She can't. The Bureau *has* sent an

independent Auditor, their most senior, to ensure that a fair and just Audit takes place. That Auditor will not make it to the Audit today.'

'Too bad for the Auditor. What was going to happen to the witnesses? You still need witnesses.'

'We found witnesses to suit our purpose. We chose you deliberately. Ala was to pretend that she only spoke the local language that was spoken at Capreae. She spent her whole life there, after all. It wasn't unbelievable that she wouldn't know how to speak the language of the Empire.'

'And this morning... when I exposed Galalla... I suppose I don't look like the kind of person who should be assisting at such an irregular Audit. What will happen to me if I do my job properly?'

'I wouldn't harm you, if that's what you're implying!' He turned around and strode a few steps away from her, looking up at a tree whose dark, dense foliage nearly blocked out the daytime stars visible through the dome. Small flowers bloomed in a garden at his feet and his white hair glowed blue under a special light that made the leaves of the tree green rather than the usual translucent shade.

'You're harming the Auditor,' Tethia reminded him, facing his back. With every word she said she wondered if she was signing her own death warrant. 'What's to stop you hurting me?'

Beris spun around to face her, his pale face flushing. 'I'm not hurting anyone. What Caesar orders his guards to do is another matter.'

'So, I won't make any long term plans, then?'

'Once you hear what Ala has to say, you won't proclaim against us. It would ruin more lives than one.'

'And yet this morning I spoke and ruined other lives. I had plans for this evening. Should I cancel my dinner reservations?'

Beris gaze searched her face. 'You were chosen because of your history,' he said. 'You were chosen because of Sheya.'

The sudden shock of hearing her daughter's name spoken aloud made Tethia rear her head back in surprise. The only person who'd ever spoken her daughter's name was her brother. To hear it spoken so publicly, by a man who was practically a stranger, shook her to the core.

Beris went on. 'We all decided that you could be blackmailed.' He caught her hand in his. 'You know that I feel something special for you. Tell me that you know that.'

She kept her head down. She wasn't going to make the mistake of looking into those deep blue eyes again.

'You're far too young for me and I'm not in your league.' She sighed. She had to be honest. 'But, yes, I know that. I don't trust it, but I know that something has happened between us.'

She heard him sigh. 'Yes, Tethia, that's the truth. But, for all that, I must tell you – if you reveal what Ala tells you during her Audit, I will be the very first to proclaim you. The same goes for your assistant. There are things Ala cannot afford to become public.'

'So, why can't your precious Ala just keep her mouth shut?' Once she'd said the stinging words, it occurred to Tethia that she thought the same of herself, every day of her life.

'Because the Auditor would know if she was lying. Because after she has spoken, the Auditor is required to go back and verify the answers to every question he asked. Because there is a list of questions that the Auditor is *required* to ask. And Ala *must* answer. There is always the risk that the Auditor would repeat her answers to the newsspeakers and we couldn't afford that. Tethia, you must never reveal what she says to anyone.'

Tethia kept her eyes down. 'You saw me this morning,' she said, trying to keep the bitter disappointment out of her voice. 'I was ordered by my superior to keep confidential everything I hear connected with the Imperial Household, the same as I am required to keep confidential the details of every Audit I attend. Surely after this morning you must know that I will do what I am ordered to do, no matter what the repercussions. I am a Law-abiding Citizen.' She pulled her hand from his. 'We might as well go back to the litter. I have to say, it's been a most romantic walk.' She stalked away from him and back to the litter.

The rest of the journey was made in silence. At the third gate, a slave opened the curtain of the litter briefly to allow a guard to look inside. 'Salve, Lord,' the guard said, bowing his head to Beris deferentially. Beyond the guard's broad shoulders, Tethia could see the rest of the guard post. They looked very serious, staffed by officers, tall and handsome, apparently chosen as much for their looks as their skill. Their hands rested on their weapons, ready to move at a moment's notice. Tethia was accustomed to waiting for the guards to feel like passing her through the gates. She'd never accompanied a member of the Imperial Household before.

'I beg your pardon, Lord, the Lieutenant must surrender his sword before he enters the Palatine.'

'Of course,' Tethia said, unbuckling the belt and passing the sword carefully to the guard.

'It will be returned to you, sir, when you return through the gate.'

'Of course.'

#

They emerged from the litter in Caesar's famous ocean court. There were frescoes on the walls of the gods of the sea, ancient legends and myths of heroes. In the very centre was a statue. Probably these days people thought it was just an artist's rendering of an attractive woman at her bath, but Tethia recognised the ancient goddess that she herself was named for: Tethys, creating the sea, pouring out the waters from the vase in her hands, holding all the waters of the earth lightly, as though her strength were so immense that even this mammoth task was not beyond her ability.

Tethia heard a bell toll, counting the ringing out of habit. It was still only the sixth hour of the day. She reached out to grasp Beris's sleeve.

'Wait,' she said, keeping her voice low, not sure if she was afraid of the Palatine guards, the bodyguards, Beris himself or all three. 'It's too early,' she said. 'Ala's appointment isn't for another hour.'

Beris gave her a thin-lipped smile. 'It's all the time we saved not having to wait at checkpoints,' he said.

She looked down. It was better not to see that bitter smile. 'But what do we do now?'

Beris shrugged. 'I can't even control you when you're doing your job and I'm your senior. What hope do I have of telling you what to do in your free time?'

'First,' Tethia replied in a low voice that no longer held any hint of deference, 'you're only my so-called senior because of a six-week training program. It's your first day and I've been doing this job for thirteen years.'

'How fascinating,' Beris replied and faked a yawn.

'And secondly, leaving us in a strange environment where we could be prosecuted for doing the wrong thing is just plain mean. I never thought you were mean.' She looked up at his face, boldly meeting his eyes.

To her surprise, it was Beris who looked away, letting out his breath in a heavy sigh. But that was nothing to the surprise she felt when he replied.

'I'm sorry,' he said, looking back to her. 'I'm forgetting my manners. Here.' He dug in his pocket and produced a small coin. 'This is a freedom token. Until the audit is over, Caesar has granted you freedom of the Palatine. You are free to go wherever you wish. I will bring you to Ala's quarters when the bell rings for the seventh hour. I believe you will be most entertained at the banquet. There is someone there with whom you are already acquainted.'

Beris clipped his heels together and gestured politely for Tethia to accompany him across the courtyard. She went with him, feeling like she should be ashamed of herself. Kela followed dutifully behind.

'Sir, may I ask a question?' Kela asked.

'Of course,' Beris replied.

'It's only just the sixth hour. Most citizens take morning Mixte at the third hour and the midday meal isn't until the eighth hour. How is it that there is a banquet at this hour?' She spoke carefully, formally. She barely sounded like herself.

'Morning Mixte is only a light meal, Corporal, typically taken by Tiedmen, Freedmen and the lower levels of society all the way up to Citizens. Councillors and Consuls usually break their fast in a more substantial manner. Caesar and those in his household are not accustomed to taking light meals. There is no hour of the day or night when the banquet hall is empty.'

'Sir, if I may ask...'

'I said you could.'

Kela's voice was quieter than ever. 'Will Caesar be there?'

'Impossible to say,' Beris replied. 'Caesar is bound neither by the rules of the Palatine, nor the Laws of our land. Caesar goes where and when he wills.'

Tethia tried very hard not to be overwhelmed by the luxury of the palace, but it was nearly impossible to retain her composure when the whole complex was built expressly for the purpose of impressing the most seasoned member of the Imperial Household. Successive generations of Caesars had added to the grandeur of the Palatine and Tethia hardly believed there was anything left to embellish. The floors of the courtyard were paved with white marble. The columns that supported the porticos were made of rich, purple marble, the Corinthian ornamentation at their heads gilded with pure gold.

In the villa in Valdennes where Tethia had grown up, the walls were covered with frescoes, but they were nothing like those she saw in the palace. These were rendered so carefully that for a moment Tethia was deceived, believing that the long room truly opened onto a lighted garden. Scenes from ancient myth and legend lined the walls – some rather more explicit than Tethia had ever seen before. Gods and creatures half-man, half-beast cavorted on a ruby background, limbs entwined until Tethia's embarrassed gaze wasn't sure where one ended and the next began.

Looking at the frescoes, however embarrassing, was better than looking at the people in the room. They were every bit as licentious as the painted figures on the walls. The chitons of the women were so thin and fine as to be barely decent and some of the men were little better. Her gaze was caught by a man reclining in a pile of... a pile of women, it seemed, since the cushions beneath them were nearly obscured by the number of limbs and the sheer volume of gauzy chiton that draped over the muscular man who reclined, bare-chested and laughing in their midst.

Tethia was not a religious woman, hadn't been religious since an Edict was passed ten years ago severely restricting the practice of religion in New Rome. Still, the first epithet that came to her lips was a blasphemy. 'By every god and his dog!' she cried, then bit her tongue in embarrassment. She turned abruptly to Beris. 'Get me out of here before he sees me!'

'But I thought-'

'Get me out of here!' She didn't realise she'd raised her voice, but the bare-chested man heard her. And she heard the shock and discomfort and sudden sobriety in his voice when he said her name.

'Tethia?' He struggled to sit up, dislodging a nymph who fell back onto the cushions with an inelegant 'Oomph!'

'Tethy, fancy seeing you here!' he proclaimed, loud enough that everyone in the room heard him and many turned their eyes. He opened his arms expansively, as though expecting her to run into his embrace.

She had no choice but to turn and face him. He was much taller than she was and much closer than she'd realised, her eyes precisely level with his nipples so it was a relief to keep her eyes cast so low they were nearly shut. 'I'm here on business,' she replied shortly. 'I see I don't need to ask what you're doing here. It's obvious.'

She hated him for laughing and endured the bear hug she was engulfed in. She tried not to inhale as she was pressed up against him. 'Join the party,' he invited. 'You never know. It might be interesting to have some fun for a change.'

'Thank you, but no,' she replied primly, standing still in his arms. She hated sounding prim and she always did around him. 'I have an appointment.'

'I know. That's why I thought I'd come here today. I don't get to see you often enough.'

'I *work* for a living,' she reminded him. 'And from the looks of it, you didn't come here today, you got here yesterday and haven't left yet.'

He shrugged. 'Same difference. It's always a party up here. Look.' He let her go and turned, shoving one hand into his pocket and raising the other to point at a middle-aged man reclining at the table, seemingly doing his best to eat his weight in rich food. 'That's your Auditor.'

Tethia cast a quick glance at Beris. 'He'd want to be careful,' she said darkly. 'He'll get a terrible stomach-ache.'

'Aren't you going to introduce me?' Kela asked. Beris's eyebrows went up at the impertinence but he didn't say anything. Tethia sighed.

'Fine,' she snapped. 'Merrim, this is my sexy assistant, Kela Sirron, Corporal, who could probably be induced to shed her unTied status for the right offer of marriage and as many babies as her husband's status permits. So, three babies if it's you. Ten if she happens to catch Beris's eye back there. Kela, this is my brother, Merrim, who would be getting his brains bashed out every night in the arena if he had any brains left to lose.'

Merrim grinned and bowed his head. 'Salve, Kela Sirron. I am Merrim of Valdennes, at your service.'

Kela bowed, bending at the middle in a deep obeisance. 'Salve, Lord. At your service.'

Tethia felt more than saw Beris bend close behind her to whisper, 'So, who's serving whom?' and was hard put to it to keep a straight face.

'So, Tethy, what time's your appointment?' Merrim asked, drawing close to her again and taking her hand. 'Do you have time to party with your big brother?'

Tethia tried to give no sign that he'd just pressed a small, folded slip of paper into her hand. She shrugged. 'I always have time for my family,' she replied lightly, quietly horrified that she'd just told a lie in public. She turned to Beris. 'Thank you for escorting us. Salve.' She bowed, deep and low.

Beris's jaw clenched. He took a sudden step towards her and stopped sharply. 'Salve?' he repeated. 'That's it? I don't think so.' He turned on his heel and walked away.

Tethia shivered a little. For a moment there, she'd thought he was going to kiss her again.

'Come, sit down,' Merrim urged. At a gesture from him, the lovely ladies on the couch dispersed.

'Won't they miss you?' Tethia asked acidly.

'They're slaves, Tethy,' Merrim replied. 'They do

what they're told. If they have feelings and opinions, no one wants to know about them.'

'If?' Tethia repeated.

'Don't play word games with me, Tethy.' He sat back down, resting on one elbow and reaching out to the table with the other hand. 'Have a drink.'

With an ease obviously born of long practice he poured her a dish of wine and passed it to her, balancing the wine dish by the base below the stem. Tethia took it awkwardly and resented him for making her look awkward.

'And you, Corporal?' Merrim asked, turning to Kela, placing her on his other side and turning his back to Tethia. He lowered his voice in a manner he probably thought was sexy. 'What can I do for you?'

Kela giggled – at least, Tethia supposed it was her, since she couldn't even see her beyond the broad outline of Merrim's back. She took the opportunity of opening the note he'd given her, rolling her eyes a little at the childishness of note passing.

After reading the first line she set the wine dish down carefully. The note was brief, scrawled in tiny letters on a fragment of paper.

"Sheya is alive today but is scheduled to be terminated five days from now. She is being held in the

Lygian branch of the Starlight Project."

Trying not to draw attention to herself, Tethia picked up the dish of wine again and quickly crumpling the note into a tiny ball, she swallowed it, following the small wedge of paper with a deep swallow of rich wine.

She tried to remember what Beris had said earlier about the Starlight Project. It was where unCounted children went, he'd said. Where... she remembered what he'd said with a growing horror. Where they experimented, looking for a cure for starsickness. And the things he'd said in the garden, implying that she could be blackmailed.

Well, he'd been right.

Tethia tapped Merrim in the centre of his back, thrusting an imperious finger between his shoulder blades. He jolted, then turned to face her.

'I'm going,' she said. 'Where would I find Beris, party-boy?'

'Probably with Ala, preparing for the Audit,' Merrim replied. His glance dipped to her hand and saw that she'd gotten rid of the note.

'Will anyone stop me?"

Merrim sighed gustily. 'You're talking about paying a visit to one of the most powerful women in the world. I'm sorry, Tethy. It just won't happen. You'll be arrested at best, probably Audited to find your reasons for approaching private quarters and you don't want to disclose those.'

Tethia stood where she was, wavering for a moment. 'Too bad,' she said. 'I've got to try. You should understand better than anyone.'

Merrim nodded. 'I understand.' He added mysteriously, 'That was the point.' He got to his feet. 'Come on, Kela. It's back to work for you.'

'Yes, Lord,' Kela simpered. Tethia couldn't help the roll of her eyes this time.

'You don't need to come with us,' Tethia said as Merrim snagged his shirt where it lay in crumpled folds beneath the table.

'Your welfare is important to me,' he said simply, shrugging the shirt on and tucking its billowing white folds into the blue trousers that only Citizens were permitted to wear. 'I always have time for my family.' His fingers paused on the buttons. 'However, unlike you, I can say that with a straight face. Come on.'

Instead of heading back out the main doors of the banquet hall Merrim led Tethia and Kela through a smaller door at the side of the room that opened onto an unexpectedly plain corridor.

'Why is it so bare?' Kela asked.

'The slaves come through here,' Merrim closed the door behind them.

'How do you know about it then?' Tethia asked, her voice quiet but sharp.

'This corridor also leads to guest accommodation, those not of sufficient status to have their own quarters on the hill.' His voice was still low and that irritated Tethia beyond measure.

'Why are you whispering?' she asked in a normal voice. 'Beris said I had the freedom of the Palatine until after the Audit. We don't have to skulk around in the servants' quarters. I don't know why you think I'd be arrested for simply trying to do my duty.'

'But you're not doing your duty, are you?'

'As far as an Auditor is concerned, that's all I've ever done.' She looked directly at him, staring hard until he had to drop his eyes. He drew in a deep breath and sighed it out.

'The freedom of the Palatine, Tethy, means that you can stay in the banquet hall and enjoy the party. You could go to one of the temples if you really wanted to, but they're mostly deserted these days.'

'I'm not religious.'

'You used to be.'

Tethia shrugged, feeling surprisingly free to express herself in this deserted corridor with the two people she trusted most in the world. 'Ever since the last Edict I haven't been. I will believe anything Caesar wants me to believe, because what I believe in most is the "Or Else."'

Merrim looked at her for a moment. 'One day, if you ever give yourself time, you ought to think about what that attitude makes you.'

'Anyway,' she said quickly, trying to divert his attention, 'why would anyone who was attending a party want to go to a temple when Caesar has expressly spoken against public religion? What's the point of "freedom of the Palatine" if all you can do is eat or pray?'

'There are also a series of cubbies set aside for visitors.'

'So, I can eat, pray, or sleep? No wonder no one would expect us to leave the banquet hall.'

Merrim rolled his eyes. It had been more than a decade since anyone had dared roll their eyes in front of Tethia, but she found the experience oddly amusing. 'You're so ignorant. You *can* crash in one of the cubbies and sleep in privacy... or you can do whatever else you want in privacy.' He watched the disapproving look settle over her face with his own amusement. 'That's why they're popular.'

'So, why are you here, anyway?' she asked, again hoping to divert his attention.

He cast a glance at Kela. 'Maybe you and I ought to talk privately?' he suggested.

'I have no secrets from Kela. She has been my best friend for ten years. I speak more freely to her than I do to you.'

'And does she know... about the person in the note?' Merrim asked.

Tethia nodded. 'She's known about Sheya for years. That's how I know I can trust her – I've never come to work and found a yellow card on my desk to tell me to report for Auditing.'

'Fine. We found out yesterday that Sheya was scheduled for termination.'

Behind them, Kela gasped. She put a hand on Tethia's arm. 'Oh, I'm so sorry,' she said.

Tethia shook her off. 'We have five days,' she said bluntly. 'I have no intention of ever allowing that to happen, so stop getting all emotional.'

'Ala has things to say to you,' Merrim went on. 'You need to listen to her. We arranged for a false report to go to your office, pretending to be from Caesar and asking for you to translate for the Audit, when obviously Ala is quite able to speak for herself. Beris has arranged to get rid of the Auditor and will take his place so that what Ala says will not be made public.'

'How do you know Ala?'

Merrim shook his head. 'That's not important, is it?'

'It might be, if it looks like you're keeping a secret from me.'

He gave her a very direct look. 'I'm a famous sportsman, Tethy. Does it never occur to you that sometimes very influential and powerful women might want to meet me? This isn't my first visit to the Palatine.'

Tethia's lip curled. 'You're disgusting.'

'I do what's necessary to get on in the world, Tethy, just like you do. We just cope in different ways, that's all. Now look, I brought you out here so we could have a little privacy, but servants might be along here at any moment. We need to detain the Auditor. I want you to go in there and tell him that Ala has summoned you for the Audit. Take him to the Library – you've been there before, haven't you?'

Tethia nodded. 'I go there to translate documents

sometimes.'

'Good. Show the guards your freedom token and go through the Reading Room and to a door directly under the map of Capreae. This key will open it.' He pressed a flat key into her hand. We will be waiting for you beyond the door.'

Tethia felt a little sick at the thought of leading a... well, a *comparatively* innocent man to his death. Merrim read the look on her face with ease.

'We're not going to kill him,' he reassured her. 'We've got better plans.'

'I don't suppose I need to know, do I?' Tethia replied, not believing him. 'Still, for Sheya, I would do anything.' She smiled bitterly. 'Come on, Kela. Let's go lead a man to his doom.'

They went back into the banquet hall and found the Auditor, a slave girl reclining so close next to him that there wasn't even the space for a breath to pass between them. Tethia stood over him imperiously.

'If you're finished carousing,' she said drily, 'you still have a job to do, so if you don't mind...?'

The Auditor looked up, disconcerted by the authority in her tone. 'Who are you?' he mumbled, his mouth full of pastry, crumbs falling onto his black tunic.

'I am Tethia of Valdennes, Lieutenant, unTied, and your translator for this particular Audit. So, if you don't mind leaving the lady here, we can get on with our job.'

The Auditor pulled himself up from his reclining position. The slave turned aside to someone else and Tethia had a moment of revulsion for the lives these women had been forced into. Some of them might have come from decent families before being chosen by Caesar.

The slaves of Citizens were children sold by destitute families, either for cash or in payment of a debt; others were prisoners of war taken in one of the Empire's many military victories. The slaves of Caesar were sometimes purchased, but sometimes Caesar just took what he wanted. If he saw a girl on the street and desired her, then he took her. And this room was probably where many of them ended up afterwards, clinging first to one guest, then to another, spending their youth smiling at strangers.

'I suppose I'd better get going then,' the Auditor muttered. 'I'm Starga of Rumiae, Lieutenant, but you may address me as Auditor.' He finally got to his feet. Tethia wondered if the sheer size of his paunch made balance problematic, for he swayed for a few moments.

'Certainly, Auditor. If you've got your feet yet, we'll be going.'

The Auditor shot her a glance but Tethia had thirteen years' experience in shooting her mouth off at inappropriate moments, so she was already positioned meekly with her eyes cast down and her hands demurely holding the manila folder in front of her.

'This way, please, Auditor.' She turned and glided from the room, not waiting to see if the Auditor was following. It took her a few wrong turns before she realised where she was, but she kept gliding ahead as though she knew exactly where she was going. Some guards intercepted them when she exited a courtyard heading to the Library.

'Sir! Auditor!' one of them cried, snapping to attention. They showed the utmost respect. Tethia supposed that anybody might be just about anybody on the Palatine. After all, who was Caesar when he wasn't wearing his golden mask? 'May I see your pass, please? You are entering a restricted area.'

She'd been through this before, although always before she'd been accompanied by a slave who'd provided the pass for her. Now she was the one providing the pass for Starga of Rumiae and she didn't like the feeling. She passed across the token that Beris had given her, giving her the freedom of the Palatine. The guards handed it back to her and she slid it back into the pocket of her grey tunic.

'Enter freely, sir, Auditor,' the guard said, standing by the door with their spears held tight and straight to their sides. Tethia, Starga and Kela passed through. Tethia noticed that no one had asked Kela for any identification. Apparently, the safest position was that of the most junior. She'd keep that in mind.

They entered the Library. Tethia proceeded confidently to the door under the map of Capreae. The map was huge, drawn on the skin of an enormous animal, cured and dyed to show the map to best effect. The door itself was nothing out of the ordinary, a simple metal panel that slid back into the wall. She pressed the flat, circular key Merrim had given her against a panel beside the door and it slid open silently. She hadn't expected it to be this easy. She looked through it with some trepidation. Something was bound to go wrong any minute now.

Ahead of them was a set of steps. The passageway wasn't well lit and it was impossible to see how far down the steps went. Still, Tethia had her instructions. She stepped to the side to allow Starga to enter.

'This can't be right,' the Auditor protested.

Tethia turned. 'You said something, Auditor?'

'We shouldn't be in the dark, surely. You must have

taken the wrong turning.'

'Then why do you suppose the key let us in, Auditor? If you will follow me, please. We don't want to be late.' She turned again and started descending the stairs. 'Even on the Palatine, Caesar shows good faith with his people by observing wastage and conservation laws. How many people did you expect to come this way? Caesar's niece must be protected at all costs and who would look for her underneath the Library?'

Finally, she heard him start to descend the stairs behind her and drew in a silent breath in relief. 'I suppose you might be right – why else would the door open?'

Kela's light footsteps followed the Auditor's heavy tread down the stairs.

At the foot of the stairs there was another door – that explained the darkness. Trembling slightly, Tethia held out the key again and pressed it to a spot that roughly corresponded to where the panel had been on the previous door. Although there was only minimal light, Tethia was quite able to see – not that she would ever let on to someone like the Auditor. It played to her advantage more often than not if her adversary had no idea that she wasn't as blind as he was.

The door slid open, as the one in the Library had

done. The sudden light was a shock. Tethia stepped aside, as Merrim had warned her, and quick, strong hands reached past her and grabbed the Auditor. Even she was barely even able to see what was happening, but she could make out enough to know that the fat lump on the ground, currently being sat on was probably the Auditor, while the slim, rangy figure that sat on him, a hand over his mouth, was probably Beris. The mountain of a man that stood over him, fists still clenched by his sides could only be her brother. Behind her, close enough to stir a dark curl of hair over Tethia's ear, she heard Kela sigh.

'So, what are you going to do with him now?' Tethia demanded.

'Shut up!' Beris hissed.

Hearing rough language coming from Beris's lips shocked Tethia into silence. She clamped her lips together.

Merrim closed the door that led to the steps. 'Come on.' He grabbed Tethia by the arm. Unbidden, she let out a hiss of pain as his fingers dug into the sore spot where Tannep had thrown her against the wall earlier. Merrim let go of her at once. 'Did *he* hurt you?' Merrim demanded, pointing at the fallen Auditor. Beris looked up sharply.

Goaded, Tethia put a finger to her lips for silence.

'It was an Officer in Special Services,' Kela

whispered, her voice barely audible but crystal clear. 'He hit her this morning. It was a wonder he didn't break her arm.'

'What?!' Merrim snapped, his voice lower, but sharp as a knife. He looked from Kela to Tethia with fury burning in his eyes. 'I hope you broke his damned neck!'

'He's my superior,' Tethia replied in a similar low whisper. 'Breaking the neck of a superior officer would severely injure my chances for promotion.'

'It's not worth it, if you get severely injured yourself,' Merrim replied.

'What's his name?' Beris asked. His voice, while as soft as theirs, held a quiet, dangerous note in it that made Tethia suddenly aware of his powerful position as a Consul's son, friends with the woman who was to bear Caesar's child. It sent a shiver down her spine.

'Tell me,' he urged.

'Tannep Baen, General,' she answered.

'Tannep Baen, General' he repeated, and she knew that he wouldn't forget. 'Help me get him up, Merrim. We need to get him to Nesta.'

The Auditor was still conscious, but only barely, Tethia judged, from the way he wove on his feet. There was a long corridor ahead of them with doors opening out from it every few paces. Each door had a number on it.

'What is this place?' Tethia asked.

'Re-Ed,' Merrim replied shortly, holding the Auditor up and guiding him along the corridor. 'We're lucky they haven't been too busy. These rooms are only used for overflow and storage.'

Re-Education. Tethia's blood ran cold and a memory skittered just under the surface of her mind. It was gone before she could get a fix on it. A few doors ahead of them a door opened and a face peered out.

'If you're finished having your conversation can you bloody get him in here? My arse is on the line, too, you know.'

Tethia thought she was prepared for what she would find. She'd imagined all kinds of horrors. No one knew exactly what the Re-Educators did, but everyone knew at least one person who'd returned from Re-Ed a different person from the one they'd been when they went in. They could fine-tune a personality like a musical instrument, the saying went, only a lot of people came back flat.

After all, the passions that drove a person were usually what got them sent to Re-Ed in the first place. The Re-Educators simply removed those passions and the problem was solved. That a Re-Ed could never be trusted was also well known. They were loyal to the Empire, no matter what. Many people found themselves issued with yellow cards after a Re-Ed returned to work.

So Tethia expected a torture chamber, maybe dripping still with some poor sot's blood, maybe sterile and silver, but above all, she expected lots of sharp edges and pointy implements of a mysterious nature.

Instead it looked like a Medic's office. There was the desk with the State-issued computer, the chair with ergonomic back support for the long hours spent sitting, the tidy cupboards that held who-knew-what and a hard table for the patient to lie on. The person who'd hurried them on stood in the middle of the room gesturing to the table.

'Get him on the bed,' the Re-Educator urged, the businesslike tone at odds with the rotund body and a face that looked like it smiled often. They watched Merrim heaving at the Auditor. 'Nesta Palatine at your service. Salve.'

Merrim pulled at the Auditor, pulled him off his feet, grunting at the huge weight in his arms. His muscles bunched under his shirt as he heaved the fat man up onto the table. Beris was there to push the Auditor's legs up and stop him from rolling off the narrow bed.

'Gods and dogs,' Merrim cursed. 'Don't ask me to

do that again. He-'

'Stop complaining,' the Re-Educator murmured. He reached out a pudgy hand to Merrim and touched his arm. All of a sudden, Merrim went very still and silent.

'What did you do to him?' Tethia demanded.

'Don't do that to my friends!' Beris cried at the same time. 'Merrim are you all right?'

'I'm fine,' Merrim said, his face still a little blank.

Beris eyed Tethia. 'Why don't you stand over there?' he suggested. 'I'd rather you didn't get within arms' reach of a Re-Educator again.'

Tethia nodded and did what she was told. 'For once, I agree with you. What did you do to him?'

'If you don't mind,' Nesta Palatine said, 'I'd like to get to work so you can all get out of here alive. Anyone who disagrees with that statement, please come here now so we can get this over with.' Nesta held out a hand and waved it in a vaguely threatening manner and laughed when they all cringed back. 'People are so funny.'

The Re-Educator waved at Starga's fat belly. 'Now, let's fix Auditor Starga of Rumiae, get all those troublesome memories in order.' Nesta glanced back at the four others in the room. 'Don't worry. By the time I'm done with him, he'll think he's had a heavy night with one of the party-girls. He'll wake up thinking he missed the Audit altogether. He's going to think he had a much better day than the one he had planned.'

'And then what?' Tethia asked. Both Beris and Merrim gave her frustrated looks.

'He'll be disciplined,' Nesta replied, hands moving over the Auditor's head, seeking a specific spot behind the ears among the fall of ashy blonde hair. 'Disciplined, Audited, castrated and sent back to work doing entry-level Audits. He won't do it again, even if he wanted to.'

Tethia drew in a shocked breath. She turned to Beris and her brother. 'You're barbarians!' she cried. 'You can't allow that to happen!'

'I'll take care of it,' Beris said, taking Tethia's hands and urging her to face him. 'It won't come to that.'

Tethia looked up at him. He clearly believed what he was saying. She didn't, but what did her opinion matter? She closed her eyes and bent her head, feeling sick.

Tethia had expected that Re-Education would take much longer, days, weeks, but it seemed that it only took Nesta a few minutes to work.

'A new Re-Educator might take a long time to do this work,' Nesta said. 'I've been doing this for years, Lieutenant. The fact that I have certain... natural gifts in this area doesn't hurt.'

'Natural gifts?' Then a thought struck her. 'Did you know what I...' her voice trailed off, afraid of sounding like a hysterical idiot.

'You're not the type to become a hysterical idiot,' Nesta replied. 'And yes. And again, yes. I'm a mutant, like you. Well, not exactly like you. I can enter a person's mind at will, see what they're thinking and channel their thoughts and memories into less turbulent waters. My gifts are precise and powerful.'

The Re-Educator straightened, let go of Starga's head and turned to face Tethia with an arrogant expression. 'Your powers are slight. Animals listen to you, but only out of the goodness of their hearts.'

'You're a *mutant*?' Kela asked, horror lacing her voice. In the close confines of the room, in the position they'd all adopted out of Nesta's reach, Tethia felt Kela shrink away from her.

'I'm no mutant,' Tethia denied. 'I'm good with animals, that's all.'

Merrim's hand fell heavily onto Kela's shoulder. He'd known about Tethia's abilities since they were children and a grave expression was on his face. 'And you wouldn't dream of telling anyone, would you?' he said. It wasn't a question.

Kela looked up at him, her pale eyes searching his face. 'No, Lord. I wouldn't.'

'I can fix her for you if you like, free of charge,' Nesta said.

'No!' they all chorused, Kela shrinking further and further away from the others.

'Fine, then. This one won't wake up until tomorrow. I'll get the orderlies to take him out to one of the cubbies on the Surface. And if any of you get caught on the way out, I was forced to do it. Have a nice day.' Nesta bowed politely before reaching out to turn on an IV pump. The small beep it made when it turned on caught Tethia's attention, but the moment passed before she had a chance to think too much about it.

Beris was speaking. 'We have to get back to the Surface,' he said. 'If the guards see any of you then you'll be taken.'

'Can't we just have a token, like we did to get in?' Tethia asked.

'The guards will know it's false. This is the most highly guarded area in New Rome. It isn't hard to get in, who cares who gets *in* to Re-Ed? Getting *out*, now, that's the trick. If you try and exit through the Capreae door, you'll set off an alarm. If you get seen, it will be clear you're not Re-Ed staff.'

'Don't you ever get Servicemen in here to assist you?'

'Servicemen, yes, unTied people, no. And I'm sorry, but you're not built to pass yourself off as a man. Only Re-Education staff come here. Even I, dressed as an Auditor or as a Consul's son, wouldn't be exempt from reprisals for breaking in. No, I have a plan for escaping, but you'll need to pay attention.'

A few minutes later they were standing on Nesta's desk while the Re-Educator continued to type at the computer. Merrim was the first to climb into the air-conditioning duct, leaning down to pull Kela and Tethia after him as Beris held them up towards the ceiling. The women squeezed past him and held onto his ankles as he leaned down further to pull up Beris. Even his legs strained to pull the other man up into the duct.

'Gods and dogs, you're heavy,' he grunted.

'Stop complaining,' came Nesta's voice, already seeming far away.

Beris led them through the ducts, each of them taking care to be as silent as possible. The ducts varied in size, some large enough for Tethia to sit up, others so narrow that Merrim had to press himself close to the floor and pull himself along by his arms. It seemed to go on forever, the air that had at first felt like a soothing touch of the outside world soon chilling the sweat on their skin to clammy discomfort as they slowly climbed higher and higher.

Finally, Beris stopped at another opening.

'This grate will lead to my own quarters.' He peered through the grille, then looked sharply back up at the others.

Tethia, her eyesight sharp in the darkness, could read the fear on his face. She shimmied closer and looked down. She saw nothing to be frightened of, just a servant moving about his room. She bent her head closer to the grille and watched the woman. It took her a little while to realise what was wrong. The woman wasn't putting things away – she was looking for something.

She was dressed like any other slave in the Imperial Household, a white chiton with a red belt, and a veil covering her head. From this angle, it was impossible to see her features, but it was clear she was a tall, powerfully built woman, not that this distinguished her from so many other slaves. She left the room before Tethia could see what she was doing.

'Go now,' Beris urged. He pulled the grate up and jumped through the hole, rising to his feet and lifting his arms to catch Tethia. She didn't imagine the moment that he held her tight to himself before letting her go, but she didn't understand it. He caught Kela and put her away from him immediately. Merrim tried to land lightly but it just wasn't possible and he hit the floor with a heavy thump and an involuntary groan.

'Go,' Beris repeated. 'Merrim, you know what to do.' He looked at Tethia one last time then turned away, heading to the door.

Merrim took Tethia's hand and drew her and Kela with him into the next room, then the next, looking for something. The third room led out onto a courtyard, full of beautifully groomed plants and shrubs reaching tall, white stems to the dark, starry sky. He reached down to pull a grate from beneath a garden. 'Quick,' he whispered, turning his head as the sound of heavy knuckles knocked on a distant door. 'Get in.'

Kela jumped in without hesitation. Tethia followed her, her skin crawling at the thought of where they were going. Merrim followed them, landing with a splash. Tethia met Merrim's eyes, her face curled in distaste.

'It's just a drain, the water's clean. Don't be so

squeamish.'

They went through the drains for what had to be at least a kilometre. Kela and Tethia tried to walk at the sides to avoid the small rivulet of water that ran in the middle of the tunnel. Tethia's ankles twisted from the constant pressure of walking on an angle, so she eventually joined Merrim walking in the very centre of the water.

'There's a reason for everything, see,' he said, insufferably smug. Tethia ignored him and just hoped that the beautifully polished boots that she'd put on with her uniform that morning wouldn't be completely ruined. She had no idea how she'd describe this incident on a requisition form.

As they walked, following the twists and turns of the drains, Tethia realised something. Naturally, she had to share this immediately with Merrim.

'How do you know where you're going?' she demanded, keeping her voice quiet. They were walking in the dark, Kela following along clumsily but at least it meant there weren't any grates above them opening to the surface, where guards might hear her speak. 'How long have you been planning this?'

'I told you, we only found out yesterday.'

'We?'

Merrim hesitated. 'Me, Beris and Ala.'

'And are you close with Ala?'

'None of your business, Tethy. She's only been in New Rome for six weeks. We're six-weeks' worth close. She came to see me in the arena one night and called me to her the next day.' He shrugged and she watched the movement of his shoulders in the darkness as he walked ahead of her. 'We heard about Sheya yesterday.'

'Yes, but would you care to tell me why Caesar's niece was notified that one insignificant girl was going to be terminated? There must be hundreds just like her.'

Merrim's steps slowed. 'Ala can see the future,' he said, very softly. 'So, she's like you. She said that Sheya is vital to the future of the Empire. Without Sheya the world descends into darkness.'

Tethia rolled her eyes. 'I've never met a future-teller who didn't speak like that. One of them told me once that I'd get married and live among the Eridai clans on the very borders of the Empire. I've been to Eridea. It's pretty and their culture is… interesting. But I'm not going to leave Service. I'm not going to leave New Rome. Who would? I worked hard to be unTied. I'm not about to give that up. Anyway, I'm Sheya's mother. I don't need to hear this end-of-the-world nonsense to be convinced to save her.

As for the rest of you, I don't care what motivates you, so long as I get my girl safe.'

'What would you do if you found her?' Merrim asked. 'You couldn't live with her. You'd never be allowed to be a mother to her.'

'I don't expect to be a mother to her. But I will make sure she's safe, that she has *someone* to keep her happy and warm. I don't need her with me. I need her to be safe.' She didn't hear the note of desperation in her own voice, but Merrim did. He turned and put his arms around her, holding her tightly. Tethia buried her face in his shoulder and for a moment allowed herself to tremble with fear.

After walking an age through the darkness, punctuated with brief shots of light from the buildings above, Merrim stopped at a grate that seemed no different from all the others.

'This comes out in the gardens,' he said. 'Get out here and then find the third gate. Use the token Beris gave you. Tell the guards that you were having a romantic stroll in the gardens and that he was called away, that you need to get on for your appointment with Ala and they will supply a slave to take you to her quarters. Beris and I will try to get there. If anyone asks, you were at the banquet, you went for a walk and now you're going to Ala, nothing more. Keep it simple and you're less likely to get confused.'

'How do I explain my wet boots?'

'However you like. Maybe he kissed you and you were so overcome with passion that you stepped into a fountain.'

'You've never actually kissed a girl, have you, Merrim?'

'If that thought makes you happy, then believe what you will.' She saw the flash of his teeth in the reflected light from the garden above. 'Now get.' He held out his hands, linked together, and Tethia and Kela stepped into his cupped hands and he boosted them up through the grate into the marvellous garden above.

Tethia and Kela made their way through the garden.

'I'm not prejudiced against mutants,' Kela said suddenly.

'Sure you're not. You acted like I threw acid at you.'

'It was a shock. I know that mutants can be of use to the Empire. After all, look at the Re-Educators. They're employed by Caesar. And future-tellers are at every fair.'

'And some mutants are taken away from society never to be seen again.' Tethia made a sharp sound of disbelief. 'They probably go to the Starlight Project.'

'The what?' Kela asked.

'Don't you remember Beris mentioning it, after Galalla's audit? He said that the Empire uses unCounted children in the Starlight Project to try and find a cure for starsickness.'

'Oh, yes.' Kela didn't sound interested, so Tethia didn't push it any further. Before today, she would have told Kela that Sheya was in danger. After seeing her reaction to hearing that her friend was a mutant, Tethia wasn't sure she wanted to confide in Kela anymore, until she was sure she wouldn't find a yellow card at her desk.

'I didn't know you were certified as a linguist in only two years,' Kela said, clearly comparing her own ambitions to Tethia's achievements. 'How did you learn so fast?'

'I was a General's daughter. I grew up travelling the Empire, one battlefield at a time. My tutors were prisoners of war. I could have been certified earlier than that, but I couldn't be unTied until I was twenty-one. Right after Caracalla I made sure I would be able to be unTied as soon as I attained my majority.'

At the third gate the light was almost a shock after the dim garden. The guards were just as tall and handsome as the other guards had been earlier, still standing erect at their post, their hands still on their sword hilts.

'Salve!' they cried when they saw Tethia and Kela approach.

'Salve, brothers,' Tethia replied, her tone formal. 'I am Tethia of Valdennes, Lieutenant, daughter of Meropius, General. I am commanded to present myself-'

'Thank you, Lieutenant.' The guard's voice, while pleasant and cultured, was not the kind of voice that bore interruption. 'Our duty is to guard the gate. We know who has been commanded to pass through it.'

'As you say, brother.' She met his eyes squarely. He was only a Lieutenant, the same as her. She wasn't going to look down and mutter "sir" to someone of her own rank, whatever their gender. 'I'd very much like to perform the duty I have been commanded, so if you don't object to letting me in, I'd appreciate it if you could do yours.'

She handed him the token that Beris had given her. He passed it under a scanner as the guards inside the Palatine had. It still cleared.

'If you would be so good as to wait,' the guard said, his tone tight. Apparently, he'd wanted nothing so much as to turn her back, but with Beris's token it seemed that denying her wasn't an option. Tethia waited, shifting from foot to foot with a soldier's surreptitiousness, hoping that the guards wouldn't notice her wet boots.

#

She'd expected a guard to escort them but instead it was a woman – a slave. Usually slaves were dressed in neutral clothing and not permitted the privilege of gender unless their master assigned it to them for the purpose of maintaining the modesty of the women under their care. This slave was dressed like a woman, but she carried herself with a confidence Tethia had never seen in any woman before, slave, free or unTied.

Since Ala had spent most of her life in exile on Capreae with her mother – after her mother, once the wife of Caesar had been found guilty of adultery and sent into exile – Tethia had expected Ala to be under guard. Tethia knew from her file that Ala had been allowed to return from exile after the unexpected death of her mother but all the same, Ala had spent most of her life keeping company with a woman guilty of sedition.

Since Tethia and Kela were to be escorted by one of the women of the house, it seemed that Ala had somehow gained Caesar's trust to the point where she was not guarded. Instead, for all the difference it made, she was protected. For all her tainted blood Ala was still a Citizen. Her mother had been both the sister and the wife of Caesar. Since her mother had been unfaithful – or at the very least, charged with being unfaithful – Ala was denied the peerless privilege of being known as Caesar's daughter, instead being granted only the title of being his niece.

The tall woman gliding across the marble plaza was dressed in a white chiton with a red belt and brooch holding it all together, pinned neatly at one shoulder. Up until the day she joined Service Tethia had worn much the same, except her belt and brooch had been blue, as befitted the daughter of a Citizen. That was before Caracalla, when women hadn't been allowed to be Citizens in their own right. These days Tethia wore her uniform – pressed grey trousers, white blouse and grey tunic with a leather belt – on duty and off. It was her right as a Citizen and a Serviceman.

The woman inclined her head to Tethia, making her veil billow from where it was held with concealed pins in the mass of her dark hair. Gold pins glittered from near her ears.

'Lieutenant, Corporal, if you please, I am known as Mira.' Tethia blinked. A slave with a name was unusual, but perhaps the slaves of Caesar had more rights than others. 'I am Ala's personal attendant, her mother's companion, and faithful servant of our Lord, Caesar. Salve.'

Tethia inclined her head. 'Salve, Mira.'

'Lieutenant, if you please, may I take you to my mistress?'

'That *is* why I'm here,' Tethia snapped.

Mira bowed again, the billowing of her veil irritating Tethia almost beyond measure and showing gold studs near her ears. Even the trembling of her hands was irritating. Tethia and Kela followed the woman across the immense court, the floor paved with marble that had a rippled pattern. Tethia had heard of that – the Caesar who built the palace had been a megalomaniac who liked to think that the ripples in the marble meant he was a god who could walk on water. These were more enlightened times – no one believed the Caesars were gods anymore. Very few believed in the gods at all.

Once they'd passed through the tall pillars that supported the portico around the courtyard, Mira led Tethia through a maze of passages and surprisingly small rooms, no bigger than the room Tethia occupied at the barracks. Finally, Mira stopped just inside an apartment that was no richer or more ornamented than the next.

The decorations told Tethia one vital fact: Ala had satisfied Caesar's mistrust of her sufficiently enough to bring her out of exile, but she didn't have his favour. Was that another reason why she was afraid of this Qualification Audit? Had it been arranged as a means of enabling her to succeed to the high honour of bearing Caesar's child, as a means of sending her back to Capreae in disgrace... or as a means of getting her out of the way in a more permanent fashion?

Ala was still in bed, covered with blankets and furs, even though in the dome of New Rome the temperature outside remained at a constant pleasant ambience. Ala had spent her life at Capreae. She was accustomed to temperatures that varied depending on winds and waves and other vagaries that Tethia, brought up in the protected environments of New Rome and her family villa, had never understood. Thankfully, the weather didn't require her understanding and continued regardless.

'No, no, no,' Ala whispered, her voice muffled by the furs, but even in the small syllables her heavy Caprese dialect was obvious. That was why Tethia, ostensibly, had been chosen to translate for the woman's Audit. Mira moved quietly about the room, doing this task and that, her hands always busy as befitted a good servant.

Tethia waited with all the external marks of patience, but inside she was a seething mass of nerves. Where was Beris? He'd said he'd be here. Had someone found Starga? Had Nesta betrayed them?

Ala sat up. 'Mira? You don't need to stay. The linguist and her assistant will be sufficient chaperonage for my Audit.'

'But the Auditor isn't here yet, my lady. Wait a little longer, until the Auditor comes.'

Ala's eyes met Tethia's hopelessly.

'It is very important that an Audit be private,' Tethia said. 'The Auditor will not agree to proceed unless absolute privacy is guaranteed.'

Mira pinned a hard stare on Tethia that nearly withered her. 'I have nursed Ala practically since her birth, sir' she said with all the dignity of a high-born slave. 'There have been very few moments in her life when I was not present. I doubt very much that anything important happened in the brief periods when I had to leave the room.'

'That is for the Auditor to decide,' Tethia said smoothly, taking refuge in professionalism.

Mira looked from Ala to Tethia and back.

'It will only be for a little while, Mira, dear,' Ala said. 'As you said, I doubt very much that anything interesting will happen while you are out of the room. And, after this Audit, I will be Qualified to bear the child of my Lord Caesar, to keep the Imperial bloodline pure. That is the purpose of my life, isn't it?'

'It certainly is.' Tethia was shocked by the hard look that Mira gave her mistress. Mira pursed her lips. 'All right. I will leave. I will be in the courtyard if I am needed. You need only to say my name and I will hear, mistress.'

'Thank you, Mira.'

Mira left the room, pulling the door nearly closed behind her. Tethia followed her and pulled it all the way shut, hearing Mira's 'Tsk!' of irritation.

'Can we speak freely?' Tethia asked, looking around the room.

'As long as Mira doesn't hear.' Ala's heavy accent vanished, and she spoke in even, cultured tones. 'You know how they say some people aren't all they seem? Mira's more than she seems. I've known her all my life and only just realised it.' Ala sat up straighter in the bed and raised her hands to run them through her wealth of pure white hair. Her skin was paler than Beris's, the blue veins visible beneath the finest tissue of skin that Tethia had ever seen.

'Is Beris coming? Did things go all right with the other fellow?'

'I hope so,' Tethia replied. 'I can't be sure.'

'We don't have much time,' Ala said. 'Your daughter is on Capreae, in Lygia, in the Starlight Project. She has been useful to them, so they have allocated her in a control group to test the danger of exposure to the stars. She hasn't yet been hurt, but she was disobedient. In five days, she will be terminated and they will conduct an autopsy to finalise the data she has provided. You must-'

The door opened. Ala clutched the furs tighter to her breast.

Three men entered the room, two guards and the Auditor. Tethia's heart sank. It wasn't Beris. It was Merrim.

If Ala could truly tell the future, then Tethia knew why Ala had been disturbed. There was danger here, but not from the guards. They were tall and handsome men, twins, looking ever more identical in their scarlet uniforms. They stood to attention to allow the false Auditor to pass through. Tethia watched Ala drink him in and she tried to look at him dispassionately.

He was tall, but no matter how she looked at him, he wasn't handsome, his grey eyes the same shade as

Tethia's uniform – and the same shade as Tethia's eyes. His nose had been broken more times than anyone could count and there was a recent scratch under one eye that Tethia was surprised the guards hadn't noticed. His face was too square, his full moustache only adding to the predominance of horizontal lines on his face with heavy eyebrows shooting a straight line across his brow.

His features appeared harsh, which was a surprise to Tethia. She hadn't thought he had it in him to look so stern, though he had to, if he was to pass himself off as an Auditor. Most Auditors were as tough as diamond chips, but Merrim, however harsh and stern his expression, couldn't hide the compassion in his eyes when he looked at Ala, crouched fearfully beneath the furs. He proved it when he spoke, almost immediately.

'Don't be afraid, sister, my name is Starga. I'm not going to hurt you.'

Ala peeped out from under the furs. 'You won't?'

Tethia rolled her eyes as she translated the heavy accent that Ala hadn't had two minutes ago, unable to resist the impulse, but Merrim replied gravely. 'No, little sister. I'm not going to hurt you.' He turned to the guards. 'Thank you. You may leave us now.'

The guards cast a glance between them and one of

them muttered in a tongue that Tethia found difficult to translate – it must be some regional dialect. 'He must be new, cut him some slack.'

The other one replied, 'That's no excuse for being an idiot.'

Tethia agreed with the second guard, but kept her mouth shut. This was the most dangerous moment of the day. He might be a pain in the neck, but she didn't want to see him executed. Their mother would never forgive her.

The first guard replied, speaking before the other had a chance. 'We're sorry, sir, but the ladies of his Excellency's court are never left unguarded with a man.'

Merrim's gaze slewed to Tethia, seeking confirmation of the guard's words. He was a terrible actor. Tethia smirked at him. His expression barely changed but she could tell he was just aching to stick out his tongue. The big baby.

Tethia schooled her expression into one befitting a Lieutenant in Special Services, casting her eyes down as befitted a woman.

'I am Tethia of Valdennes, Lieutenant, Auditor,' she began, her tone respectful. 'I am the linguist the Services sent to assist you in understanding Ala's Caprese dialect. Salve.'

'Salve,' he replied. His grey eyes twinkled. 'Nice to meet you, Lieutenant.'

Smart arse. If he was going to be that way, she wasn't going to cut him *any* slack. Idiot.

'Why don't you proceed with the Audit, sir? I will follow your lead.'

The grey eyes ceased to twinkle. He walked towards Ala's bed, passing close by Tethia. He muttered 'Be fair,' which made her feel a bit of a heel.

'Fine,' she muttered back, then in a louder voice, in the Caprese dialect, 'Ala, my name is Tethia. I am here to translate for you, so the Auditor understands you. Just speak normally and I will translate. The Auditor will ask you a series of questions, beginning by asking you about your life in Capreae and your return from exile when you were allowed to return to the Eternal City six weeks ago. Once the Auditor has asked you about your life, he will ask you about your hopes for the future, how you feel about children, what you believe to be effective discipline. You must answer honestly, because the Auditor will return to his office and check each and every fact. If the answers you give are incorrect, you will not pass your Qualification. If your answers are untrue, then you will not pass your Qualification.'

'All right,' Ala whispered, as though she had any choice in the matter.

Merrim stood at the end of the bed and teased the whole sorry tale out of the girl. If it wasn't for the fact that Tethia knew for sure that he could never attain the position of Auditor, she might have even believed him in the role. He asked the questions compassionately until Ala was not only sitting up in the bed but accepting a cup of hot, sweet tea, which was in itself a triumph since Mira, who brought the tea, explained that Ala had been refusing to take fluids since the previous day.

When Mira left, confident that Ala was answering her questions like a good girl, Ala turned the interview. By the end of it, Tethia knew more than she had ever expected to know. She knew why Caesar spent so much time on Capreae and why Ala's mother had committed suicide to gain her freedom. Merrim's expression had remained unflinchingly compassionate and Tethia's voice remained professionally impassive, but when Merrim finally rose to his feet and folded his notes into his briefcase, Tethia didn't need to look to know his hands were shaking. Kela stood in the corner of the room, quiet tears falling from her eyes.

The guards, close enough to hear every word, turned to murmur quiet words to one another in their own language. Tethia's ear, more attuned to listening to foreign languages than her own, automatically took note of their words.

'He's a Citizen and an Auditor – we can't! And she's a woman...'

'Every Serviceman knows that one day he may be called upon to die for the Emperor. Today is her day. We have our orders.' There was a pause, the first guard clearly not convinced.

Tethia watched him out of the corner of her eye. She edged closer to Merrim and deliberately trod on his foot. He looked up from Ala in surprise.

The guard spoke again. 'We serve the Emperor. We cannot allow this to become public!'

The pause was shorter then. 'For Caesar, then,' the first whispered.

'For Caesar!' It was a shout. Tethia was near enough to Kela to grab her arm and yank her away from the swiftly drawn swords. She screamed, which was a sure way of drawing the attention of every guard within earshot. Tethia reached to draw her own sword, cursing when she remembered that it had been taken from her at the third gate.

The other guard ran towards Ala, who didn't

scream, who just sat up in bed holding a cup of tea in shaking hands. Merrim caught him in a tackle, rushing at him head down and arms wide, catching him about the middle and crashing him into the opposite wall.

The fallen man's sword went flying and Tethia raced for it. She dodged beneath the swing of the other guard's sword, blessing her short stature – he was used to fighting men. He wasn't a Palatine guard for nothing, though. He came back instantly with a swing at her legs.

She managed to get a little distance away, which was why he didn't break both her legs, instead only giving her a glancing blow across her ankles. Her boots protected her feet somewhat, but it still hurt. She fell, trying to aim her fall for the other guard's forgotten sword. He and Merrim were wrestling, the guard's training a solid match for Merrim's years of professional boxing.

Merrim managed to pull away from the guard long enough to draw back a powerful right arm and hit the man squarely on the jaw. The man collapsed beneath him. Merrim turned to help Tethia but she already had the sword in her grip and she and the remaining guard were circling one another. She couldn't afford to give Merrim any of her attention, but he understood.

He turned to Ala and lifted her clear of the covers

just as Tethia made a sudden lunge at the guard, again taking advantage of her short stature and, angling her sword upwards, thrust under the hard leather breastplate. The guard dropped his sword, his legs collapsing beneath him. He moaned as he fell, clutching at Tethia's sword, still in his belly.

Tethia leaned in to finish him off. He made an instinctive move to protect himself and Merrim's voice rang out, 'Tethia, no!'

Tethia ignored him.

'That wasn't necessary!' Merrim shouted. He turned back to face Tethia but before he even took a step, she'd already dispatched the guard he'd knocked unconscious. 'What have they done to you?' he demanded.

They stood there for a moment, frozen, staring at one another. Ala lay still in Merrim's arms and Kela's gaze flickered back and forth between them.

'We don't have time for this now,' Tethia said, her voice even and controlled. 'We have to get out of here. How did you get in?'

'Through the sewer.'

Tethia tried not to respond, but the words bubbled out of her automatically. 'Merrim, you are hands down the grossest person I have ever met. Fine. Let's get going.'

#

Merrim led them through the maze of Ala's private apartments, slowing suddenly to a walk as he came out into the loggia of a public courtyard. He set Ala on her feet then stood back and offered her his arm.

'This is all very romantic,' Tethia snapped, 'but I don't want to die today. My schedule is full for the next five days, so can we please get moving?'

'Our only chance of remaining undetected,' Merrim said in a smooth, controlled voice that wafted over his shoulder as he escorted Ala along the loggia, 'is by appearing that we are ordinary visitors to the Hill. So, promenade, damn you!'

'I'm a soldier,' Tethia replied, 'dressed in my uniform with my assistant accompanying me. The best I can do is a slow march.' She stood straight and proceeded along the loggia with all the dignity she could muster. Kela followed suit.

A slave came out of a doorway, carrying a pile of linen. Tethia felt her muscles tighten as the slave approached them, but she didn't show by any word or sign that she'd seen anything amiss. She walked straight past them, efficient and quiet, walking so close to the wall of the loggia that she was barely noticeable.

A man came out of another door, dressed in the white shirt and blue trousers of a citizen. There was a piece of paper in his hand, his attitude that of a man on an important errand. He didn't even look at them.

They'd made it to the end of the loggia, close enough to see that there was another courtyard ahead of them. Even from a distance, Tethia recognised the ocean court. From a distance, the rippled effect of the marble was even more stunning.

There came the sound of a heavy gate opening followed by the sound of marching feet. Beneath the sound, Tethia heard the lighter sound of running feet, going through the drains. Looking for *them*.

'The guards often pass around here,' Ala whispered. 'Maybe it's nothing. We just have to get past the next courtyard then we'll be able to get through the gate. If we make it to the gardens, we can get into the tunnels.'

'*If?*' Tethia echoed quietly.

A shout echoed across the courtyard behind them.

Tethia started but kept marching. Ala half turned.

'There's only two guards,' she whispered. 'Quick, we need to get into the next courtyard.'

Merrim held out his arm, but Ala slapped it away.

'Run!' Ala cried.

They ran, making it into the next courtyard just in time to see the last of the guards pass through an open gate to their left. There was a pack of dogs that accompanied them, not leashed but famously obedient, the Hounds of the Palatine. Two slaves started to pull the gates closed.

'Quick!' Ala cried. 'Inside!' She pulled at a door, tugging at the heavy carved wooden panel with all her strength to try and open it. Merrim came to her aid, but the door wouldn't budge.

They were too late, anyway. The guards behind them saw them and followed them, shouting that they'd abducted Caesar's niece.

The last of the column of guards passing through the gate turned, then shouted. They ran towards the small group.

'Run!' Ala cried. 'They weren't supposed to see us! We'll be captured!'

The guards pointed to the small group on the other side of the courtyard and shouted orders at the dogs. In a heartbeat, the dogs were running towards them, slipping lightly over the patterned waves of marble, barking loudly. The pair of guards who had followed them from the smaller courtyard was running towards them, closer, but slower than the dogs.

'They'll kill us!' Ala whimpered.

Tethia stepped in front of the others, shaking off Merrim's sudden, desperate grasp on her arm. 'Be ready,' she said. She raised her arm towards the dogs bounding towards them. She looked directly at them. 'Stop!' she cried.

Merrim, Ala and Kela watched in amazement as the famed Hounds of the Palatine tripped and stumbled in their efforts to stop as quickly as possible. They fell on their haunches, slipped and skidded on the marble, and all the barking stopped.

The courtyard seemed very quiet for one brief, breathless second, then the shouting resumed. The guards started running towards the group, yelling at the dogs to get moving. Some of the dogs got up, but they just started milling in a circle. The two guards from the courtyard had paused for a moment, but now they started running towards them again, drawing their swords as they ran.

Tethia raised her arms and lifted her face to the sky. 'Come,' she whispered.

A cloud appeared on the horizon, black and moving erratically. Tethia raised her arms higher. 'Come and help us. Come, all of you. Come.'

'Who are you talking to?' Kela shrieked.

Tethia turned to her, lowering her arms, and for a moment her expression was so distant that Kela shrank back. 'They're coming,' she replied.

'Stay back!' Merrim ordered and shoved Tethia behind him as he faced the guards.

The black cloud on the horizon swelled suddenly. It was closer than it had seemed. It dropped onto the two guards. They cried out; their running steps faltered and they fell. The black cloud fell with them. The men were screaming now.

'What is it?' Ala's voice was heavy with disgust. The men lay still, the black cloud dissipating.

'Bugs,' Tethia replied simply. She fixed Ala with a smug smile then turned back to the dogs wandering aimlessly around the centre of the courtyard and made a shooing motion. 'Go!'

The dogs were too far away to have heard her, but they went anyway, running back to their masters with renewed vigour. After a moment, it became clear to the guards that the Palatine Hounds weren't running back to them to return peacefully – they were attacking. Some of the men tried to turn and run, but they were Palatine guards, the best of the best. Those who tried to run were slaughtered by their comrades. The others faced the dogs with weapons drawn.

'Go,' Tethia urged again. She took her attention from the dogs for the briefest of moments. 'We should run, too, maybe,' she suggested. She didn't wait to see what they were doing, taking off at a run across the courtyard as fast as her feet could carry her. 'Go, go,' she urged the dogs.

Before the dogs reached the guards with their deadly swords and spears, the dogs broke away, turning, running instead for the gate on the other side of the courtyard where Tethia was headed. For only a moment she was surrounded by the pack before they outpaced her, racing through the gate.

Merrim, Ala and Kela followed on Tethia's heels. Tethia was still whispering, using what little breath she had to call the birds.

They appeared swiftly, large and small, white magpies and translucent swallows and sparrows and, wheeling high above, a lone falcon. They descended on the guards, flying in their faces, the small beaks attacking where they could. The guards swung at them with their swords but found that their enemies were too small and swift to defeat. Still, many small bodies fell to the ground and Tethia felt the shock of each death, huge in proportion to the size of the body on the ground. And still, she kept running.

The gate was unguarded. It led only to the gardens, but Ala said that was their destination. They ran through the entrance. Kela turned as they passed through and shoved at the gate to close it. It was a huge thing, carved of solid wood but it ran on a rail embedded into the ground. Merrim shoved the other door closed.

A bare second before the doors closed, one of the Palatine Hounds raced through the narrow opening to run rings around Tethia. Tethia reached out to the dog's mind and was shocked by what she found there. The Hound had not always been a dog, it had once been a man.

Merrim reached for the bar, the solid length of engraved steel that historically barred the gates of the Palatine. It was heavy: it usually took three men to lift but Merrim's strength was immense and the situation was urgent. He lifted the bar, straining and crying out with effort, dropping it onto the metal arms that cradled it against the door.

'That won't hold them long.' Tethia's mind was still half-entangled with that of the dog.

'Stop being so damned pessimistic!' Merrim replied. 'Keep running.'

They ran into the gardens. It was darker there, stranger-lit with the special lights Beris had shown Tethia, that assisted the growth of the plants.

'Can we hide here?' Kela asked.

Ala shook her head. 'They'll comb the Palatine for me. I'm too valuable to lose. They'll do anything to get me back.' Tethia stared at her for a moment, surprised by the arrogance of the statement, combined with the pretty vulnerability of the girl with her long white hair tumbling over slender arms revealed by a white chiton.

'Then we'd better run,' Tethia suggested. 'Where are these tunnels?' As she spoke a dozen cats sped along the top of the wall by the third gate. They dropped down into the ocean court, yowling and hissing as they attacked. The guards cried out at this new assault, the sound carrying over the wall. Tethia imagined a Palatine guard held at bay by a spitting cat and smiled to herself.

'Quick, the tunnels are over here,' Ala called. She led the way, an ethereal figure in filmy white against the darkness of the gardens.

The others followed. Among the dark foliage and closely spaced trees, the entrance to the tunnels was nearly invisible, for all that it was well maintained and clearly put to frequent use. The gravel path that led to it diverted unobtrusively from the main path, going behind a copse of trees whose trunks were as dark as the night sky. The garden rose into a hill behind the copse of dark trees and set into the hill was a door, stained dark and nearly invisible. Ala pressed her thumb into a space beside the door frame and the door slid open silently.

'Follow me.' She looked over her shoulder, the light from the anteroom beyond the door spilling out to illuminate the thin fabric of her chiton, the slender limbs and the white hair falling in disarray over her exposed shoulders and arms, giving her only the barest modesty. Tethia heard Merrim draw in a quick breath; heard, too, Kela's quickly smothered sound of disapproval.

They followed Ala into the antechamber and she closed the door behind them. She opened the door that led out of the anteroom then drew back in horror.

Mira stood there, her tall figure casting a shadow over Ala's slight form. She laughed. Ala cowered.

Merrim grabbed Ala by the back of her chiton and yanked her away from Mira. He drew back his other arm and hit Mira so hard it was a wonder she didn't die.

The slave crumpled. Still holding Ala by the back of

her chiton, Merrim shoved her into the hallway, forcing her over Mira's prostrate form. She stepped carefully, as though the slave might reach up and grab her at any moment. Not far away came the sounds of marching feet, from inside the corridor at first but quickly echoing out in the garden, the sound of dozens of booted feet crunching over gravel.

'Get in there!' Merrim shouted at the top of his voice.

'Are you insane?' Tethia cried softly.

'Do as you're damned well told, woman, or by the gods I'll break your neck!'

Tethia flinched away from him. She'd never heard him use that tone of voice before and for a moment she was frightened. The marching feet were close, now. They must be around a corner, only a few seconds away.

'Open the door!' Merrim thundered.

Kela jerked open the door, her eyes wide. Still holding a wide-eyed Ala, Merrim shoved Kela ahead of him into the little room she'd revealed. It was nearly identical to Nesta's office: a small desk, a chair and an examination table. Merrim followed them and slammed the door behind him. He pulled the desk away from the wall and shoved it against the door. A bookcase was up against one wall. Merrim grabbed it and nearly threw it at the door as a barricade.

'Get to the other side of the room!' he shouted and the women clustered in the corner. He strode towards them. Kela and Ala shrank back, but Tethia had been fighting with Merrim since they were children and she wasn't going to cower before him now.

'What in the name of Caesar is wrong with you?' Tethia demanded.

'Tell them I coerced you,' Merrim said, grabbing her so roughly she knew she'd bruise. 'Tell them *I* killed the guards. Do anything you need to do to make Sheya safe. She's my flesh and blood too, you know.'

He hesitated, but the heavy thud that sounded against the door as the Palatine guards attempted entry galvanised him into action. 'I have to knock you out,' he said, 'or they'll never believe it. You others, you need to tell them I abducted Ala and you tried to stop me.'

Tethia stood as tall as she was able. 'I'm ready,' she said.

Another thud sounded at the door. The desk moved across the floor a little, but the bookcase still held the door closed.

Merrim gave Tethia a searching look, then,

unexpectedly, he grinned.

'I've wanted to do this for thirty-three years,' he said. 'You always were a pain in the neck.'

He drew back his arm. Tethia didn't even manage to curse him, his eyes or his ancestors before she was unconscious.

#

When Tethia woke up, she was in an infirmary: white walls around her; stainless steel implements; extraordinarily uncomfortable bed. Her whole head throbbed, like Merrim had shoved her jawbone up through the back of her skull. She muttered a curse and thought better of it when the movement of her mouth aggravated the abused tissues.

Her very own Auditor was sitting by the bed, dressed in his black tunic and cloak with silver braid on the collar. She recognised him. She'd translated for him once or twice, but he was completely featureless, like the best kind of Auditor.

Tethia said all the right things – the things she'd been saying for fifteen years. She didn't even allow herself to remember what she'd learned about Sheya's scheduled termination. She didn't dare allow anything to show on her face. Finally, the Auditor reached the question of Merrim's actions.

'Why do you think he let you live?' he asked. 'He didn't hesitate to kill the guards.'

'My mother would kill him if he did.'

The Auditor looked confused, which was shaky ground. If she tried being too smart with an Auditor she might never come out of the Infirmary. Tethia sighed and said, 'He's my brother. I'm sorry I made a joke about it, but I thought it would be in my file somewhere. Somewhere near the front, seeing as sportsmen are such public figures. I'm surprised you didn't recognise his picture.'

'I don't follow sports,' the Auditor replied, making swift notes in his book. Tethia wondered what he was writing. She wondered if he, like her, always wore his uniform.

By the time the Auditor left it was afternoon. It would only be a few hours before Tethia would see the reflection of the pink light from the distant nebula shining through the window. It was always unnerving to have to look up at the nebula, the tune to the old children's song echoing through her head.

"Starlight, starlight, underneath her skin!

From the other side of the globe

Skin burned like a tattered robe,

And her hair on the ground behind her.

Don't let her give you the starlight!"

Fifteen minutes after the Auditor left the room, a junior Serviceman arrived at the door with a note. He stood to attention while she read it, trying to maintain her dignity and not show the pain she felt from her throbbing jaw and bruised shins from the fight with the Imperial Guards. She was sore from where Tannep, General had shoved her against the wall earlier, too. The painkillers had only been administered after the Auditor left and hadn't taken effect yet.

'Tethia of Valdennes, Lt. dtr of Meropius, Gen., Salve. A date has been set for your court martial on the seventh day of this month.'

Tethia's eyebrows rose in surprise. Today. She glanced out the window. She wasn't sure what time it was, but if the nebula wasn't visible it couldn't be the night hours yet. She'd never known that the wheels of justice ground so fast. Maybe they made exceptions for people accused of abducting Caesar's niece. It was a wonder they bothered with a trial at all. A summary execution wouldn't have surprised her.

Tethia was escorted to the courtroom by two large Servicemen. She stood between them, feeling very small, but glad she was still in her uniform. At least she still had her dignity.

The court martial was devastatingly swift. In fifteen minutes, she was stripped of her rank, dishonourably discharged and escorted by armed guards to a cubicle where she was ordered to change out of her uniform and into the white chiton and blue belt worn by Citizen's daughters.

Her fingers trembled as she folded the fabric at her shoulder and pinned the brooch in position. There was no mirror. She was glad of that. She couldn't bear to see herself like this anyway.

She exited the cubicle looking like any other Citizen's daughter, feeling even smaller than before and as though something had broken inside her. She'd thought they would let her go after that, turn her onto the street, but the guards were still very businesslike.

'Where are you taking me?' she asked as they escorted her into a secure vehicle, her voice as small as she felt.

'Speak when you're spoken to, woman,' one of the guards reminded her sharply.

Tethia's temper rose. She looked him square in the face and said firmly, 'I may no longer be an officer – Corporal – but I am still a Citizen and you will address me by my name.'

For an answer he struck her across the face. It wasn't a large vehicle, but it was big enough that Tethia managed to land one solid thump on the guard before being restrained. She heard her dress rip where the brooch pinned it at her shoulder, but she didn't care. Even when her hands were manacled, she felt it was worth it. She was restrained, but she didn't feel quite so small.

She was a bit sorry she was such a mess when she realised they were taking her to the main arena in New Rome for another trial. It seemed bizarre to her that she should have a civil trial immediately following her court martial, but there wasn't anything she could do about it. She walked meekly between the guards, who held her arms tighter than necessary in a grip sure to leave more bruises to match the ones Merrim and Tannep, General had already given her.

They waited in a small room built into the space beneath the seating of the arena, no larger than necessary to hold two guards and the accused. Tethia assumed it would be a quiet trial – who would care about her enough to attend her trial? Especially given the late afternoon hour and the short notice, she expected only to have the judge present, along with the dozen standing jury members, most of the seats in the court's arena empty… but she had forgotten Merrim was involved.

When Tethia entered the court, the trial appeared to have been in progress for some time. Merrim stood in the centre of the arena, the judges accompanied by members of Caesar's household up on a dais at the opposite side of the circle. Merrim swayed on his feet as five thousand spectators looked on.

The jury stood in the arena, on the same level as Merrim, but ranged around him in a circle. It was a full jury – one hundred and fifty Citizens, all watching in fascination as a sporting hero faced trial.

Tethia was escorted to the centre of the arena, to stand next to her brother. 'You look like you've been in a fight,' he muttered.

'I was,' she replied, then cast the briefest glance she dared at the judges before lowering her gaze and assuming a modest posture. They looked very grim and stern. Her heart beat a little faster, but she refused to show her fear. Only Caesar had the power to order executions, she told herself, the memory of thc two Palatine guards she had killed preying heavily on her mind.

'Where is Kela?' she asked.

'She's already been tried.' Merrim spoke low and barely audible above the roar of the crowd. 'It was all I could do to keep them from executing her. She remains in Service, but she is to be sterilised.'

Tethia's knees went weak. Kela may have been an unTied Citizen but she'd always longed for a family of her own. It shouldn't have been a surprise that she'd be sterilised as punishment. As someone who'd been accused of a crime, she would never pass a Qualification Audit anyway.

As for her own fate, at best she would receive the same sentence. Sheya would be her only child. It was one thing to decide that her career and her Citizenship was more important than having children, it was another thing to have the decision taken out of her hands. At least, with Caesar absent, the judges would not be able to order their executions.

There was a sudden fanfare and the crowd rose to their feet. With a sinking feeling in her heart, Tethia looked up. On the dais at the opposite end of the circle the judges in their blue robes had all risen to their feet. They turned. A door behind them was opened by a slave and a man emerged. He was tall and plump, his skin soft and pellucid white, even from a distance, almost shining beneath the purple robe. On his face was a golden mask.

Caesar had arrived.

Behind Caesar, she glimpsed a familiar face, hair light and lovely curling around his face. As she watched, Beris leaned forward to whisper something in Caesar's ear. Behind the golden mask it was impossible to read Caesar's response.

The leading judge bowed to Caesar and turned to pin Tethia with a stern gaze. 'State your name!'

'Tethia of Valdennes, daughter of Meropius General, Citizen.'

'You are charged with adultery. How do you plead?'

'What?' Tethia was an adult, a professional. She never shrieked, but she came close. 'Not guilty! He's my brother! That's disgusting!'

'Quiet, woman!' Tethia bit her tongue to keep it still. She'd looked straight up at the speaking judge and he favoured her with a pitying gaze. 'You are not charged with indecency with your brother, but rather against your father's honour. While a daughter is a virgin in her father's house, any actions of impurity are considered a crime against her father. Do you deny that while you were a virgin in your father's house you had a sexual relationship that resulted in a child?'

Tethia stood very still. Everything around her faded away – the gasps and jeers of five thousand sports fans, the disapproving looks of the jury and judges, even Merrim's whispered apology for sharing her secret. All of it didn't matter anymore.

She'd kept her secret for fifteen years. Things could never be the same now, not after the world learned about Sheya. Her conditions were broken. Without warning, she was back in that moment when they took her baby out of her arms, telling her that Sheya would be cared for. Lying to her face.

'I don't deny it.'

She didn't need to be told to lower her eyes. She couldn't look up for anything. Five thousand voices roared – now the whole world knew. The noise seemed to go on forever.

One of the judges must have held up a hand for silence because the whole arena went quiet to hear him speak.

'Merrim of Valdennes, Citizen, in the absence of Meropius, General, you are the nearest male relative of the adulteress Tethia of Valdennes, and therefore responsible for her conduct. You have spoken eloquently regarding your reasons for breaking and entering a government facility. You have been less forthcoming regarding the circumstances surrounding your impersonation of an Auditor, the murder of two Palatine guards, the abduction of the niece of Caesar and the assault of her nurse. This court will adjourn for today and reconvene tomorrow at the fifth hour to proclaim your sentence.

'Tethia of Valdennes, Citizen, there is clear precedent for your case. This court is not unsympathetic to your plight. As an adulteress, you are stripped of your Citizenship and your status as an unTied person. As a mark of respect for your father's military exploits, you will not be required to name the father of your child before this public court, however you shall do so privately. You shall be removed to your family home in Valdennes until such time as the father of your child is ready for you to join him as his wife. Transport will be provided for you to Valdennes.'

He gestured to the slave behind him, who rang the gong to signal the end of the hearing. The judges rose to leave the court, waiting patiently in their blue robes for Caesar, and then the members of Caesar's household, to depart. The crowd, five thousand strong, rose silently to their feet. Once the judges left, the people started talking again as they crowded towards the exits.

The guards came to collect Tethia and Merrim. They looked at each other; both feeling that it was wrong to part without some significant words passing between them but neither seemed to know what to say.

They were different guards this time and were gentler. As they led Tethia away, she heard Merrim shout something over the general hubbub. She twisted to look at him, her arms still held fast by the guards. He shouted it again, but she wasn't able to hear him. That made it seem even worse. It was the last thing he ever said to her, and she missed it.

#

As a general, Tethia's father had been able to purchase a villa not more than three hours away from New Rome, so Tethia arrived at her mother's door by midnight. The nebula was high in the sky now. The white render on the walls outside the villa was bathed in its pinkish light. A slave, eyes musty with sleep, answered the door and woke up abruptly at the sight of the guards.

The slave ushered both guards and Tethia into the reception room. Tethia's mother was already there, seated at her loom, but turned sideways on the stool, ready to face her daughter as though she had been waiting for this moment for years. A host of expressions passed over her face at the sight of her daughter. 'Tethia! What happened to your uniform?'

'My Lady, salve!' one of the guards said, pressing a fist to his chest in a gesture of respect. 'If I may be so bold, this letter has been provided by the court to inform you of the situation.' He passed her the letter.

Tethia stayed next to the other guard. He didn't restrain her so long as she didn't make any fast moves, out of respect for her father, probably. Tethia watched her mother's expressions – confusion, dismay, the searching look as she tried to remember back to that time fifteen years ago, horror, disgust. Then, worst of all, blame, probably when she came to the part about Merrim's pending sentence. Tethia looked down. She blamed herself, too.

The guards left, but so did Tethia's mother. A slave remained to escort Tethia to her room. Tethia looked at the slave and she shook her head.

'Go prepare my room,' she said, mainly to get the

slave out of her way. She went after her mother.

'Mater,' Tethia called. Shey-Leen kept walking.

'Mater, stop! This is important!'

Shey-Leen halted at once but didn't turn around.

'Haven't you done enough?' she whispered.

Tethia halted, too. There was so much she wanted to say and Shey-Leen was the only person on the planet who made her feel like she couldn't say anything. 'Haven't I suffered enough, Mater? All my life, haven't I suffered enough that you need to punish me more?'

'*Punish* you?' Shey-Leen spun around. There were tears on her face. She was the perfect Citizen's wife. She could cry her heart out and no one would know, so long as she kept her face to the wall. 'Tethia, please, just get it over with. I'm ready. Name the father of your child.' She said she was ready, but she closed her eyes.

Tethia hung her head. 'Rinnarius of Valdennes,' she whispered.

'What?' Shey-Leen's voice was sharper than Tethia had expected. Tethia looked up.

'You must have known, Mater. He was the only one.'

Shey-Leen just stared at her, utterly wordless, but a light of hope was kindled in her eyes that Tethia resented.

'The court convicted me, Mater. The whole City saw the trial. I was publicly shamed. Isn't that punishment enough?'

Shey-Leen still stared. Finally, she spoke. 'You don't belong in this house anymore, Tethia. You have a child. You should be with your husband.'

'No! Absolutely not!'

Shey-Leen hurried across the marble floor to take Tethia's hands in hers. 'If you were ever an obedient daughter, then you need to be obedient in this. You're not a daughter anymore, you're a wife. You should join Rinnarius *in Lygia* as his wife. He was always a good Citizen. He will honour the law.'

Tethia was so shocked the room reeled around her. Shey-Leen knew. She had to know. Lygia was where the Starlight Project was holding Sheya, on the Island of Capreae. Tethia's mind spun, too, and her only anchor was the firm grasp of her mother's hands. The slaves were everywhere, they heard everything. Even in her own home, Shey-Leen had to be careful. She had always been careful.

'Yes, Mater,' Tethia said.

Within the hour she was on the train out of Valdennes, heading for Lygia, the small port on the western side of the Island of Capreae.

#

Tethia had slept for a few hours on the way to Valdennes and she reasoned that she would be able to sleep on the way to Capreae. She took with her only a slave, since it was unseemly for a Citizen's daughter to travel alone, and the token given her by the Court that would oblige Rinn to accept her. The slave flung a few of Tethia's old things into a suitcase, insisting that these things would be needed and hurried after its mistress.

The journey, after disembarking from the train on the main line, was difficult. They had to change trains several times, since Capreae was usually only visited by those who were rich enough and wasteful enough to order a private train. The newsspeakers paced up and down on the trains. Tethia called one over.

'What news of Merrim of Valdennes?' she asked.

The newsspeaker told her all about the trial, about the famous boxer's whorish sister. Tethia bore it in silence, the images of the story crowding her mind as she listened, hoping for news, but judgement had not yet been passed.

Tethia had only seen Capreae on maps. Servicemen didn't go to Capreae. Even Citizen's daughters didn't go to

Capreae. It was where Caesar went, where the very rich or the very influential might go for a holiday. It was not a place where a Citizen's daughter would go to visit, even if her father was a General.

Capreae was an island, separated from mainland New Rome by a narrow strait of notoriously rough water. Tethia had travelled the Empire in her work as a translator, but never before had she seen the island where Caesar sent his disgraced relatives... and where Caesar himself spent most of his time.

The island was the pointed peak of an underwater mountain range that projected from the rough, dark water in irregular spears of jagged rock. Carved into the sides of the mountain were dwellings, temples, even broad, pleasant plazas that looked out onto the sea and the lights of the mainland. The more disgraced the family member, the more desolate the jagged lump of rock they were exiled to.

The journey had taken all night and the pink light of the nebula had faded to below the horizon by the time they arrived at the seaside town of Suruae. Tethia had worn both veil and mantle for the journey, not liking being out under the nebula any more than the slave, who had spent the journey cowering in the train with its hands over its head.

The train deposited them at the last station near the

coast. Tethia stood on the wharf, her mantle close about her in the raging winds and looked out at the sea, the wind whipping the water into a foam that nearly covered the water entirely.

'Help you, sister?' a man asked, approaching her with a politeness she didn't expect. She didn't realise that he had been watching her for long moments, while her mantle was blown tight against her body, her ankle-length chiton blown high on her calf.

'I need to get to Capreae,' she said, keeping her eyes lowered. She wasn't sure she wanted to make eye contact with a strange man under these circumstances anyway. 'And I need to get there as soon as possible.'

'No sooner than tomorrow, sister. Storm's up.'

'I don't care if the storm is sideways,' she snapped, keeping her eyes fixed on the boards of the wharf. 'I need to get to Capreae right this instant!'

'No-one'll take you, sister. Not in this storm.'

'I'll pay any price.' She reached into her chiton, fighting the folds of fabric moving in the wind to find her purse and brought it out. 'Any price you name and then some.'

'You'd be paying the price to the man's widow.'

Tethia had to raise her voice to be heard against the

wind. 'I need to get there!' she shouted. 'And I will, even if I have to swim.'

Tethia heard the pause while he shook his head. 'No, sister. Not today. Not in the storm.'

'Any price!' she shouted, looking up at the burly man with his serious face and his dark blonde hair flying in the wind despite the leather thong that held it back in a ponytail. 'I will give you any amount you name.' She raised herself up on her toes to scream, 'I will pay any price!'

She swayed towards him. He caught her briefly by the shoulders then pushed her back onto steady feet. 'No, sister,' he repeated. 'The storm is too bad. Tomorrow.'

She flung herself at him then. 'Today!' she screamed, incoherent with fear for Sheya. Every moment mattered. She would not let a storm stop her. Not even if Caesar permitted every single god to rise from their eternal sleep could they stop her.

She battered the man around the face and shoulders with her purse, her thick mantle and bitter rage hampering her movements. He caught her wrists this time and held her away from him.

'My daughter is dying!' she screamed. 'I have to get there!' Face white, heart stilled with fear, she wrenched herself away from him. Her mantle slipped from her shoulders, caught in his hands. She turned, took a dozen quick steps, and catching a life preserver from a pole she leaped into the roiling water.

The water closed over her head. She couldn't hear anything from the wharf, not even her own pounding heart, nothing but the water. She kept her arm wrapped in a tight lock around the life preserver and forced herself to still so it could raise her to the surface.

She broke free with a great gasp and started kicking. Thin threads of shouts reached her from the wharf, but she had no energy to spare for them. All that mattered was reaching Sheya and if it meant that she died on the way – well, so be it.

She swam for what seemed an age. She swallowed as much water as air, sobbed as much as she breathed, and despaired of ever seeing Sheya again. Everything she had suffered, knowing that she had been the reason her best friend had all her hopes and dreams literally cut from her body, seeing Merrim shackled and beaten in the arena, knowing what was going to happen to him, the rift between her and her mother – all of it had been in vain, because she was going to die here, in the dark water, under the cold, dim light of the stars.

She was pulled under the water again. She lost her grip on the life preserver. She was so cold that she couldn't hold on to it anymore. She could barely breathe against the cold that gripped her tight around her chest. And suddenly she realised that it wasn't the waves pulling at her.

Silhouetted against the sky was a boat. A man was in the water with her, pulling at her chiton until she was close enough for him to grasp, pulling her tight against him while they were both dragged back to the boat.

Tethia was never later able to remember details of the journey to Capreae. Lying on the slick boards of the deck, the heaving waves crashed over the edge of the boat to wash over her body. The man who had saved her – the same man she had spoken to on the wharf – dragged her along the deck into the relative safety of a cabin. Her slave was there to make disapproving noises and try to rub her dry with a towel. The seawater seemed to have penetrated all the way to the marrow of her bones and her skin remained clammy.

The slave threw Tethia's mantle over her wet chiton, folded her veil beneath her head for a pillow and she slept. Then the slave knelt beside its mistress's supine form and prayed to every god it could remember by name for deliverance from the depths of the sea that were opening wide to swallow them.

Hours later, the ship limped into the harbour at Capreae. Tethia was sitting up now and the slave was still on its knees, thanks and praise replacing the desperate pleas for preservation.

'You'd better stop that,' Tethia whispered, poking the slave in the thigh nearest her. 'You must know that Caesar disapproves of religion. And this is Caesar's island.'

The man who had jumped into the sea to save Tethia insisted that she and her slave wait until the boat was properly moored at the wharf. The sea was still rough but not as deadly and fierce as it had been on the Suruae side of the strait.

'Where to now, sister?' he asked Tethia as he helped her onto the wharf. This wharf was better lit, not quite lovers-light, but not the stranger-lighting of the Suruae wharf.

'Thank you, I can make it on my own,' she croaked.

The man threw back his head and laughed.

'Sister, you couldn't make it to the end of the wharf without someone to hold you up. I've got a skipper this side of the strait. Seeing you want it so bad, I'll take you where you want to go.'

Tethia cast a quick glance up at him. His clothes

were still wet from the constant assault of the spray from the sea. He was right. She needed help and he was likely the only one who would give it. No one would care anything about her, here on Capreae. She gave the sailor the address.

'I'm going to meet my husband,' she said.

'You said,' he replied. She looked up at him again in surprise, sure she hadn't mentioned Rinn. 'You said your daughter was sick,' he added. 'Course I knew you was going to meet your husband.'

Of course. Tethia's lip pulled. Telling Rinn he was married was sure going to be fun.

The sailor suddenly took a step away from her and bowed politely. 'I forget,' he said. 'It's different at sea. Salve, sister. I am Garrig of Suruae.'

Tethia lowered her eyes. 'Tethia of Valdennes. Salve.'

'Where can I take you, sister?'

Tethia kept her eyes down, hoping that her discomfort didn't show on her face. 'I don't know the address,' she said quietly. 'I know he is working on an archaeological dig somewhere on the island, near Lygia.'

Garrig was gracious. He didn't even allow a moment for her to feel his pity. He spoke briskly.

'Certainly, sister. Come with me?' He held out a polite arm and Tethia took it. The slave followed them as they left the wharf.

The dig was further out of town than she'd expected. They didn't arrive until late afternoon. The dig was a tiny settlement of tents and other temporary accommodation that lay sheltered in the space beneath soaring mountains. Garrig pulled the skipper up outside the first demountable. They both sat there in silence for a moment.

'Want me to come in with you?' Garrig asked. She sensed his pity, but he gave no outward sign of it.

'No,' she said quietly.

Garrig got out of the skipper to help her down the step in an unnecessary, but polite gesture. As an unTied person she hadn't had this kind of courtesy for years. She wasn't sure if she liked it or not. Holding her head high beneath the long veil, her mantle over her shoulders, she walked proudly towards the demountable. The slave followed her, pulling the suitcase from the transport.

PART TWO

It was darker here than it was in New Rome, with no public lighting to stain the sky. There was no dome over Capreae, so the stars were brighter than Tethia had seen in a long time, the sky enormous. She felt exposed, but at least it was morning and the nebula was safely radiating its pink light onto the other side of the world.

The stranger-light of the compound reminded Tethia more of her childhood in Valdennes than she cared to admit. Her steps faltered. The slave slowed behind her, dragging a bag that seemed much heavier than was necessary. Tethia had no idea what the slave had even packed.

'Stop dawdling,' Tethia snapped. 'I'm not going to hang about here under the sky for no good reason.'

'But the bag-'

Irritated beyond bearing, Tethia slapped the slave across the face. 'I didn't ask for your opinion. Stay here with the bag until I summon you, then.' She turned and strode away, determined not to call the slave until at least the eighth hour, heading for the largest demountable. She knocked briefly then flung the door open.

It was a dining room – if it could be described in such grand terms. A trestle table ran along the middle of the room, collapsible storage lining the walls. Two people were sitting at the table, drinking coffee. Looking up surreptitiously, Tethia tried to recognise the boy she'd known fifteen years ago.

The man at the table was nothing like the Rinn she remembered. If this was him, then she didn't recognise him. So, she simply stood in the doorway with her eyes modestly lowered, and gracefully dropped her mantle from her shoulders and folded it over her arm.

He rose to his feet. 'May I help you, sister?'

Tethia stood straight – and tall, insofar as she was able – her shoulders back and her head high. 'I am Tethia of Valdennes. I am here to join my husband, Rinnarius of Valdennes.'

'Husband?' the man gaped. He covered his shock quickly. 'Forgive me, sister. It appears I am not so well acquainted with your husband as I thought I was.'

Tethia smirked, her eyes still modestly lowered. 'As I haven't seen him for fifteen years, brother, you probably know him well enough. Where is he? I have to present myself to him as custom demands before we begin our co-habitation.' Let him stew on that, she thought vindictively.

'He stayed went early to the site today. If you'd care to wait-'

'I do not. Take me to him.'

The man cast a quick, almost imperceptible glance at the unTied person seated at the head of the table.

'Certainly, sister. If I may introduce myself, my name is Morgan of Mellior. Tethia of Valdennes, salve.' He bowed again. 'I work with your husband. This unTied person is Jael, the architect of the dig.

Tethia bowed once in greeting. 'Salve,' she said curtly and turned back to Morgan. 'Well?'

He gestured for her to precede him and they left the room. They passed her slave along the way, standing nervously beside the fallen suitcase. 'Did you want your slave to join us?'

'Leave it. It needs to learn obedience.'

Morgan's step slowed but he must have known what bad manners it was to intervene in the disciplining of a slave. 'Of course,' he replied.

Under the star-studded sky, Tethia rolled her eyes behind his back.

Once Tethia had an idea where they were going, the site seemed obvious. There were a few caves on the lower hillside that were lit from within, but one was enormous and flooded with lovers-light. It was better lit than the residential area, which was only stranger-lit. The mouth of the cave was clearly artificial, chiselled out of the rock of the mountain.

Tethia felt a stirring of curiosity as they drew nearer and she could make out carvings around it, pillars carved into solid rock, massive bas reliefs that seemed to support the entire mountain. Who would build such an edifice? Why? What good did it do to pretend a mountain was a dwelling?

Shrugging off the idea on the grounds that if ancient people were weird it wasn't her problem, Tethia kept her eyes out for her husband. Though she would sooner die than admit it to anyone, she was nervous. She hadn't seen him in fifteen years. Back then she'd been in love with him. What would he say, what would he do when he saw her?

She recognised him at once, though he was very different from the clean-cut new recruit she'd last known. He was positively scruffy, she thought with distaste, his shoes dirty, his shirt rumpled, his hair a little long where a dark lock fell into his eyes. He pushed it back impatiently, driving his fingers into his hair and scrubbing at his scalp.

'Back already, Morgan? I thought Jael-'

'Your wife is here, Rinn.'

'What?'

Hidden behind Morgan, Tethia saw Rinn's shadow as he leapt to his feet. She stepped forward.

'There's been a new development in your life, Rinn,' she said. 'I thought you ought to know. We got married yesterday, you and I.'

Rinn looked from Tethia to Morgan and back again. 'What in the gods' names is going on?' he demanded.

'I'll be back at the Refectory,' Morgan said hastily and beat a retreat.

They waited for him to get out of earshot before continuing, looking at one another, sizing one another up. Tethia's heart pounded. She felt more ashamed than she ever had in her life, but she would rather die than let him see it.

'I had a baby,' she said, lifting her chin to look him straight in the eye.

She saw… she saw so many different emotions fleet over his face: disbelief, anger, regret, even a shadow of guilt.

'I didn't particularly want to marry you at the time,' she said, her voice offhand, though her heart felt like it broke with each lie she told. 'So, I gave her up. I promised the Auditors that I would never speak of her. As a woman of questionable virtue, I would never Qualify to have any other children, so I sought status as an unTied person.' She drew in a deep breath. 'Yesterday my baby became public knowledge and that breached my conditions. I had to go before a court. I was charged with adultery since I was a virgin in my father's house at the time when I fell pregnant.'

'So-called virgin,' he mocked. She stared at him. His lip was twisted in a sneer. She wanted to kill him.

She drew in deep, steadying breaths, trying not to think of her training as a soldier, when she'd been taught how to kill a man. She'd been in battle before, quelling rebels over in Stansis. Rinn wouldn't be the first man she'd killed. He wouldn't even be the first man she'd killed this week. And life would be easier, so much easier, if she was a widow…

'You know enough to know that that statement makes you an arsehole,' she snapped, choosing to save his miserable life. 'What choice did I have? Answer me that, and sneer as you do it!'

He had the grace to look ashamed. 'I'm sorry,' he said, staring down at his feet like a woman. He scuffed a dirty boot on the dirt floor. 'It was a low blow. But cut me some slack. I never thought I'd ever see you again! I have my own life here, my work – my work is important! I don't need some helpless female hanging off me wasting my time. I'm concerned with important things here! I don't need some silly woman boring me with discussions of how to get around wastage laws so she can buy more shoes!'

Tethia allowed a silence to fall between them, then said, 'If that statement is supposed to be proof of your male superiority, I suppose I should tell you that it makes you look like a backward, sexist jerk.' She smiled serenely and folded her hands together.

Tethia and Rinn stared at one another.

'You've changed,' he said finally.

'What did you expect?' she asked. 'I'm nearly twice as old now as I was then. I've lived more in the last seventeen years than I did in the seventeen years before that. I've been independent, unTied. I've been in the Special Services since the moment I attained my majority, travelled the world, done exciting things.'

'It hasn't improved you.'

'I can't say much for your manners, either,' she snapped. 'You don't have a choice in this any more than I do. I'm staying. And you needn't worry I will ever, ever discuss something as trivial as shoes! In fact, we needn't discuss anything, ever. All I have to do is be physically present in your house. Now, I've presented myself to you, that's my only responsibility. Now it's all official. Now that you know, I'll go back to camp and leave you alone.'

Rinn flung himself back into his chair. 'Go back to camp, then, I'm busy. But I should warn you, I've only got a room at the dig, not a house.'

Tethia saluted. 'Sir, yes, sir!'

He scowled at her. 'Are you going to be a pain in the neck for a little while until we get to know each other, or are you going to be a pain in the neck for the rest of our lives?'

'Sir!' Tethia cried, delighting in the knowledge that it irritated him. 'For as long as we both shall live, sir!' She made an about-face and marched from the cave. On the way back to camp she passed the slave standing with the suitcase. She walked straight past it.

Tethia flung the door of the refectory open again. Again, startled faces turned to her, the unTied person sitting at the head of the table frowning a little more than last time. 'I'm staying,' Tethia announced. 'What's for breakfast?'

The woman with the frown – Jael – ordered Morgan to show Tethia to her new quarters. He hesitated at the door. 'Shall I call your slave?'

'Why are you so concerned what I do with my own property?' Tethia asked. 'I will call it when I am ready.' And he let it go at that.

Rinn's quarters were much smaller than Tethia had expected, despite his warning. She'd assumed he had some kind of managerial position, from the way he'd been so absorbed in paperwork at the cave, thought he would have had one of the demountables for his quarters. Ala had said that he was an administrator at the dig. It was only reasonable to assume he would have ample room for at least one other person.

Instead he had a single room, no larger than the room Tethia had occupied at the Special Services barracks back in New Rome. And now they had to share it.

There was a metal locker beside the bed, strewn with papers. A trestle table served as a desk, again strewn with papers. A pile of scrolls was stacked untidily beside the locker. The bed – a narrow, single cot – was unmade and, unlike every other surface of the room, not covered with papers.

Instead, the objects on the bed were things that Tethia had never seen before – small cylinders made of stone and various metals, finely carved and engraved, ranging in size from as large as her forearm to no bigger than her little finger.

Morgan made a sound of disapproval. 'What's *that* doing in here?' he asked, snatching something small off the rumpled quilt. Tethia couldn't quite see what it was since it fitted into the palm of his hand and he quickly slid it into his pocket. All she saw was a glimpse of gold.

'Enjoy your morning,' Morgan said laconically before leaving the room and closing the door behind him.

Tethia looked around the room, at the little locker, the desk, the tiny bed that wouldn't accommodate both of them, even if they *were* lovers. Maybe it would have been better to stay in solitary confinement back in Valdennes. She drew in a deep breath, repeating to herself why it was vital she come to Capreae in the first place. It was worth it.

Worth anything.

Once she'd got her priorities in order, she scooped all the little things off the bed. She noticed in passing that they were covered with writing. After fifteen years as a linguist she couldn't help but read the strange script. The one in her hands was a description ancient laws, very similar to the legal documents she was sometimes sent to translate at the Palace.

Tethia rolled her eyes, putting all the cylinders on top of the papers on the desk. She knew better than to tidy the papers, she thought, smiling a little wryly to herself. She made the bed then lay down on top of it, despite the fact that it was barely past the third hour. She was more exhausted than she would admit to anyone, so tired she might lie down to die if she hadn't had Sheya to save.

She needed her rest, she rationalised. It wouldn't be a *bad* idea to get a little rest. She wanted to be at her best for the fight with Rinn that would inevitably ensue when he returned. And then she needed to find a way to get out, to find the Starlight Project, to find Sheya.

She hadn't expected to sleep, only to rest, but she'd underestimated the stress she'd been under. She didn't wake until Rinn returned to the room an hour later. He closed the door softly behind him and looked her over slowly.

'Can you tell me about it?' Rinn asked, his voice quite different from earlier.

Tethia's heart pounded that little bit faster, but not from any pleasure. She dreaded what she had to say to him. Maybe, if she told him the truth, he might be able to help her, but she would need to tread carefully. If he reacted the wrong way, she might find herself speaking to another Auditor.

'It was a little girl,' she said softly. 'I deliberately kept any knowledge of her from you. I got rid of you long before I started to show.'

'I always wondered why you were suddenly so keen for me to accept that posting to Farris.'

'You weren't in a position to marry. You weren't a Citizen yet and I hoped that I was going to be able to hide it away and pretend it never happened. I named her Sheya and I gave her up for adoption shortly after she was born.' Tethia shrugged, lying on her back in the cot. 'They told me she'd be looked after.'

Rinn let the silence lengthen after this statement, aware there was more to come.

'They lied. I'd assumed because she was the daughter of a Citizen that she would have the same rights as I did. It turns out that illegitimacy negates any rights she might have had. She became one of the unCounted.'

Rinn breathed in sharply. 'How do you know that?'

'We found out recently-'

'Who's "we"? Some new lover of yours? One in a long string, I suppose? I know what unTied women are like!'

'You *are* a backward, sexist jerk. It was me and my brother. Merrim, remember? Your friend before you disappeared? He and I found out that Sheya was not given to another family. Instead she was sent to the Starlight Project.'

Rinn sat down on the chair, turning it so he could face her directly. She'd expected to see his face full emotion, but it was wiped blank. 'And what do you know about the Starlight Project?' he asked.

Tethia thought through her options carefully. Back when she was young, she'd loved him with all her heart. Now... now she wasn't so sure she could trust him. She shook her head. 'Not much. Have you ever heard anything about it?'

Rinn shook his head, too. 'There isn't much I could tell you about it.' Tethia thought that wasn't exactly an answer. 'But you've found something, haven't you?' It wasn't a question.

'All I know is that Sheya is scheduled for termination in four days. She's going to be killed, Rinn. I need to save her. I don't even know where to start looking, but I can't let this happen.'

She was surprised by the touch of his hand on hers. 'I know,' he said. 'I understand.' For a moment the blank expression slipped, and his eyes blazed into hers. 'I will do anything to save her. But I don't see how you could do… anything. After all, you know nothing, no-one, you have no information, no skills that might help!'

'I have a mother's determination,' she told him fiercely, sitting up on the bed to better meet his eyes. The room was so small they were close enough to kiss. 'I swear by all the gods I will find her. And if anyone has hurt her, I swear I will kill them.'

Rinn glanced up at her, his dark eyes clashing with her grey ones. 'If you don't, I will.' He shifted quickly to sit on the edge of the bed beside her. 'We have to do something about this!' he cried. He reached for her hand.

Tethia pulled it away and scooted back to press against the wall. 'You don't say. What do you think I was doing when I was arrested?'

'You weren't exactly forthcoming earlier.'

'I suppose I wasn't.' She shrugged. 'I had a busy day.' She paused. 'I couldn't find out if Sheya was alive, but I found out she is here on Capreae.'

Tethia bounced a little as his sudden backward motion made the cot move. 'So that's why you came. I wondered.' He stood up. 'You must be hungry. Breakfast is ready. If you want to get refresh yourself, and I would recommend it, the facilities are down the hall to the left.'

Now alone in the little room, Tethia remembered that she'd left her things outside. She slipped her feet into the light sandals that were considered appropriate footwear for a respectable matron, reflecting that her service-issue boots would be far warmer.

There was a small pile of objects in the middle of the compound. The slave had wrapped itself in Tethia's warmest shawl and curled up to sleep with its head on the suitcase.

Tethia nudged her with her foot, kicking at the slave's leg. 'You, wake up.' The slave opened its eyes, its shining, colourless pupils picking out Tethia's shadow above it in the stranger-light of the compound. It drew back in fear and dismay.

'Get up,' Tethia commanded. 'Bring all this stuff inside. My room's in that building.' She pointed. 'It's through that door, second on the left. Make the bed, too. My husband doesn't know how.' She ignored the slave's furious blushes and turned to stalk back to the dormitory.

As Tethia stepped into the demountable, she had to go up a small flight of steps and she felt something catch on the hem of her chiton and pull it upward. She twisted to free it and caught a brief glimpse of a leer on a man's face. He was standing behind her, bent over, the hem of her chiton in his fingers.

'Let me fix that for you,' he murmured. 'All free now. In you go, sister.'

Instead Tethia climbed back onto the ground. Like most people, he was taller than she was, but she fixed him with a stern glare. 'I understand that mistakes happen,' she said in her most reasonable voice, 'but understand this: touch me or my garments again and I will break your fingers. Is that clear?'

He smirked and Tethia strongly considered breaking his nose now rather than his fingers later. She climbed the few stairs again, trying to rein in her temper. His hand was raised to hold the door open behind her when she turned.

'I was in the military for thirteen years. It was my duty as an officer to keep my word. Rest assured that while my status may have changed, my character has not, and I will not hesitate to do whatever is necessary to defend my honour. Be told.' She swept inside with a ripple of her mantle and jerked the door out of his grip, slamming it behind her.

There were a dozen people around the table now. Rinn was already seated and an empty place lay beside him, an extra chair squeezed in at the corner of the table. Tethia sat down, the leg of the table uncomfortably between her knees.

'Allow me to introduce everyone,' Morgan said. Tethia didn't look up, but she heard the smile in his voice. There wasn't much point being introduced, since she wasn't supposed to make eye contact with anyone, but she appreciated that he was making an effort. 'You've already met Jael, the architect of the dig. Going clockwise around the table, there is Andred, our transport officer; Eleron, our cook; Lesara, who is doing her doctorate in archaeology. At the other end of the table are Tiedmen and Freedmen associated with our work.'

'Salve,' Tethia muttered, as the others muttered likewise.

'Will your wife be joining our work, Rinn?' Jael asked, his tone abrupt.

'I don't know,' he admitted. 'Do you have any

skills, Tethia?'

Tethia looked up long enough to glower at him. The effect was ruined somewhat by his failure to even look up. 'None whatever,' she replied. Her skills were none of his business. 'If you'd care to provide me with a travel pass, I'd like to go shopping today. I need to buy some shoes.'

His lips quirked in an unexpected smile, but he still didn't look at her. 'Do whatever you want,' he said dismissively. A little thrill went up Tethia's spine, though she wasn't sure if it was excitement, fear or hatred.

Rinn reached to his belt and untied his money pouch. He tossed it across the table to her. 'Try not to spend it all at once.'

'Depends how annoyed I still feel when I get to town,' she replied sweetly.

After breakfast, Tethia went to the small tent that Morgan was erecting in the compound. She hadn't told him to do it and was annoyed that he had dared contravene her orders to stay outside, so she ignored him.

'You! Slave, get my things! And go tell Andred I want the transport running in ten minutes.'

The slave's rumpled head emerged from behind the canvas, its long hair falling around its face. 'Mistress, will you be ready in ten minutes?'

Tethia aimed a kick at the slave's head which failed to connect when the slave drew its head back smartly. 'If I'm not ready in ten minutes you'll be sleeping under the stars tonight.'

The slave scampered from the tent. Tethia heard it cry as it went, 'Yes, Mistress!' Ten minutes later both Tethia and the transport were ready, and Rinn was waiting beside it.

Rinn saw her coming out of the sleeping quarters. He blinked in surprise at the sight of her.

'Well, what of it?' Tethia demanded.

'Nothing,' he replied in a tone that clearly implied that there was, indeed, something. 'I've just never seen you in a mantle before.' He looked her up and down, taking in the long swathe of fabric that covered her head and shoulders then falling down in folds over the rest of her body to the level of her knees.

'Married women are supposed to wear a mantle,' she replied, her voice dry. 'What else would I wear, when I'm apparently a married woman?'

'There's no need to be smart,' he replied sourly. 'It was just an observation, that's all.' He turned and got into the transport. He didn't say anything else for the whole trip into Capreae.

The main settlement on Capreae was located near the port, so the transport wove down steeply curved paths as it made its way down the mountain. There were scattered houses along the way, many of them built into the side of the mountain itself. Some of them were simple dwellings, some nothing more than doors at the mouth of a cave. One or two were carved villas set into the mountainside, carved with pillars and porticoes and spaces in the mountain that must lead to private inner courtyards like the one in the villa in Valdennes. What surprised Tethia was the gardens.

There were very few gardens in New Rome. In some of the plazas there were arcades of groomed trees, occasionally Kelsis plants in small gardens, stretching tall, pale stems toward the nebula and ending in small florets of palest green. The gardens on the Palatine were unlike any Tethia had seen before and here on Capreae were plants she had read about, but had never seen for herself. These plants only grew in places where the ambient light was controlled and living in the dome of New Rome most of the time, or in places where civil unrest required the local Councils to order higher levels of lighting. Tethia had never seen bioluminescence in real life.

It was breathtaking. The plants came in all shapes and sizes, clustering around buildings and walls, soaring up to make hedges or spreading out to create carpets, not of leaves or flowers, but of light. The light that radiated from the leaves and stems of the plants seemed to come in every colour of the rainbow. Here a hedge was electric blue, here a soft pink, a carpet of flowers pale yellow, a shrub glowing rich amber. As they drove past the villas and their magnificent gardens of light, both Tethia and the slave craned their necks to catch yet another glimpse of the thrilling colour.

The town itself was set into the harbour. Tethia hadn't even noticed it the day before. The harbour was a symmetrical half circle and the lights of the town built on the steep mountainside reflected splendidly onto the dark waters still frothed with luminescence from the storm.

Rinn drove Tethia and the slave to the broad central plaza where lovers-light outlined the arcades of groomed trees around its border and the well in its centre. These days most houses had indoor plumbing but the poorer houses, generally those inhabited by Freedmen, still required the householder to travel to the well twice daily. At this hour, the well-cover was firmly in place. Only a terrible housekeeper would have failed to fetch water by this time.

Tethia wrinkled her nose at the cooking smells that assailed her while the slave next to her sniffed appreciatively. Half the shops that ringed the plaza were restaurants and food kiosks. The same Freedmen who couldn't afford plumbing also couldn't afford a kitchen so most of the household food would be purchased already prepared.

Tethia's upbringing in the villa in Valdennes had accustomed her palate to delicate flavours, masterfully blended by a skilled chef. The food in the Officer's Mess had been bland rather than delicate, but it was filling. The food the Freedmen preferred was highly flavoured, to cover the rancid taste of spoiled ingredients, if the heavy odours surrounding her were any indication. Tethia looked at the slave next to her then dug into the money pouch that hung on her belt.

'Here,' she said ungraciously. 'Why don't you get yourself something to eat? I'll meet you back here at the eleventh hour.'

The slave glanced at the clock in the Civic Hall tower, well-lit and large enough to be visible from a long distance. It was only the sixth hour, plenty of time to spend the contents of Rinn's wallet.

Tethia and Rinn faced each other across the space of the transport.

'I'll return here at the eleventh hour,' Tethia said.

She felt strangely uncertain. 'I will find her, Rinn.'

Rinn tapped out a pattern on the metal casing of the transport. 'I suppose.' He opened the door and got into the driver's seat. 'I'll be here waiting for you at the eleventh hour.' He closed the door behind him before she had a chance to reply.

Tethia didn't care. She had enough to do without worrying about Rinn. She went into the bath house and let her mantle drop to her shoulders.

In the first room was a pair of guards, two unTied women, dressed alike in sensible clothing suited for accosting any male who dared to breach this feminine sanctuary. Not even Caesar was allowed into the women's baths. Tethia nodded at them politely but didn't speak. If she was female then she was permitted entry, it was as simple as that.

Beyond the guardroom there was a reception room where a massive woman – a little fat, maybe, but muscular and big built – sat behind a desk. Her jowls rolled over her thick neck, her hair, dark, lank and short streaming flat around her face and framing an impressively large bulbous nose. In front of her was a money coffer. That was the key to passing this second gate keeper. The poorest women in the country might pass the first gatekeeper but certainly not the second.

Tethia strode confidently to face the woman, aware that standing to her full height she was nearly as tall as the massive woman was sitting in her chair. 'My name is Tethia of Valdennes, salve,' Tethia said in a ringing voice. 'I wish to rent a cabinet for the day.'

The woman looked her up and down. 'Seventeen Singles and a Bifid for the day. If you want to rent it for a week, it's a Century.'

Tethia reached into the pocket that was carefully concealed among the folds of her chiton and covered by her mantle. She drew out a Century coin.

'For the week, then,' she said.

The woman nodded, as though she'd guessed as much, and held out her hand. Her hand was soft and white, the fingers surprisingly delicate and tapering. She didn't take the coin, waiting for Tethia to give it to her. She slipped it into the money box in such a way that Tethia couldn't see how much money was inside, unlocking and locking the box with a key she withdrew from the depths of her bosom. If she wasn't on such a serious mission Tethia would have laughed at the production of the key, only emerging after the woman inserted her hand into the front of her chiton all the way to the elbow.

'Follow me, sister,' the woman said and, not waiting to see if Tethia was keeping up, made her way through a maze of small corridors and rooms, finally stopping at a small cubicle. 'This is what you get for a Century a week,' she said, gesturing inside.

Tethia looked around. The room was tiny, even smaller than Rinn's quarters at the dig site. There was a narrow bed that folded up against the wall, a tall cabinet with a mirror on the door for clothes and toiletries and a series of hooks on the wall. Tethia had seen hundreds of similar rooms on her travels. Well-to-do women purchased a room and decorated it to suit their tastes, other women would share a room with family members, each taking turns to attend the bathhouse – after all, the bathhouse was where you went to gossip *about* your mother in law, not to enjoy her company.

'This will suit me well enough,' Tethia admitted grudgingly. The woman passed over the key to the cabinet and strode away, the rolls of fat over her hips swaying with each step in an almost hypnotic movement. Tethia went into the cabinet and closed the door behind her. It was dark except for a sliver of light that came in from over the door. A Century a week bought the cabinet, it didn't buy light. Wastage laws still applied, even on Capreae.

Tethia took off her outer garments, the mantle and plain white chiton with a blue belt that marked her as the wife of a Citizen and emerged from the cubby wrapped only in a towel. She was trembling. She had no idea how she was going to proceed. She felt unsure of herself for the first time in thirteen years. Even when she'd abandoned her status as a Citizen's daughter to become an unTied person, she hadn't felt so uncertain. Even yesterday, when she threw herself into the sea at Suruae, she had felt a certainty that it was the right thing to do. Now, facing a group of women wreathed in steam and terrycloth, she trembled.

The bathhouse was busy. Even in the corridor, women bustled past her, chatting with one another in very sharp voices that indicated that their mothers in law hadn't arrived yet. Once Tethia opened the door to the caldarium, she had to draw back for a moment. The room was full of steam, forming a superheated cloud that obscured the room at shoulder height. Most of the women in the room were sitting on the marble floor, beneath the cloud of steam, splashing themselves with cool water and scrubbing at their skin with rough cloths. The room was so long that the end of it disappeared into the steam. It had to be massive, though, simply from the constant, loud hum of voices.

Tethia went into the centre of the room, where a

group of women clustered around a fountain. She snagged a small bowl from a shelf by the door and ducked her head to avoid the intense heat of the steam. The fountain ran with cool water and was a relief after the heat of the steam.

Tethia gave an exaggerated sigh as she splashed herself with the cool water. 'Aaaahhh, that's sooo good,' she murmured, tilting her head back in sensual delight.

There was a young woman on her own, right beside Tethia, who smiled at Tethia's obvious posturing.

'I know, right?' the girl replied. 'I had to wait all week to come here. My husband is a Medic and he hates me coming to the bathhouse. He says it's full of germs.'

'Unlike the hospital,' Tethia commented, and they both giggled. Tethia splashed some more water over her chest and shoulders. She was starting to get used to the heat and the water from the fountain felt cold on her skin. She shivered.

'I've only just arrived in Capreae,' she said. 'Last night, from Suruae.'

'In that storm?' The girl's pale eyes grew wide. 'You're lucky you weren't killed!'

Tethia looked around, then leaned forward conspiratorially. 'I nearly did,' she confessed. 'It was so rough on the boat that I fell into the sea.'

'No! Really?' The girl's hand covered her mouth in a polite gesture of shock. 'How terrible!'

'I thought I'd be chilled to the bone for the rest of my life.' It wasn't even a lie. Tethia didn't reach for the cool water in the fountain again. The chill of that dark ocean was already in her bones. She didn't have to fake the shudder that ran through her. 'I was so afraid I'd get starsickness from being out under the nebula.'

The slave, huddled under a pile of shawls in the dig compound that morning, flashed into Tethia's mind but she pushed it away. The slave needed to learn a lesson, and there were always more slaves where that one came from.

'I hear that the hospital here is making great strides in treating those with starsickness, so at least I'm in the right place,' Tethia went on. She shuddered again. 'Disgusting disease.'

'Oh, it is.' The girl leaned forward, too. 'My husband says it turns people into mutants. Apparently, they're trying to treat the afflicted, but so far nothing can stop the mutations.'

Tethia turned back to the fountain and allowed her hand to trail in the water that now felt sharply cold.

'I heard that's what the Starlight Project is for – trying to find a cure for starsickness.'

'Oh, yes. Everyone here in Capreae knows someone who contributes to the Project in some way. People think that we're all Caesar's favourites out here on the rock, but we try to do our part for the Empire.'

'I'm not sure I'd like to get too close to one, though,' Tethia said. 'I mean, they don't just let the subjects wander around, do they? Surely they're all locked up for the safety of all concerned?'

'Oh, yes, they never leave the hospital. They keep them all far underground, so they don't suffer any more radiation from the nebula.'

'Thank Caesar for that,' Tethia said, with full irony. Then she turned the conversation to inanities and let the girl take over the rest.

Newsspeakers wandered through the bathhouse, their white, sightless eyes no threat to the modesty of the women. Tethia asked one for news of Merrim of Valdennes. He had been found guilty, as she knew he would, but was still awaiting sentencing.

Tethia emerged from the bathhouse an hour later, her skin glowing fresh from scrubbing and shining with the oils used by the masseuse and still a little too warm from the steam.

She went straight to the hospital. From what the girl

in the bathhouse had said, the Starlight Project operated out of one of the wards. There was no point waiting until night and for everyone to go to sleep. The hospital was a major research facility. It would be just as illuminated at night in the pink glow of the nebula as it was during the dark day. At least in the daytime Tethia wouldn't need to worry about protecting herself from the radiation.

Tethia made her steps bold as she approached the hospital. There was no need to affect the slow, modest walk of a matron now that she was dressed as an untied person. Some young men jeered at her short hair, the sign of an unTied person, as she passed through the parking lot at the front of the hospital, commenting on which parts of her clothing she should untie first. She ignored them. Plenty of people barely old enough to remember life before Caracalla still hadn't adjusted to the changes it had made in society. There was no point engaging them. After all, she didn't know the area. Where would she hide the bodies?

She strode straight up to the puddle of light at the gatehouse and rapped her knuckles against the glass to get the attention of the guard. He'd seen her coming and bent his head deliberately to his computer screen.

He jumped at the sudden noise and glared at her. She stared him down. 'I'm looking for a patient,' she announced. 'My niece, Sheya of Valdennes.'

'I thought unTied people didn't have families.' He took a moment to sneer.

'I wasn't hatched from an egg.' Moron. She contained it, but barely. He had no right to the information that she was now a respectably married woman.

The guard ignored her sass, which was probably just as well. He tapped Sheya's name into his computer. Tethia watched the keystrokes, greedy to even see Sheya's name spelled out in front of her. She'd been silent for so long, starved for the sound of her daughter's name.

'Nope, nothing.'

'What if you look for her by matronym? Daughter of Tethia of Valdennes. She's fifteen.'

'Nope.'

'What about by patronym? Rinnarius of Valdennes?'

'Nope.'

Tethia paused to allow the stricture in her throat to pass. 'What if her father was listed as Meropius, General, of Valdennes?'

The guard sniggered. 'Your sister gets around, doesn't she?'

Tethia slammed her hand flat against the glass, right

at the level of his head. It was a wonder it didn't smash. She would have smeared his nose across his face if she could have reached him. The guard jumped back. Maybe he had seen that look on one too many people's faces.

'No!' he shouted. 'Your sister and her bastard baby aren't on this system, now get out of here before I call someone to take you away!'

Tethia's response was pithy, but what it lacked in length, it made up for in clarity.

She strode away from the guard's cubby, through the pools of darkness in the stranger-lit parking lot. She'd been ready to smash the guard for not being able to help her. Her hands still trembled with rage when she saw a familiar slim figure emerging from a skipper.

'Hey!' she cried, too overwrought to keep her voice down. 'Salve, Beris!'

He turned, but there was something different about his expression. It was blank. He spotted her and gave no sign of recognition. She ran up to him because she wasn't built for stealth.

'Salve, Beris!'

'Salve, sister,' he replied politely, with an incline of his head that a Consul's son wasn't required to give to anyone below the rank of General. Even now his manners were impeccable. 'Can I help you?'

'Beris, it's me.' She stopped short just within arm's reach. 'Tethia.' As though he might have forgotten in the last twenty-four hours. He might not have always liked her, but she was sure she'd made sufficient impression for him to remember her name and face twenty years from now. His blank, polite expression could only mean one thing.

Her hands were still trembling, but the rage was swiftly being replaced by horror. 'Beris, surely you recognise me?'

He peered at her more closely in the stranger-light. 'I'm sorry, sister. Were you a patient at the hospital?' He turned away from her to retrieve a cup of incita and a wrapped lunch from the skipper.

Tethia's hands clenched into fists. She wanted to take the cup of incita from him and fling it in his face. Maybe some third-degree burns would wake him up. She'd heard that sometimes intense pain or a shock could cause the Re-Ed cover to falter. 'Beris, have you been Re-Educated?'

He dropped the incita. 'Gods and dogs,' he muttered, stepping back quickly so the coffee didn't splash all over his immaculate boots. When he spoke again, his voice was slightly louder, which for Beris was the equivalent of a shout. 'What are you talking about, woman? Who do you think I am, that I'd ever be in need of Re-Education? I'm a Consul's son, not some... some *person* who goes around accusing strangers of being Deviants in parking lots! Salve!'

He turned and strutted away, looking down to check his boots were still clean.

'Beris!'

'You can call *me* Beris, baby.' Tethia hadn't noticed that the group of young men who'd cat-called her earlier had come up behind her. 'I'll be anyone you want me to be. I know unTied women can sometimes get confused about the name of their current lover, when there are so many.'

'Piss off.' Tethia didn't turn around, that would be a mistake. She shouldn't have even responded, but she was at her limit.

'Afterwards.' He grabbed her shoulder and spun her around to face him. The other young men were gathered around him. One of them grabbed her and the man who'd spoken slapped her across the face. He grabbed hold of her chiton and pulled hard, ripping the fabric free of the brooch, his nails scratching her neck. They tried to pin her arms behind her, but she managed to get one fist free. Thirteen years in the military, a genetically bad temper and one very bad day all culminated in a blow that…

Didn't land where it was supposed to.

Someone else had grabbed her from behind. Tethia spun, ready to throw another punch that would definitely land this time. Just before she broke his nose, she realised that it was Beris who was holding her and she let her momentum throw her into his arms. He dragged her back, a moment before the hospital security arrived to take the young men into custody.

Tethia, angry, but not an idiot, began to cry, quiet, pathetic sobs that made Beris put his arms around her and murmur comforting nothings.

They didn't even ask her any questions. Security just took the young men away while Beris guided her towards the hospital. He led her into a cubby, lined with medical supplies, with a hard, narrow bed in the centre of the room. Tethia sat on the edge of the bed and buried her face in her hands.

Beris closed the door. 'You can stop that now, we're alone.'

Tethia looked up, checking. 'Bastard,' she muttered.

'I'm not going to turn you in, but you can stop with the language. Even an unTied person knows better than to speak like that. You were probably a Citizen's daughter once.' He took supplies from the shelves, his back to her.

Tethia took the handkerchief from her pocket and wiped away the conjured tears. She snivelled, an unfortunate result of the tears. 'Being a Citizen's daughter isn't all it's cracked up to be, not before Caracalla, not after. You have to ask yourself why so many of us seek classification as unTied people rather than women. Maybe it's something to do with the fact that fifteen years ago, under the law, we weren't even human. *Some* men still don't think we're people.'

'Well, I'm not one of them.'

'I know. Even Re-Educated, you're still not cruel.'

'I wish you'd stop saying I've been Re-Educated.'

'Why should I give assent to a lie? You wouldn't.'

Beris stared at her, then dropped the medical supplies he'd been holding into a small dish. 'Who are you?'

Tethia was about to give her name, hoping it might jog his memory, but she was in a precarious position. Her trial, thanks to Merrim, had been very public. It had probably even been reported all the way out here in Capreae. She remembered Beris's pale face at the trial. Re-Education only took a moment. For all she knew, he'd been Re-Educated before the trial even took place. It would explain why her trial was the first injustice he'd ever allowed to pass unremarked.

'Lerina of Mellior,' she replied. 'UnTied businessperson.' She'd given her real name in the parking lot. She could only hope that he hadn't recognised it from her trial. It had only been yesterday.

Beris ripped open a packet of sterile equipment and began to lay it out on a trolley. 'I suppose I don't have to introduce myself to you. You seem to think you know me already.'

'Not well,' Tethia admitted. 'I only knew you for a short while. I-' she stopped again. She couldn't tell him that she was assisting with Ala's Audit. There were no circumstances where an ordinary person would assist at an Audit. They would never even go near the Palatine. They would never meet someone of Ala's status, nor of Beris's. 'We met in New Rome, when you went to Audit Ala.'

'Audit Ala?!' That brought his head up. 'I refuse to believe Ala would *ever* be the subject of an Audit!'

'She wasn't a Deviant.' Tethia's voice was low. Even the suggestion was obscene. 'It was a Qualification Audit. She'd been recalled to New Rome because she was to be given the honour of bearing Caesar's child.'

Beris went pale, and not for the first time, Tethia

wondered exactly what the relationship was between him and Ala. Although Beris was still a young man, probably ten years Tethia's junior, Ala was much younger than he was, probably not even at her majority. They'd both grown up here, in the solitude of Capreae. Ala was Caesar's niece, Beris a Consul's son. They might have been anything to each other. He pulled on sterile gloves with excessive force.

'That didn't happen,' Beris muttered, his gloved hands busy arranging the materials on the sterile trolley, the tremor in them visible as he picked up first one instrument then another before putting them back down again. 'It didn't happen. I've been on Capreae all my life. How could such a thing have happened without my remembering it? I came in to work this morning... the guard said....'

He stopped fiddling with the instruments and locked eyes with Tethia. 'The guard asked if I'd been on holiday, since he hadn't seen me for a few months. But I'm sure I came in to work yesterday, the same as always. I remember it.'

'Maybe yesterday wasn't yesterday. The Re-Eds are...' a memory came unbidden to Tethia's own mind, as out of place as Beris's recollections of yesterday. 'The Re-Eds are very good at what they do.'

Maybe Beris wasn't the only one to be Re-Educated. That would explain why he'd been so familiar with her, practically from the first moment they'd met at the train station.

Beris pulled the trolley over to Tethia.

'Lift your chin,' he ordered. 'I'll clean the wound first. Who knows what kind of filth he had under his fingernails?'

Tethia shuddered at the thought and obediently lifted her chin.

Beris swabbed at her skin with antiseptic. 'Why did you come to the hospital, anyway? Were you looking for me?'

Tethia sighed and Beris raised her chin with the tips of the forceps under her jaw. 'Not exactly,' she admitted. 'This is so awkward, trying to explain it to you, but you might be the only person who can help me. You're a good man, aren't you, Beris?'

'I like to think of myself as a good person.' He dropped the forceps into a kidney dish. 'I suppose we all like to think of ourselves as good people.'

'Yes, but you really do care about people, don't you?'

'Why else do you suppose I became a Medic?'

Tethia laughed, but it wasn't funny. 'I've known plenty of Medics who aren't in it because they care about people. Have you ever seen someone who suffers from starsickness?'

'Of course I have.' He picked up the dressing carefully. 'We get a lot of starsickness in Capreae because there isn't any shielding. We have whole wards full of people suffering from starsickness. Disgusting disease.'

'They're trying to find a cure, though, aren't they?'

'I suppose so. It's probably the major threat to the health of our society today. I'm not much involved in research, but I've heard about a project in progress here in Capreae, trying to find a cure. Why are you so concerned about starsickness?'

For one moment, the very shortest of moments, Tethia considered not telling him about Sheya. She'd spent half her life pretending that Sheya didn't exist, keeping her a secret. Yesterday she'd stood in front of a crowded stadium and admitted her secret to all of them. She'd been more ashamed than she had ever been in her whole life, but it was worse, now, admitting it to a man she respected and admired, here in a quiet, private room.

She kept her chin high, because she'd rather die than show her shame.

'I had a baby,' she said. 'Sixteen years ago. I was not married. The child became one of the unCounted. I always believed that she was being cared for, maybe by some kind, childless couple. An older couple, maybe, who would spoil her and lavish affection on her.'

Beris sank back onto a stool, but he never took his eyes from her. Tethia went on. 'It gave me comfort, and hope, to think that she was happy, that she was safe, that she had the kind of life and the kind of family that I wouldn't be able to give her. Yesterday I discovered that all those comforting hopes and dreams were not true.'

Tethia finally dropped her chin. If it had been hard admitting her infraction, it was nearly impossible to speak the words she'd read on Merrim's note. 'She was sent here, to the Starlight Project. They have been using my little girl for medical experiments, Beris. And in three days she is going to be killed.'

He didn't gasp or cry out, he didn't mutter some denial. 'You utter bastard,' she breathed. 'You knew!'

He brought up his hands just in time to stop her as she flew at him, trying to beat at him with her fists while he held her arms.

'Stop it, or I will have to call security.' He didn't raise his voice. The moment he raised his voice, security would come anyway. 'I didn't know about your daughter. I would swear before a whole stadium that I don't know you. But I knew that the unCounted were part of the Project.'

'How could you know about such evil and stand by?' Her voice was as low as his. She wrenched her arms away and he let her go. 'I thought you were better than that. I thought you were better than all of us, and you've been standing by and letting evil grow right in front of you. People like you are the reason the Starlight Project exists! People who just go about their lives and don't think twice about what is happening around them. People who only care about the things that affect them directly, and into the dark with everyone else!'

'They are test subjects, Lerina,' Beris replied. He tossed the sterile instruments he'd used into a bin and bundled up everything else on the trolley. 'Starsickness is a terrible disease. Thousands of people die of it every year. Many suffer from hideous mutations. Research is necessary to save lives. Nobody is doing these things for fun.'

'She is my *daughter!* Do you expect me to just let her go, because starsickness is a terrible disease? It is her *life!*'

Beris threw the bundled up equipment into a bin. 'I'm sorry you're upset about this. The Starlight Project is our best hope for saving lives. Without it, thousands will die every year from starsickness.'

'That doesn't make it right!' Tethia cried, forgetting to keep her voice low. 'My daughter may be unCounted, but she is a person, not just a missing digit in a census.' She hopped down from the bed and paused at the door. 'I thought you were a better man than this. Vale, Beris.'

#

Tethia closed the door on Beris and put him out of her mind. She was inside the hospital. That was more luck than she'd bargained for. There was no way the guard outside wouldn't remember her and he wasn't going to let her in again.

The Starlight Project had to be located in the hospital. It was a research project. They would need access to labs and medical equipment and medical personnel. It wouldn't be in the main part of the hospital, that would be reserved for people requiring medical care. It would be somewhere separate, somewhere most people wouldn't go. The test subjects would be isolated from the other patients, maybe in a deep basement, or a building set apart from the main section of the hospital.

She'd had a lot of time to think about this in the bathhouse, and the long hours on the train coming to Suruae. She wished she'd had the foresight to keep one of her uniforms somewhere so she would be able to access it. It was going to be difficult to find a good enough reason to be in that section of the hospital.

She stretched out her mind, reaching for the smallest thoughts. She could sense the people around her, but they were mere presences. The smaller the mind, the more power she had to take control. And take control she did.

The hospital was about to have an infestation.

Tethia walked purposefully. When she passed a reception desk, she stopped. 'Can I have a piece of paper, please?' she asked. 'And a pen? Thanks.' She scribbled on the page, then returned the pen, again offering thanks. Folding the paper, she continued on her way. She kept the main entrance behind her, aiming for the back of the hospital, and taking every staircase that led down. In all the stories she'd ever heard about someone breaking into a hospital there had always been a convenient rack of lab coats and masks available for disguise. All the staff in this hospital apparently got dressed at home or in a locker room instead of the hallway. What were the odds?

One man stopped her. 'Hey, where are you going?' he asked.

Tethia raised the folded piece of paper. 'Delivering a message, sir.'

'I haven't seen you here before. Do you work in the hospital?'

'No, sir. I'm here to deliver a message.' Maybe sass wasn't her best friend right now. She smiled and dropped her gaze to dilute the effect, but he remained suspicious.

'Who from?'

There was no disguising the fact that she was dressed as a Citizen's wife, so the answer was obvious. 'From my husband, sir, to one of his colleagues.' She smiled again, daring to raise her eyes. 'To tell the truth, sir, I haven't been this way before. My husband gave me directions but I'm terrible with directions. You know what women are like. I know the Project is down here somewhere, but I forget where I'm supposed to go from here.' She even bit her lip.

He dropped a heavy hand on her shoulder and she was careful not to flinch – thirteen years in Service had taught her that much. He turned her around, then pointed down the corridor. 'You head down this way, then through the door on the left. They'll ask for your security pass at the next marker. You *do* have your security pass, don't you?'

Tethia laughed a little and turned her head to find herself uncomfortably close to him. 'Of course,' she said.

'Off you go, then, sister.'

'Thank you, sir.'

Tethia glided away, making sure to walk like a respectable matron instead of an unTied person with things to do and people to see. She cursed herself as she went. A security pass? How in the name of Caesar's Mask was she going to get her hands on a security pass? And what could she possibly say at the door to make them do anything other than arrest her?

In the end, she just walked past. There were two guards standing outside the door, armed and alert. They looked like they meant business. She couldn't think of a single thing to say to them that might allow her into the protected area. She went through the door at the very end of the corridor and found herself outside in the dark again.

She wanted to scream. But screaming wouldn't help, so she didn't. She knew where the Project was, at least. That was progress. She walked around the area. It was concreted all around, surrounded by chain link fences, with large pieces of strange machinery that could serve any purpose from the ventilation of the building to the disposal of unCounted bodies.

Meanwhile, a similarly uncounted horde of insects were finding their way between cracks, coming up from the floor, out of the walls and down from the ceiling, to look around the interior of the Starlight Project. Tethia let her mind join theirs, following their small thoughts as they scuttled along corridors and into rooms. Eventually, she sat down. It was tiring, following so many thoughts. The back of the hospital was built at the edge of the town, so there were just hills and natural scrub beyond.

And then, a small thought that had Tethia leaping to her feet. One of the insects was passing beneath her feet. Through a ceiling, under the ground. Tethia followed it, stepping slowly as the roach scuttled through cords of wiring and insulation. The Project wasn't just in the hospital. It extended underground, into the bedrock of the surrounding hills.

Tethia paced out the borders of the Project, climbing among the scrub, the plants catching at her chiton and the dirt marking her hands and face when she slipped and fell on the steep incline. She didn't realise how late it had become until she heard the sharp sound of the warning bell, all the way from the centre of the square. The nebula was rising.

She hurried back around the hospital. It was a large complex and the exterior wasn't designed for easy access. She was going to have to hurry.

By the time Tethia finally made it back to the square, the nebula was already visible over the horizon. She felt like her skin was already prickling from the radiation, even though all the experts agreed that the dose of radiation was too slight to feel symptoms from a short period of exposure.

Rinn was waiting beside the transport, a dark cloak wrapped close about him, his face hidden by the deep hood. The slave was already in the transport, its outer garment wrapped around its head and face.

'Where the hell have you been?' Rinn demanded, striding forward. He grabbed her arm tightly. Tethia let him pull her close so she could hiss in his face.

'You know damned well where I was, Rinnarius!'

'We agreed to meet at the eleventh hour-'

'Surely it must have occurred to you that maybe I might be a minute or two late?'

He slapped her across the face.

Tethia had been slapped plenty of times before – slapped, punched, shoved by her father and her superior officers, but she wasn't ready for Rinn's blow. He'd never raised a hand to her before. She let her head rock to the side from the force of the blow.

'Don't you dare interrupt me again,' he gritted.

Tethia turned her head back to face him. So many thoughts raced through her mind. She was quite capable of killing him. She might have joked about her not knowing where to hide a body, but after her day on the hills, she even knew where she would leave him. It would be so easy.

But then, she would have to abandon her search for Sheya. She needed his permission to be in public, needed his transport and his respectability. So, she lowered her gaze and murmured, 'Yes, sir.'

It was enough to please him.

'That's better,' he said. 'Get in the bloody transport.'

'Yes, sir.'

\#

They were both late for the evening meal. Jael waved away Rinn's apologies and excuses that sounded false even to Tethia's ears.

'You look like you've been very *active* today, sister,' Andred said. Tethia ignored him, addressing herself to the food. 'In fact, you look exhausted.'

'It was a long day of shopping,' Rinn replied, with a sidelong glance at Tethia. 'She needed some shoes.'

'Really? I didn't think buying shoes was quite so... physical. And you were quite late coming home, weren't you? Did you make your new husband wait for you, Tethia?'

Rinn slammed his fork on the table, making Tethia jump. 'That's enough!' he snapped. 'If you have anything you want to say to me, Andred, you'll say it to me. You have no reason to address my wife so familiarly.'

A sly look entered Andred's eyes. 'Oh, I don't know. She was unTied for a long time. UnTied women are all the same. Why else was she back so late today?'

Tethia and Rinn spoke simultaneously.

'How dare you!' Tethia cried while Rinn shouted, 'That's enough!'

Rinn rose to his feet. 'My wife has never gone anywhere unaccompanied and has never acted with impropriety.'

'Except for the reason you were married so suddenly, right?' Andred smirked while the rest of the group looked on in fascination. He nudged Eleron, sitting next to him and the other man sniggered. 'I follow boxing. It's very interesting, especially that boxer who went on trial for his sister's adultery yesterday. Still waiting for sentencing, I believe, but it doesn't look good. The newsspeakers talk of nothing else.'

Rinn's face darkened and he turned to look at all the interested faces around the table. 'If you were all so concerned you could have spoken to me directly. Are you forgetting that I was also involved in that crime? Tethia may have committed adultery, but *I* was the one who defiled the property of Meropius General. I was lucky that I wasn't caught while the General was alive or he'd've castrated me. Instead, I was lucky enough to find myself married to a beautiful woman. I wish I could be sorry for what I did, but how could I be sorry when it has brought me everything I value in the world today?'

He turned to look down at Tethia. She was gazing up at him, astonished. The look in the dark eyes he turned to her appeared sincere and surprisingly tender. He turned back to Andred. 'Insult my wife again and you'll answer to me.' He allowed a heavy silence to follow his words before turning back to Tethia. 'Now, my dear, would you like to take a walk before we retire?'

'Certainly, dear. Whatever you say.' Despite thirteen years in Service those were words that had never passed her lips before. She put her hand in his and rose daintily from the table, simpering at Rinn as she went.

Rinn's hand was firm holding hers and he set a pace walking to the caves that made her skip to keep up.

'Rinn, are we running?'

He stopped suddenly, seeming to only just realise that she was so much shorter than him that she had to raise her arm like a child to hold his hand. He slowed his pace until they were inside the shelter of the cave.

'Sorry – I was upset.' He pushed the hair off his face in that rapidly-becoming familiar gesture. 'And I'm sorry you had to hear Andred carrying on like that. I know you think I'm sexist, but I hope you don't think I'm anything like him. I'm sorry-' he stopped, and she was surprised by the anguish that rippled across his face. He continued in a very soft voice, 'I'm so sorry I hit you earlier.'

Tethia examined his face. She wasn't even sure how she felt. There was still a chance he wasn't going to survive the night, even with a pretty apology. But then, he had been her first love. She'd never felt about anybody the way she'd felt about him. And there wasn't a man she knew who didn't slap his wife occasionally.

The thought crossed her mind involuntarily that Beris would never strike anyone, whether he thought he had the right to do so or not. She pushed the thought away. Beris was not the man she had been married to.

'I'm sorry I was late,' she said. 'I spent the day trying to find the Project, trying to find a way in. Sheya was all I could think of. Knowing that she is safe is everything to me, Rinn.'

'Of course, it is,' he replied, smoothing a hand down her cheek. 'The girl I knew would do anything for the people she loved.' Rinn's gaze strayed from her to the mountains. 'I wish I'd married you back then,' he said. 'Then we'd have our own home by now and Sheya would be safe with us, instead of gods-know-where.'

Tethia pulled at his hand to bring his attention back to the present. She didn't want him fantasising about some perfect life with her. Any man who could strike her so easily was not someone she wanted dreaming of a forever after with her in it. 'Maybe you were right. Maybe she is safe somewhere. She still has time. If I can just get to her, I know I can save her.'

He raised his hand to rake through his hair again. 'But we there isn't anything we can do!' he gritted out. He turned back to face her and she was astonished to see that there were tears in his eyes. 'Gods help me, I'd do anything to try and stop this. I've been trying all day to try and find a way around it.'

Undone by the sight of his tears, Tethia raised a hand to his arm. He put his hand over hers, and then all of a sudden, his arms were around her and he was crying into her shoulder. His shoulders shook under her hands. Somehow these tears made her think more of him – if he could cry, then he must have a heart in there somewhere. He must care about her little girl. He must not be as bad as she had thought. Maybe he'd only slapped her today because he'd been so worried about her, because he was already so worried about Sheya…

He was holding her tightly and she felt the moment he realised he had a woman in his arms, not just an object to comfort him. 'Tethia?' he whispered. He drew back and his gaze searched her face for one long moment before he kissed her.

Tethia stood very still. She was his wife. He had the right to kiss her. And if she protested, he might stop her going out tomorrow.

His lips were firm, demanding her surrender and she gave it. She began to fall into his passion as he kissed her and kissed her, in the dark barely protected from the nebula, until she was dizzy and his arms around her were the only stable point in the world. Everything else had faded away and nothing existed but his lips on hers, his hands against her body.

'Let's go back to our room,' he whispered while his lips explored her neck and the lobe of her ear. 'We'll be more comfortable there.' He didn't wait for her to reply, just swung her up in his arms and strode back to the dormitory block.

Inside there was the single lamp, hanging from the point of the ceiling, just over his head. She could barely see him, just his silhouette against the light. Seeing didn't matter. She closed her eyes and waited for his kiss.

'Tethia,' he murmured again as he lowered her to the bed. Now that he was further from the light, she could see him clearer. He was looking at her so closely it was like he was examining her. His hand drifted over her body, coming to rest on her stomach. 'We might make a baby tonight.'

The thought jolted her out of her daze. 'Rinn...' she started to sit up but he sat on the bed next to her and his weight on the bed halted her movement. 'Rinn, I'm not sure I want another baby.'

'But we have to-'

'We do not *have to*.'

'Tethia,' he sounded confused. He probably was.

191

Everything was always much simpler to him than it was to her. He'd always found it easy to fit in to the world and conform to social standards. 'We've lost so much. She was – she could have been everything... to both of us. She could have brought so much joy into our lives.' She couldn't see the tears in his eyes, with the lamp still above him, but she could hear them in his voice. 'If we have another baby, we won't have lost everything. We're still young – there's time.'

'You can't replace one baby with another!'

'Don't you think I know that?' He raised his voice to match hers. 'Nothing could replace her, that doesn't mean we can never have any other children.'

'What could she possibly mean to you? You never even met her! I felt her growing and moving in my body, held her in my arms, fed her at my breast. I was the one to lose her, not you!'

Even as the bitter words left her mouth, she regretted them. His tears had been real, there was no doubt in her mind about that. He jerked back suddenly as though he was stung. He stumbled to his feet.

'You're right,' he said in a gritty voice. 'I didn't lose her. But neither did you. You gave her away, like she was some birthday present you didn't want. You chose to do that to us – to all three of us. You didn't even tell me she was alive. You stole from me any chance I might have had to be her father. Even if we save her, by the gods, it will never be what it could have been.'

Tethia couldn't reply. She couldn't defend herself against the charge. He was right. 'I'm sorry,' she whispered, then raised her voice in sudden anger. 'But I gave her up because I couldn't care for her – not because I didn't want her! I wanted her to have the best life possible.'

'Why didn't you tell *me*? I would have married you. I loved you! Didn't I say it often enough?'

Tethia didn't reply at once. She sat up, averting her face. 'I couldn't face having another baby, Rinn. I couldn't bear it.'

'Well, I *do* want another baby, so where does that leave us?'

'You can't force me to have a baby.' She kept her voice low, well aware that it would be the easiest thing in the world for him to force her to at least conceive a baby. 'You may have a right to my body, but these days I have a right to choose if I have a baby.'

'You took away *my* right to choose. Why is it acceptable for you but not for me?' He turned away from her, his hands raking through his hair again. 'And by the gods, would you stop cringing away from me? I'm not going to rape you. Quite frankly, I'm not in the mood anymore. I'm going back out to the caves.'

He left the room. Tethia relaxed her head back onto the pillow, then turned her face into it and wept for the first time in sixteen years. She wasn't even sure if she was crying because she was grieving, or if it was because she was relieved he was gone.

#

Tethia had spent fifteen years being posted to every corner of the Empire. She was used to waking up in a strange bed. She was even used to waking up in dormitories with a bunch of soldiers snoring away in the nearby bunks. Today there was only one snore, a soft one, coming from the floor beside the bed. It was a struggle to restrain herself from leaping out of bed or running away, maybe or maybe not pausing to bash in his skull on the way out. She shivered with the force of the emotion and tried to keep herself from screaming.

To dispel the nervous energy, she rolled over and looked at Rinn. He was lying on his back, his mouth open, chin on his chest, gently occluding his own airway. His dark hair was longer than it had been when Tethia knew him last. Back then it had been freshly sheared into an approved military style. He had been a fit young man, but he was leaner now, his belly concave beneath the whipcord-muscled arm he'd thrown across it.

Tethia crawled out of bed, needing to scoot to its foot to avoid stepping on the archaeologist on the floor. She turned to look at him for a moment. For once, his dark hair was fallen back from his face, revealing his lean profile. He still had his head in a position likely to occlude his airway permanently. Tethia battled with twin temptations – first, to boot him awake to stop him snoring and second, to tilt his head just a bit more and let him choke. She considered both options but in the end, she just left him to it.

When she got back to the room, Rinn wasn't there. He wasn't at breakfast either. Of course, the others noticed. Tethia had expected it would be Andred but instead it was Jael who asked the question outright.

'Where's your husband this morning?'

'You'll have to ask him that.'

'It's not like him to be late for meals,' Jael pressed.

'I wouldn't know.'

'Ooh,' cooed Andred, 'trouble in Paradise, eh? I'm free, today. Need another ride into town to do your secret stuff, sister?' Andred asked.

'It isn't secret. Clearly you've never spent any time with a woman or you'd know that many women spend several hours a day at the bathhouse. There is food and entertainment there, better than what can be found in the plaza.'

'Sure – entertainment.'

'I believe I was on the verge of threatening to shove your teeth down your throat last night, Andred.' Rinn's voice came from the doorway, clear and sharp as though he'd been well rested and awake for hours. 'Come outside now and we'll settle this once and for all.'

'Uh...' Andred looked around. Everyone else at the table suddenly seemed fascinated by their food. Tethia found that in itself fascinating. 'I didn't mean it – I'll be more... mindful of my manners, in future.'

'No,' Rinn said. 'You've been insulting my wife and that insults me. I have a right to demand satisfaction, by the law. You'll come outside now and face me, whether you're a coward or not.'

Andred's face flushed. 'I'll show you who's the coward.' He stood up suddenly, shoving his chair back.

Rinn merely held the door open and gestured for Andred to precede him through it.

Once the two men were outside, all the uninterested faces around the table dropped their facades and rushed to the door. Jael held them back. 'Tethia – there's space for you. Don't you want to see?'

Tethia shook her head, not deigning to even look back. 'No, thank you. My brother is a boxer. I've had years to realise how much I dislike the sport.' She heard the thump of a fist against flesh, heard a man's groan, heard the muffled cheers from the crowd gathered at the door. She knew the fight was over when the others scurried back to the table. She rose to her feet and went through the door, calmly descending the stairs.

Before her, Andred lay sprawled in the sand. Rinn was striding towards her and her heart gave a funny thump to see him. It was like the first time she'd seen him, like she was seventeen again and he was the most handsome boy she'd ever met – and he'd smiled at her as he smiled at no one else.

She was stunned by the surge of attraction she felt for him. And after all, he was her husband. It was only right for her to be attracted to him. He looked... magnificent, all male and strutting with his victory. His hair was messier than ever, his face shining with a mixture of determination, triumph and possessiveness. He held out a hand to Tethia and stood there, his head thrown back, waiting for her to come to him.

'Come on, Tethia,' he said, 'I'll drive you into town.'

'Whatever you say, my dear,' Tethia said – that was twice, in two days! – and put her hand into his, allowing herself to be led to the transport. As he handed her into the transport, she deliberately held her chiton high to show him a flash of leg and he laughed at the coquettish look on her face.

'You used to do that all the time,' he said, swinging himself into the driver's seat. He pressed the button that brought up a divider between them and the slave in the back seat. 'Sometimes I thought I saw your legs more than your face.'

'You saw a lot more than my legs.'

'Yes, but not often. In fact,' he started the engine, 'it was only twice, if I recall.'

Tethia smiled at him. She liked him like this, more like the boy she remembered. 'You recall correctly.'

'I was pretty sure I remembered it right. I had a lot of time to reminisce over it.'

'I'm sure you've had plenty of other women flashing their ankles at you.' She kept her eyes on the road this time, as they pulled out of the dig site.

'I'm a history teacher, Tethia. I tend not to drive women wild.'

'I find that hard to believe.'

That made him laugh. 'You're good for my ego today, love. But you must know, you were way out of my league. The only reason I managed to get so close to you was because I'd been wearing you down for seventeen years.'

'You must have started young. I was only seventeen, as I recall. You were only a year older than me.'

Rinn turned to face her briefly, then there was a quick silence in the transport. 'I've loved you all my life,' he said seriously. Tethia turned to face him. She swallowed deeply, but before she could reply – and what would she have said? – he went on, 'You don't need to say anything. I understand. I just wanted you to know that there's never been anyone else for me. I'm sorry we argued last night.'

'I'm sorry, too, but Rinn-'

'I know. I do understand. I know all this...' he waved one arm around to encompass the whole world, it seemed, 'all this has been hard. Of course it's been hard. I don't want to make it any harder on you. If having more children would make you unhappy, then I accept that. We have our whole lives ahead of us. We've got plenty of time to discuss...' he shook his head. 'Everything, I guess, everything we've done and everything we plan to do. We can make our plans together. Our marriage doesn't have to be unhappy, just because the Court mandated it.'

Tethia sat in silence for a moment, thinking. 'You didn't seem happy to see me when I arrived.'

'I wasn't thinking about you, then. I was in the middle of my work. Some things weren't going so well. I don't know.'

'I won't hold a grudge, don't worry,' she teased. He was getting grim and she wanted to keep him in his good mood. It was so much easier that way.

That brought his head around. He hadn't expected her to forgive him so quickly, that much was clear from that boyish, surprised look on his face again. He swung his gaze back to the road quickly. Tethia smiled – no, smirked – to herself.

The trip into town wasn't unpleasant, but Tethia breathed a silent sigh of relief when they pulled up in the square. Rinn seemed reluctant to open the door for her, but finally he pressed the button to let her out. 'I'll be here at the eleventh hour to bring you home, then.'

Home? 'Sure,' she said, uncertain, but with a bright

smile.

She spent the morning at the bathhouse that day, figuring that since she'd been telling everyone that she was spending her days there she had better spend at least a little time watching the performances and listening to the storytellers. They were entertaining enough, but Tethia itched to get going. Days at the bathhouse had been interesting when she'd been a Citizen's daughter. Now that she'd had thirteen years as an unTied Citizen, she couldn't imagine spending the rest of her life simply being entertained. She slipped out of the bathhouse around lunchtime and headed for the hospital.

This time, Tethia didn't waste her time going into the hospital itself. She wasn't sure how she would get past the guard, so she walked up the road by the side of the hospital instead. She was ready with a cover story. 'Me? Oh, I'm just going to visit a friend, since women don't have interests or lives beyond gossip. You know how women are.' Canned self-loathing and laughter to follow.

But no one even drove past, much less asked her where she was going. The road quickly petered out to a dirt track, then a driveway after going through a small gate. There was a large villa at the top of the hill, and the driveway appeared to be completely private. It would be harder to explain herself to anyone coming down a private road, so she wrapped her dark mantle tighter around her and sought the skies for a bird's thoughts to ride.

There – an eagle. Tethia joined her mind to the eagle's with surprising efficiency. It felt strangely familiar, almost like coming home. The bird was even pleased to meet her, its thoughts sharp and joyous as it wheeled in the dark, star-studded sky.

The path was steep. Tethia eventually had to stop and sit by the side of the road, keeping her mantle close about her to hide her white chiton. The eagle circled her once, admiring her camouflage, before flying further afield, over the scrubby, rocky hillside.

Tethia followed the eagle's thoughts as she rested, scanning the ground for any signs of human activity. When she saw it, a jolt passed through her body and she found herself on her feet with no memory of standing up. She turned away from the driveway and began to hurry through the scrub. That was it. It had to be. It just had to be.

It wasn't much, but it definitely wasn't natural. The eagle had passed a small, shiny patch of ground, perfectly square and cleared of weeds. Within the eagle's memories was a cage that rose through the square and stayed above ground for several hours or days. And inside the cage…

humans. Tethia couldn't get any further details from the eagle's memories. Humans weren't good to eat, therefore too boring to remember. Her heart was pounding as her sandals skidded in the dirt beside the square.

There was a release button to one side – Tethia couldn't believe her luck. She'd had time to think about this, though. This was a secret Project, but it wasn't clandestine. It was officially sanctioned by the government and probably had Caesar's seal all over it. They didn't think they were doing anything wrong, just like Beris had tried to convince her yesterday. They were just doing their jobs. They probably even saw themselves as heroes because they were trying to eradicate starsickness. If a few, or even many, subjects were lost along the way, then that was an acceptable loss in the name of science. They didn't see their work as murder.

The Project wasn't underground because it was secret. The young woman in the bathhouse had given Tethia information readily enough. The Project was underground so it didn't contaminate its data. The purpose of the Project was to find a cure for starsickness. Naturally, they would need to study the subjects away from the contamination of radiation from the nebula. They would need a control group that had never seen the sky. They would also need to expose other subjects to the nebula for carefully timed periods to find out how much exposure would result in cellular damage or mutation.

And this was it. This was where the subjects were exposed to the nebula. And since it was just another day at work for the scientists, of course they had a release button on the outside of the doors. What if something went wrong? She wasn't trying to break into the lair of a supervillain, just a laboratory. And laboratories everywhere were very keen on Occupational Health and Safety.

She pushed the release button, keeping herself to the side to avoid being seen, just in case someone was below and looking up. The smooth square split in the middle and the two doors slid open. They covered a dark tunnel. Tethia looked down carefully and saw nothing. It was just a tunnel.

She'd been right about the Occupational Health and Safety, though. There was even a ladder, set into a recessed section of the tunnel wall. The cage would rise, but anyone on the ladder would not be crushed if the cage happened to go past them. It seemed so bizarre that a Project whose purpose included terminating its human subjects would be so concerned about the health and safety of its researchers.

But then again, she said to herself, as she tried to

kick her chiton out of the way of her sandals as she descended the ladder, whether or not your life was worth preserving depended entirely on who you were. Unbidden came the thought of her slave, cowering outside, covering itself with shawls and cloaks to protect it from the nebula.

No… not it. Tethia's foot slipped on the ladder and she held in a short scream that made her chest hurt. The slave was human. The slave was male. He. *He* had covered himself with shawls and cloaks to protect himself from the nebula that wasn't even visible in the sky anymore.

She pressed her face against a cool metal rung of the ladder.

'*Just jump, woman, you're almost there!*'

The voice shocked her so much that she couldn't hold in the scream this time. Her foot went down without pushing her chiton out of the way first. The fabric slipped between the ladder and her sandal and she cried out again. Her hands slipped against the smooth metal. She lost her grip on the ladder and fell backwards into the dark.

She only fell a few feet but landed hard on her back. She gasped, all the air driven from her lungs.

'*Stop being such a wimp,*' the voice said. Tethia rolled to look beneath her and received her second shock.

She was lying on top of the cage.

Her daytime-vision was excellent, one of several mutations she'd successfully hidden throughout her career. She could see as clearly in the dark as she could in the light of the nebula, or in artificial light. She'd used it to her advantage more than once, but she hadn't seen this cage beneath her while she was looking down into the tunnel. Now that she was lying – extremely uncomfortably, mind you – on top of it, she could see that its surface was louvred to carefully grade the amount of exposure to the nebula the subjects received.

The subjects. The cage wasn't even full, but both the subjects were looking up at her. A hasty pull brought her chiton to a respectable level and one of the teenage girls inside looked away just long enough to snigger silently. Tethia rolled over onto her stomach and gripped a slat.

'You have to help me,' she whispered urgently. 'I'm looking for a little girl. Her name is Sheya. I have to find her.'

She gazed down into the cage. As Tethia watched, one of the girls locked eyes with her and rose to her feet. She kept her eyes trained on Tethia, looking straight up. Standing at her full height, she tossed her hair back in an unnecessary, haughty gesture.

The gesture she made with her hands was

universally offensive.

The other girl, sitting at her feet, her white hair reflecting in the light of the stars, looked down. She sighed. The standing girl nudged her with her foot. The seated girl sighed again.

'*So what?*' she said in a regretful voice. '*What about us, we don't get anything, but we should totally rescue whoever you think is more important than us? We'll just stay here. We're in a starstruck cage, it's not like we're going anywhere.*'

The whole thing was delivered in a monotone.

'Are you all right?' Tethia asked? 'Have you been hit in the head recently or something?'

The standing girl snorted. She made another gesture, just as offensive as the first and sat down.

The pale girl looked up. 'I'm Dubhia.' Her voice sounded different this time, quieter, sweeter. 'This is Perry. They stopped her talking and now I get to say all the rude things she wants to say. I'm not a rude girl, so anything I say that's upsetting, that's Perry talking.'

'Perry… is that the girl who's rude even when she's not talking?' Tethia asked.

'That's the one.'

Tethia shook her head. She knew that the subjects

might be horribly disfigured from starsickness. She'd even considered the possibility that they were mutants, like she was. She hadn't expected sass.

'I'm looking for someone.' She curved her hands around the louvres beneath her. 'She's my daughter. She's in terrible danger, she's scheduled for termination!'

'As opposed to the rest of us, of course, who deserve to die.' The voice was different. That must be Perry.

'She's only a little girl, fifteen years old!' Tethia cried.

'Fifteen years *old* is *NOT* a *little* girl!' This time there was a curious tone to Dubhia's voice. This time she and Perry had spoken at once.

Tethia drew in a deep breath and let it out slowly, but when she spoke, she still sounded sarcastic. 'You're right, fifteen years old is very grown up. Now tell me where I can find my daughter!'

'Screw you.'

'I'm glad I'm not your mother,' Tethia snapped. 'You must be an awful disappointment to someone. Now answer the damned question!'

Dubhia looked down. Perry shrugged. *'Who knows how many of us there are? We're from the Western shire. We only see foreigners when it's Founder's Day and when the Councils meet. When we get together we don't really talk about how many of us are going to die soon.'*

Tethia, despite her excellent daytime-vision, had to blink to clear her eyes. It had looked for a moment like an emotion other than anger had crossed Perry's face, but that had to be a trick of the dark. It was gone before Tethia could classify it.

'You have to tell me how I can get in,' she said. 'Sheya is my daughter. I'm sorry about what's happening to you. I would help you if I could. But she is my *daughter*. She means everything to me. I have to save her or I can't go on.' Despite herself, her voice started to shake. Because she was lying down, the tear that fell didn't roll down her cheek. It fell straight into Perry's hand, who stared at it like a diamond fallen from the sky.

'*Only if you save us, too,*' Perry said. Dubhia's head whipped around so she could stare at Perry, even as Perry's words came out of her own lips.

'Oh, please,' Dubhia whispered. She reached out to touch Perry's hand and there was a moment of silent communion between them.

Perry stood up again. '*Promise,*' she said. '*You have to promise.*'

They were just little girls, really. Perry might have

attitude enough for a regiment, but she was still only a little girl. Hadn't she said as much? If one was to matter, then all had to matter, and the little girls in front of her had just as much right to live as Sheya. She couldn't turn away from them.

'I promise,' Tethia said. She tried to reach through the louvres, but they were too close together and she could only fit her forearm through. 'How can I get you out?'

'*Well, for starters, you can stop wasting your time trying to pull us through the bars,*' Perry said. '*Get back up and go to the side of the cage. There's a section cut out of the tunnel wall where the overseers can access the cage to take measurements. Go through there.*'

Tethia followed the instructions.

'*There's a release mechanism. Pull the panel off the wall, no, higher. Moron. Yes. Now key in this sequence.*' Tethia obediently typed in the code, trying to ignore Perry's casual name calling. The panel was easy to reach from her current position but the people in the cage would never be able to reach it. The careful attention to Occupational Health and Safety, while designing procedures intended to kill human beings was sickening. The problem wasn't just that the Project was evil. The problem was that it all seemed so normal to the people administrating it.

There was a quiet *snick*. Perry leaped to her feet. Dubhia followed, but more slowly. *'Now the release button and we can all get out of here,'* Perry said. Even her voice, coming from Dubhia's mouth, was trembling. Tethia pushed the button… and the doors slid apart right in front of her, revealing a room with rails extending into the middle of it to support the movement of the cage.

She stepped through. Perry, leading Dubhia by the hand, was right behind her. *'Quickly,'* Perry muttered. She hurried around to another access panel by the side of the door they'd just stepped through. *'We're so close, so close. They'll be back any minute.'*

'What are you trying to do? Can I help?' Tethia asked. She put a hand on Perry's shoulder but Perry shrugged it off.

'I'm trying to retract the cage so we can get out through the tunnel. It's a fail-safe, see?'

She gestured to the tunnel. Tethia looked but didn't see anything. 'See what?'

'Whenever the cage is open, the fail-safe comes down and blocks any exit via the tunnel. If I lock the cage, the doors will shut before we can get out. I need to retract the cage into the room. There's a maintenance cycle, I've heard them talk about it. It's the only way the tunnel can be

accessed.'

'Wait, you can't do that!' Tethia grabbed Perry's shoulder, so firmly that Perry could not shrug her off. 'I'm trying to get *in* to the Project, not escape it.'

'I think you'll find that getting in is the easy part. Getting out, now, that's the trick. Let me go!'

'You said you were going to help me find Sheya!'

'I said I was going to help you get in. You're in. They're going to kill me. Of course I want to escape.'

'But how do I find Sheya?'

'That's your problem. Dubhi, get ready, here it comes.'

The cage slid out of the tunnel onto the rails on the floor. *'Come on, Dubhi, time to climb.'*

Tethia turned away from the two girls as their slight forms disappeared into the tunnel, their dark jumpsuits already blending with the shadows of the dark day above. She leaned over the computer and began to search the system.

The system was not easy to navigate. It was a corporate computer system, filled with redundancies, dead end file paths and duplicated information. After all, she didn't even know Sheya's name. She found some subject files, organised by date of birth, but there were eight subjects who shared Sheya's birthday. Each one was identified by two letters and a series of numbers.

She had no time to do more than skim the list when the door to the office opened. Two guards rushed in, followed by a man in a lab coat. In the hallway, a red light blinked from above the open office door.

Tethia grabbed the keyboard from the desk, ready to use it as a weapon. The guards approached her, arms spread wide to cage her in.

'You're making a mistake,' Tethia said. 'I'm not one of you.'

'That's painfully obvious,' the researcher said. 'What's your assignment number?'

'My what?' One of the guards tried to take advantage of Tethia's distraction. He ended up with a keyboard across the face for his trouble. When his companion went down, the other guard rushed to apprehend her. A quick swipe of his hand knocked the keyboard from her grasp. Tethia grabbed his arm, pulled him forward sharply and cracked her forehead against his. He grunted. She swept her leg around his to bring him down.

She made a tiny noise of shock. She'd lost track of the researcher: he was behind her, and if the little sting in her shoulder was any indication, he'd just won this round. She fell to the floor, landing directly on top of one of the guards. The last thing she saw was the researcher safely disposing of the syringe in a sharp bin.

#

Tethia expected to wake up in a cold, dank cell. Instead, she woke up in a room that smelled of disinfectant. She lay on a cold, narrow bed, and as her vision cleared and details emerged, she saw that she was alone in what looked like a hospital room.

There were monitors attached to her chest beneath a hospital gown. The temptation to remove them was strong, but she didn't want to draw attention to herself. She still had to find Sheya, and maybe even find a way out. She sat up, noting a pain in her side she was sure she hadn't had before, and slid off the bed.

The door opened, without so much as the courtesy of a knock. Another man in a white coat entered the room.

'How did you know?' she asked.

'Motion sensors.' He gestured to a small unit in the corner of the ceiling. 'So, you're awake. We couldn't find your tattoo. What's your assignment number?'

Tethia sighed and sat back on the bed. 'I don't have an assignment number.'

'Hmm.'

'Hmm is not particularly helpful, you know.'

'Fortunately, or unfortunately, haha, depending on your point of view, we're not here to help.'

Tethia sat very still. 'What are you here for?'

The man sat in the chair beside the bed, pulling a small unit from his pocket. 'That depends entirely on what you're here for. Shall we start with your name?'

'Lerina of Mellior,' she replied, her hand moving to her side to try and find the source of the pain. There was a dressing, a foreign ridge of fabric beneath the hospital gown. She couldn't remember being wounded. Her skirmish with the guards hadn't resulted in her receiving a wound. Her side was aching, but she was determined not to show weakness.

'Hmm.'

'I wish you'd stop doing that.'

To her astonishment, a broad grin split his face. 'Hmm,' he said. 'What about the people you're working with, who are they?'

'What now?' Tethia thought she was being funny, maybe even being a bit cute. She wasn't ready for what happened when he pushed a button on the unit in his hand. Pain suddenly radiated from the new wound in her side, slicing through her abdomen and arcing through her bones. She fell back on the bed, shaking.

'Answer the question, Lerina.'

'I'm not working with anyone!' she shouted. 'What did you just do to me?'

A quick tap of the button and a smaller pain shot through her. 'I'm sorry, Lerina, you don't get to ask questions here. We caught the Medic you were working with. We even caught the two subjects you attempted to liberate.' Tethia, laying back on the bed, closed her eyes. So, Perry and Dubhia hadn't made it either.

The researcher went on. 'It doesn't make much difference *why* you were trying to break into the Project. After all, we have many uses for the average person in the street who has been exposed to the sky all their lives. It makes it difficult to extrapolate data, but at least it gives us an idea of how our research could be applied to the general population without wasting one of our valuable subjects.'

'You can't keep me here. I'll be missed.' Tethia lay her hands ready against the wound in her side, prepared for the sharp lance of pain that went through her.

'No one would dare look for you, Lerina. Do you

know anyone who doesn't fear a yellow card turning up one day? We won't even have to Re-Educate your relatives. People are so used to keeping silent that we barely have to remind them of the dangers of speaking out. It's just a few – just people like you.'

'I'll escape.' She closed her eyes. 'I've been in worse situations than this before. And when I get out, I swear by all the gods that I'm going to destroy you. Stop it, you bastard!' This time the pain was so intense she arched her back so sharply that only her head and her heels remained in contact with the bed and her voice rose in a scream.

'If you want to die a messy death in the squalor of the holding cells then I suggest you continue speaking out of turn, Lerina. I'm a Medic – I'm obliged to help people, but you're not a person anymore. You're a research subject now. Be grateful I even addressed you by your name. It may well be the last time.' Tethia's eyes were still closed but she heard him rise, walk to the door and pause. 'If you try to escape you will be shot and it will be my greatest pleasure to sign your certificate of death.' He slammed the door behind him, and she heard both the sound of the lock and the murmur of conversation between the researcher and a guard outside.

Tethia kept her eyes shut tight. Her side was so very sore. She'd been a hostage before, had people tell her she was utter scum and that they wanted her dead. What difference would it make if they tortured her and killed her, anyway? She had nothing to live for. All she had was Sheya. Even if they killed her, at least she knew that she'd done her level best to save her baby girl.

The others came in shortly. They strapped her down to the bed and pushed the bed out into the corridor. She tried to get a sense of where she was, but she was too distracted by pain and the ceilings didn't differ much from one another. The room they wheeled her into didn't appear much different from the one she'd left.

A woman entered the room, so close behind Tethia that she had to have been either following the party or waiting for them. 'Hi there,' she said, sounding unforgivably chipper. 'I'm Savaa and I'm going to conduct a series of tests. This will go much more smoothly if you co-operate.' As she spoke, she was briskly opening packages of wires and probes, which she attached to Tethia's skin with an efficiency that made her expertise apparent.

'Just let me check your IV…' she snapped open a package containing a loaded syringe and shot a cool surge through Tethia's vein. 'Excellent.' She discarded the syringe and connected a new one. 'This is the sedative. I'm going to be administering this in a few minutes because, believe me, you're going to want to be unconscious for most of this. Unfortunately,' and she smiled at Tethia as she drew a device down from the ceiling, attached on a long, rotating metal arm, 'I need your input for the first few stages. Just scream for me when it gets too painful, OK?'

Tethia stared. Savaa turned on the device and Tethia couldn't help screaming.

'Hmm, would you look at that?' Savaa mused, entering the data.

Tethia woke in a cold, dank cell, if you could call it waking. It was no less than she'd expected. She shifted. Her entire body ached now from being cramped, but she couldn't be sure how long she had been there. She sensed that a good deal of time had passed since they'd tortured her. She didn't even know what they'd done to her after they'd finally given the sedative. As she tried to unknot her limbs, she felt again that dreadful pain in her side, joined now with many other pains.

The movement washed her with pain. She was in complete darkness, in a cell that made no concessions to its occupant. She didn't care about her location, though. All she cared about was the pain.

She lay on her back on a cold, hard surface and tears seeped from between tightly clenched eyelids. Nausea rose in her throat and she rolled to raise herself onto her left arm, sobbing at the pain the movement generated as she vomited helplessly. She collapsed, unable to hold herself up anymore. Her face was only a fraction from the mess she had brought up and she sobbed in helpless disgust and impotent anger as well as in pain.

She cried out, then just cried when she felt a cold hand touch her ankle. It was not a violent hand and seemed to feel almost soothing. A gritty male voice, thin with its own pain said, 'Please don't cry.'

'What did they do to me?' she tried to ask but couldn't talk properly. The pain in her side suddenly overwhelmed her; overwhelmed even her anger.

She drifted in and out of consciousness. The man with her in the dark was unkempt and half-bearded, his face thin and taut with fear. He groped around in the dark to find her and dripped sour tasting water into her mouth. Her thirst was such that she didn't care about the taste. She felt like she was dying and there was nothing she could do about it but she was grateful for the man's presence. He looked terrible but there was something soothing about him. He cared for her, though he himself seemed very ill and racked with fear that he could not hide.

After many sleepings and wakings, Tethia slipped into a state where she was awake but unconscious of the world. The pain was as bad as ever and she was unable to move. How much longer until I die? she asked herself as she longed for it. She felt more alone than she ever had in all her life, but the aloneness didn't seem to matter. The pain took up all her thought. Perhaps I am in a coma, she thought as she gazed unblinkingly at the wall. Her legs and arms twitched occasionally but not as she wanted them to. She heard a choked groan come from her throat intermittently but had no control over it.

The thought came: 'I should have killed myself.' It was what an Imperial soldier was supposed to do, die before being taken captive. 'At least it will end soon,' she told herself. Death, she felt, was very close. She didn't mind. She welcomed the all-encompassing blackness and it consumed her.

\#

Tethia heard the door open but really didn't care. She felt like she was wrapped in fire, enshrouded in burning ice. Anything outside the pain was optional.

'No more room service,' someone said. 'Your allocation of resources is up. From now on you will be joining the other subjects at table and at labour.'

The man beside Tethia, holding her hand tried to protest. 'But she can't possibly-'

'Not my problem, mister. Get your arses out of the cell. We need it for someone else.'

So, he carried her. He didn't get far. He was weak, too. A dozen steps of freedom and he fell to one knee. He lay Tethia on the ground as gently as his shaking arms would allow. Then he collapsed next to her.

Tethia's eyes were open. She couldn't move her head, but she had a fantastic view of the ceiling. She saw the others approach, heard a whispered conference, and then many hands slid her and her companion onto a stretcher.

Moving onto the stretcher was too painful to be borne. The fire overwhelmed her and Tethia fell into the all-consuming flames.

When she awoke she felt slightly better. She opened her eyes: another ceiling. Amazing. She drew in a breath and it was a surprise when it didn't burn. She tried to sit up, putting a hand quickly to the wound in her side and encountering someone else's hands already there.

'Don't you dare ruin this!'

That was Perry's voice. Tethia looked around. If she wasn't so determined not to show weakness in front of a teenager she might have shrieked. She was lying on a… a bier, she supposed was the only word for it. She was still wearing her filthy chiton. She must look like she was being sacrificed, she thought. She would have screamed if anyone but Perry and Dubhia were standing over her.

There was a low murmuring and Tethia was disturbed to realise that it was the sound of many voices chanting softly together. Around her stood a ring of people, all dressed alike in black jumpsuits, watching avidly as Dubhia bent over her, hands at Tethia's waist. Perry stood at her head.

Dubhia's head was hanging down, her soft, white hair hiding her face. Her hands were laid gently over the wound in Tethia's side and from the wound emanated a feeling of comfort and ease that she couldn't recall feeling once in her entire life.

Tethia relaxed, letting her head rest on the stone bier for a little while. Perry nodded at her encouragingly, eyebrows raised to show sincerity.

That'll be a first, Tethia thought to herself, closing

her eyes and enjoying the pleasant feeling. It was like being washed in warm water, and as the waves receded, all her pain went with them.

When the waves of sensation gave way to normal feeling, Tethia sat up. The dark-clad crowd cheered. She looked around sheepishly: that was Beris on the other bier. Dubhia was leaning over him now, but there was something strange about her. She seemed much more bent over than any young woman ought to be, even allowing for the extra flexibility of her age. It almost seemed like a widow's hump on her back.

Tethia swung her legs over the side of the bier and reached out towards Dubhia.

Perry got there first and slapped Tethia's hands away. She shook her head violently and made a series of gestures that Tethia had no hope of interpreting. As Perry put her hand on Dubhia's back – and it was even more obvious by now that Dubhia was even shorter than before, more frail, more fragile – Dubhia took her hands from Beris and turned back to Perry. Tethia only saw Dubhia for a moment before she collapsed into Perry's arms.

Beris sat up, his face radiant and refreshed. The crowd cheered again, the sound swallowing Dubhia's soft cry as Perry tried to slow their fall.

The two girls sprawled on the floor, Dubhia in Perry's arms. Dubhia had changed so much. If Tethia hadn't seen her before, she would have sworn that Dubhia was an old woman lying in the arms of her granddaughter. Perry placed her hand on Dubhia's cheek and leaned forward to press a kiss to the wrinkled brow.

Even as Tethia watched, Dubhia grew young again, her skin filling out, her wrinkles disappearing, her eyes brightening. When she looked up, her eyes first caught Perry's and Perry smoothed the hair away from Dubhia's face, both now teenagers again. Perry looked up, catching Tethia's eyes upon them.

The crowd around them was still cheering and a man was approaching Beris. Tethia barely had time to hear the raspy voice coming from Dubhia's throat.

'She is my voice. I am her strength. Together, we are the best we can be.'

Someone clapped Tethia on the back. She cringed away from it, even as she registered the friendly intent. 'So, how do you like being alive again, huh?'

'It's amazing,' she replied, slipping off the bier, as much to avoid the friendly touch as to get off a piece of furniture designed for dead people. 'Where am I?' She glanced at Beris, who seemed to be quite happy for dozens of strangers to pat him on the back. 'Where are we?'

'You're in the Colony,' the clapper replied, which wasn't as hugely helpful as it was probably intended to be.

'In the Project?' Tethia asked.

'The Colony,' a man said behind her, his voice harder than the clapper's.

'Sure, sure, the Colony,' Tethia muttered, moving forward a few steps to get away from the man behind her. She edged her way towards Beris. When he saw her coming, he held out his hand in welcome. She breathed a sigh of relief, possibly the first deep breath she'd taken without pain for some time and moved more swiftly towards him.

Beris gripped her hand, but gently. 'Well, I guess we're both alive, huh?'

'I guess,' Tethia replied.

Beris surprised her with a wide grin. 'All the signs do seem to indicate it, Lerina!' She surprised herself with a tentative smile.

'Beris, what in Caesar's name just happened?'

'I woke up a bit before you. They didn't push me so far – they wanted me to live so I could help collect data.' A quick, hard look passed over Beris's face, making him look much older all of a sudden.

'We are in the Project, Lerina. We are now subjects, both of us. The people here say they are subjects of the UnderKing, not subjects in an experiment. The researchers…' he looked away for a moment, unable to meet her eyes as he said it, 'they exposed you to a limited dose of radiation to see how much it would take before you died. They expected you to die. You received… a massive dose. But this girl, she's a Sickness Swallower. I've heard of them in very old books, but I've never come across one before. She took your sickness into herself and it took the strain into her own body. She aged before my very eyes.'

He shook his head. 'I've never seen anything like it. Sickness Swallowers usually come in pairs, one to take the sickness away and one to bring her back to herself. It creates a very close bond between them, or is the result of a bond, the literature was never very clear on that point.'

'So, you've read a lot on this, I suppose?' Tethia teased.

Beris's face was serious as he nodded. 'Yes. By Caesar's Mask, I wish I hadn't. All that literature – it had to come from somewhere. It probably comes from here, in the Project. They'd do anything to test exactly what it takes to break the bond between a Sickness Swallower and her auxiliary. Gods help us, those poor little girls. They're just children.'

Tethia followed his gaze to look at Perry and Dubhia. They both looked like they had recovered. Someone had started to sing. Dubhia leaned her head on Perry's shoulder. Perry was smiling as she joined the song.

Tethia moved closer to Beris, resting her shoulder against his, not quite brave enough to rest her head on his shoulder, but the weight of his arm against hers was a comfort she hadn't had in many years. They listened to the song together, a sad, sweet melody about exiles together, facing their exile and their grief with courage.

When the song concluded a man went up a small set of stairs to a dais. 'My friends!' he raised his arms to get everyone's attention. 'This is a day of great joy!' He paused, to allow the people to cheer, which they obediently did. He gestured to Beris and Tethia, standing close together. 'We have two new members of our Colony! Everyone, please welcome Beris and Lerina!'

Another cheer.

'Beris and Lerina, would you step forward, please?'

Beris still had a hold of her hand, otherwise, Tethia was sure she would have turned tail and hid. He had to pull at her hand a little, but she knew it was safest to fit in – hadn't that always been how she kept herself safe? They

ascended the stairs together. The man above them held out
his hands.

'New brethren!' he cried. 'Give me your right
hands.'

Beris let Tethia's hand go and put his hand into the
stranger's readily enough. Tethia's skin crawled as she did
so, but she tried not to show it. She'd done plenty of things
before that had made her skin crawl. This was no different,
she told herself, and she was closer to finding Sheya than
ever.

The man raised their arms. Tethia's mantle slipped
from her shoulders and her gaze followed along her own
arm as it was raised. She would have recoiled in horror if
he hadn't had such a tight hold of her hand. He must have
foreseen her reaction. Instead, she was left cringing away
from her own hand. She'd been marked.

Her arm was bare, from the shoulder of her dirty
chiton pinned by its blue brooch. Her skin was pale, well
adapted to her dark world. On her forearm, clearly visible,
was a blue mark. She stared at it in horror. It was a tattoo,
like a slave's. There were small symbols she didn't
understand. She tried to think back, but she couldn't
remember receiving a tattoo, even during that dark, terrible
time when she was dying of deliberately-induced

starsickness.

Beris wasn't even looking at his tattoo. He must have known it was there. He'd probably been conscious when he was marked. Tethia wished she could rip her own arm off to escape from the terrible, small symbols that she didn't even understand.

'They are one of us now!' the man went on, ignoring Tethia cringing beside him. She wondered how many people had cringed in her position and was nearly overcome by a wave of nausea.

'What is *wrong* with all of you?' Tethia cried, looking out at the identically-garbed group. 'There are so many of you – why don't you try to escape?'

He held her hand even tighter as there was a susurration of anger from the crowd. 'Escape what?' he asked, pulling her so his face was close to hers. 'Escape life? Here we are safe from the deadly sky above. We are surrounded by our friends and family and we have the honour of serving the UnderKing. What else could we ask for?'

'Freedom!' Tethia shouted, taking advantage of her face being so close to his.

'Were you really free under the nebula? You were near death. You know nothing of our ways, how dare you come into our community and try to tell us how to live? Why would we want the freedom to live in a world that is deadly to our kind?'

The crowd cheered. He was speaking through gritted teeth into Tethia's face, so the crowd would have barely been able to hear him. They must have heard this all before. They didn't even want to be free. Tethia just stared. The man, satisfied with her lack of response, turned back to the crowd with a large smile.

'My friends, we have another cause to celebrate! Our own beloved Meriah, MA-55, has been selected for promotion!'

The crowd cheered again, even more enthusiastically. The man let go of Tethia's hand, muttering, 'Get over yourself,' through his smile as he shoved her to the side with Beris.

'Meriah, will you come forward, please?'

An older woman, wrinkled cheeks blushing shyly, stepped forward. 'Now Hallenus, you know I hate a fuss.'

The man's smile, already broad and fake, stretched even broader. 'Meriah, I'm afraid you can't get out of it this time!'

A couple of people in the crowd laughed, but it wasn't a nice laugh, others joined in nervously.

'Everyone, Meriah has been with us a long time in the Colony. She has served the UnderKing faithfully and well and has earned her promotion to the dark. In three hours, Meriah will go from here to the Court of the UnderKing! Meriah, sister, we wish you well and may all your days be dark.' He raised his hands to clap conspicuously.

The applause that followed appeared genuine. Tethia looked around. People were smiling, clapping, some were whistling. Someone started singing again and this time everyone joined it.

'What are they singing about?' Beris asked, bending close to whisper into Tethia's ear.

Even with her extensive background in languages and linguistics, Tethia couldn't recognise all the words. She listened closely. Here and there she caught a word and the slow, pensive tune helped to give sense to them. She turned to Beris to answer. 'It's a song of goodbye,' she replied. 'Beris, I think Meriah is going to be terminated.'

Beris looked across at Meriah, who was holding hands with Hallenus now, her eyes modestly cast down, swaying gently to the rhythm, but not joining in the song. In the crowd, people were putting their arms around their neighbours and swaying together as they sang. They were looking around at each other, too, as though they were reminding themselves of their own good fortune, that it was not their loved ones who were going to be "promoted" today.

'Beris, I think I'm going to be sick,' Tethia muttered. She wasn't exaggerating. She ducked away from Beris and through the crowd. No one tried to stop her. She found a quiet spot away from the group, who were all still facing the blushing Meriah and singing together. She collapsed to her knees and vomited.

She hadn't expected Beris to follow her, but there he was, his hand gentle on her shoulder, soothing her. He cleaned her up, using a corner of her mantle, which had slipped to the floor when Hallenus raised her arm. The mantle was as filthy as the rest of her clothes, and it probably wasn't the first time it had been used for a similar purpose, but she felt better. It felt awfully nice to have someone look after her for a change. She started to cry.

Tethia leaned against Beris and his arm came around her shoulders, stroking her gently. 'Don't cry, Lerina. I'm still here.'

She turned her face to bury it in his shirt. One arm went around his neck. 'I'm so glad you're here with me,' she admitted.

#

'Hey, LA-97, BS-109, get up. I don't know what they told you about life in the Colony, but it clearly doesn't involve as much sitting down and self-indulgence as you two seem to think. As of five minutes ago, you two were employed in the community kitchens, so that's five minutes overtime for you to make up at the end of your shift.'

Tethia looked up. A fat man wearing an apron stood over them.

'Follow me, or you'll go without privileges.'

'What privileges?' Beris asked.

'Food, for one,' the man replied. 'Now hurry up. I'm wasting precious time from my own break just to kick your sorry butts to the kitchen. We've got to cater for Meriah's Promotion Party.'

Beris helped Tethia to her feet. She still felt disgusting and her stomach roiled. She couldn't stop herself from brushing at the tattoos on her wrist as if she could wipe them away. As they hurried along behind the fat man, through winding, spherical tunnels, Beris took her hand in his and kissed it, his eyes meeting hers for one heartbeat in the gloom.

They spend the next hour washing dishes.

Tethia had never washed a dish in her life. That was what slaves were for. Even in Service she'd always had an hourly slave to look after her needs. All she'd ever had to do was dress herself and coming from the privileged life of a Citizen's daughter, that had felt like it was quite enough. She'd never even tied her own sash until she'd entered Service.

She'd expected Beris to be the same. He was even more privileged than she had been as the daughter of a General. He was the son of a Consul. He probably lived in a villa high on a hillside somewhere with its own dome and a private temple, from the days before Caesar declared against religion. And yet he approached that sink like he knew exactly what he was doing.

They fell into a rhythm, Beris washing the dishes like he'd been a slave all his life and, once Tethia got the hang of it, she dried them. It couldn't have been ten minutes before Tethia started complaining.

'My feet are sore,' she muttered, 'Aren't your feet sore, Beris?'

He didn't even pause, scrubbing grime from an enormous pot. 'I suppose. I've had sore feet before today, though.'

'I feel like I'm in the bathhouse from the wrist down,' Tethia said. 'Aren't your fingers getting wrinkled?'

She wasn't ready for him to laugh. He smothered it quickly, but he wouldn't look back up to meet her gaze, peering very closely into the big pot. She suspected he was hiding a smirk.

'And what, may I ask, was so funny?'

He turned to face her, still scrubbing. She'd been right. He was smirking. Smirking from ear to ear, like he was having a great day and she'd just told a joke. He held up a hand. 'I guess my fingers *are* getting wrinkled. I have to say, though, I was afraid today was going to be a whole lot worse than this.'

'We're washing dishes and we're slaves, Beris. How much worse do you suppose it could possibly get?'

He chuckled again. 'Well, to begin with, I'm already cleaner than I usually am after ten minutes at work. No one has bled on me – or worse. This morning I thought you were going to die. Mid-morning, I thought I was going to die, too. Now we've both been raised from the dead. All things considered, it really could be a lot worse.'

'We're slaves in a secret government project, Beris. Don't you think this is depressing?'

The pot was clean. He tipped it over and put it on

the grille to drain. He surprised her by grasping her chin with wet fingers and kissing her firmly. 'Right now,' he said, his face only inches from hers, 'not only am I not depressed, I'm even happy.'

She stared at him as he went back to washing dishes. She could still feel his kiss on her lips. Something woke inside her that she'd forgotten. She hadn't made anyone happy in a long time. She began to wipe the pot, her heart a little warmer in her chest.

Eventually the dishes were done. The sounds of the Promotion party continued through an open door, but now it was dancing and more singing. Tethia wiped the last plate and bent double over the draining grille to ease the pain in her lower back. Beris, with unerring accuracy, lay his hand on the sore spot and began to massage away the pain.

'Don't get too comfortable.' It was the fat man again. Tethia straightened up, Beris's hand migrating to hold her waist. 'You've still got the rest of your shift to go. An order has arrived. I want you two in the pantry to put it away.' He pointed.

Tethia sighed, but the dramatic gesture backfired. The man just watched her chest rise and fall with interest. He grinned. 'You can do that as often as you like, sister.

Doesn't mean you don't have to do your work, though. Into the pantry. Now.'

They did as they were told. The pantry was massive, banks of shelves marching back into the darkness at the back of the room.

'Psst! Hey, come on! This way!'

Tethia and Beris both looked around. Tethia hadn't realised how dark it was in the storeroom until she noticed that she could see Perry and Dubhia quite clearly and Beris's gaze skimmed right over the girls.

'Did you really mean it about saving your daughter?' Perry asked.

'Of course I did.'

'Well, come on then. Get up. Unless you want to stay here the rest of your short life, until every last one of us is "promoted."' Perry's voice, even coming from Dubhia's lips, was distinctive. Dubhia's face was apologetic, but her voice was still acerbic.

Perry whirled and stalked away. Dubhia was slower. 'Sorry,' she whispered. 'She's not always like this. We've got a group. It would be really nice if you could come.' She held out her hand. Tethia took it.

'No disrespect, but I *do* think she's always like this,' Tethia replied. 'Let's see what your group is like, then.'

Perry was already far ahead of them. Dubhia hung back just far enough for Tethia and Beris to follow her through the long banks of shelves to a far corner.

Beris stumbled at one stage, grabbing at Tethia's shoulder. 'How can you keep your feet in all this darkness?' he asked.

Tethia wasn't about to say she could see in the dark. Beris hadn't recoiled from her when they were under the Palatine and Nesta had revealed her abnormality, but Kela had, despite her assertion that she wasn't prejudiced against mutants. Beris had been understanding, as if he met mutants every day, and for all she knew he did, but that was Beris before he was Re-Educated. He might have changed – she couldn't risk telling him.

'I'm following the girl,' she said. Beris took her word for it, and he placed one hand on her shoulder to guide his way as they continued along the corridor.

Perry and Dubhia led them to a small room, where boxes and crates were piled high, ready to be put away in the pantry. A man and a woman, closer to Beris's age than Tethia's, were sitting on the boxes, waiting for them to come in.

'*I have to apologise,*' Perry said, ushering Beris and

Tethia through the door. '*These two are probably duds, but they're the best we've got.*'

'What are your allocations?' the woman asked. 'I'm TR-133 and this is LK-01, but you can call me Triss and you can call him Loki.'

'Fancy naming your child after a foreign god,' Tethia muttered, and received a small kick in the heels from Beris, a silent plea for her to behave. It made her even more smug to remember that her mother had named her after an ancient god... but it wasn't a foreign god, so that was OK.

The man snorted. 'You're pretty arrogant for someone who hasn't even received a name, yet.'

'My name is Lerina,' Tethia replied. She wished now that she had never lied to Beris, but at least if she continued to use a false name, her indiscretion couldn't be traced back to Rinn, and that way get back to Sheya, or to Merrim, or to her mother.

Beris took a step forward and made a small bow, his manners impeccable. 'My name is Berisus, son of Caelus, son of Amerenus, Consuls of Capreae for three generations. Salve.'

'Take your Salve and stick it up your-'

'Loki, no!' Triss cried. Tethia cast her eyes down

modestly to hide the smirk.

'I suppose you don't even have any powers, do you?' The man held a little ball and tossed it from hand to hand, slowly, as if the conversation bored him beyond measure. 'You both look like a fine pair of followers. I bet the both of you followed the rules your whole life long until the moment you were dragged down beneath the soil.'

'What powers do you mean?' Beris asked. 'Why are we all standing around in the dark here? Are you afraid to turn on the light?'

Loki made an unpleasant noise. 'Well, that answers that well enough, I suppose. If you had any powers, you'd know about them. We can safely say that vision isn't exactly your strong point.' He lounged back on the pile of boxes like it was a dining couch at the Palatine, eyeing Tethia and Beris with a cynical gaze. 'What about you, sister? Are you a dud?'

'Yes, sir,' Tethia said. He sighed heavily and rolled his eyes. Tethia was struggling to hold onto her temper. She'd been through a lot today. For at least part of the day she'd probably been dead. She had no idea how long she'd been sick, no idea how much time had passed in this communal grave beneath the hospital. She had no idea how she was going to help Sheya and no idea if Sheya was even still alive. If Loki made one more smart arse remark she was going to kneecap him. She would, of course, keep her eyes modestly downcast as she did so.

For good measure, though, in the meantime, she sent her attention outside of herself and found a small army of ants at the back of the boxes. She encouraged them to come forward, just enough to climb up his back and march down the back of his uniform.

'I don't even see why we need them,' Loki said. 'They're duds. What use can they be to us?'

Perry arranged herself on a box, crossing her slim legs in front of her. She shrugged. *We can always use them as human shields.* Dubhia sat cross legged at Perry's feet and leaned against her knees.

Triss was pacing around nervously, keeping an eye out. She barely seemed to notice the conversation, except when Loki threatened to go too far. She turned and approached Beris. She touched his arm gently, but he wasn't able to see in the dark and Tethia felt his sudden start of surprise.

'I need you to come with me,' she said. 'We don't want them to catch us.' Beris followed her. They didn't go too far away. She guided him into stocking the shelves while Tethia looked on in surprise. Triss was acting as if nothing was untoward, as though she was merely doing her job.

The door slammed open. Tethia jumped like a damned coward. She peered through the forest of shelves and caught sight of the fat man, far away. 'You damned well better be stocking those shelves!' he shouted.

'Yes, sir,' Triss murmured, even though there was no way for the man to hear her clearly at that distance. He slammed the door again, leaving a sudden, breathless silence in the cavernous pantry.

Loki was still tossing that damn ball up and down. Suddenly he threw it at Tethia.

Tethia was smart enough not to dodge it. She'd planned to pretend surprise when it struck her in the shoulder, but it hit her in the face and it set off the last curb she could keep on her temper. She bent and scooped it up, a tiny light ball with the power off, and hurled it back at Loki as hard as she could. 'What kind of childish move was that?' she demanded. 'I never did anything to you. I came here trying to help you and you've done nothing but act like the kind of human excrement who belongs in a place like this.'

Loki just caught the ball, smiling. He twisted it to turn the power on and even the small light made the room uncomfortably bright for a moment to Tethia's eyes. In the moment when Tethia's eyes were adjusting, he leaped to his feet, hand raised to strike her.

Tethia grabbed his arm before the blow could connect and swept her foot around his ankles to bring him to the ground. She could have used her leverage on his arm to slow his descent. She didn't.

He surprised her by laughing, flat on his back, his arm still in her grasp. 'Can't see in the dark my foot,' he wheezed.

'Maybe I lied,' Tethia said. 'You should know that when I say I don't tolerate bullshit, that isn't a lie, so be told.' She let his arm go, giving it a shove for good measure. 'Tell me about your little rebel group. I suppose you're the only four in this dank little hole who don't fancy the idea of being "promoted." So, what do you plan to do about it and why did you ask us specifically to join you?' She glared at Perry. 'And don't give me that "human shields" bullshit, either. I haven't had a great day and I'm really not in the mood for this.'

Perry just shrugged. Dubhia smiled.

'Don't make me tap my gods damned feet,' Tethia snapped.

'OK, fine. Yes, we're the Resistance. There are

more of us, but they're not going to meet you. You don't need to know everything.'

'I don't really care what you think I need to know or not. I don't particularly care about your little Resistance. You can all be *promoted* for all I care. I'm looking for someone. A little-' she caught Perry's sharp eye, 'a young girl, a young lady. She would be fifteen years old now. Her name was Sheya when she was born.'

'None of us have our birth names,' Dubhia said. Her voice was soft and pleasant, a contrast to Perry's. 'When we came to the Project we were allocated assignment numbers instead.'

'You should already know that, LA-97.'

'Lerina,' Tethia snapped. It might not be her real name, but it was better than being numbered.

'Within our brethren we are given names. Just like you, Lerina, have been given a name.' Dubhia shifted forward. 'I'm curious, the names you have now, Lerina and Beris, are they the same names you had in the world under the nebula?'

'Under the nebula?' Tethia blinked, feeling foolish

'That's right,' Beris said, covering for Tethia's uncertainty. He and Triss had joined them again, just in time for Tethia's temper to abate a little. He put his hand on

Tethia's shoulder. 'Who gives you your names?'

'Lector RS gave me my name,' Perry said. *'He told me he named me after my mother.'*

'Lector?' Tethia asked, still feeling off balance. Beris's hand on her shoulder was a welcome point of stability and she leaned towards him, barely even noticing that she did it.

'Perry is Lector RS's favourite,' Dubhia said, looking up at Perry briefly.

Perry shrugged. *'It's convenient.'*

'He seems so nice.'

Perry looked away. *'Yeah. Seems.'* She wouldn't even face Dubhia as she said it.

'Sounds like someone I know,' Tethia muttered. She raised her voice to a normal level. 'What is a Lector?

The man replied. 'The Lectors teach the children. I was a Lector.' Triss looked at him sharply and he met her gaze with a growing smile. 'For a little while, that is. My name is Loki.' He threw off a poor salute, without getting up. 'LK-01 at your service. Salve!'

'Zero One?' Tethia asked. She remembered that Triss had mentioned their allocations previously, but the numbers hadn't made an impact on her until now. 'Does that mean you've been here from the beginning?'

'By the Under King, can't you even read?' Perry demanded. She stalked across the room. *'He showed you his Marks. It should be obvious that he was born here, in the first year of the colony, and has never been under the nebula.'* She pointed to the woman. *'Triss came here at the age of twelve but hasn't been under the nebula since. They're both Controls, isn't that obvious?'*

'No one controls me,' Loki muttered. He fished a small packet out of his pocket and took a cigarette out of it. One handed, he slipped the cigarette between his lips and touched a finger to the tip. A small point of light flared where he touched the end of the cigarette. He grinned at Tethia's astounded look. 'I, sister, am *not* a dud.'

Perry was standing by his side and holding his wrist to show Tethia his Marks. She dropped his wrist and plucked the cigarette from his lips. She ignored his surprised, 'Hey!' and ground it beneath her boot. *'Sure, no one controls you,'* she said. *'No one controls you, but no one else wants to be stuck in here while you Break the Rules. And if I only had my voice back, I could make you bark like a brand new dog if I wanted to.'*

'What do you mean, if you had your voice back?' Beris asked.

Perry shrugged, but there was barely restrained

violence in the casual movement. *'I can tell people what to do. The UnderKing finds my power useful. It's the only reason I'm still alive.'*

'But you can't speak…' Beris's voice trailed away.

'I was… disobedient. I was silenced. One day my voice will return and that day will be a very bad day for the man who did this to me.'

'What do your Marks mean, Perry?' Tethia asked. 'You've got a lot of little marks on your arm. What does that mean? Have you been out under the nebula before?'

Perry didn't answer. She just pushed her sleeve down further to cover the tattoos. *'None of your damned business,'* she snapped.

'Perry, stop it, you know I don't like to swear,' Dubhia complained. Even when she complained, her voice was sweet.

'We'll let you know when we need your help.' Perry walked around Beris and Tethia. *'We have our plans. Be ready.'*

Dubhia was close behind, along with Triss. Loki lingered a moment, still tossing the illuminated light ball. 'I just bet you were in Service, weren't you, sister? You were one of these unTied people I've been hearing about the last few years.'

'How do you know that?'

'I'm a good guesser. I'm curious about the world above. If you're free this evening, come to Dormitory One. I would be interested to hear your perspective on life above.'

Tethia stared at him as he followed the others. 'I would sooner swallow my own tongue,' she said, very softly, so only Beris could hear her. Then she raised her voice. 'Wait! I need to know, before you go...' she trotted after them. Loki looked over his shoulder and paused. 'What's the date? How many days is it since I first came here? Perry and Dubhia were in the cage the first day I arrived, I need to know how many days it is.'

One day, she thought to herself. *Please, say it was only one day. Sheya only has two days. Any more than two days and I couldn't stand it, please, please, please.*

'Oh, let me think,' Loki murmured. 'If that was the day that Perry and Dubhi nearly escaped, that would be about a week ago.' He grinned. 'Remember, Dormitory One.'

He was gone before Tethia started breathing again. She would have stopped breathing altogether if she'd had the power. Her breath sawed in and out against her will. It came out too loud and made a rasping cry on the way in.

Beris found her, in the dark, and put his hands on her shoulders.

'Lerina, what is it?' he asked.

She moaned, the noise like an animal's cry. Her mind was completely blank. The darkness inside her couldn't be any more complete if she'd lost her sight.

'Lerina, what's the matter?' Beris demanded. He grasped her by her shoulders, trying to hold her in place while she rocked back and forward in time with the swaying demands of her unbalanced world. 'Lerina, what's wrong?'

A rough breath in. 'She's dead. My daughter's dead. My daughter's dead! *My daughter's dead!*' She started to scream.

The door slammed open again.

'What's all this ruckus?' the fat man bellowed. Tethia only saw his vague outline and in that moment he stood for every person, every nameless, faceless person who was just doing their job and kept the Project going. She wrenched free of Beris's grasp and sprinted towards the fat man.

She saw the terror in his eyes as she attacked him. She would have killed him if Beris hadn't been able to drag her away. She'd wanted to kill him, wanted to feel his blood on her hands, wanted to rip out something vital, the way something vital had been ripped out of her.

Guards came and took her away. They took Beris, too, shoving him away from the man he was trying to save. She was shackled, Beris shackled beside her. The pair of them were whipped, as Tethia remembered seeing slaves whipped so often in the courtyard of the villa in Valdennes when her father was alive. She didn't hold in her screams. She howled, whether the lash touched her skin or not. The only thing that stopped her screaming was the blessed darkness of unconsciousness. And still the lash stung, because the required number had not yet been reached.

She woke up with Dubhia kneeling beside her cot. With a painful gasp, Tethia caught hold of the girl's hand. She pressed the back of Dubhia's hand against her brow and wept, broken hearted.

But Dubhia's power could heal anything, it seemed. The girl put her hand on Tethia's head and slowly drew the pain away. Perry stood behind Dubhia, her face inscrutable, watching Tethia weep.

#

The next morning, Tethia was awakened by a

sudden loud noise. She jerked upright. She was in a room with about twenty other people, all in varying stages of jerking upright from their own deep sleep. A light was switched on and every person in the room made a sudden movement to shield their eyes. Each person had their own narrow cot; each person had their own rough blanket. There seemed to be nothing in the room except for cots, blankets, and people.

Beris was next to her, also sitting up in his own narrow cot, covered by his own rough blanket. He was blinking owlishly in the sudden bright light. He arranged his face into what might have been a small smile. 'I guess it's time to start the day. How are you?'

Tethia swung her legs out of bed. 'I'm alive, I suppose. What do we do now?'

'I don't know,' Beris said. 'But I'm gonna go out on a limb here and say we're probably going to go to work. We are slaves after all.'

He wasn't wrong. After a quick, uninspiring meal, they were each sent to their work. Beris was sent back to the kitchen and this time Tethia was sent to the laundry. If she'd felt overwhelmed in the kitchen, it was even worse in the laundry. The work was just as hard and there was no Beris to try and cheer her up. A pair of guards watched her closely all day. Well, she couldn't blame them for that.

She did what she was told, answering to her new allocation of LA-97 as if it was her name. She wore the same black jumpsuit that all the other colonists wore, the marks that she had been given as tattoos emblazoned across the shoulder of the jumpsuit. She didn't make trouble. There was no point. There was no point trying to do anything anymore.

In the evening, she saw Beris again. There were both too tired to talk. Tethia glimpsed Perry in the communal dining room the next morning, from a distance. Neither gave a sign they recognised the other and then it was back to work again for another day.

Tethia very quickly lost track of time. One day followed another. There was nothing to make one day different from any other day. There was nothing to hope for; there was the mere fact of the passage of time. Most nights, in the dark room with all the other slaves in her quadrant – even though they called themselves Colonists, they were still slaves – Tethia lay on her narrow cot and tried to keep her weeping quiet. Every night, she found a new reason to cry. Sometimes she cried because she never had a chance to meet her daughter. Sometimes she cried because she blamed herself for giving Sheya up in the first place. Sometimes she cried because her life in the Colony was so miserable and the thought that this was the only life Sheya had ever known was nearly unbearable.

One night, as she was weeping quietly into her cot, a hand touched her on the shoulder. She rolled, suddenly hopeful that Beris had heard her weeping and was going to offer comfort, but it was not Beris was kneeling by the side of her bed, it was Perry.

Perry gestured the Tethia to follow her, rising to her feet then turning to walk out of the room. She turned back for the briefest moment, laying her hand over her heart in a silent, sincere gesture of apology.

Tethia wiped her eyes on a corner of her blanket, then got up to follow Perry.

When she reached the hallway, she was surprised to find that Perry had already walked halfway along it. Perry turned and gestured for Tethia to follow her again. Tethia hurried along behind the girl.

Perry led her to a small room and she closed the door behind Tethia when she entered. It was dark, but both of them could see in the dark. Perry looked desperate. She put her hands together, in a pleading gesture.

Tethia stared at her. She raised her arms in an exaggerated shrug and gestured randomly back at Perry while saying, 'I don't know what you're trying to say to me. Why don't you go get Dubhia? Then you'll be able to speak with her voice.'

Perry slapped one hand down into the palm of the other, making an emphatic negative gesture and then clapping her hand over her ear and opening her hand again. *'Don't gesture at me. I can hear you.'*

Perry held up a hand for patience. This time she started off by cupping her hand around her ear again, begging Tethia to listen and pay attention. She indicated herself and then slowly and deliberately drew a finger across her throat and then pointed upwards.

Tethia brought her hand up to her mouth. 'Perry, you're not going to be promoted?'

Perry nodded. The girl was as hard as nails, but as she caught Tethia's eyes, she started to cry. She formed a space in the crook of her arm and then pointed at Tethia.

'My baby?' Tethia asked.

Perry nodded, then ran a finger down the tear tracks on her own cheek. Tethia nodded. 'Yes, I was crying for my baby just now. I know she's not a baby now, she's a young woman, but to me she will always be my baby.' She paused, trying to speak delicately, although it didn't come naturally to her. 'Did you ever know your mother?'

Perry shook her head. Another tear made its way down her cheek and fell into the space she still held for an imaginary baby. Tethia felt the tears spring into her own eyes.

'Your mother would be heartbroken for you, Perry.'

Perry took a hesitant step towards Tethia. She pointed to Tethia, then ran her finger down her cheek again. She raised her eyebrows to make it a question.

'Oh, Perry, of course I would cry for you.' She took a gamble and opened her arms. Perry rushed into them, burying her face in Tethia's shoulder, shaking with silent sobs. Tethia wrapped her arms around the girl. Someone, somewhere, would grieve for Perry, as she had grieved for Sheya. Perry had the right to a mother's tears. It was the right of every child. Tethia let her tears fall into Perry's hair, so like her own.

Tethia stroked Perry's hair. 'I promise you; I won't allow this to happen.'

There wasn't much time. Perry's promotion party was set for the following afternoon. Tethia couldn't see Perry that morning, she was kept fully busy in the laundry. The guards still watched her; it was impossible to get away. The only time the guards allowed her to leave her trough was lunchtime, when they escorted her to the communal dining room.

After lunch that afternoon, Hallenus went up to the dais again and called for everyone's attention.

'My friends, we are greatly honoured yet again! This is the second week in a row when one of our members has been honoured with promotion to the court of the UnderKing.' Beris had looked up to catch Tethia's eye across the table. She gave a small nod, to indicate that she was well aware of what was happening. They rose to their feet, along with everyone else, and looked up to the dais where Hallenus was drawing their attention.

'PA-62, why don't you come on up here?' Hallenus had his arms open again, and Perry had to proceed, even though her steps dragged. Hallenus just smiled at everyone. 'Teenagers,' he said. 'They never like to do what they're told, do they?'

The crowd laughed, obediently, but every single person there could see that Perry was deeply reluctant. She didn't blush happily as Meriah had. Her face was pale and the fear was plain in her eyes.

'What a lucky girl you are!' Hallenus cried. 'You've been so lucky all your life. You're only teen years old and already you have been on dozens of missions in the service of the UnderKing and his court. You were blessed with very special abilities, PA-62. It was such a shame that you didn't always use them for the right reasons.'

Perry thrust out her arm, pointing to Dubhia. Dubhia opened her mouth, but one of the guards who had been assigned to watch Tethia was right behind her. He grabbed Dubhia from behind and clapped his hand over her mouth. Perry turned back to Hallenus, anger overcoming the fear in her face. She waved her arm at Dubhia, who was being dragged from the crowd.

'No, no, PA-62,' Hallenus said. 'We don't want to hear the tricks that DA-44 can play with her voice. We're here to honour you today, even though you don't deserve it.' Hallenus turned back to the crowd. 'Usually, the person being promoted would spend one last afternoon with their friends and family, but as we all know PA-62 has no friends and no family, so she will be leaving us immediately. PA-62, the good Medic here will take you to your new home in the court of the UnderKing.'

Dr Matasin stepped forward. Tethia was half afraid that he would seek her out in the crowd and was ashamed of herself that she was afraid of simply being looked at. Matasin didn't even bother to look at the crowd though. For all Tethia knew, he was responsible for bringing half of them there.

'Time for you to come with me now, PA-62.' He held out his hand.

Perry shrank back from his extended hand, then turned and tried to run into the crowd. The guards were there to capture her. She fought them and let out a single wordless sound of horror. From a distance, Tethia also heard the same cry coming from Dubhia's throat. The crowd just watched in silence. Tethia started to push her way through the crowd. Beris was right behind her.

Matasin caught at one of Perry's flailing hands. From the moment he touched her hand, she stopped fighting. Tethia realised that Matasin must have powers of his own.

In that moment, Perry went with him willingly. Hallenus raised his hands to lead the people in gentle applause. Tethia and Beris passed into the corridor beyond the crowd. Behind them, the people had started to sing.

'Where are we going?' Beris asked, hurrying along behind Tethia. 'We don't even know where they're going to take her. Even if we did know where they were going to take her, we don't know any way out of here.'

'I don't know the way out of here,' Tethia replied, still hurrying ahead of him in the dim corridor, 'but I do know where he's going to take her.' She turned and flushed the briefest grin at Beris. 'And to think, I thought all the time I spent in here was wasted. Matasin will take her to his office. He will put her in a little cage and raise it up to the surface so she can be exposed to the nebula. He'll leave her there, observing to see how long it takes before she dies of starsickness. He's a scientist. He isn't going to waste resources.'

'How do you know this?'

'It's how I got in. I may have been unconscious when they dragged me out of there, but I spent the last several days taking bloodstained linen in and out of the laboratories.'

'What are we going to do when we get there?' Beris caught her hand, trying to slow her down. She shook him off.

'I don't know.' She shrugged. 'Bust some heads, maybe? I'm not going to let them hurt that little girl, I don't care whose daughter she is.'

Beris faced her for a moment, then nodded. 'You're absolutely right. Doing nothing is how all this evil grew so much in the first place. We have to do what we can.'

Tethia led them by way of the kitchen. Given that the promotion party was just starting and the kitchen had apparently been given zero notice, the atmosphere was intense. There were people everywhere, running around and shouting directions at one another. The washers up were engulfed in huge clouds of steam from the sudden rush of hot water into the washing troughs to get the glassware washed and back out into the cafeteria for the party.

The fat man in charge of the kitchen caught sight of Beris and Tethia and gave a gusty sigh of relief.

'Thank the UnderKing's hairy – knuckles. We need another pair on trough three.'

'Yes, sir!' Tethia and Beris replied, hurrying smartly over to the trough. They each took a knife from the piles of dirty implements on the bench. Beris took a meat tenderiser and weighed it in his hand like a mace. On the way out of the kitchen, Tethia snagged a lid off a large saucepan. Beris raised his eyebrows. Tethia raised the lid like a shield. It didn't feel dissimilar to the kit every Serviceman was issued, including a short sword and a shield.

As they grew closer to the laboratory, they started to move more carefully, staying closer to the walls, utensils at the ready. Tethia stopped suddenly and scooted back past the last corner, dragging Beris with her. She pressed her back against the wall and cautiously peered around the corner.

There was Perry. Matasin was still holding her by the hand and she followed him, quietly compliant. None of them have seemed to be concerned that someone might come and try and attack them. Everyone acted as if this was business as usual. This was normal. Once Matasin held Perry by her hand, he could see no reason why she would try to escape. They walked at a leisurely pace, no need to rush. After all, this was just another day's work for them.

There were only five of them: Perry, Matasin, the two guards and another young man who wore a lab coat, the same as Matasin did. Tethia thought back to the first day she had arrived in the Colony. Hallenus had been furious when she had suggested trying to escape. The crowd had also been angry. This was their life, this was their world. They had been brainwashed into believing that they were serving the UnderKing. Why would anyone try to escape if they thought they were going to be promoted?

Matasin knew that Perry was disobedient. Perry herself had admitted that the reason she couldn't speak was because the guards had silenced her after she was disobedient. They had to expect some protest… but then, Matasin also knew that when he touched Perry, he was able to control her. Perry had said that one of her powers was controlling people with her voice. It appeared that Matasin had a similar power, only associated with touch instead of voice.

Tethia watch as they went into the laboratory and closed the door behind them. She turned back to Beris. 'Now, let's go.' She led the way.

She didn't bother trying to kick the door down or trying to pick the lock. Instead, she just knocked. The door opened. Tethia tried very hard not to think about the fact that when the guard opened the door, his face was open and friendly, like anyone opening a door who doesn't expect a saucepan lid to the face. He fell straight backwards, his expression suddenly blank.

'What the hell do you think you're doing?' the young man cried. He leaped towards them, but his posture was one of defence rather than attack. He thought he was one of the good guys. Behind her, Tethia heard Beris attack the other guard with the meat tenderiser. Tethia raised both knife and saucepan lid, but she didn't have a chance to make her attack.

The moment she had come through the door, Matasin had thrust his hand into his pocket. He found the small controller that she had seen him carry before. He pressed the button. The sudden pain that lanced through

Tethia's middle made her double up in agony. She dropped both knife and saucepan lid. Beris cried out in pain and fell to his knees.

The guard came up behind Tethia and pushed her to the ground. Her hands dropped uselessly in front of her. She tried to draw them in, so she could raise herself back to her feet but Matasin was too quick for her.

The doctor walked towards Tethia. She was still on the floor, but she read the intent in his face and tried to scramble away. She wasn't fast enough. He hurried his pace and brought his foot down on her hand. She cried out in pain and heard Beris raise his voice in protest.

'Leave her alone!' he cried.

Matasin rocked back and forth.

Tethia screamed as her bones cracked under his boot, felt fire race along her arm. She knew, though, that the terrible anger that burned in her heart would protect her a little from the pain – for only a little while, but she had to act fast. She hadn't been a soldier for thirteen years for nothing.

The others were at the other end of the room, on the other side of the cage. She was half hidden from their view. In a sudden lunge she brought her other arm around and grabbed Matasin's ankle, tugging sharply. It brought his foot off the floor, but it was her body twisting, curling into a ball on the floor before extending in a kick that caught his other foot that brought him to the ground.

He let Perry go and she backed away to cower in the corner of the room, wedging herself behind the cage.

In a lithe, twisting motion, Tethia brought herself to her feet. She was wearing sandals, not boots, since she worked in the laundry, which meant she couldn't do as much damage as she wanted, and being so small she didn't have much weight to bring to bear but it would still be enough to stop him. She stood above the Medic and, with a lightning swift move, brought her foot down on his throat, letting the whole of her body weight follow.

He didn't scream, just made a strange noise that Tethia had never heard before. Beris rose suddenly from the floor and flung himself at the guard. They struggled and fell to the floor, rolling around in a deadly display. Blood spurted as the guard got in a good blow and broke Beris's nose.

Perry was still wedged behind the cage, watching the young researcher closely. She brought her hands up to grip the bars of the cage. Tethia bent and retrieved her knife and took a step towards the young man.

Perry's voice suddenly rang out, clear and sharp

over the grunts and cries of the fighting. *'Stop it!'* she cried. A strange, imperative tone entered her voice. *'Stop fighting! Just stay still! Let us go!'*

All at once the room went quiet. The guard froze, crouched over Beris, his arm raised, a knife in his hand. The researcher looked as shocked as everyone else at the voice coming from his throat. Tethia herself was struck still and there was a terrible silence from Matasin. A sudden chill came over Tethia, but she ignored it. She focussed on releasing herself from Perry's command. She'd had years of practice from earliest childhood, learning to disobey the same commanding tone in her father's voice.

'Let's go,' she said. 'Quick, it's easy, behind the cage and up the ladder to freedom.'

Perry shook her head.

'You've got to be kidding me,' Tethia muttered. 'I thought you wanted to escape.'

'No,' Perry said through the young researcher's mouth. *'Not without Dubhia. And Triss and Loki, if we have time.'*

'Please don't kill me,' the young man whimpered. He fell to his knees and held out his hands pleadingly to Tethia. He apparently didn't even know who was speaking through him.

'We're not going to kill you,' Beris said. He grabbed the researcher by the collar and hauled him to his feet, grunting at the effort. 'What's your name, boy?'

'Valorius, sir,' the young man replied.

Tethia and Perry both sniggered. Valorius clapped his hands over his mouth as the snigger left his lips.

'We're wasting time,' Tethia snapped. 'Where are your precious friends? And you, my brave lad, keep your fool mouth shut or you'll never speak for yourself again.'

They had a brief argument over what to do with the guards. Tethia advocated a swift death for them both, but Beris refused to allow it.

'They'll only raise the alarm,' she warned.

'I don't care, Lerina. We're not killers. We're not going to come out of this worse than them.' His voice was strained and his eyes were bright, despite the rapidly swelling and bruising skin around them. This really mattered to him.

She let him have his humanitarian moment. She couldn't bear to dim that light in his eyes.

Perry led them away from the laboratory, running down the corridors. Dubhia, Triss and Loki were back in the pantry again, gathered closely together, whispering.

'Hey, I'm back!' Perry announced, whispering

through Valorius's lips. All three turned sharply. Dubhia's face lit up and Tethia was heartily ashamed that she'd ever suggested leaving the others behind. Dubhia threw her arms around Perry, her lips shut tight to hold in the cry of joy that might bring attention to them. Perry held Dubhia tightly for a moment. *'Come on, let's go. I've got my voice back. We've even got this fine fellow to help us.'*

'Please, stop doing this to me,' Valorius wailed, but even he was careful to keep his voice low. He didn't fear being caught nearly as much as he feared Tethia, and she kept her steely gaze on him to keep it that way.

'We'll be lucky to get back to the lab without anyone seeing us,' Tethia warned. 'Those guards will have cone to by now.'

'Now that I have my voice back, we have another way out,' Perry said. Valorius looked very strange, cringing and smirking at the same time.

'And what would that be?' Tethia planted her hands on her hips.

The smirk on Valorius's face overwhelmed the cringing.

'We walk right out the front door and drive off in their own transports.'

Tethia pinned Perry with a hard stare. It wasn't

difficult coming up with a hard stare. Whatever the hell it was that Matasin had implanted in her side had caused some serious damage and she was struggling to pretend that she wasn't badly hurt. Her hand hurt more than she could say. She knew she was pale and that made her voice sharp.

'I suppose you have a plan? I'd very much like to leave here and I'd very much like to have these bloody injuries treated-' Tethia drew herself up short. When they stopped, Beris had to lean up against a wall. He was even paler than she felt. He closed his eyes for a moment and his chest heaved with a ragged breath. He put his hand over his heart.

'Mate, you don't look so good,' Loki said.

'I wasn't quick enough finding my voice,' Perry admitted, her voice soft and apologetic, coming from Dubhia's mouth.

Beris grimaced. 'You probably saved my life,' he admitted. 'Gotta look on the bright side… at least he only stabbed me once.'

'Beris, no,' Tethia whispered. She took the few steps between them quickly. 'Beris, show me.' She put her hand very gently over his.

He tried to smile, but it came out lopsided. He took his hand from his chest – it came away stained with blood.

The dark fabric of his jumpsuit was torn and glistened with the shine of fresh blood.

'Oh, by the gods, Perry, you'd better have a plan to get us out of here,' Tethia whispered. She couldn't take her eyes off Beris's face. A month ago, she hadn't known he existed. They'd been through so much together now that it was impossible to imagine a life without him in it. 'Oh, God, we have to get you to a hospital!'

'You're in a hospital,' Valorius said. They all turned to face him and he quailed. 'Sorry.'

'Perry – Dubhia, you have to heal him-'

'We don't have time,' Triss said. 'It will take hours to heal him. Heal him when we're out of here and safe. Right now, we need one of you to drive. None of us have ever driven a skipper before. Perry is the only one who has ever been outside before.'

'Well, a dead man isn't going to be much use to you, is he?' Tethia snapped. 'I'll drive. But if Beris dies, I swear by all the gods, I'll kill the rest of you myself.'

Perry's lips trembled for a moment. *'Stop complaining,'* she said, and the tremor in her voice matched the tremor of Valorius's hands. 'I can get us out of here.'

'What about me?' Valorius complained. 'You have to let me go. I'll be no good to you-'

'Shut up,' Tethia snapped. 'The sooner we get out of here, the sooner you can forget we ever met.'

The four of them had chosen the pantry as a meeting place because of its proximity to the loading docks. Guards stopped them – twice! – but each time Perry opened Valorius's mouth and issued commands. Valorius, trembling, showed the guards his ID, and if they weren't so busy following Perry's commands that might have been helpful.

Through the large, double doors that led to the loading docks, they could hear the low hum of a transport vehicle. They gathered in the dark, just outside the doors.

'Let me go now,' Valorius whispered. 'I've helped you get here, now let me go.'

Tethia stopped to think. She wanted to do what the boy asked, but a hostage was a valuable commodity. On the one hand, a hostage would make it easier to demand a vehicle, but on the other hand, walking into a public area holding a hostage in a headlock would make her an instant target for any snipers. If they let him go, they might be able to lie their way out, they might not even need to fight.

She knew she was justifying it to herself, but she didn't care. She'd thought a lot about what Beris had said to her. If he died, his words would be branded on her soul.

And he was right. It was important that they didn't come out of this worse than the people they opposed. If he died, it would be imperative that she honour him with her life. Whatever choices she made today would not be choices she would regret. There were times when a code like that would be death for a soldier, but she wasn't a soldier anymore.

'Yes. You've done your part,' she said. She let him go and the young man immediately sprinted away down the corridor.

'Why did you let him go so easily?' Loki asked, leaning against the wall beside Beris. 'We could have used a hostage.'

'I had to make a choice,' she replied. 'It had to be a choice I could live with. Follow me.'

Beris touched the shoulder of her abused arm and it was all she could do not to scream. With her good hand she grabbed his hand and moved it to her waist. 'Here, hold my belt,' she instructed, her voice tight from the pain. She reached out for the door release panel. She paused for a moment when she touched the cold metal, whispering a silent prayer to any gods who cared to listen that it might be open. She placed her palm over the sensor.

The door opened.

Silently promising to offer sacrifices to any and all gods paying attention, she peered through the widening crack. There was a dim light in the large bay beyond, so even Beris could make out some details, looking over her shoulder. There were only two vehicles – one large transport in the middle of the room and one small skipper on their side.

The trouble was that there were six people in the room, some working at incomprehensible tasks in the shadows of the far side of the bay and three working on the skipper itself, near enough for Tethia to hear their voices clearly.

She ducked her head back and pulled the door nearly closed to face Loki. 'How can we get rid of them?' she whispered, as much to herself as him.

Loki shook his head. 'We'll have to rush them.'

Tethia heard another door open – bang open, loud and attention drawing. She opened her door to peek through again. A door further along her own corridor had opened and Valorius had stepped through it.

'Good evening, brothers!' he cried in Perry's voice, waving an arm. *'You must need a break.'* His voice acquired that deeper, almost subliminal tinge that Perry's commands used. *'Why don't you all go out for a cigarette?'*

Across the space of the open door, Tethia saw Perry eyeballing Valorius. She was whispering, and the silent movement of her lips was controlling the young man all the way across the loading dock.

'You know what,' one of the mechanics said, 'I really feel like a cigarette.'

'But you don't smoke,' another replied. 'It's against the rules.'

'I know, but I'm dying for a cigarette. Are you coming?'

'You know what, I think I will.'

And they downed tools and headed out of the bay while their workmates all said 'Hey, guys, wait for me!' and 'Hey, can I come, too?' and followed them.

Tethia looked at Perry, deeply disturbed.

'Just go,' Perry mouthed, then ran towards the skipper.

'Let's go,' Tethia muttered to Beris, reaching behind her to grasp his hand. They ran, half stumbling, to the skipper and slammed its doors shut behind them.

'Women can't drive,' Beris murmured. He was barely able to sit upright in his seat.

'You'll be unconscious soon,' Tethia replied. 'Unconscious men don't drive all that well. Buckle up, I'm getting out of here fast.'

Perry and the others climbed into the skipper behind them. True to her word, Tethia started the skipper and peeled out of the transport bay into the dark day beyond. She didn't even know where she was going but she knew she wanted to get there fast.

#

'Any ideas where we should go?' Tethia asked. She didn't turn on the headlights. She was able to see their way well enough in the dark day without them.

There was a deafening silence from the backseat. 'Take the northern road,' Beris muttered. 'Go up the hill.'

'That's as good a direction as any,' Tethia agreed. 'So, Perry's that's one scary talent you've got there. How long has it been since you enslaved the human race?'

'A few years,' Perry admitted. *'And clearly I haven't used it to enslave the human race, or you wouldn't be able to be such a bitch to me.'*

'Perry,' Dubhia murmured disapprovingly.

Tethia, as an adult, had to struggle to stop herself from crying, 'Takes one to know one.'

'Anyway, I can't help it,' Perry went on. *'It's a part*

of me. Like being able to see in the dark or being good at maths. It hasn't all been fun and games for me. Lector RS realised what was happening even before I did. He had me assigned to... to a special school. I had to go out under the nebula many times... running errands.'

Running errands sounded suspiciously like a euphemism for assassinating people, Tethia thought. She wondered how many people on the wrong side of politics had spontaneously decided to suddenly commit suicide in the last few years. A girl with Perry's powers, who had been brainwashed her whole life... she would be a powerful tool in anyone's hands. No wonder they had silenced her when she was disobedient.

'Come back here with me,' Dubhia said to Perry. 'I'm going to need your strength if I'm going to do some more healing today.'

Tethia thumped the steering column, hard, with the palm of her uninjured hand. 'I'm not giving up.' She cast the briefest glance at Beris. 'No matter what.'

Beris nodded, his eyes still shut. His head was slumped back against the seat, his mouth hanging open. He looked terrible: both eyes bruised, a graze on his cheek, his nose broken and unset. His jaw was unshaven since they'd entered the Project and little trails of blood spilled from his mouth and through his new beard.

He started moaning at one point and Tethia cast more frequent glances at him, but she wouldn't stop until they reached Lygia.

'It's all right,' she said, meaning to calm him, but knowing her voice was sharp. 'You'll be all right. Not far now. I'm here.'

Not that her presence helped in any way, she thought, but a gentle hand stretched out to touch his arm and the gentlest words she could muster were all she could do. That had to count for something.

Loki was sitting in the back, staring out the back window, Triss close beside him. Tethia was driving as fast as she could go, her foot flat to the floor. She knew the danger they were in and kept a close eye on the rear vision mirror. She didn't need Loki's whispered, 'They're behind us, you know,' to tell her about the three vehicles speeding towards them.

'Where can I possibly go?' Tethia shouted. She didn't know why she was shouting. Beris was in no position either to help her or bear the brunt of her ire. It didn't stop her shouting, though. She gestured widely, letting go of the column for a moment. 'I mean, look around us! It's a dark country road! It doesn't even lead anywhere! There is no possible way I can lose them on this road. I'm already running dark.'

Beris opened his eyes, then turned a sleepy grin her away. 'No, Lerina, it leads somewhere. I told you to come this way, didn't I?'

Tethia clenched her teeth together. She hadn't meant to make it into an accusation. He put his hand over hers. It was heavy – he barely had the strength to raise his hand anymore. She was terrified he was going to die before she could get him to help. In the back of the skipper, Perry and Dubhia were sitting with their hands joined and their eyes closed.

'Don't worry, I'll think of something,' she muttered. She turned her hand to hold his and it lay, heavy and cold in her grasp. She guided the steering column with her forearms, knowing it was a stupid idea when she was going so fast, but she couldn't let go of Beris's hand.

'It will be OK, Lerina. We've just got to get home. Just past that curve where Ala broke her leg, remember?'

His voice was slurred, now. Tethia ground her back teeth together to distract herself from the threatening tears. 'We'll make it home, Beris, don't worry.'

Suddenly, her eyes opened wide. There really was a sharp curve ahead. She nearly lost control of the skipper, the back wheels skidding freely across the roadbase. Her heart began to pound heavily. There were lights ahead of her – a villa on the hillside, overlooking the whole of Capreae spread out before them. Her breath came faster. A house as grand as this didn't belong to an ordinary person. It could only belong to the consul.

And his son.

Her vision was swimming and she kept blinking her eyes hard to clear them. Beris was unconscious now and her good hand was back on the steering column. She almost envied Beris his unconsciousness. The pain in her side and in her hand was nearly unbearable. She knew she couldn't make it much further. She focussed on keeping her foot down.

When lights came into view in the distance her first thought was that she was imagining it. She blinked her eyes once more for good measure. The lights danced before her dark – accustomed eyes but they didn't disappear. She drew in a deep breath and gritted her teeth, her foot still pressed all the way to the floor.

She made it through the gates only a hair's breadth before the vehicles following them. She threw open her door and stumbled out of the skipper.

'Come quickly, Beris is injured!' she shouted. She

stumbled on the driveway and fell to her knees just as the researches and guards behind her spilled out of their vehicles. She gathered the last vestiges of breath available to her and screamed, 'Help Beris!'

She fell flat on the gravel. It was hard to hear anything through the ringing of her ears, but the commotion was loud enough to pierce her agony. Doors were opening and being slammed, many feet were running, voices exclaiming. The guards took hold of her arms and raised her from the ground to carry her to their vehicle.

'What in the name of Caesar's holy balls is going on here?' The voice was deep and booming, cutting through the cries of everyone else and making even the researchers and guards hesitate. He didn't have Perry's commanding tone, but the confidence of command laced every syllable he spoke.

'You there, let that woman go! I didn't give you permission to enter my property! I am the Consul of Capreae and if you harm any person on my property, I tell you truly, I will see you tried in the arena before Caesar himself.'

One of the researchers tried to oppose him. 'They have escaped from the Starlight Project, sir! For the safety of yourself and your family, and for the safety of these poor wretches, I beg you to allow us to remove them.'

Tethia craned her eyes open. Beris's father was an imposing figure, but more from attitude than appearance. He was middle aged and heavy, but every step he took resounded on the earth and he moved like he expected the whole world to give way before him. In his experience, it probably did. He strode over to the skipper and looked inside. Tethia remembered that look on Beris's face.

She smiled a little and let her eyes fall closed again. The researcher didn't stand a chance.

She didn't make out anymore. She heard the shouting and the protests, but Beris's father had even more guards than the Starlight Project, and there was not a living soul who could out shout him.

The guards and researchers left, promising that they would return, solely concerned with the safety of the inhabitants of the house. The Consul saw that the gates were closed behind them.

When Tethia opened her eyes again, she saw Dubhia sitting in the driver's seat of the skipper, reaching out towards Beris. Perry stood outside the skipper, reaching in to keep her hand on Dubhia's shoulder. Slaves and Citizens alike were clustered around the door. A small group of slaves were beside Tethia, too, preparing to move her onto a stretcher.

'I can do it my damned self,' she muttered, aware that it was more a moan than the snap she intended it to be.

Dubhia leaned back, allowing the slaves to get in to help Beris from the skipper, encouraging him to stand on his own two feet and walk the short distance to the villa.

Tethia put her head down for just a moment, just to rest her eyes and was startled out of her half-dreaming by the feel of slaves sliding their hands beneath her to lift her onto the stretcher.

'I can do it myself,' she moaned again. Temper was the only thing holding her up, but she was fortunate she had a lot of it. They withdrew their arms and extended hands to raise her to her feet.

Tethia allowed them to help her up, on the basis that Beris was leaning heavily on the slaves attending him. It didn't matter what the slaves thought, but Beris might still be watching and she needed her pride intact. Perry and Dubhia were struggling their way inside. Triss and Loki had already gone ahead of them, Beris's parents already inside, their voices clearly audible as they arranged the whole household around the emergency.

Beris *was* watching her. He left the slaves and headed towards her. 'Come on,' he said, 'we'll hold each other up.' Tethia allowed herself to lean on him for a moment. Those days in the darkness would take a long time to forget. 'We'll go into the villa and we can start healing those poor bones of yours.'

The slaves ushered them inside. Tethia looked around at her surroundings. They were in a salon, urged to recline on comfortable couches, surrounded by the finest furniture, the frescoes on the walls just as fine as the ones in the Palatine. Slaves busied themselves around them, offering food and drink, and more important than any of that, pain killers. They even gave her new clothes to wear. They must have asked Beris, to know to give her clothes that marked her station, she mused, as the slaves helped her bathe and dress in the clean clothes of an unTied woman. From a distance, there was the sound of music. Tethia thought she recognised a song the Colonists had sung in the Project and fancied she recognised Perry's voice.

Fresh heart came into Tethia as the pain killers they gave her took effect. A Medic entered. He examined Beris's wound. Given Dubhia's attention, it was nearly healed. He turned to Tethia. He placed a cool, pain relieving compress against the wound in her side then turned to the long, tedious business of stitching up her hand. Tethia would have gotten restless, except Beris's painkillers had taken effect, too, and he was sitting next to her. They didn't talk much, just a few words here and there, but he was a calming influence on her.

'It's been a long day, hasn't it,' he commented, a small smile on his face for her alone.

Tethia laughed, despite the sickening feeling of the needle pulling through her pain-deadened flesh. 'Sure has,' she said. Finally, the last knot was tied and, with a discreet nod, the Medic left them alone.

'You need a good night's rest,' Beris commented.

'I need a lot of things,' she replied, hardly hearing him.

'Safe to say, my place is probably closer.'

Tethia looked up at him, suddenly realising what he was saying. That small smile was still on his face, gentle and kind – but that wasn't all. There was more than kindness in that smile. He looked at her with love. Everything he was to her, was in that smile.

He wasn't asking a question. He felt utterly sure of her and under other circumstances, he would have been right. As it was, he wasn't wrong. She was already his. Nothing remained but formalities. Her heart fell because there was only one answer she could give him. She looked down at where her uninjured hand lay on her thigh, where his hand lay over hers. She swallowed deeply.

'I need to get back to my husband,' she said softly. 'I will have been missed.'

She didn't look up, couldn't. He drew his hand away.

'I thought you were unTied.'

She breathed out, then struggled to draw the next breath in. 'Not now,' she answered. 'I was – for a long time. I'm so sorry I didn't tell you the truth. In the beginning you didn't matter... and then all of a sudden you mattered too much.'

He sighed heavily. 'Bear with me,' he said gruffly. 'It takes a little getting used to.'

'I'm barely used to the idea, myself,' she admitted. 'It's a long story.'

He sat in silence for a moment. 'Do you suppose you would ever tell me the whole story?'

Tethia allowed space for her own silence and felt it stretch between them, almost physically pushing them apart. 'No, I don't think so,' she replied softly.

He sighed again. 'I suppose it wasn't a long time that we were together, in that place,' he mused. 'It wasn't a long time, really. In the scheme of things, it was barely more than a handful of memories. But it changed everything for me. I suppose I was arrogant when I assumed those days changed anything for you.'

He stood up, reaching out to the couch to steady himself when the change in position made him briefly dizzy. Tethia reached out for him momentarily but snatched her hand away. She cast her eyes down, but not out of modesty; it was because she couldn't bear to look at him and see that she had hurt him. He was right. Those few days had changed things for both of them.

'Look at me, Lerina.' His voice was softly commanding. Tethia did as he bade her, longing to hear her real name on his lips, eager to answer any command he might give her, any command that she was capable of obeying. She longed for him as she had never longed for any man. She examined his features, desperate to commit every line of him to memory.

'I don't suppose I'll see you again. Still, I want you to know, if you ever need anything – I suppose it sounds trite, but I mean it, and I want you to understand it. If you ever need anything, I swear I will do anything in my power to help you. Do you understand what I'm saying?'

'Yes, I think I understand,' she said softly, still memorising his battered face.

He looked down at her for a long moment, seized

her hand and kissed it, then walked away.

The skipper was still parked outside the villa. She climbed inside and took one brief moment to feel the agony coursing through her. Her side ached, her hand felt like it had been minced and her arm felt like the bone was burning her arm from within. Not to be outdone, her head throbbed so much she wouldn't have been surprised if it had been visible to the slaves on the veranda that surrounded the villa. She drew a deep breath and let it out slowly, focussing on what she needed to do next and started the skipper.

The dig might have only been a short distance away, but it seemed a long way with her head so fuzzy from the pain killers. It wasn't as long as the drive from the Project, she told herself. Nothing could ever be so long as the drive from the Project. She suspected that she would be using that comparison for a long time. If she could do that, she could do anything.

Still, it was a long, long time before the stranger-light of the compound came into view. She parked the skipper neatly with the other vehicles, then put her head forward to rest it against the steering wheel – just for a minute.

She woke up when the door was jerked open and

she heard Rinn cursing. When he slid his arms underneath her, she would have argued with him, as she'd argued with the slaves, that she didn't need to be carried but she was just too sleepy to care. His arms felt nice around her, anyway, and there was no-one to impress any more. She rested her throbbing head against his shoulder while he held her. She didn't even understand the words he was saying, they seemed to come from so far away. She didn't care, really. She'd made it home. That was as far as she needed to go.

She was asleep before she even felt him take a step. Asleep, that was it. She definitely wouldn't do anything as silly as fall unconscious. Or so she would have told herself if she was conscious at the time.

#

She woke up as he lay her on the bed in his quarters. 'How are you feeling?' he asked.

She relaxed onto her back. 'I feel horrible, actually. Everything hurts. It's not like you can do anything about it, anyway. Even my skin feels sore.'

'Maybe you're coming down with something.'

'I've gone as far down as I can go. The only way

out is up.'

'I don't suppose you'd care to tell me where you've been all week?' He sat up and pushed his hair back off his face. His expression was stern. 'I don't suppose you care to tell me how an ordinary, respectable woman goes missing for a whole week and comes back with wounds like a soldier?'

Tethia shrugged and considered, when it hurt, that it was worth it from the furious look it brought to his face. 'I've only been an ordinary, respectable woman for about five minutes. Old habits die hard. You're supposed to be so glad I'm alive that you don't care.'

'Of course, I'm glad you're alive!' He leapt to his feet, pushing back that errant lock of hair again.

'Good, because I nearly died. So, stop being so ungrateful and do something helpful like help me change my clothes. I've bled over these ones already.'

Maybe not a good idea to draw his attention to her clothes. 'Why are you dressed like an unTied person?'

Tethia closed her eyes. Her side hurt, her hand hurt, her arm hurt and be damned if she could think up a plausible lie. 'Can't you just help me get dressed?'

He stood by the bed and watched her for a minute. 'I don't see why I should be penalised for your lack of discretion. Maybe doing for yourself for a change will teach you not to be so *independent.*'

He left the room. She muttered to herself exactly what she thought of him, but she knew that she'd never dare to say it to his face.

#

Rinn came back hours later. Tethia hadn't even changed her clothes, just collapsed back, exhausted, on the bed and slept without even trying to take off her shoes. She woke up to the quiet sound of the door opening and watched Rinn enter. His face was cold and hard. Their eyes caught, so she saw the expression in them as he carefully slammed the door behind him.

Tethia flinched and despised herself for it.

'I *told* you, I wanted you to change back into respectable clothes.'

Tethia struggled to sit up. She accidentally put pressure on her hand as she did so and released the air in her lungs of on a hiss of pain. She brought her arm up to cradle her sore hand protectively against her chest.

'I'm sorry,' she replied. With all her being, she wanted to shout back at him, demand to know if it wasn't obvious that her hand was bandaged and the fingers protruding from the bandage were swollen and blossoming with bruises. She restrained herself.

After all, she really *was* a respectable matron now. And that's how respectable women lived, wasn't it? Restrained, in one way or another. She had left Beris behind for this, to follow the Laws, to do the right thing. She was bound to Rinn, and it was her duty to honour that bond.

She deliberately softened her voice. 'I'm sorry. My hand – I couldn't manage the buttons. I'm sorry I'm dressed like this. They were the only clothes available.' Just a white lie, after all.

He remained where he was, standing with his back pressed to the door, his hand still on the doorknob. When he spoke, his voice was still taut with anger.

'Where have you been? How dare you go away for so long? I've had to tell all sorts of lies to my colleagues.' He drew in a sharp breath after the quick rush of words. 'You made me look like a liar. You made me look like a cuckold. Can you imagine the things Andred said to me? I had to have him removed. You ruined a man's career, his whole life, because you disappeared on your little holiday.'

'Holiday!' The word burst from her before she

could stop it and her injured hand flew out as instinctive evidence. 'Rinn, I was looking for Sheya. You knew that.'

'You didn't do a very good job of it, then, did you?' he asked, a nasty sneer on his face. 'Our daughter is dead now, and it's all because you couldn't be obedient.'

Tethia drew her injured hand back into her lap and dropped her gaze. 'I know.' The tears she thought Dubhia had dried up still threatened to fall. There would probably be a lifetime of tears to threaten. 'I wish I had died in her place.'

'We all wish that, Tethia.'

She closed her eyes, but it didn't stop the tears.

'This is why women shouldn't be independent. They don't have the brains for it. *Let a woman run free and let the world run to ruin*, as they say. I bet it was a married man who said it first. You've brought me nothing but grief.'

'I'm sorry, Rinn. I don't want to be independent. I'm your wife. That's all I want.'

Some of the fight went out of him. He left the door, taking those few steps towards her the tiny room allowed. 'You'll just have to learn your place, Tethia.' She flinched again when he touched her cheek, but his hand was gentle as he raised her face to look at him. 'I'm to blame, too. I should never have let you out alone. I knew that you were too accustomed to your own way. You didn't know any better. Now, keep your chin up. Let me get started on these buttons.'

Slow tears slipped down Tethia's cheeks as he undressed her. The painkillers must have worn off, because it was terribly painful drawing the jacket over her injured hand. He noticed her small cry of pain, and to her surprise even seemed to be moved by it.

'Never mind, love,' he said. 'We'll get that hand sorted in a minute.'

He dressed her again, this time in her own nightgown. The loose fabric still felt unfamiliar. She hadn't worn such a garment for more than a decade before the trial. After she was dressed, Rinn left the room briefly and then returned with a first aid pack. Tethia doubted that Rinn would be able to do a better job with a first aid pack than a certified Medic was able to do with his whole kit, but she knew better than to protest. The worst thing she could do right now would be to mention Beris.

She consoled herself with thoughts of Beris as Rinn unwrapped the bandage on her hand. Beris would never have treated her this way. Beris would never have forced her into lowering her gaze. Beris had never once criticised her for being independent. He had appreciated her strength.

When Rinn finally unwrapped the bandage, Tethia was gratified by his sudden intake of breath. Her hand looked terrible now, bruises purpling her swollen fingers, the marks of Matasin's boot clearly visible on the back of her hand. Maybe now Rinn would show her some sympathy.

'By the gods, Tethia, this cannot be.'

'It's not as bad as it looks,' she said, although of course it was every bit as bad as it looked, if not worse. 'I bruise easily, you know that.'

Rinn crouched at her feet and held her hand gently in both of his, staring at it. 'Tethia, I wanted so much for the two of us to be happy together. I wanted us to be a family,' and just like that, there it was again: the thought that somehow everything would be all right, that they would go back and be the same people they had been sixteen years ago. But he went on and ruined it as always.

He turned her hand over in his, showing the tattoos that she had nearly forgotten about. 'Tethia, where is Perry now?'

Tethia's astonished gaze flew up to meet his. 'How can you possibly know about her?'

Rinn dropped her hand and rose from his crouch.

He had that shuttered look on his face again. 'I've known Perry even longer than you have, Tethia. I was the one who named her when she first arrived. I was the first one to ever tried her little tricks on. I know how dangerous she is. Where is she?'

Tethia stared at him.

She saw his hand go back, that she wasn't quick enough to dodge the slap that knocked her across the bed. 'Where is she?' he thundered.

He shouldn't have hit her. He should have known better. She was willing to drop her gaze, she was willing to give up her whole life and be a respectable matron. She'd put up with worse, far worse, in the Project, but at least the guards in the Project had never pretended that they loved her.

And if he wasn't going to pretend, then she wasn't either.

She came up fighting. Her left hand was out of commission, but there was nothing wrong with her right. She landed a heavy jab directly on his nose. He went back, both hands flying up to cover his face. His eyes opened wide. It had never occurred to him the woman would ever fight back.

He tried to attack her, coming for her with open

arms, but he had no idea how to fight. He was a bully. She was a soldier. She left him sprawled out on the floor.

Tethia ran out of the room and across the courtyard to where the skipper was still parked at an awkward angle in the compound. Rinn hadn't even bothered to move it. It was late in the night by now, the nebula riding high in the sky and shedding its pink light over everything. Tethia ignored it. She would worry about starsickness later. Right now, she had to get away.

She drove back to the Consul's villa, high on the hill overlooking Capreae. This time, there were guards patrolling outside the villa. They stopped her before she could even get through the gates. If they noticed that she was only wearing a nightgown, they gave no sign. These were professional guards. All they cared about was their duty.

'What is your business here, sister?'

'My name is Lerina,' she told them, 'I have business with Beris, the son of the consul. I must see him urgently.'

'Sister, it is late in the night, the consul and his son are not available. None may pass here tonight. Come back in the morning.'

Tethia slapped the steering column with her good

hand. Even it ached after the blows she had dealt her husband that night. 'I must see him now! I know why you are patrolling tonight. I am the reason you're here. I was with Beris when he escaped. I am not safe. You have to let me in to see him!'

The guards stepped back from the window and conferred amongst themselves. One of them radioed back to the villa, explaining the situation in clear and dispassionate terms. They waited for a response, hands ready to reach for their weapons, but remaining coolly polite. The wait was interminable. When it finally came, the guard's eyes opened wide.

'My apologies, Ma'am. You are to proceed to the villa immediately.' He stepped away from the vehicle and waved her through.

Beris was already out in the courtyard when she arrived. She parked the skipper with no more skill than she'd shown at any other point that night and reached to open the door. Her hands were shaking so much, tears blinding her vision, that she could barely manage the handle. The door was jerked open from outside.

Beris was there, lifting her out of the skipper and gathering her into his embrace. She raised her arms to encircle his neck and lifted her face to receive his passionate kiss.

He carried her back into the villa, kissing away her giggles, then holding her tight against him as she buried her face in his shoulder. She held him just as tightly with her good arm, a whole lifetime of dreams flooding her with a joy she'd never really thought she'd know.

#

Tethia expected him to carry her to his room. The guards and slaves watching them pass by didn't matter to her. She was quite possibly the most shocking woman on the planet now, but at least she was free to call herself a woman. She wasn't a Citizen's daughter; she'd given up that right many years ago. She wasn't an unTied person. She wasn't an officer. She wasn't a wife, not anymore, if she ever really had been. She was just herself and she didn't care what anyone else made of it.

Beris carried her through the salon where they'd had their wounds tended. All signs of the domestic medical care had been erased and now it was just a pleasant, gracious room, lit only by a small light ball on a pedestal. He continued walking. Half a dozen slaves trailed after them.

Beris dragged his gaze from Tethia long enough to ask a slave, 'Would you mind getting that door for me, Carolius?'

Tethia's eyes opened wide, but she tried to hide her shock as the slave opened the door and Beris carried her into a garden.

'Can I get you anything, sir?' Carolius asked.

'A dish of our best wine for my sweet lady and myself, if you would, please, Carolius.'

Tethia didn't have to be looking at Carolius to hear the smile in his voice. She could tell that it was a smile, too, not a smirk. 'Certainly, sir.'

The garden was extraordinary. It had its own dome, curving protectively over the courtyard that glowed with the most stunning array of bioluminescence Tethia had ever seen. The whole garden was lit by the glow of flowers and leaves of exotic plants, to the point that the glow of the nebula barely seemed to intrude into the lovely, secret spot.

Beris lowered her to her feet, keeping his arms around her and drawing her even closer for another kiss. Tethia closed her eyes and lost herself in it. When Beris raised his head she wasn't sure if she was dazed from the intoxicating light from the garden or… who was she kidding? She knew what it was from. When his eyes made their way back to hers, she was smiling.

'Do you like the garden?' he asked, turning away from her and drawing a deep breath. 'I noticed you gasped when you saw it.'

Tethia ducked her head, biting her lip to try and hold back her smiles. She couldn't stop smiling. Beris turned back to her and raised her face to his and for a moment she thought involuntarily of Rinn. That banished her smile. She'd have to explain everything to Beris sooner or later. It would be obvious once her bruises came out anyway.

'The garden is lovely, Beris.' She placed her hand on his arm. 'I've never seen anything like it. Ordinary people like me don't live like this, and you know it.'

He stroked her cheek. 'You're hardly ordinary, Lerina.'

She'd forgotten that she'd lied about her name. She couldn't tell him about that now. Could she ever tell him about her other secrets? Beris had spent his life in this lovely place. He'd grown up privileged, with everything that a child could ever want or desire. He'd never encountered opposition until he'd decided to take on one of the biggest secrets in Caesar's arsenal. Tethia closed her eyes to hide from that sweet, expectant look on his face.

She tried to focus on what she'd been saying.

'It wasn't the garden that made me gasp, though. Your slaves have names.' She laughed, but it was a nervous laugh. 'I've never seen a slave who had a name before, except for the slaves on the Palatine.'

Beris turned serious. 'All slaves have names, Tethia, whether you knew them or not. In this household, even the slaves have rights. My father has been fighting for human rights since before I was born. The whole system of slave, Tiedman, unTied person, freedman, Citizen… the whole thing is designed to keep people in their place. Come and sit with me, darling.'

He drew her to sit on a stone bench, surrounded by bright lavender flowers that spilled out over the pavers beneath them. 'A name seems like a small thing, but it matters. A person has a name. When a slave is denied the right to their own name, they are denied the right to an identity. If they are allowed no legal identity, then they are vulnerable to abuse. You've been a slave. You know a little of what it can be like. We were fortunate, you and I, when we were in the Project.'

'Fortunate!'

He was still serious as he nodded. 'Yes, very fortunate. We were beaten: beaten badly, I grant you. To be fair, though, you nearly killed that man. You were justly punished for a crime. If you did such a thing in the world under the nebula, you would have been executed.'

Tethia remembered the two Palatine guards, thought back further to how her father had died and kept her mouth shut. She'd had many years to learn how to keep that secret.

'Haven't you seen slaves beaten before? Haven't you seen female slaves bear child after child who everyone knows is fathered by the master? You have to have seen slaves tormented, and worse, by the families who pat themselves on the back for their humanitarian goodness in granting their slaves the bare minimum of food, clothing and protection from the sky. How many of those we met in the Colony were slaves or the children of slaves?' He stopped and looked at her. 'Didn't you talk to people when you were there?'

She kept her eyes down, hating him for making her assume the position. 'I don't know if you've noticed, Beris, but I don't make friends like you do. They hated me. We didn't chat as we trod the laundry.'

Beris raised her gaze again. 'I'm not accusing you of anything, Lerina.' His hand dropped to take hold of hers. 'This is important, though. I'm not going to speak a pretty lie just because the truth is uncomfortable. The Project took our names because it's a devastatingly effective tactic in depersonalisation. Atrocities were committed there and taking names away, taking identities away, was a vital part of allowing those atrocities to happen. What we do here in this house, learning to respect one another, this is a beginning. You are Lerina, not LA-97, a person, not a test subject. In the same way, the person who will bring us our wine is a person, not a thing; a man, not an it; *his* name is Carolius, not Slave, and that is the name he chose himself, it wasn't given to him by someone else.'

There was a knock on the inside of the door as Carolius politely alerted them to his presence. He came out into the garden, smiled encouragingly and lay the tray with its two dishes of wine on a small table. 'Can I get you anything else, sir?' He looked from Beris to Tethia and it was too hard not to smile back. Tethia found herself responding to the warm friendliness of his gaze.

'Thank you, Carolius,' Tethia replied and Beris added his thanks to hers.

Carolius straightened up. 'May the gods bless you both,' then he retreated and left them alone.

Beris took a dish of wine with an experienced hand and gave it to Tethia. Tethia tried to balance it on its base, the way she'd seen Merrim do at the Palatine, but she couldn't get it steady. She grabbed it by the stem, but not before it splashed all over her hand and onto her nightgown.

Beris tried to help, chuckling as he swiped ineffectually at her nightgown. Tethia tried to brush the droplets of wine away but only succeeded in spilling more. 'Beris, I'd be an embarrassment to you. I've been unTied for the last thirteen years, I'm not used to being out in society, I'm too accustomed to being independent. I'm ten years older than you – it might as well be a hundred. You'd be a fool to want me. You're a Consul's son. I'm nothing.' She tried to put the dish of wine back on the table but her trembling hand made it spill all the more. Frustrated, she tossed the rest of the wine into the garden and stood up.

'This is ridiculous,' she said. 'I don't even know what I'm doing here. I should never have come. I wasn't thinking straight. I should go away, go… well, go somewhere.' She looked around, as though a path would immediately present itself. 'If you could just get me some clothes – again – I'll be on my way. I won't bother you again and I do apologise.'

Beris rose swiftly to his feet. 'Lerina, don't, please! Lerina, listen.' He closed his eyes for one long moment and drove his hands through his pale hair. 'Lerina, why do you think I welcomed you like this? Everything we've been to one another in those dark days – don't you trust me?' He turned away from her to pace along the flagstones. 'This is just like it was in the Colony, listening to you cry, night after night.'

Tethia gaped at him. She'd had no idea that he knew she cried in the night. The pain was sudden and sharp. He'd heard her cry and hadn't opened his arms to her, and he'd been right there in the next cot. Her hands stopped shaking. Everything inside her went very still.

Beris turned to pace back towards her. 'Why do you always have to hide from me? When you came to me tonight, I thought it was a sign that at last you were ready to turn to me in your need.' He tilted his head back to look at the nebula, shining through the protective dome. 'You'll never know what it did to me, lying there, wishing you'd turn to me, wishing you'd let me comfort you.'

And Tethia just stared at him. His life had been so different from hers. She was afraid to ask for help, and he was afraid she would reject any help he offered. Well, one of them had to take the risk. She'd been a soldier her whole adult life. She could be brave, if she wanted to.

She swallowed deeply, to bolster her courage, then

hastened across the flagstones to him. She threw her arms around his waist and buried her face in his chest. 'Beris, I love you. Please don't let me do anything stupid, like leave. I need your love. I need you to comfort me. If I leave you, I'll never feel safe or happy anywhere in the world.'

His arms came around her and he sighed heavily, dropping his face to rest against the top of her head. 'Lerina, trust me. I love you. You, not some idealised version of womanhood. I don't want you to be anything but what you are.'

Beris drew back so he could frame her face with his hands, thread his fingers through her hair while he stared lovingly down at her. 'I don't care how old you are. You're not an old woman and I'm not some boy. And who cares if you haven't wasted your life learning how to balance a dish of wine? You're strong, independent, and you never hesitate to do what you think is right. And you have so much heart. You don't like to show it, but I've seen your heart in action. I love that, I love so much about you. I don't want you to become some respectable matron. I only want you to be yourself. I want you to be free to be yourself, with me.'

Beris pulled out of Tethia's arms and stepped away. He took hold of both her hands and dropped to one knee.

'Lerina, I love you. Will you marry me?'

Tethia, heart pounding, despite the fact that his proposal was hardly unexpected or sudden, clasped his hands gently with hers and drew his hands together to rest on her breastbone. 'Yes, Beris, with all my heart,' she replied.

Then he was back on his feet again, holding her close and kissing her until she was dizzy.

#

There was a pounding noise in the distance, from outside the house, followed by the sound of something breaking.

The garden door crashed open and Carolius rushed in. His face was pale in the light from the luminous plants.

'They're here!' he cried.

Beris's gaze swung from Carolius to Tethia. There was something in his face she'd never seen before: despair. His wide-eyed gaze focussed on her with passionate intensity. He was looking at her as though this one last glance was going to have to last him a lifetime. Tethia read his thoughts so clearly. He didn't expect to ever see her again.

He shoved her towards Carolius. 'Quick, take her into the tunnels!'

Carolius grabbed Tethia by the hand. He kicked at the large flagstone in the centre of the garden. One edge of it rose and he bent to raise it like a hatch, revealing stairs descending into darkness. He ran down the stairs, pulling Tethia along with him. The hatch closed behind them with a heavy thud.

Tethia tried to pull away. 'Wait, Beris-'

Carolius's face was fierce. 'This is a mark of his love for you, woman. He gives you life. Don't spurn such a generous gift. Come. We must warn the others.'

'Others?' Tethia asked, then realised: Perry. She hurried willingly after Carolius.

The tunnel was narrow, twisting and turning under the earth. A ditch ran along one side, forcing them to run close to the wall on their right side. The soldier in Tethia appreciated the design. The attackers following behind them wouldn't be able to swing their swords freely, positioned so close to the wall, while those defending the tunnels had free movement thanks to the additional space offered by the ditch.

There was a door, an interminable distance along the dark tunnel. Carolius pounded on the door, just as

Tethia fancied she heard pounding behind them. She wished passionately for a weapon, just as her heart ached for Beris, left behind. She had no idea what he was going through right now.

The door opened, revealing two small faces, gleaming even in the dark. Perry looked ready to attack, Dubhia shoved protectively behind her.

'Where are Triss and Loki?' Tethia asked.

'They have made their own way in the world.' Neither Perry nor Dubhia looked surprised at being abandoned by their friends.

Carolius didn't waste time on pleasantries. 'Follow me. We must go to the caves.' He turned back towards the dark and the others followed him.

Carolius stopped several times when they ran through doors, to lock the doors behind him. Tethia wondered exactly what went on in that villa for it to be so carefully prepared for defence. Eventually, they came out of the manufactured tunnels into crevices and natural caves.

'Go on further,' Carolius ordered. 'And cover your eyes.'

They did as they were told. Tethia nearly screamed when the ceiling of the crevice collapsed behind them. She released the tension in a thin cry of his name. 'Carolius!'

She stared at the billowing clouds of dust, making the rear of the cave impenetrable, even to her excellent vision. The grit stung her eyes. Dubhia made a sound that was equal parts cough and sob. It was impossible to tell if it was Perry or Dubhia who cried.

Out of the swirling debris, Carolius came forward, one arm curved protectively over his eyes and mouth, the other feeling his way in front of him. Tethia caught his hand and led him out of the gritty cloud.

'That will hold them for a while,' he said, moments before his knees buckled beneath him. Tethia reached down to help him but he pulled himself right back up onto his feet again. 'Got to get further.' He coughed and Tethia noticed a smear of blood on his face beneath its covering of dust. 'Got to get to the main cave. Supplies there.'

'Don't talk,' Perry said. Her voice didn't have the same commanding tone when she spoke through Dubhia. Carolius nodded, none the less, and they continued through the caves.

Tethia thought the walls of the crevice would become rougher as they progressed from the manufactured tunnels. Instead, they gradually grew smoother, until the floor they walked upon was perfectly smooth and flat and the walls around them formed a perfect archway. The path

– it could no longer be called a crevice, or a cave – ended in a massive room.

Perry found a lightstick propped in a sconce at the end of the path and twisted it. The sudden change in brightness, even from a small lightstick, burned Tethia's eyes and she had to shut them tight to protect them. When she opened her eyes, she gasped.

The enormous space was a perfect half sphere, the floor level and the walls so smooth they reflected the glow from the light stick with a polished sheen. The striations on the rock created patterns that stretched all the way around the room, the circumference of each circle smaller than the last until they reached the very centre. Tethia's gaze followed them, then was drawn back down to her own level, to where a pillar stood, shoulder high to Tethia, carved all over with tiny writing.

Following a quarter of the circumference of the room was a huge bank of storage units. In one quarter of the room was half a dozen foldable cots, in another cooking facilities.

'What is this place?' Tethia breathed.

Carolius was already stretched out on one of the cots, an arm flung over his face. 'An ancient stronghold,' he said. 'It was a god's labour trying to keep the archaeologists out of it. They've got a dig not too far from here.'

'I'm familiar with it,' Tethia murmured. She moved closer to the column in the centre of the room. A door descended across the entrance of the path. Tethia looked around. The room now appeared seamless.

Perry moved with her. They both bent to read the glyphs that spiralled upwards from the base of the column.

Tethia straightened. 'You can't possibly read this,' she said scornfully. 'This is an ancient language. A girl your age couldn't know anything about such an ancient language.'

Perry returned Tethia's gaze with scorn to spare. She didn't use Dubhia's voice for the string of obscenities she made quite clear with hand signals.

'Lector RS made sure Perry was taught as many languages as possible. It was useful in her... work.' Dubhia sounded exhausted. She was sitting on the edge of a cot, her head hanging down.

'You're right, I wasn't around when people were using this language in conversation – like you were. That didn't stop me learning.' She pointed to the text. *'The snake illuminated the world.'* She turned to bob her head self-righteously at Tethia.

Tethia didn't stop the sneer that rose to her lips. 'Are you sure of that translation? The snake illuminated the world? Really? How do you suppose that worked?'

'It's a metaphor,' Perry replied as Dubhia swung her legs up on the cot and lay down. *'People spoke differently then. It's a religious conceit.'*

'Well, full marks for using the word conceit correctly in a sentence,' Tethia snapped, her tone making it quite clear she what she thought of Perry's translation. 'You're wrong, though.' She gestured. 'See that symbol there? It doesn't mean snake, it means star. It's talking about the world being so close to a star that we didn't need any other light. We were lucky we weren't burned up. It's bad enough that the nebula is so close, but at least it's far enough away that we can survive.'

'And how would a you know how to read an ancient language?' Perry mocked scornfully. Dubhia yawned.

'Well, in this particular instance, it was about ten years ago. That's the benefit of being a grown up. You get to have what we call experience. You'll learn about that when you grow up. Caesar had some ancient documents that he needed translated and I'd spent far too much time in the library.' She shrugged. 'I was the only one in New Rome who knew the symbols, so I spent the next year or so practicing. Every now and then they call me back to translate some more, when I'm not needed elsewhere. And I'm telling you, that symbol means star, not snake.'

Perry fixed her with a hard stare while Dubhia and Carolius ignored them both. *'Fine,'* Perry said finally. *'You read it, then.'*

'The world was bright and warm in those early days, in the light of our own star. We departed, travelling across the dark, ironically measuring the distance in light years from our own star. After many dark years we will arrive at a new star and warm ourselves in its light. We must maintain our cultures intact, preserving history as living history.' Her voice trailed off and she stared at the text. There was no way she could read all of this to Perry. Her hands were shaking. 'It goes on like this for a quite a bit. I'd say the writer of this cylinder was a whinger.'

Tethia abandoned the column, cursing the names of her own ancestors for her weakness in giving in to the urge to show off. If Caesar or an Auditor, found out what she'd learned here today, not only her life, but the lives of those she came into contact with would be forfeit. This was the greatest secret in the world.

Hands still trembling, she went to the storage compartments. One contained food and water, wine and oil neatly packed away. She went to the next cabinet. Finally, weapons. She selected a sword, belting it at her waist over her stained nightgown, attaching a dagger to the opposite hip. She felt safer with the weapon at her side. The terrible secrets she'd read made them even more of a target than the Marks on their skin.

'Hey, Carolius!'

The man just grunted.

'You said the archaeologists wanted to get into this place. Where are the other exits?'

Carolius shook his head, not even opening his eyes. 'We could only ever open the one, and that's closed with the weight of the mountain weighing upon it. We're safe here. Rest. Eat. Refresh yourself. When we are stronger, we will move on to the next stage of evacuation.'

'Evacuation. They'll be right behind us, Carolius, and you know it.'

'How could they get through a cave in?'

Tethia arched an eyebrow. 'Telling us that we're safe because we're entombed isn't particularly reassuring, Carolius.' She moderated her voice when she saw Dubhia's eyes open in sudden alarm. 'You said you couldn't open the others, not that others didn't exist.'

'We're safe in here, woman.'

A pounding on the door made him sit up straight. Dubhia just lay there with her eyes wide open, hands gripping the sheets. Perry abandoned the column and ran to the weapons locker. She girded herself with deliberate movements that spoke of long practice. 'What did Lector RS turn you into?' Tethia asked.

Perry looked up briefly, but didn't answer, her face tight. She gestured to Dubhia, who got up and joined Perry near the column. She took the knife Perry gave her but held it like a dinner knife. Perry stared at her a moment, her tight face showing a thousand emotions at once. She made an emphatic gesture to Dubhia, but it wasn't clear to Tethia what she was saying. Dubhia seemed to know, though. She threw her arms around Perry's waist, holding the knife carefully away from Perry's back, and buried her face in Perry's shoulder. Perry held Dubhia gently, but didn't stop scanning the room, ready for the threat to arrive.

Tethia looked away from the couple. The expression on Perry's face was terrifying: hard, brutal and ready to wreak vengeance. She would kill anyone who tried to touch Dubhia and it was clear that it wouldn't be the first person she'd killed. For a moment, Tethia fancied that she and Perry might look alike to anybody who saw them. She'd seen that hard look in her own eyes, reflected back in the eyes and armour of her foes.

Their attackers were devastatingly quick in opening the door. They were coming from a different direction than the small group of refugees had arrived. They must have known where they were going and come at them from another entrance. They beat at the door for only a few moments, a muffled shout calling for the battering ram.

The fight was similarly brief. Their attackers were wearing the uniform of the Project, not of the Imperial Military Services, but they were just as skilled. Carolius was killed immediately and Tethia brought down the man who felled him. She killed another, diving under his guard just as Perry killed her first. It was brutal and bloody. They fought well, backing close together and trying to defend against their assailants, but there were too many of them.

One grabbed Dubhia's knife with a mailed fist and dragged her away from the others. Perry leaped after her and once they were separated, they were doomed. Tethia's sword was clashed from her hand. She grabbed for the dagger with her other hand, but she'd forgotten the broken bones from Matasin's assault. She fought, but the momentary disability was enough to give him the chance to grab her.

He caught her hand, gripping tight and the crushing

grasp on her broken fingers was unbearable. She screamed. He tightened his grip, his face gleeful. She pulled away but another guard was behind her. He brought something heavy down against her head.

She was unconscious before she hit the floor.

\#

When Tethia woke up, she was in a narrow bed, rocking slightly from side to side. Rinn was snoring louder than the engine of the train and hatred for him flooded her even before she realised that he couldn't possibly be there. She sat up and looked around. She was in a train carriage. The cabin was small, but well-appointed with bunk beds, the upper bunk containing an impressively loud snore. There was space for a desk, flooded with papers. Beyond it was a small sitting area with two comfortable chairs clustered around another table. It looked like a first class cabin on a high speed train, the same as the one she'd travelled on the journey to Lygia.

For a moment, she wondered if the whole disaster was a dream, but she hadn't shared the cabin on that journey. The slave had its own quarters.

Tethia stopped herself. The slave had *his* own

quarters.

She swung her legs over the edge of the narrow bed and looked down at herself. She was still wearing a nightgown, stained with the wine she had spilled in the Consul's garden. Her hand was bandaged afresh and the fingertips more purple than ever. She stood up and went over to the desk. No wonder she'd fancied she was back with Rinn. His desk was just as messy. She must have imagined the snore. She couldn't hear it now. Maybe it had all been a dream, and she'd just made a mess on the desk herself.

She rifled through the papers with a sense of unreality. These were the same sort of papers Rinn had on his desk: a mix of archaeology journals, scribbled notes and official reports. She dropped the papers. That was Rinn's handwriting.

'So, I guess you're awake,' Rinn said.

Tethia spun around. Rinn was sitting on the edge of the top bunk, his head canted forward to avoid the low ceiling. He smiled. 'I thought you'd sleep all day.' The effect of the smile was somewhat spoiled by the two brilliant black eyes and swollen nose. She knew a sense of satisfaction. If nothing else, she'd done that to him.

Tethia breathed faster, even though the air didn't

seem to get past the tight constriction of her throat. 'What are you doing here?' she gasped. 'Where are we – what happened?'

Rinn climbed down the ladder. He came towards her and put his hands on her shoulders. 'We're in a train, love. We're going to New Rome.'

'But... how? Perry?'

'She's safe.' He smiled encouragingly.

She stared back. 'Rinn... what the hell?'

He let her go, just long enough to slap her so hard across the face that it rocked her head to the side. She would have lost her footing if he hadn't grabbed her again.

'I don't like my wife swearing, Tethia.'

Tethia just stared, her chest heaving with every breath.

'We're in a train going to New Rome. You were disobedient. You were very naughty, in fact. But women need a firm hand and I was at fault, Tethy, I really was. I should never have allowed you to leave the dig at all. I just thought it would be a nice pastime for you. Everyone needs a hobby.' He smiled again. 'I didn't want you getting bored.'

'Well, I certainly can't say I was bored,' she replied with a nervous laugh.

Rinn let her go and went over to the sitting area. Tethia swayed with the movement of the train. 'Come, join me, love,' he said encouragingly, indicating the other chair.

Tethia did what she was told.

Rinn pressed the button for the slave. Tethia just sat in the chair while he ordered refreshments. 'I know this is a lot for you to take in. I don't want you to worry. You're going to be safe. I know you've got those filthy Marks on you, but that won't matter. You're my wife. No one will dare touch you if you're mine. Ah, here we are.'

The refreshments had arrived. Rinn acted like a civilised gentlemen, every inch the high-born Citizen, while Tethia knew that he'd had to pay for his Citizenship and had to earn it with military service. He hadn't been wrong when he'd said – a lifetime ago, when he was driving her into Capreae – that she was out of his league. She'd been a Citizen's daughter, with every right and privilege available to a woman. He'd been the son of a merchant. Even as a woman, as a girl who hadn't even attained her majority, she'd still been his social superior. She'd gone on to a career of distinction in the Services as an unTied person.

He may have bought his Citizenship, but he hadn't become much of a man. And now he was flaunting his power in her face.

Tethia sat up a little straighter in her chair. She may not have spent much time socialising with adults, but she'd been a very well-trained little girl, and she could sit nicely and drink her tea with the best of them. She took the cup he offered her with a low, gracious murmur of thanks.

'You sound like a powerful man,' she purred.

Rinn sat up a little straighter, too. 'I've attained a certain position,' he boasted.

'I'll just bet you have. You've grown far beyond your early promise.' He took a sip of his tea. It must have tasted like liquid pride. She leaned in for the barb. 'Still, you're only an archaeologist, though. How could you possibly protect me against the might of the Starlight Project?'

She'd been ready for him to throw his tea in her face. Instead, he just leaned back a little, a self-satisfied smile playing around the corners of his mouth.

'I'm not just an archaeologist, Tethia. I'm a member of the Starlight Council. I let you have your little quest because it kept you occupied and away from all the men at the dig. I don't just know about the Starlight Project. I run it.'

Tethia gaped and hated herself for it when he

preened. 'Why didn't you tell me this before?'

Rinn shrugged. 'Why should I? You're only my wife. You don't need to know everything. Now, though, you need to know that I can protect you, even when you're naughty. I never thought I'd get married, but since I am, I want to be a good husband.' He drew in a deep breath and wouldn't quite meet her eyes. 'And, speaking of you being naughty, there's something you have to apologise for, isn't there, Tethia?'

Tethia held onto her cup. It was the only weapon at hand, and she wasn't going to rule out killing him. 'Apologise?' she asked. 'For knocking you on your arse, you mean?'

He pursed his lips and put his own cup down. He leaned forward. 'I let you think you got the better of me so you could learn the value of obedience.'

Tethia couldn't help the chuckle, even though she knew she'd pay for it. 'You mean, you *meant* for me to give you such a fantastic set of shiners? And people say women are illogical!'

She was still chuckling when he launched towards her and pushed her shoulders into her chair. She stared up at him, the laugh dissolving into a baring of teeth. He didn't hit her, though, just pushed her then jerked away from her to pace around the cabin.

'Who touched you?' he demanded.

'What?'

'*Who touched you?!*' he shouted.

Tethia shrugged. 'Dozens of people, I suppose. The guards. Carolius, the decent man who died trying to protect people he didn't even know by name. Perry. Dubhia. Beris. Dr Matasin, before I killed him. Before that, probably dozens of people in the Colony.'

'*Who raped you?*' Rinn shouted.

Tethia stared at him. 'No one. Not for years.'

Frustrated, Rinn strode towards her and grasped her nightgown from her lap, lifting the section that had been stained with wine, then flinging it back down.

'Do you think I don't remember seeing a stain like this on your nightgown before?'

Tethia kept staring, but she hardly saw him anymore. She'd been seventeen. It wasn't long after Proxima died. She'd gone to Rinn afterwards, not knowing where else to go. She hadn't told him what happened, but he'd seen the stain on her gown. He'd comforted her, his shattered expression enough to make her think fondly of him for more than a decade, even though she never dared to pretend her baby was his.

'No one touches what's mine,' he ranted. 'Tell me who it was and I'll have them killed. *No one* touches what's mine.'

Tethia looked down, just as shattered as she'd felt the night she'd gone to him when she was seventeen. She'd given him every possible chance. He would never be a good man; no amount of rationalisation would ever make him into a good man. The desperate hopes of a cornered teenager and the fears of a woman who had never been safe with a man had persisted in blinding her. Those hopes and fears were a part of her, but it was time to move past them. She had to focus on getting out of there, focus on saving the two little girls with no one to look after them.

'No one touched me, Rinn. Someone gave me a glass of wine and I spilled it. Look, you can see the stain isn't stiff enough to be blood. It isn't dark enough. It's only wine. No one touched me. No one would dare touch *your* wife.'

Rinn turned away from her to pace around the tiny cabin again, stopping to grip the bars of the upper bunk and press his forehead against the cool metal.

'What about Perry, Rinn? Has someone hurt her? Is she as safe as I am?'

He didn't turn around, just gripped the bars tighter.

'She's in the next compartment – safe… for now.'

'For now?'

'I can't save Perry. I'm sorry, Tethy, gods know I'm sorry, but I can't save her. She's too powerful. She's disobedient-' he turned, with a forced smile. 'Like you. But Perry's dangerous. I was the only one who could even begin to control her. We tried taking her voice away, but last night she escaped and Valorius told us she'd used his voice to command. We thought she could only speak through Dubhia and she can't command with Dubhi's voice.' He gave a short bark of laughter. 'Dubhi can barely control her own bladder. Perry was so useful to us.' His face grew stern. 'If she can't be obedient, she is a risk, not an asset and we can't risk her.'

'Rinn, she's just a little girl!'

Rinn came back to place a heavy hand on Tethia's shoulder. 'I know how much she means to you,' he said, his voice deep and serious. 'She's had a special place in my heart all her life because of what she would have been to you. I thought she was Proxima's daughter, though, not yours. I never knew you were pregnant. All I knew was that this was the daughter of Meropius, General.' He sat down in the other chair again, leaning forward and resting his forearms on his thighs. 'I received her into the Project when she was just a baby. I was the one who named her; Perry is short for Proxima.'

'Rinn…' Tethia's voice was embarrassingly thin and reedy. 'I have to see her…'

He shook his head. 'You can't, Tethia. You've already been terribly naughty. I have to get you off this train so I can hide you somewhere. Perry is too dangerous to save.'

Tethia buried her face in her hands and wept.

After a moment, Rinn got up, patted her on the shoulder. 'You have a good cry, love. I'll be back in half an hour. When you've dried your tears, I want you to get dressed and ready to run when I tell you. I can keep you safe, but I can't keep you in public.' He left the cabin, locking the door behind him.

Tethia was ready when he returned. She had dressed in the Service uniform he'd left for her. That in itself told her both his plans and his confidence in her. There wasn't much point in dressing her as a Citizen's wife if he wasn't going to accompany her. She ate all the little sweets the slave had brought with the refreshments, drank all the tea, even though it was cold. It might be her last meal for some time. It might be her last meal, full stop.

The door slid open and Rinn entered. 'Good girl,

you're ready.'

She just nodded.

He looked at his watch. 'It's time.'

The train lurched to a sudden stop. Tethia nearly stumbled, grabbing hold of the upper bunk to steady herself. 'What was that?'

'That's our diversion. It will give you time to run. It's daytime – you should be safe from the nebula for hours yet. We're passing through the suburb outside Valdennes. You can jump off the train and lose yourself in the streets. Go to your mother's and I'll come and get you on the return trip.'

She nodded firmly. 'Good idea.' She followed him out of the cabin and stopped suddenly. 'Which of these doors is Perry's?' she asked in a small, feminine voice.

'We don't have time to talk about Perry! Let's go!' he caught her wrist and tugged her to follow behind him. Tethia used his grasp on her hand to pull him back towards her, until his back was pressed against her front and her arm held his hand across his chest, pulling him down until he was nearly off his feet. The broken shard of a teacup was pressed tight enough to his throat to draw a small trickle of blood. 'Tethia! What-'

'Shut up, you piece of filth,' she gritted. 'I asked

you a question, pig. Which of these doors is Perry's?'

'You've lost your mind!'

'If you won't tell me, I'll just kill you anyway.' She pressed the shard tighter into his flesh, feeling the small give that told her she'd broken the skin.

Rinn squealed like the pig she'd just called him. 'On the left, on the left!'

Tethia turned him to face the door. 'Open it.'

Rinn swiped his palm across the lock and the door swished open. Perry and Dubhia were inside, sitting on the lower bunk. Perry leaped to her feet, a look of fierce glee on her face. *'There's something I've been longing to tell you, Lector RS,'* she said. Dubhia's expression was just as fierce as Perry's and for once the voice didn't sound strange coming from her mouth. Perry took a few swift steps forward and brought her fist around to crash into Rinn's jaw.

He went slack in Tethia's grip. She dropped him before he crushed her, and he coiled up in the hallway. 'I don't think he's going to listen right now,' she said to Perry.

'I think he got the point. Are we escaping? That's my favourite thing we do together.'

Tethia smiled broadly and stepped back from the

doorway for the two girls to run past them. Rinn groaned at her feet.

Perry and Dubhia jumped over Rinn's prostrate form and ran down the corridor. The door at the junction of two carriages was open. Perry jumped down, then helped Dubhia to the ground.

Tethia heard the word behind her. '*Disobedient!*' She didn't see him, but she sure felt the blow Rinn landed on the back of her head.

She only woke up once more on the journey to New Rome. She wasn't in a first class cabin anymore. She hadn't even known that a class like this existed. And, maybe, on an ordinary train, it didn't. The carriage was empty, except for half a dozen prisoners sitting on the cold metal floor. There was dried food and water at one end of the carriage, but all the prisoners were shackled to the wall. She didn't even recognise the mess of a man shackled across from her until he spat towards her.

'This is all your fault, woman!'

'What?' Tethia squinted through a swollen eye that she was sure hadn't been swollen before she was knocked unconscious. What a brave man her husband was. He'd worked her over, but only after she was unconscious. A name swam into memory. 'Andred?'

'If it wasn't for you, I would never have ended up here.'

'That sounds like bullshit to me.' Tethia closed her eyes again. 'The way you were going, it was only a matter of time.'

Rinn had said something about this, though… what was it? That's right. *'I had to have Andred removed.'* Tethia had thought he'd meant he'd had him fired. From the looks of it, he'd not only had Andred removed, he'd removed quite a bit from Andred.

'It was *your* husband who did this to me!'

'Me, too. And are we really talking?' Tethia made that huge effort to open her eyes again. 'After all that's happened, can't we just be honest and admit we despise one another?

'You'll join your brother soon, bitch.'

She closed her eyes again. It still hurt, but it didn't hurt as much. 'What are you talking about?'

'I told you before, I follow the boxing. Your brother's trial was big news. His execution was big news, too. So sad. Such a promising young man. You know, I always thought it was funny that your mother had two girls when she first married Meropius, then a boy so late in life, just when the older girl was old enough to… well, you catch my drift.'

Andred went on talking but Tethia wasn't listening anymore. She already knew who Merrim's mother was. Had been. And now Merrim... a sob rattled in her chest and she let out the air in a moan. She couldn't hear Andred because all she could hear were her own sobs.

#

Tethia woke up briefly when they took her out of the train and put her on a transport. She was probably going to trial again. Taking her to New Rome for her trial was not a good sign. There was no reason why they couldn't try her in the small arena in Lygia... except if it was a capital crime. When that thought occurred to her, she paused for a moment to consider what she might have done to merit execution. In hindsight, it wasn't a short list.

Given her previous record, they might realise that she had killed the guards on the Palatine Hill and aided and abetted the abduction of Caesar's niece. That was not one but two capital crimes right there. Then there was breaking into the Project, conduct unbecoming to a Tiedwoman, unlawful purchase of goods without authorisation, assaulting a respectable member of society... come to think of it, she was also guilty of withholding sex from her husband and that was a crime, too. No wonder they were taking her to New Rome for trial. She'd be standing there all day.

It was early evening when they took her out of the train. The pink light of the nebula drove a faint glow through Tethia's swollen eyes. Tethia dozed, her head dropping onto her chest until she woke herself up by snoring as loud as Rinn ever had.

This trial was going to be worse than the last one. At her last trial she'd at least had some dignity. Since the accused were tried in the same clothes they were arrested in, at her last trial she'd been wearing the clothes of a respectable Citizen's daughter, regardless of how dishevelled she'd been when she arrived at the arena. She'd stood, straight and proud under the glaring lights and dared the jury to convict her.

Now she was going to have to stand under the same glaring lights, exposed and vulnerable in her stained nightgown. Rinn had given her the clothes of an unTied person for her attempted escape: he'd changed her back into her stained nightgown when she was unconscious. The knowledge that he had undressed her while she was unconscious, that he'd deliberately put her in the most shameful attire passible, made her skin crawl and left an acid taste in the back of her throat. The crowd was sure to be as great as before, fascinated by the ongoing drama. Tethia imagined them talking about her, calling her "that boxer's sister" and saying that it was "proof that women can't be trusted to be unTied."

She'd been mistaken, though. They didn't take her to the arena, or to the prison adjoining it. There was no window in the transport, but she heard the roar that could only come from the arena when the games were on. It was the only place in New Rome large enough for such crowds to gather.

When it appeared they were going straight past the arena, Tethia went very still. Going to the arena for trial was a bad sign. Not going to trial at all was worse. She tried to think where they might be taking her: a civilian prison, a military prison... a facility for research... execution... Re- Education... Her breathing sped up, despite her efforts to control it and her heart, completely beyond her control, thudded heavily. She swallowed hard, letting her straining eyes stay shut for one long moment. Sheya was alive. Sheya was safe. Dubhia would look after her. She was free, at least.

Tethia's breathing slowed, even her pounding heart slowed. *Sheya is safe*, she told herself. She tasted her daughter's new name on her tongue. *Perry is safe. Perry is strong. Perry can look after herself now.* So that was all right, then. It wasn't all she'd asked of the world, but it was the most important thing.

At least she'd seen her. At least she knew that Perry was free. If she focussed on that, then what was ahead of her was bearable. She closed her eyes again, the better to see the grey eyes and gamine face, the capable, quick hands, the voice that could be so soft, but so determined and could come from anyone. Her determination she had inherited from her mother and from her grandmother, too.

Tethia had a sudden memory of the look on her mother's face as Shey-Leen had told her that her father was dead and that Tethia must never, never tell anyone, that she must say he was missing, she must remember this. Tethia had felt betrayed. Her father was dead, the man who had caused her more suffering than any man she'd met since. Now he was dead and there was no revenge for her anymore. And Shey-Leen had allowed it to happen. Tethia could never forgive that.

But Perry was the important thing. Perry was safe. Perry was strong. Perry would survive. Tethia chanted it to herself as they led her from the transport along a wide, open avenue lined with columns that pointed to the sky like a row of leafless trees. She looked around. These columns looked familiar. She caught sight of a high wall, and in the distance, a gatepost.

They'd taken her to the Palatine Hill. She swallowed hard to ease a suddenly dry throat. So, it was to be execution without trial, then. Her breathing came faster, and she scanned her surroundings for a possible escape. The guards gripped her arms tighter. They'd probably done this a hundred times.

She thought, inconsequentially, of the nightgown she was wearing and resented that she should have to face her last moments dressed so shabbily. Her mind flew to a thousand regrets and reproaches.

She should have told Rinn that she was pregnant so many years ago, demanded that he marry her and divorced him in short order. She was a Citizen's daughter and he hadn't yet received his Citizenship. She'd had the right.

She should have killed Meropius herself and not left her mother to do it. She should never have let the relationship between herself and her mother grow so cool.

She should never, never have given Sheya up. She should have sought her out earlier, should have been more discreet in her approach, should have been smarter and not gotten caught. All her life seemed to sum up to very little and her regrets were overpowering. She began to struggle.

The guards' hands tightened like iron around her arms. She struggled harder and they lifted her off her feet.

Stop it!' one of them growled from behind her. 'It'll be worse if you keep this up!' He put a heavy hand on her shoulder.

'I've got nothing to lose!' she hissed back, then turned her head and bit his hand.

He cried out in pain, but he didn't let go. The guard tightened his grip, his finger finding a vulnerable pulse point and Tethia passed out. Again, she thought wearily, as the world faded around her.

Tethia woke, surprised to wake up at all. She was lying on a hard bed. On examination, she found that her arms, legs and body were strapped down. When she tried to raise her head, she found that was strapped down, too.

'Good afternoon, Lieutenant.' The voice was oddly, pleasantly androgynous, professional and impartial, but it sent a chill down Tethia's spine.

'Get it over with!' she snapped. 'And it's not Lieutenant anymore.'

'But it will be, and it won't hurt me to get in a little

practice.'

'What? Hurry up and kill me already.'

'You don't need to worry, Lieutenant. We're not going to kill you. We're going to fix you. After all, you are an exceptional linguist. Your case went before Caesar himself. You should be thankful. He found your approach to life... intriguing.'

Tethia looked around but the speaker was out of sight. At least she could open her eyes again. 'I might as well say it, but I will never, never give up looking for my little girl. You can do anything and I will never, ever give up.'

The speaker laughed. The laugh sounded familiar. Tethia shivered again. Whoever he was, he thought the situation was genuinely funny. 'Of course you will. You all do. You forgot about looking for her before. It was just unfortunate that you had managed to get a message to your brother before we got you here to Re- Ed last time, still more unfortunate that it was to you that Caesar's niece should choose to so freely reveal the details of the Starlight Project. But never mind, we can take that all away. This time we'll patch every person you've come in contact with. The memories will be flying from here to Capreae tonight. This time tomorrow, you'll wake up thinking you've had no more than a bad dream, and even that will pass soon enough. This time tomorrow the world will have forgotten all the sorrow you've brought it, leaving only a useful Lieutenant.'

The speaker moved into view. They were middle aged, but the heavy frame and smooth skin gave a youthful tone that belied the experience in the eyes. Their skin was pellucid-fair, the blue veins running in clear lines beneath it, the eyes the palest blue, hair the fairest white. They were only there a moment then they moved out of sight for a moment. There had been a resemblance to someone she knew, but they'd moved before she caught it.

'Who are you?' she asked.

'I'm the only one here with your best interests at heart, Lieutenant, so you would do well to listen to me.'

There was a drawl in the voice, an accent. Accents were Tethia's bread and butter. 'Have you lived in the Imperial household long?' she asked, determined to get the upper hand somehow. The fact that getting the upper hand while strapped to an examination table was going to be difficult was not lost on her.

She tried to place the voice, tried to place the face. There was something about the white jowls that rolled down from the square jaw that reminded Tethia of Ala, but it wasn't Ala's delicate face.

Tethia tried to keep herself under control. 'Even if you kill me, it won't matter.' She turned her eyes back up to the ceiling. 'My daughter escaped. If she is free, then I don't care what you do to me.'

The Re-Educator moved back into view for just long enough for Tethia to see the smirk. 'Then you'll be disappointed, Lieutenant, because we've been doing this a very long time. All the subjects are tracked through their Marks. It was a simple thing to follow PA-62 to her location. Within the hour, our forces had raided their hideout and taken all the subjects back into custody.'

Tethia's heart sank, so far and so fast it was as though that vital organ had deserted its place altogether. 'Sheya's back in the Starlight Project?' she asked, her voice a broken, disbelieving whisper.

'No.'

'No?' She couldn't help the flash of hope, the rise in her voice.

'No, Lieutenant, your daughter is dead. The subjects were terminated immediately following their arrival in custody. Now, don't take on,' he continued when Tethia let out a thin wail. 'Their function in the project was to show the effect of environment on an individual's risk of dying from starsickness. Once they'd been exposed to the sky, between fifteen and *forty-five* years' research was *wasted*. To wilfully destroy *decades* of research like that! It was criminal.'

'No,' Tethia moaned. 'No!'

The Re-Educator continued speaking as though Tethia were being unreasonable. 'They were no further use to the Project and it's not as though either of them was a Citizen, or even a person under the law. They were either illegitimate, deformed or unwanted. They didn't even have the right to live in the first place.'

Tethia gritted her teeth and tried to blink back the tears. Suddenly, passionately, she hated herself for not giving Sheya a better life, for not being able to save her from an early death. She would never forgive herself for this.

'Oh, by the gods,' she wailed for the second time in as many days, 'just kill me now. Let me die.' Then she just cried, lying flat on her back, strapped into position, tears running down the sides of her face and into her hair.

The Re-Educator stood there staring at her for a moment. 'You disappoint me, Lieutenant. I expected more. Re-Education will do you good.'

Tethia lay still on the bed. No matter what anyone

said, there would never be any life for her again. From somewhere in the room, she heard a little beep as the Re-Educator started to adjust an IV pump. There was a small sting in her elbow as the IV went in and oblivion was waiting for her.

PART THREE

Tethia woke late, bleary eyed and heavy with dreams, and more important than any dream – late! She dressed quickly, with an efficiency born of fifteen years of military service. She didn't hurry – that would be unseemly. She made her way quickly to the Special Services Headquarters, her face calm, impassive even, presented to the other commuters on the train. Inside, she was screaming. She had to shove her way past a newsspeaker to get out of the train and hurt her hand. It throbbed like she'd done some damage.

Every checkpoint she passed, she turned a bland

face to the inspector, holding her ID card ready in her hand to save every second she could. She didn't go to her office, going instead straight to the conference room, sliding into her seat just in time to leap to her feet as Terreus, General entered the room.

She gazed straight down, aware that he'd seen her reverse direction but he didn't say anything. She sat, polite and civil as assignments were handed around, receiving hers obediently, keeping her eyes downcast as was seemly for a woman, even though she was a Citizen, an officer and unTied.

The General droned on. The man was a deadly bore, the kind of person who always wore his uniform. Tethia struggled to stay awake, the manila folder not nearly exciting enough to keep her mind off her dreams. Her head had been reeling with them this morning, so close and real that it was hard to tell them from reality. It all seemed so jumbled! Running along dark streets, chased by shadowy foes. A face from the past, mixed in with a crowd of faces both half familiar and fully foreign. There were whispered messages, lost in the shock of sudden waking and under it all was Sheya.

That wasn't a surprise. Tethia hadn't seen her for fifteen years and had met her only the once but she seemed to be behind every dream that passed through Tethia's sleeping mind. Funny how some people can make such a difference, Tethia mused, eyes still on the manila folder.

There was nothing in the meeting that required Tethia's attention. She watched the manila folder until she nearly fell back into dreams again. Her head nodded for one dreadful moment, jerking back up to the sudden thump of her heart. She cast surreptitious eyes to left and right but no one seemed to have noticed. Her heart continued its heavy thumping, keeping time with the rhythm of pounding feet remembered from her dream.

Terreus, General knocked his knuckles against the polished wooden tabletop to signal the end of the meeting before Tethia's heart rate had returned to normal. She rose and saluted in sync with the others, even though she kept her eyes downcast, and left the room promptly, holding the manila folder that contained her assignment. Same old, same old, she told herself. Another day translating in the archives.

#

She took the train to the Palatine Hill, watching with discreet interest as more and more passengers disembarked. The train was nearly empty by the time it reached the hill.

At the first gate she presented the guard with the token that had been given to her among the other contents of the manila folder. They sent a silent slave to guide her through the gardens. She had always taken a different route, through a long cavalcade of offices. It was a special treat to be allowed to see Caesar's gardens. The pleasant, stranger-lit space was calming and by the time she reached the third gate, Tethia felt more her usual self. She presented herself to the guards with cool professionalism and stood rigidly to attention while she waited for a slave to take her to the library.

The slave arrived at the third gate after only a matter of moments. She was tall, solidly built woman who walked across the patterned marble as though she were a goddess walking on water. The white veil billowed from artfully concealed pins in her white hair. She stood patiently, waiting for Tethia to speak first.

Tethia bowed her head, deciding to be polite, since this was a member of Caesar's household. 'My name is Tethia of Valdennes, Lieutenant, salve. I am authorised to visit the Library today, to translate documents from the First Age.'

The slave bowed again, the veil billowing around her plump arms as she straightened. Her manners were impeccable. 'Lieutenant, salve. I am known as Mira, personal slave to the gem of the Imperial household. I will be your attendant today. If you would care to follow me, it would be my honour to assist you.'

Mira led Tethia to the library. Tethia had been there before, translating other documents from the First Age. The Library was the largest in the world, although some of the oldest documents described a library even larger. Every now and then an ancient manuscript would be referenced by one of the histories in Caesar's Library. Tethia's job was to translate the oldest materials in the Library, to create a catalogue of documents available and to pass on a translated copy of the documents to the steward of the Imperial household.

The pair passed quietly up the massive flight of stairs and below the columned portico. Inside the Library it was cooler than outside, to protect the fragile manuscripts from the damaging effects of heat and humidity. The main area of the Library was a massive reading room lined with books, rising up three galleried stories above floor level.

Mira led Tethia from the main room, through a door that discreetly nestled behind a row of books and into the long hallway beyond. Doors and other hallways branched off from this one, each marked with a symbol to denote its purpose, but the symbols meant nothing to Tethia. Then finally one last room, lined with shelves piled high with scrolls, a large desk in the centre of the room with space for at least a dozen scholars. Now it was set up for only one, a pillow in place ready to hold a book open without damaging the spine. A length of fine cord to hold the pages open and a pair of gloves for handling the paper were left where Tethia had placed them on the pillow the last time she was here.

'If you don't mind, Lieutenant,' Mira said, her voice hesitant and soft, 'I am commanded to stay while you attend your work in the Library.'

'Stay, if you like,' Tethia said, already standing at the shelves that held the oldest books and examining the remnants of lettering on the spines. She turned to face Mira and smiled sympathetically. 'I understand. We are both under orders. I hope you won't be bored, though.'

'I have work of my own, Lieutenant.'

Tethia chose a volume and carefully removed it from the shelf. She was careful to use her right hand to handle the volume. Her left hand was still terribly sore from when she'd had to shove past the newsspeaker on the train. She placed the book on the pillow and opened it, very gently turning the pages until she reached the point where she had been up to last time she was in this room. She opened her briefcase and drew out the computer that was allocated her for her employment and started the mechanical work of translation.

An hour later she looked up from her work when the small alarm went off to remind her to take a break. She drew in a deep breath and started the stretches she always did. She looked up and noticed Mira, seated at opposite side of the desk. There was a small book open in front of her and she moved her finger along the line of text as she read. Tethia smiled.

'You're lucky you brought a book,' she said. The words sounded very loud in the empty room. They were inane, futile words, really, but sometimes, after a long time quietly translating Tethia would say anything, just to see if her voice still worked.

Mira looked up, her finger pausing on the page. 'You've been hard at work, Lieutenant. Is it anything interesting?'

Tethia shook her head. 'I'm afraid not – not interesting to me, at any rate. It's just a copy of legal documents from the earliest ages of the world.'

'That must be interesting, surely?'

'I never wanted to be a lawyer.'

'But you could, couldn't you? Since Caracalla?'

Tethia shrugged. 'I suppose I could. I just never wanted to.'

'So, what does interest you? If translating doesn't interest you, then why do you do it?'

'Why does anyone do what they do?' She shrugged again, slightly discomfited by the questions. She'd never talked so intimately with a slave before. The fact that a slave of the Imperial household ranked only slightly lower than herself made the situation only more bizarre. 'It puts food on the table, keeps me warm and out from under the sky.'

'What would you do? If you could do anything?'

'Anything?' Tethia raised her eyebrows. 'I don't know. Sleep for about six months straight. Eat very unhealthy food. Spend time with my family.' She paused. 'And I'd travel. I've seen a lot of the world, being a linguist in Service, but there is so much more I'd like to see.' She looked down at the book beneath her cotton-gloved hands and absent-mindedly stroked the page. 'And there is so much of the history of the world that I don't know, that no one knows. Imagine what it would be like to be a part of that, to discover a history that has been hidden from human eyes since the foundation of the world.'

'Surely there is a book in this room that you would find interesting.'

'Of course. But that isn't what I'm paid to do. I have a specific assignment from my superior. There is enough work in this room to keep an army of linguists busy for a hundred years. I couldn't possibly translate everything here, so I have to prioritise what I read. At the moment, I am told to prioritise legal documents. So here I am.' She paused and for one daring moment looked directly at Mira. The woman was staring right back at her, in contradiction of her earlier exquisite manners. She didn't look away when Tethia locked gazes with her. 'What would you do?'

The question seemed to shock Mira and she broke the challenging eye contact. 'I – I don't really know. I've never... never really been free. I've always… had my duty.'

'If you could do anything, though.'

Mira looked up past Tethia to scan the books lining the walls. 'I'd like to sit on the beach, on my own, listen to the ocean and watch the dark waves washing up on the white sand, watch the stars wheeling over the water.'

'You couldn't do that for the rest of your life,' Tethia criticised. 'After a few hours you'd be terribly bored.'

Mira's gaze came back to Tethia. She smiled, a little sadly and sighed. 'Lieutenant, if I ever dared to do what I wanted to do, the rest of my life wouldn't be much more than a few hours long. I've... I've often wished that I could have children, but it is impossible. I read your file, Lieutenant, if you will forgive the impertinence. What is it like being a mother?'

There was no reprimand Tethia could give Mira for reading her file. Sheya was a matter of public record. 'I can't say,' she replied. 'I was only a mother for a few minutes.'

'But it left a mark on you, didn't it?'

Tethia stared at Mira, caught in her penetrating gaze. She couldn't help but be completely honest. 'It changed everything. And it changed nothing. And it makes me angry beyond everything I've ever known that I can't do one damned thing about that. I don't even know if she's alive. It might be the way it is, but it's not right.'

Mira stared right back at Tethia for the longest time, then lowered her gaze back to her book. 'I'll let you get back to your work, Lieutenant.'

Not long after that, another slave arrived, making a low obeisance at the door and another when he reached the table. 'Mira, my Lady, Caesar himself calls for your attendance.'

Mira closed her book and stood up, bowing to the slave briefly. 'You may return and tell Caesar that I will attend him with all speed.' She looked wryly at Tethia before she left and whispered, 'See?'

Another slave replaced Mira. This one had no pert questions and sat quietly, idle, allowing Tethia to get a lot of work done, but Tethia missed the other woman's presence. There was something about the slave that commanded attention and respect that impressed Tethia. She might never admit it but the slave's questions – *Mira's* questions – had been thought provoking and the room seemed very silent without the inaudible sound of her finger moving along the lines of text as she read.

Tethia took her hourly breaks, as her supervisor had mandated and when the noon bell rang at the eighth hour, she obediently put aside her work and ate the sandwich she'd brought with her. The slave, sitting very still in her chair did not speak, neither to comment that she was hungry, nor to comment that she was not. She had no meal.

Tethia held out half a sandwich tentatively but the woman didn't even respond. Not that a slave in the imperial household would be allowed to accept a gift: it might imply partiality. Still, Mira would have given a reason.

When the bell rang for the eleventh hour Tethia closed her computer. The slave stood up, ready to escort her. The slave's face was blank. Tethia wondered what the woman's name was but didn't dare to ask. It was strange, she thought, putting the book back on the shelf, her preoccupation with slaves today. She'd never really thought much about slaves before. It didn't matter what the slave's name was. It was only a slave, after all. Yet, somehow, it was hard to think of slaves as 'it.' She was being progressive even referring to the slave as "she."

This time the slave didn't lead her by way of the gardens. Tethia was sorry – she'd looked forward to seeing their cool, dark spaces again. This time she took the route she'd taken before – corridors, hallways and tiny rooms all the way. By the time the slave deposited her at the first gate Tethia had no idea how she'd got there. Considering the wonders she'd seen on the way there it was disappointing to see nothing whatsoever of note on the return journey.

The rest of the trip was uneventful, but for one small incident. As she was getting off the train at the Special Services station she happened to look down the carriage and saw her mother, sitting only a few rows behind her. 'Tethia!' Shey-Leen called, in an embarrassing display that caused more than one other passenger to look her way.

Tethia raised one hand in a rueful salute acknowledging the greeting and quickly exited the train. She turned to look when she was on the platform. Shey-Leen had tried to get out at the same platform as Tethia, the slaves accompanying Shey-Leen struggling to keep pace with her. What business could Shey-Leen have at the Special Services complex?

She got her answer only an hour later. Tethia was handing her notes and her computer over to her senior officer – a very, very formal Terreus, General. Tethia stood to attention with eyes downcast while the General sat at his desk and slowly, slowly read her report. Her report was a one-page summary of the translations she'd done that day and a log of her travel expenses. Terreus read it over, slowly, slowly, until Tethia's feet and legs ached and even her fingers tingled from being held straight and low by her sides.

A knock sounded on the door. Tethia's hopes rose, but Terreus ignored it. She sighed inwardly. He must be determined to punish her. The knock came again. The General hesitated. Tethia saw, in a lightning-fast glance, when he looked at the door and decided that he was too bored to continue reading the same words over and over.

'Come!' he called.

A young private entered and saluted, crying, 'Sir!'
He was as tall as the General but leaner, fresh faced and
hard: everything a young soldier should be. In thirty years,
he'd be the one behind the desk. Punishing some other
lackey, Tethia thought sardonically, because she'd be
standing here until she was dead, and given the current
condition of her aching feet, she wouldn't last more than
another five minutes.

'Yes?' Terreus barked.

'Message for the Lieutenant, sir!

Terreus hesitated. The bastard, Tethia thought.
Finally, he nodded. The private handed Tethia the data
sheet, saluted the General, shouted, 'Sir!' once more before
doing an about-face and leaving the room.

'Aren't you going to read your message?' Terreus
asked, his voice suddenly silky.

Tethia's gaze snapped back to him in exasperation.
'No, sir,' she replied smartly. 'Since it's a private message,
I thought I'd read it in private.'

'Who's the message from, Lieutenant?'

'I don't know, sir. You'll notice I haven't read the
message yet.'

'Watch your tone, Lieutenant.'

'I am a Citizen, General, as well as an officer under your command. That allows me the right to freedom of private communication. Even as my Commanding Officer, *sir*, you may not infringe on that right.' She eyeballed him. 'With all due respect, sir.'

#

'So,' Kela said, later that afternoon, reclining on Tethia's bed and watching her do her hair, 'I saw you were escorted back to barracks under guard earlier. Did you do anything exciting?'

Tethia pinned down an errant strand of hair. 'I told my superior officer he had no right to read my mail.'

Kela frowned. 'Of course he doesn't. Why would he even assume that?'

'Because he's an arsehole.'

Kela laughed and rolled onto her stomach. 'Tethia, being an arsehole is not the reason why *everyone* does *everything*.'

'Of course not,' Tethia replied placidly. 'Just most people and most of the time. Hand me another pin, would you?'

'That would mean getting up. Sorry.'

Tethia fixed her gaze on Kela in the mirror. 'See?' she said. 'Arsehole.'

Kela laughed again and sat up. 'Fine,' she drawled, throwing her head back to show what a huge effort it was. She massaged her belly like it was sore. Sitting on the edge of Tethia's desk, which was currently being used as a dressing table she armed herself with a fist full of pins. 'Was it a love letter?'

Tethia rolled her eyes. 'Who do you suppose would be sending *me* a love letter?'

'You never know.' She sat back further on the desk to rest her back against the wall. 'You might have some old flame who's never got over you deciding he can't live another day without you in his life. Or some new flame you made such an impression on that he can't wait to see you again.'

Now it was Tethia's turn to laugh. 'Not likely. It was from my mother. She's in New Rome and she wants me to have dinner with her.'

'Any special reason?'

'Not that I know of. Another pin? Thanks.' She wrestled with a curl, trying to pin it down to make it look like a longer, more elaborate hairstyle. 'Mater hates seeing me look like an unTied person. At least my hair's grown fast since the last time I got it cut. I usually keep it so short I couldn't pin it at all.' She took another lock of hair and rolled it around her finger.

'She might have something important to tell you.'

'Not any more likely than some passionate lover arising from the woodwork. You know what these family things are like. They bore you to tears, but you can't get out of them unless you're dead at the time. Even then, sometimes.'

'"A passionate lover arising from the woodwork"? Tethy, that's a very... explicit... image.' Kela wrinkled her nose and they both giggled. 'Speaking of men-'

'We weren't.'

'What ever happened to that brother of yours?'

'Merrim?'

'Got another brother with muscles like oiled steel?'

'That's a very *gross* image, Kela.' Tethia reached around behind her for the veil she'd thrown over the back of the chair. She was sitting on the edge of it and it was only because of Kela's help that the veil didn't rip. 'I'm not sure what he's up to. He's always going somewhere with some boxing thing. I was never much interested in sports.'

'You've got that crooked.'

Tethia sighed gustily. 'I hate dressing like this. I

feel like I'm only half a person already.'

'You could get married. Find your *other* half.'

Tethia turned to aim a level stare at Kela, aware that the effect was ruined by the traditional veil and chiton. 'We're soldiers, Kela. Things can get very confusing in battle. Don't make me shoot you.'

'Your veil is still crooked.'

Half the trouble with dressing like a demure Citizen's daughter was the fact that she got stopped at every single checkpoint and asked why she wasn't accompanied by a responsible male. When she left the barracks, she had to prove that she had lawfully gained entry and when she purchased a ticket at the train station she was asked to show identification. It happened several more times on the way to the restaurant, so when the maître d' inquired politely if the good sister was accompanied and if not could he please see some kind of authorisation, she was just about ready to shoot someone. She held out her Service ID, which she'd kept ready in her hand. There was no point putting it away. Besides, rummaging inside the folds of the chiton was embarrassing.

'Tethia of Valdennes, Lieutenant, *unTied*,' she snapped. 'I'm only dressed this way to meet my mother. Here. Shey-Leen of Valdennes, wife to Meropius, General.'

The maître d' bowed. 'Certainly, Lieutenant. This way, if you please?'

She followed him into the restaurant. When she sat down, she forgot to pull her veil out of the way, and it pulled her head backwards. She drew it out from underneath her and gritted her teeth in frustration at Shey-Leen's long-suffering look from across the table. The maître d' was still standing by the table. Shey-Leen gave her order. They both waited for Tethia.

'I'll have whatever's most filling and most economical,' she replied, deliberately trying to embarrass her mother. 'I'm only on a Lieutenant's salary, after all.'

The maître d' bowed again and went away. The two women looked at each other for a moment. Tethia picked up a fork and used it to tap out an impatient rhythm on the tablecloth.

'All right, I'm here,' she said, straight up. 'What did you want?'

Shey-Leen took a moment to respond.

'I have had it just about up to *here,'* and Tethia whipped her hand up like a salute, 'with people hesitating. Why can't you just come out and say what you mean?'

'Fine.' In that moment Shey-Leen sounded like her daughter. 'I'm here to find out why *you're* here, Tethia.'

'I work in New Rome, Mater. I don't find the commute from Valdennes as exciting as Pater did.' The tapping fork found the edge of the plate.

'Stop that.' Shey-Leen put a hand on Tethia's to stop the incessant ringing of the fork. 'If you were in your right mind the last thing you'd be doing is drawing attention to yourself.'

'Just because I'm unTied doesn't mean I'm not in my right mind, Mater.'

'No, but the fact that you've been Re-Educated does.'

Tethia put the fork down, slowly and carefully. 'What makes you think that?' she asked quietly.

'The fact that you're here in New Rome, Tethia,' Shey-Leen replied. 'That tells me that you have no knowledge of the events of the past month or so.'

'I suppose the last month was terribly exciting.'

Shey-Leen's gaze slewed away from her daughter for a moment. 'I'm not sure exciting is the word, but it certainly hasn't been boring.'

'Go on,' Tethia urged. 'Enlighten me.' She picked the fork up again and rocked it back and forth quickly over her middle finger until its outline was a silver blur.

'All right. I know that I have a granddaughter. At

least, I did, before she was murdered.'

Tethia went cold all over. The fork fell to the floor. Shey-Leen let the words sink in. She watched her daughter's face across the table. Tethia went very still and a mask came down over her features. Finally,

'Who?' she asked, her voice hollow.

She didn't care why, nor how. All she needed to know was the name of the person against whom she would exact vengeance. When Shey-Leen didn't respond at once Tethia pressed, '*Who*, Mater? I need to know who to kill.'

'You can't kill this person.'

Tethia replied quickly, her voice low and urgent, 'If any soul on this earth has hurt my little girl then I tell you truly, I will get even with them. *Who,* Mater?'

'Caesar. Caesar gave the order. You can't-' she looked around and lowered her voice, 'you can't *kill* Caesar.'

'If Caesar is mortal then I can indeed do just that.' She stood up. 'I'll ask you for more details later, Mater. Right now, I have work to do.'

'Tethia, don't be foolish!' Shey-Leen also rose to her feet. 'Stop jumping in with both feet. Stop and *think* for a moment.'

Tethia stared blankly at her. 'No, Mater. I can't sit

still on this. Not when it's my little girl.' She felt like her whole life stopped suddenly, went backwards and she was there again, watching her mother kill her father but there was a bizarre sense that she and Shey-Leen had switched places. 'This is my decision to make, Mater. I cannot live with myself if I don't act on this.'

Shey-Leen sighed heavily. 'Give me just one minute, Tethia,' she said. 'There is more you need to know. Look, just sit down.' She sighed again and sat down, raising her eyes to the ceiling before lowering them to her daughter. 'Sit down, please, have a drink of water and *listen* to me.'

Tethia sat down. She drew in a deep breath. 'All right. One minute.'

'All right,' Shey-Leen echoed. 'Have a glass of water. Let me tell you what I know. Just don't make a scene or you'll be shot before you can do anything about Sheya. The maître d' is watching you.'

Tethia couldn't help the quick slew of her eyes to look at the maître d' where he stood at the front of house. Shey-Leen was right. He *was* watching her. She tried to control her breathing, tried to act normally and not make a scene. It was hard to act normally when the whole foundation of her life had disappeared.

Everything she'd done, every single thing over the past fifteen years, had been either for Sheya or because of her. She'd always hoped that one day she would be able to prove herself a fit mother, prove that she could be a good influence on her child, so that maybe one day she might meet her, see that beautiful small face again, the blue eyes, the little tip tilted nose.

All of a sudden, the image before her eyes changed: there was blood and the baby was screaming, screaming like a grown woman and Tethia wanted to vomit. She closed her eyes, though nothing made the image go away. She felt her breathing come faster but she couldn't control it. She leaned forward, rested her elbow on the table and put her face into her hand.

'Mater, I can't bear this,' she whispered, and was never sure if Shey-Leen heard her or not.

'Here's your water,' Shey-Leen said. 'Drink up, daughter.'

Tethia opened her eyes and raised her face. She knew that she was paper-pale. Her hand felt so weak she could barely hold the glass. Shey-Leen was right. She was in no fit state to charge the Palatine right now. She took a deep swallow of the cold, fresh water. 'You said you had other things to tell me.'

'You were arrested, Tethia, you and Merrim. He took responsibility for what you'd done. The truth came out about Sheya and you were sent to Lygia to marry her father, that irresponsible boy.'

Another image came and went, faster than she could see it, like something from a dream. She knew what she had to say. 'You and I both know who Sheya's father was, and it wasn't Rinn, Mater.'

Shey-Leen looked away. 'I did what I could, Tethia.'

'It was too late. You should have listened when I told you the first time-'

'We don't have time to talk about that now. *Listen*, Tethia. You found out information about the Starlight Project and passed it along to us. You went to Lygia and you tried to save Sheya. There is more we can do, here in New Rome. We need you with us tonight. We may not be able to save Sheya, but there are thousands of others who need our help.'

Tethia smiled grimly. 'Sorry, Mater, you'll have to give my regrets to everyone.' She stood up. 'I have a date with Caesar tonight.' She wavered on her feet. 'Only I don't feel so good.' She focussed, in the last moment available to her, on her mother. 'Mater, what did you put in my drink?'

'Just enough,' Shey-Leen replied softly, and leaped to her feet in time to catch Tethia and slow her slide to the ground as she fainted.

#

When Tethia woke, disgustingly nauseated and with a splitting headache, she was lying on a cot, in a naturally formed cave. She looked around.

'I'm sorry I had to drug you, daughter. It was for your good, for the good of so many unCounted children who need someone on their side.'

Tethia had an odd feeling of déjà vu, like she'd been in a cave recently, but living in New Rome she would never find herself in such an environment. It was very strange. She sat up, as much to dispel the feeling of déjà vu as to dispel the nausea.

'We have little time to waste, daughter. We must join the others. All will be made clear.'

Tethia followed her mother out of the small niche that served as a bedroom and into a tunnel that led to a larger cage. There were dozens of people there, all talking together, and the hum of conversation echoed from the walls of the large cave. She had that odd feeling of déjà vu again as she passed through the mouth of the cave, but it was gone before she could put her finger on it, leaving her with a lingering sense of unease. The cave was reasonably well lit; every person there carried a lightstick or a globe in a holder. They were perched high on rocky outcrops or seated on the rough stone floor of the cave. Many of them turned to look at her as she entered.

'This is my daughter,' Shey-Leen announced into the sudden silence, as though that were passport enough.

Tethia had spent the first twenty years of her life being introduced by her relationship to others and she wasn't going to stand for it. She put up with all the disadvantages of being unTied so she wasn't going to allow Shey-Leen to introduce her like a dutiful Citizen's daughter. She was aware that her own name and rank might be a danger to her in this place, so she announced,

'My name is Lerina,' in a voice that rang from every corner of the cave. 'I am here to join you tonight.'

Shey-Leen made a slight movement next to her, but she'd been privy to Tethia's use of the alias before and knew better than to let on.

She wasn't ready to hear the name return to her in a similarly ringing cry, 'Lerina? Lerina, thank the gods!' A man shouldered his way through the crowd and came at her so fast she barely had time to glimpse him before he had his arms around her.

'Who in Caesar's name?' she muttered, but it was muffled against his shirt, a button scraping hard along her cheek. All the same, that sense of déjà vu was so strong it was nearly overpowering, strong enough for her to finally catch a detail – they were together in the dark. He had been hurt but he was still trying to look after her. His hands were gentle, and his voice was kind. She could even hear his name. She whispered it.

'Beris?'

'Lerina!' He drew back to examine her, dark eyes skimming over her in a purely medical manner. 'You aren't hurt?' He threw back his head to let out a heavy breath, as though he hadn't taken a deep breath since he'd seen her last. 'I've been looking everywhere trying to find a trace of you. I joined the rebels because I was sure you'd make your way here. How did you escape?'

Tethia shook her head. She had no idea what had happened beyond what little she'd seen of him in that one moment when they'd been together in the dark, but if her mother was right then she hadn't gotten away at all. They'd let her go. Shey-Leen saved her from having to lie.

'Excuse me, young man,' Shey-Leen said, putting a hand on Beris's shoulder, 'but would you mind not putting your hands on my daughter in front of me? I don't wish to take action, but I will if I have to.'

'Action?' Beris asked, eyes flicking back to Tethia. He let his hands drop from her waist and took a step back. 'Forgive me. I was carried away in the moment.'

'So, you two have met?' Shey-Leen asked, moving their small group to the side of the cave where they could gather in a rocky nook.

Beris grinned. Tethia might not be able to remember much about him, but she was pretty sure that grin was only for her. 'We went through a lot together in Lygia. My Lerina. My darling.' The look he gave her was as warmly intimate as a caress. He turned away, mindful of her mother's eye. 'Oh, look, Freedwoman Sorha's here.'

'A Freedwoman?' Tethia asked. She'd never heard of such a thing before. Women could be daughters, wives, even unTied, but they were never Free.

The assembly fell silent as they watched the elderly woman approach the podium.

'Brothers and sisters,' she announced, 'the rebellion is proceeding according to plan. The first and second Units are engaged on the Palatine Hill and remain undetected.

Units Three to Nine are progressing with their engagements in the media. Some of you may have noticed a slight change in tone in the newsspeakers for the Daily Review and I'm proud to say that it's the work of our own companions at Re-Ed. Units Ten to Twenty have been finding challenging environments in health care, although they assure us that they are slowly and surely contributing to a changing mindset regarding the care of the unCounted.'

She paused, allowing time for the cheering to die down, then she sobered. 'I do, however, have unfortunate news. Unit Twenty-One has been arrested. If the government follows its usual policy, then our brothers and sisters will be Counted and executed. There is, however, a risk of Re- Education, so you must all remember that even if you should meet Varn, Folly, Ferin or Meri again, they are no longer the people we knew. They will be changed into government-controlled pawns and will be under the strictest surveillance. Any communication between us and them must, from this time forward, be considered to be compromised. Let's pause for a moment of silence, to remember our fallen comrades.'

Beris bowed his head. Tethia looked around surreptitiously, noting that every single head in the room was respectfully lowered. All except – a shock went through Tethia at the sight of the woman's face. They had met – she knew for certain that they'd met. She knew with equal certainty that the name had been deliberately wiped from her mind during the process of Re- Education. The woman was looking at Beris with a small, curious smile on her face, which Tethia filed away for future reference.

Beris raised his head. Looking surreptitiously through lowered lashes with the ease of long practice, Tethia watched him in that one unguarded moment. He looked out at the people assembled before him, his expression grave. It seemed to Tethia that he was almost counting them, placing each person in their place in his memory. She thought of the title used for surrendered children, the deformed, the unwanted, the different: the unCounted. From where Beris was standing right now, every single person in front of him mattered. He had numbered them all. They mattered.

'They are gone,' Sorha said, her voice rich and sincere, 'but they are not lost. We will remember them. We will create a world worthy of their sacrifice.'

Another flash of memory: Beris had said something similar once. They were in a garden together, the plants blooming with luminescence. As Tethia listened to

Freedwoman Sorha speak, encouraging, cajoling and ordering the group to speak for the sake of those who had no voices, to act on behalf of those who didn't have the right to exist under the law, the thought crossed her mind again that all of this must have been going on for some time.

Sorha dismissed most of the group, asking that Unit Eight stay behind. 'You're with us, now, Lerina,' Beris said as Tethia looked around, unsure if she'd just been dismissed or not. Shey-Leen, with a stern look at Beris, departed.

The group that stayed was larger than Tethia had expected, given that Unit Twenty-One had comprised of only four people. At least a dozen people remained in the cave when the others had filed out. It was a lot darker now that so many had gone and taken their lightsticks with them.

'We have an unprecedented opportunity tonight,' Sorha said in a low, conspiratorial voice that made everyone lean in just that little bit closer. 'Both adults and children who are enrolled in the Starlight Project are being moved in small groups to a new, more secure, location. During transport these groups are vulnerable, and the Project cannot afford either the publicity that a large convoy would attract or the security necessary to guard such a large group would require. The first of these groups will be moved tonight, from the Suruae mountains to somewhere in the north. In collaboration with Units One and Two we plan to attack the convoy as it passes through Croyes.' She drew a small data module from a fold of her chiton and opened up the viewing screen, tilting it so they could all see. 'Here's the plan.'

\#

When Sorha had finished outlining the plan of the ambush, she sent those of the group who were allocated to caring for the rescued subjects to the first aid point so they could prepare the site. Beris turned to Tethia and spoke in a low, intimate voice that was just for her ears.

'While I admit I'd rather send you with them, Lerina, where I know you'd be safe, I've seen you in action. I know you'd never forgive me if I denied you your part in tonight's work.' He grinned. 'On a more selfish note, you're good in a tight corner and I want you with me.'

Tethia couldn't help but smile back. Whatever they'd shared in the dark, whatever else they'd been through together, he clearly knew her well.

'You know me,' she drawled in a droll voice. 'Don't you?' She didn't hold back her smug grin, either. Beris could take that grin and assume anything he wanted from it.

'Before you get carried away with my unmarried daughter, there is someone I want her to see first,' Shey-Leen said.

Tethia smiled at Beris and allowed her mother to lead her through a makeshift door to a niche that served as a room and reveal her brother.

'Merrim?' she asked. Memories started to return. She took a step back, overwhelmed by the flood. Ala's Audit. The Trial. Andred, telling her that Merrim had been executed. She took a dozen quick steps forward and threw her arms around him. 'Oh, Merrim, thank the gods you're alive!'

She heard the rumble of laughter deep in his chest and his arms came around her to hold her uncomfortably tight. She welcomed the tight embrace. She felt like she was coming back to life and everything that mattered to her in the world today was in that little room.

By design, rather than by accident, Tethia ended up sandwiched between Merrim and Beris, crouched behind a pile of boulders in the rough, rocky country outside the town of Croyes. At one point, Beris's hand slipped down to squeeze her hand. She turned to look at him, conflicted by her feelings of joy in such a dark moment, and squeezed back.

Eventually, three skippers appeared in the distance, their headlights visible as they crested the distant hills. Beside her, Merrim and Beris tensed so much that they were practically vibrating. Her own hand tightened around the grip of the weapon she'd been loaned. Her breathing sped up to match her excited heart.

The boulders lying beside the road provided the perfect place for the rebel snipers to take out the driver of the first skipper and enable one of the rebels to get inside to steer it to block the road to the rest of the convoy. The other drivers and guards sitting next to them fumbled for their weapons and returned fire.

'Why are the guards so poorly prepared?' Tethia asked, but her voice was lost in the sound of gunfire. Beris put a hand on her shoulder to hold her back until it was time for them to fulfil their part of the plan.

'Steady,' he whispered, his voice close to her ear.

When the gunfire settled, Sorha cried, 'Let's go!' and leaped from her hiding place, running down the hillside. Merrim, Tethia and the rest of the rebels were half a pace behind her.

It was barely even a fight. The drivers and guards were facing overwhelming odds and quickly fell to their knees in a gesture of surrender.

'Well done,' Sorha said warmly, commending the rebels who stood in a ring around the drivers, their weapons trained on the defenceless men. She turned an excited face to her comrades, smiling widely, her eyes bright. 'Come on,' she said. 'Let's set our family free!'

They went around to the back of the skipper. The doors were locked, but one of the drivers had immediately dropped his keys in Merrim's hand when Merrim raised an arm and the man recognised the famous face behind the battered fist.

Beris unlocked the doors of the first skipper, so excited his fingers were shaking. He threw the doors open with an expansive gesture.

There was no one inside.

'What's this?' Beris muttered, stepping up into the skipper, Tethia close behind him.

Inside the skipper were racks of shelving with varying sized boxes neatly strapped into position. The boxes were labelled with a series of numbers and letters that made no sense to Tethia. 'What do these numbers mean?' Tethia asked, lifting one of the smaller boxes from a shelf. It was heavier than she'd expected. She turned so Beris could read the number and opened the lid.

'Lerina, no!' Beris cried, lunging towards her and snatching the box from her hands. It was too late. She'd seen what was in there. She stumbled backwards in horror, a loud ringing in her ears obscuring all sound, all thought. Her uncertain steps took her too far and it was a long, dizzying moment before she realised she'd fallen off the back of the skipper. Merrim was behind her and caught her roughly, twisting with her to set her on her feet, but her feet wouldn't hold her.

'Tethy, what is it?' he murmured.

'Get her out of here!' Beris shouted, holding the little box with one hand, close to his chest.

Still held upright by Merrim's arm, holding her nearly the same way that Beris held the box, Tethia suddenly felt overwhelmingly sick and started to retch. She would have vomited if she'd eaten anything since the sparse lunch she'd had in the archives that afternoon.

'What is it?' Merrim asked Beris, since Tethia wasn't answering. He turned his head and shoulders away from her to avoid her convulsive movements although he still wasn't able to let her go.

'Just get her out of here!' Beris turned to put the box back on the shelf. Tethia saw him out of the corner of her eye. She put her hands down and gripped Merrim's arm where he held her. Beris jumped down from the skipper and slammed the doors behind him. 'Keep her away,' he ordered.

Tethia and Merrim watched him stride across the dusty road to where the drivers were still held under guard. The rebels watched him, the light of expectation plain in their eyes. Something of the horrors he had found must have shown in his face because their hopeful smiles faded, and they looked at one another for support in their confusion.

'Who is the leader among you?' he demanded.

The drivers and guards looked at one another, still on their knees, their hands behind their heads.

'Who is in charge?' Beris thundered.

'We just drive the trucks,' one of them murmured. 'Honest, we just drive the trucks.'

Beris stepped forward and grabbed the man's collar, dragging him to his feet only to knock him to the ground again with one powerful blow to the man's face. The driver fell back down to the ground, legs sprawling beneath him awkwardly. His hands went to his head, coming away wet with blood.

'What did you think you were transporting?' Beris shouted. 'You must have been given information of some kind – and yet you dealt in this... this *filthy* trade!'

'We're carrying medical supplies,' one of the guards said, moving a step forward, inching ahead on his knees.

'You're carrying *human beings!*' Beris shouted. 'Children – babies! They deserved life! They deserved every joy that life could give them! And you stand by and allow... allow *atrocities* to be committed because you think it's not your problem.' He was breathing heavily. 'Well, it's your problem today.'

Beris drew his weapon from its holster. 'Whatever you choose, your lives will never be the same. You either join us, serve our Cause and spend the rest of your lives making reparation for the evils you allowed to happen, or I swear by every god and every name under the earth that I will shoot you here and now.'

'Whatever you say,' they said. 'We'll do whatever you want.' 'Just don't hurt us,' most of them said, but one didn't say it. One watched Beris closely and thought he was unobserved. He lunged towards Beris, eyes fixed on the weapon pointed towards one of the other drivers.

There was a shot and the man fell dead at Beris's feet.

'I didn't,' Beris said, raising the weapon as though it had betrayed him.

'I did,' Tethia said. Her voice was still shaken but her aim was true. She moved until she was standing beside him, not taking her aim from the other prisoners for a moment. 'You're not a murderer, Beris,' she said softly. 'If you'd killed that man, you'd never forget it.'

'And you will?' he didn't sound as though he believed it. It was a nice, if grim thought, that there was at least one person in the world who didn't know half the things she'd done.

'Maybe not,' she conceded, 'but I'll still sleep at night.'

There was a cry from behind them. Beris turned, though Tethia kept her eyes glued to the prisoners who had drawn into a very tight little group, as far from the body of their fallen comrade as possible.

'Boss, there's kids in the back of these trucks!'

They took the children to the first aid station and managed to keep the contents of the first skipper secret. There were twelve children in all, of different ages. Some went quietly, willing to allow anything to happen because they had never had control over anything in their lives. Others fought them all the way, unwilling or unable to believe that such a thing as freedom could even exist in their lives. When told that they would be placed with families not one of them showed any joy. One of them asked outright, 'What will that be like?' and the rebels realised that they had no idea what a family was.

#

The atmosphere in the caves was a curious mixture, Tethia thought, after the children were settled, either in little cots with their new mothers next to them, or back on the trucks and being ferried to their new homes. The children had shown the same mixture of emotions. Some were elated, some fought, some wept and some just went where they were sent.

It was the last group that worried Tethia the most. Their whole lives they had been told what to do, where to go, what to think. She remembered seeing people like that in the Project, so easy to command. Tethia wondered if all that early influence would ever be overcome. Would they ever live normal lives? Would they ever really make a decision for themselves, experience the terrifying pull of their own wants and desires, make their own mistakes and learn from them... take control of their own lives?

She thought every choice she'd ever made. Was she truly in charge of her own life? How often had she been led into decisions? As a Serviceman she'd known that she'd lived her life under orders and she'd been content with that, but she'd thought that she'd *chosen* to obey orders. Suddenly thinking that perhaps the choice had never been hers was a sombre thought.

Perhaps the others were caught up in the same wild ride of emotions. Someone brought out a crate of wine and started urging others to drink. Some others drew out instruments – a flute, a harp and one tiny woman whose powerful, operatic singing voice echoed from every corner of the large cave where so many people were gathered.

The elation gradually overcame the other ambiguous emotions. The music was all old songs that each one of them had probably heard their nannies or Maters singing in their childhood. There was a reason why these songs had persisted, from the earliest days of the world. They were infectious, the beats impossible to ignore, the words telling stories that were common to the human experience.

Despite the music and the dancing and the increasing elation of drunkenness, a part of Tethia remained outside of it all. Looking around, still, she saw that she wasn't the only one. Most of the ambivalent faces were women. Leaving Beris's arms after a dance Tethia wandered over to one of them.

'Why are you here?' she said bluntly.

'My son,' the other woman replied quietly. 'You?'

'Daughter.'

The woman nodded. 'I haven't seen you before today, but Beris seems to know you. I knew him back in Lygia when he was still at school.'

'We've been through a lot together.'

'You did well tonight.'

Tethia didn't know what to say. Still in her mind was the memory of what she'd seen in that little box and her stomach turned. The moment she'd seen it she'd remembered everything that the Re-Education process had tried to eliminate, not just last time, but the time before that.

She remembered going to translate for Ala's Audit, breaking into the Palatine Library and hearing about the Starlight Project for the first time. The trial, her marriage to Rinn, the abduction and her imprisonment… no wonder they'd managed to erase it all so easily. But she'd remembered more than that. She remembered what happened before Ala's Audit.

It had been just another day at work. She'd been translating documents at the Palatine again and they were more legal drivel about the First Laws... except now, with all her memories intact, she knew that there were powerful secrets hidden in those Laws. She caught the train to the Palatine Hill as usual, but this time there was a woman with a baby, sitting opposite her. The baby must have been brand new, lying limp and adoring in its mother's arms. Mostly, the pair had sat quietly, allowing Tethia to peruse the documents she'd been provided that morning containing her orders for the day and her travel passes, but a sharp noise from the mother made Tethia look up.

The baby had woken and was looking up at its mother with huge, dark eyes. The baby had spread its lips in a sudden smile – Tethia caught the last of it before the baby's lips went slack again as it gazed at its mother. The mother had cried out in joy, an endearment still falling from her lips as she brought the baby closer to her and bent to place a sweet kiss on the tiny, tip tilted little nose.

Tethia stood up immediately and got off at the next station. She wasn't even anywhere close to the Palatine and had to wait for the next train. Her face was composed, as always, but inside she was roiling. That kiss... that was the kiss she'd wanted to give her own daughter. Thoughts of Sheya, never far away, had flooded her. She'd stored up every memory she'd been granted with her little girl and every moment that was blurred in her memory broke her heart anew.

She'd gone on to work, spent the day translating in the library again, but in the evening, she'd gone back to barracks and that night she was on the roof of the Palatine Library. She'd found the same information as she'd found the next time she'd gone with Merrim, but there was more that she'd learned. That first night she hadn't been caught and she hadn't been alone.

But then, the next morning, the Deviants were Yellow Carded and taken away from Special Services. They'd been Tethia's comrades, who had lost loved ones the same way she had. They were her friends and she'd watched them be taken away to die while she tapped her foot impatiently.

The party went on for hours and when it was over the rebels paired off or gathered into small groups and slowly their numbers dwindled until it was late enough for Beris to leave with Tethia, Merrim tagging along with the woman who had been staring at Beris during the minute of silence. Tethia recognised her now: it was Ala.

Her face was still pellucid-fair, the veins streaming delicate and mysterious beneath the cultured skin. Whatever illness that had assailed her during her Audit appeared to be completely gone. Now she was energetic and excited, with no signs of the weakness or confusion she'd shown when Tethia first saw her. She joined them in their merriment, dancing with Beris, Merrim and anyone else willing to tap their toes to the beat, her face flushing rosy like any peasant's. Now she leaned on Merrim's arm, raised protectively around her as they left the large cave and went into a smaller one, a rough curtains screening it from the tunnels so it could serve as living quarters. Shey-Leen had long since left them and retired to her own quarters.

It was pitifully simple and uncompromisingly ample and Beris welcomed them into it as though it was a palace. Once past the rough tunnel it changed into a sculpted, architectural living space, furnished simply but adequately. They settled in, Tethia sitting daringly close to Beris. Merrim, in a flagrant display of a double standard, seated himself with his arm still around Ala.

Tethia scooted away from Beris, sitting herself at

the opposite side of the couch, ignoring his startled sound before lying down, supporting her feet in his lap. He relaxed again, a fond look coming over his handsome face, his hand dropping to caress her ankles, lingering unconsciously on the place where her bruises had been from where the Palatine Guard struck her with his sword.

Beris had no memory of that day anymore. It had been taken from him when he was Re-Educated. At last, Tethia remembered their first meeting – when Beris was working with the rebels and Merrim introduced them. They'd known one another for weeks when she had gone to translate Galalla's Audit for him, but she'd forgotten that until her memories returned today.

'What a night!' Merrim explained exuberantly, throwing his head back in exultation. 'I can't believe it all went so smoothly.'

'Not so smoothly,' Ala murmured, curled under his arm. 'One of the guards won't ever come home.'

The room was struck with a sudden silence. Tethia stayed where she was, determined not to react.

'I make no apology for what I did,' she said.

She felt Beris's tension. 'If Lerina hadn't done what she did, then I would have,' he replied tightly. 'And if neither of us had reacted, then I would be dead now. And maybe one of you.'

'Does that make a difference?' Ala asked. Merrim drew slowly away from her and she cast him a reproachful glance. 'Whatever your motivations, it was still murder. How is that any different from what they do?'

Tethia sat up and put a hand on Beris, holding him back when he might have leaped to his feet. 'I killed a man in battle. He was trying to get Beris's gun. He initiated the action. I responded and did what was necessary to keep us all safe. That is very different from taking the innocent – children, babies and people who never did anyone any harm – very different from killing them to see what's inside them.'

'What was in the box?' Merrim asked suddenly, his voice sharp. He knew her better than anyone. He'd felt her stomach revolt as she'd reacted to what she'd seen. She drew a deep breath, more unsettled by what she'd seen than she was willing to let on, even to him who knew her best. She raised her face to meet him directly.

'A baby,' she replied.

He stared at her blankly for a moment. 'But you left it in the box...'

'It was in pieces. There was nothing left to save.'

Another silence. Merrim started to say something

several times but the words always stopped in his throat.

'They killed it and cut it up for their research,'
Tethia said baldly. 'They put the pieces into a little box,
preserved in fluid in case they want to cut it up some more
later. How many little boxes were in that truck? How many
trucks do you suppose there will be? The children in the
other trucks, what do you think they were going to do with
them in the end? What do you suppose their purpose was, if
not to die?'

'I'm sorry – I didn't know,' Ala whispered.

'How could you?' Tethia asked rhetorically. 'But
now you do, what will you do about it? We need to make a
stand and make sure that this never, never happens again.
No one will be safe in this world until we change it.'

'How could we change the world?' Ala asked. 'We
can save a few people, change a few lives, but we couldn't
change the whole world.'

'Every single one of us has the power to change the
world,' Tethia replied, dogged. 'We stand up, we say to the
world that we will not tolerate this anymore. It's over. And
we do not allow it to ever, ever happen again. We are one
people, with one law and one goal. That is the oldest of the
Laws, the very First Law. That Law is inscribed on a
column of stone at the heart of our world and we don't hear

it spoken, but it's true. We stand together, as one people, and we enforce the law.'

'The Laws are already enforced. That's what the police are for.'

'Didn't you hear what I just said? We are *one* people with *one* law, *one* goal. If we are *one* people, then every individual matters. No one can be unCounted because we are all one. We have *one* law, not one law for Citizens, another for Tiedmen, Freedmen and slaves. We cannot abuse one portion of the population simply because it suits us.'

'And what goal?' Ala asked.

Tethia paused, sitting back a little. She knew that what she was going to say would be a shock. 'Our world was not always dark,' she said. 'Once it was fixed in position around another planet, close enough to a single star that it was naturally light during the day and the planet revolved the same way it does today so it was naturally dark during the night. Our planet was sent on a journey. It is intended to arrive at another star, where it will again turn from light to dark in the natural course of a day. That is our goal. Our ancestors made this planet so that we, their descendants, could make this journey. That is why we must conserve our resources, why we must all work together, for the sake for the survival of our planet, our culture and our history.'

'Oh, come on,' Merrim drawled, 'you're making this up now.'

'Who could make this up?' Tethia retorted. 'I can show you all kinds of proof. Look up at the stars themselves and look at the records of their movements and you will see. If you go into the caves in Lygia you will see there a pillar with this Law inscribed on its face. All around the sides you will read the history of the world and the destiny of the world.'

'How did you see that?' Ala asked. It wasn't until later that Tethia realised that she'd implied that she knew the pillar Tethia was talking about.

The temptation to cast her eyes down was strong, reinforced by thirty-three years of practice, but Tethia resisted it and looked Ala in the eye. 'I was there,' she said simply, avoiding explanation. 'I saw it with my own eyes.'

Beris stood up and started to pace around the little room. 'You're right,' he said, his voice grave. 'We need to do something. And you're right. We need to do more than ambush a convoy here and there. We need to stop this thing. But how can you stop something as big as the Starlight Project?' He made a despairing sound. 'By all the gods, Lerina, you *know* how big a project this is. Our numbers are growing every day, but we still can't match the Project, numbers wise. If we tried anything we'd be crushed, and our cause would lie in ruins.' He swung to face her, as though she were the only face in the room. 'We can't afford that.'

'You're right,' she said gently. 'We can't match them in brute force. But this isn't about brute force. It's about changing people's minds. We don't need to defeat the army. We need to convince them.'

'Unit Three is working with the media-'

'I'm not talking about slipping a story into the media here and there, Beris. There's another way to reach the people.'

He'd hardly heard her and the fact that he couldn't hear her over his own thoughts was infuriating. 'We'd never get past the censors,' he muttered, looking away, as though the answer lay in the smooth, polished surface of the walls.

Tethia rose to her feet and stood before him. 'I know who can get past the censors,' she said plainly, speaking simply so that her words had no chance of getting lost. 'I know who can reach everybody.'

'But even if you *could* tell the world about our

Cause, Caesar would just order the legions to destroy us.'

Tethia put her hand on her face, the familiar touch bringing his gaze to meet hers again, to make sure he was listening. She spoke slowly, looking into his eyes. 'Then we must kill Caesar.'

Ala's gasp echoed loud in the tiny room and she pressed her hand tight to her mouth as though to recapture that startled rush of air. Beris ignored her, still looking deep into Tethia's eyes.

'But that still wouldn't do you any good,' he said, his voice deeper than usual. 'The next Caesar would simply be another member of the Imperial Household. You wouldn't necessarily change anything.'

'Caracalla was fifteen years ago,' Tethia said. 'A woman can fill any position now, under the Law. Maybe it's time we had a woman Caesar.'

Every eye in the room turned to Ala and she stared back at them, her face pale, her eyes wide.

Their discussions took them deep into the night and after a time a cautious elation filled them, like nothing that had gone before at the party. They separated at last, Merrim escorting Tethia to a room of her own to sleep. It was vital she sleep, he said, and offered her his own accommodation while he spent the night in the barracks where many of the rebels slept if they were unable to return home.

#

Tethia lay awake, staring around the dark room, barely illuminated by shadow lights near the ceiling. It was possible that she'd just lived the longest day of her life, she thought, trying to place each event in its proper place. If you included the memories she'd recovered during the ambush, then the day had gone on for weeks. Everything seemed muddled, as though each event was separate and out of order from the ones that preceded it. Once she'd managed to put everything into some kind of timeline, she sat up, snaked her legs free of the covers and got out of bed.

She went down the hallway to Beris's room, moving quietly and surely on bare feet. She pushed the door open without knocking. Beris was asleep, curled up on his side like a child, or a widower in the first flush of grief. She whispered his name to wake him and waited for him to respond.

When he opened his eyes, Tethia could see that for the first few moments of wakefulness she was still part of his dream. He didn't seem surprised to see her there at first, just gazing up at her and waiting.

'I couldn't sleep,' she whispered.

He stared up at her for a moment, then moved sideways in the bed, lifting the coverlet for her to slide in next to him. He held out his arm so that she could snuggle next to him. She put her head on his shoulder and allowed his arm to come around her.

'I suppose I got carried away today,' she murmured and felt his chest rise and fall in an incongruous laugh at the ridiculousness of it all, then draw in a deep, slow breath.

'Are you thinking of the guard?' he asked.

'It's not the first time,' she replied. 'Probably won't be the last.'

He was quiet a moment, allowing her statement to fill the room. 'Who are you, Lerina? How does a person get to be like you? I've seen you do things that amaze me. I've never seen you show fear, not even when you were nearly dead. I've never seen you hesitate or back down.' He paused again, this time for effect. 'And I know that some of the things you've told me haven't been the truth.'

'Like what?'

He rolled his eyes. She couldn't see it, but it was such a strenuous move that his neck flexed. 'Like your name. I heard what your brother called you. Like the fact that you're unTied. Or maybe not unTied. Like your family. Like why you're even here. I'd like to think that you're here for me, but you were following this trail long before we even met. We went through fire and the dark together. All those nights in the Project when you cried – you never once turned to me. I would have given anything for you to let me comfort you. And yet you've never even told me that you could see in the dark.'

'I didn't think you realised.'

His voice was dry. 'It's not flattering to know that you think I don't care.'

Tethia smiled ruefully. 'I wouldn't be here right now if I thought you didn't care. I made my own decision to be here, right here with you tonight, because I know how much you care. No one sent me, or even invited me.'

'I already know you're determined,' he replied. 'Tell me something I don't know.'

'My name is Tethia of Valdennes,' she told him, quietly and carefully. 'I've been a soldier in the Special Services for most of my life – translating, mostly, but I go where I'm sent.'

He let her speak, didn't ask questions, just waited for whatever she was willing to tell him.

'My life is probably very exciting, but it was no more than a way to fill the time for me. I wanted independence. I got... well, I got a version of what independence could be. I learned to live without Sheya. But it was just passing the time. My life didn't count because my daughter was unCounted. That's all the unCounted are, isn't it? Numbers that don't exist. I figured out what the numbers meant on those boxes we found tonight.'

'By the gods,' Beris whispered. 'That look on your face.'

Tethia turned her face into his warm skin. 'I'll never forget that as long as I live. I think that, for the rest of my life, there will always be a part of me that will never stop screaming. In Caesar's name – that tiny little hand-!'

Beris tightened his arm around her but she could barely feel it. The memory of what she'd seen in the box was too strong. For one terrible, fractured moment she could almost feel the surprising weight of it in her hands, the same way she'd once felt Sheya in her arms. She'd been so small, but so heavy, drawing on the very fabric of life itself and stretching it deeper, fuller. Nothing would ever be the same again. Whose baby had been in that box? she wondered. Whose dreams would forever go unfulfilled? That story could never be made right, it could only end in vengeance and justice.

'Please, don't think of it,' he begged, pressing a kiss to her hair.

'Even if I could, I would never forget it,' she said. 'That baby has to matter. If my baby is to matter, then they all must matter. I held my baby in my hands-' she turned closer to him and took his hand, drawing it towards her, exploring the wide palm and strong fingers, tracing around his nails. 'I held her again, not a day ago, not even knowing who she was. I bullied her and shouted at her without remorse. And after all I did to save her, they killed her. She only ever saw me as a stranger, yet another stranger who hurt or betrayed her, the same way that everyone else has always done.'

'But I thought you'd never met your daughter again?'

'I saw her. I met her. I spoke with her. Well, sort of.' She gripped his hand tightly, drawing it to her heart. 'You saw her, too. You can probably guess which one she was. She's just like her mother.'

'Perry?'

'How strange you should guess so quickly,' she mused, not really caring. 'When I never knew she was mine until today. Her full name is Proxima. My husband named her after my sister. The name I gave her as a baby was quite different. Not that her name makes any difference. She's gone.'

'Lerina, listen-'

'Oh, please, I don't want to listen. Please, can't you just help me forget? I need to see something before my eyes other than that paper-white little hand.'

She let go of his hand and snaked her arms around his neck, bringing his lips to hers for a kiss he eagerly shared.

#

Tethia woke and was confused for a moment. The fact that she was in an unfamiliar room, with a man snoring next to her would seem to imply that she was in a barracks on some deployment, but the snoring man was actually in the bed *with* her and her colleagues weren't idiots. It wasn't even a proper snore, really, not like Rinn's-

The thought brought her up short and had her bolting out of the bed. She turned and saw Beris and her heart rate slowed. She'd forgotten for a moment that she was safe. How long would it be before she could stop jumping out of bed in fear?

She looked around the room and picked up her clothes from where they'd flung them over the side of the bed. As she dressed, she heard the bell for the tenth hour of the night. Three hours until the lights were raised for dawn.

Once she was dressed, she turned back to Beris. He'd rolled over and stopped snoring, curled on his side again, hand reaching out to where she had lain. It was the same position she'd found him in. He still looked like there was something missing, only now it was nice to think that the "something" was herself. She'd never really been missed before.

She sat on the bed beside him and whispered his name.

'Beris, I have to go,' she murmured, her hand stroking the silky skin of his bare shoulder.

'Don't go,' he said, automatically, reaching out to her.

'I have to. Merrim will be furious. Mater might suspect something and believe me, you don't want to get on her bad side.'

'I've barely spoken two words to your mother.' He took hold of her hand and brought it to his lips, giving the fingers a sweet kiss.

'That's about as many words as she and I

exchanged in the last fifteen years.' She couldn't tell him why. She'd spent fifteen years building walls around her heart and mind. They couldn't all be demolished in one fell swoop, no matter how romantic the idea might be.

It was very pleasant having Beris put her back to bed. Given the late hour, he was brazen, carrying her through the public hallways while she tried not to giggle at the fear of getting caught. He put her down on the single cot Merrim usually slept in, lifting the blanket to cover her and tucking her in. He knelt by the side of the bed.

'Will you sleep now?' he asked in a whisper, trailing a caressing hand down the side of her cheek.

She nestled into his touch, seeking it. 'I'll do my best,' she said. He bent to kiss her, then left her alone. She turned onto her back and stared up at the ceiling again but this time her body was exhausted and her mind was calm. She fell asleep within minutes.

#

Tethia woke at the first hour, two hours before the general rising bell. She went into the public area of the caves and asked around until someone provided her with paper and a pen. She found a shadowy corner and spent the next hour writing letters; to Merrim, to her mother, to Perry, and one letter where she poured out her heart and soul to Beris in a way she'd never been open and honest with anyone else. She even wrote a letter to Rinn. It took a lot longer than she thought it would.

Beris, Merrim and Ala found her in the communal dining room for breakfast. Shey-Leen had gone back to the villa in Valdennes and Tethia had had no idea that her mother was going until she was gone. Tethia tried not to care, drinking in the air of cautious excitement between the others. They were all aware that they might not survive the day. They were also hopeful that by the end of the day the whole world might be different. They were all back in uniform: Tethia in her Service uniform, Beris in Auditor black, Ala in a proper chiton with the gold belt that could only be worn by members of Caesar's family, Merrim dressed the same as any other Citizen in blue trousers and billowing white shirt.

They left immediately after breakfast. It took three hours to get back to New Rome when they abandoned the skipper in a public parking space. They didn't linger for tender goodbyes in case someone passing by might wonder why an unTied person was in the arms of an Auditor, why a woman of Caesar's household was dallying with an ordinary Citizen.

Beris walked in the direction of the Auditor headquarters. He had documents to file, motions to raise, ready for what they hoped would happen tomorrow. Tethia went back to Service headquarters, astonishingly late and not caring, while Merrim and Ala caught the train to the Palatine.

Tethia didn't bother to go into her office. If this all went wrong, she didn't want to implicate Kela, whom she felt had suffered enough already. Besides, after the way Kela had reacted to finding out that her favourite Lieutenant was a mutant, Tethia wasn't sure Kela could be trusted to fight for the rights of the unCounted. She went straight to Terreus's office and knocked on the door.

The General was ready for her, but he made her wait again. Tethia could afford patience this morning and shifted very subtly from foot to foot to keep the circulation going.

Finally, he looked up. 'You could have everything, you know.' He closed the manila file in front of him. 'You're an exceptionally talented linguist, your background as a decorated General's daughter is impeccable, your personal life above reproach. You're the perfect unTied person. You could be a beacon to others who want to advance themselves. You're living proof that women don't have to be bound. And yet, your behaviour lets you down at every turn. If you had known how to keep your temper in check you might have been sitting in this chair today, disciplining a promising young Lieutenant.'

Tethia hadn't expected fatherly disappointment. She knew that Terreus had only been in charge of the Special Services branch for a few weeks, although he thought he'd been there for years. He thought he knew her well, she knew that they'd barely even met.

Somewhere between the day Tannep Baen had thrown her into the wall and when she'd returned from Capreae, Terreus had been Re-Educated, as had everyone in the Special Services building. Tannep Baen was gone. Tethia didn't know where he went, but she knew why he'd gone and who had made it happen. She'd always thought that only individuals were Re-Educated, but of course that wasn't true. Otherwise, what would stop their families and friends from breaking the Re-Education? No, Re-Education was a large-scale business. Large swathes of the population were Re-Educated all at once, to maintain the usual level of social control. When she had been Re-Educated, so had everyone they thought she'd been in contact with. The only reason she'd ever found out about Sheya was because Re-

Ed had no idea she'd gotten a message to Merrim first.

'I'm sorry I'm late, sir.' Tethia kept her eyes cast down.

Terreus shook his head. 'You know the penalty for tardiness, Lieutenant. Take hold of the straps, please.'

Tethia gritted her teeth and did what she was told. It was for Sheya, she told herself. For Perry, and Dubhia, and all the other unCounted and uncountable people who had no voice in the world. This wouldn't be the worst thing she'd ever done for her daughter. She gripped the straps above her head tightly, determined not to cry out.

Terreus didn't call the slave. He applied the lash himself, giving Tethia three strokes that didn't sting as much as she'd expected them to. He felt sorry for her, she supposed, as the whip struck her back through her uniform. He was within his rights to strip her to the skin before the lashing. After today, one way or another, she would never enter the Special Services building again. Her career was over.

After Terreus put the whip away, he gave Tethia her assignment: another day translating at the Palatine Library. Tethia thanked the General for the beating, as she was supposed to, took the manila folder containing her orders and caught the train to the Palatine.

Beris met her at the Palatine station. He bowed politely. 'Salve, Lieutenant, my name is Berisus.'

'Salve,' Tethia replied, bowing her head in return. 'I am Tethia of Valdennes, Lieutenant, daughter of Meropius, General, the Serviceman who will be translating for you in this Audit.'

'Pleased to meet you,' Beris said cheerfully. 'Shall we?'

Tethia muttered under her breath, '…and don't you dare ever tell me that I didn't give you my real name…'

Beris managed to hold back his smile, but the look in his eyes was something special.

They entered the Palatine through the gardens. They waited, dawdling slowly, until Ala and Merrim brought Nesta to them.

'Don't look at me like that, Lieutenant,' Nesta complained. 'What did I ever do to you?'

Beris had to hold her back. Nesta just laughed.

'Don't bother, Lieutenant. By the time you got within arm's reach of me, you know you would have changed your mind already.'

'You Re-Educated me!' she shouted, unable to control herself. 'Twice!'

Nesta laughed again. 'My dear Lieutenant, I've Re-

Educated you a dozen times. I've followed your career with interest. The last few times they brought you in, I put the lightest possible block on you. I was curious what you'd do. Unfortunately, you're spectacularly easy to Re-Educate. I never thought the block would last as long as it did.'

Nesta's face was suddenly furious. 'Do you think you're the only person in the world who's lost someone? I had a brother-'

Lips pressed tightly together, Nesta turned away. 'I know what you're here for. I was the one who suggested it months ago, but you didn't want to break your conditions.'

'What are you talking about?' Ala asked.

Nesta sneered. 'You think you've got the reins, don't you little girl? With all your plans and your schemes, do you think the rest of us haven't got our own petty ambitions, too? Re-Ed runs the world. We don't care who wears the mask. Come now, Lieutenant. Tell me your sad story. I've got other things to do, you know, and it'll take time to get it all out to the newsspeakers.'

Tethia stared at him. She'd never had anything to do with anyone who lived on the Palatine before and the complexity of their political intrigues infuriated her. She told Nesta everything.

Nesta went back to Re-Ed, to feed the information

to the newsspeakers. Within twenty-four hours the Re-Education of the world would be complete. The whole Empire would hear Tethia's words, whether they wanted to or not. The whole world would be angry tomorrow.

Tethia, Beris, Merrim and Ala went back to the rebels' hideout and they waited.

#

The newsspeakers took Tethia's story and spread it everywhere. One of the newsspeakers came with the crowd who descended on Croyes. He only had to pass by a person to share the story. It wasn't projected orally, but mentally, and for the first time, Tethia was aware of the mental images being projected by the newsspeaker and the story continued in her mind long after the newsspeaker had gone past her.

Tethia saw her own image in her mind, the same, but different, because this was how Nesta saw her. Her face was like flint. 'My name is Tethia of Valdennes, and I am Sheya's mother. I was a Lieutenant in Special Services. I was disgraced two weeks ago. Many of you saw my trial where I was found guilty of having an indecent relationship with a man while I was a virgin in my father's house. I conceived a child.'

The mental scene shifted. Tethia was younger now, but they saw her only briefly because she couldn't take her eyes from her baby. Sheya, all big eyes and tip tilted nose, in all her winsome babyness gazed into the listening minds of every person who passed a newsspeaker.

'Because I was unmarried, my baby, my Sheya, was taken from me. She became one of the unCounted. She was sent to the Starlight Project. I tried to get on with my life. You keep living, after something like that, but a part of you stays with your child and it always will. It must, because they were a part of you. We all love our children. That is who we are as humans. We show the best of ourselves when we love and the love of a mother for her baby is universal.

'I showed my love for my baby by giving her up. I wanted her to have a good life. I wanted her to have a good family, the family I couldn't give her. I dreamed about what she might be like.' She allowed parts of her fantasies to rise in her mind. Sheya as a baby, taking her first steps. Sheya as a toddler, running away from a loving father just so he would chase her and smooch a big kiss into her belly when he caught her. Sheya as a little girl learning to count and counting everything in sight, getting half the numbers wrong.

The scene shifted to the darkness of the countryside, the headlights of a truck in the distance. 'Today,' she said, 'I found out exactly what goes on in the Starlight Project. Our children are Counted, then they are killed.' The sound of tears was in her voice, projected by the newsspeaker, the tears she'd never dare shed in her waking life. Here, it was necessary that the whole world know how she had suffered.

She showed them the inside of the truck, all the little boxes on shelves, and she showed them what the boxes contained.

'This must never, never happen again. As a people, we cannot allow it.' She took them now to the pillar, marching through the tunnel as she spoke. 'When the Empire stands together the whole world pays attention; when we march, it trembles; when we fight, evil and injustice fall down before us.'

They reached the large cavern where the pillar stood, squat and powerful in the very centre. She reached out a hand to point to the ancient glyphs. 'This pillar is the oldest law in the world. It is the basis of our world.' She walked around, letting her finger follow the symbols. 'One people, one law, one goal. This is our First Law. And if Caesar does not follow this Law and allows his people to be exploited, then Caesar no longer has the right to rule.'

She let that sink in, repeated it. 'One people, one law, one goal. We must stop the Starlight Project. We must demand a Caesar who will honour the laws by which he governs. I have lost everything. But there are other women out there today who might be mothers tomorrow and we cannot allow this to happen to them.'

\#

And then in the evening, everything was different. The slaves started arriving first, coming before the nebula rose, arriving with one light struggling to serve for twenty people, walking along rough roads in the dark. And then, the Tiedmen and Freedmen, then, in a rush, it was as though every Citizen in New Rome decided to join them. There were hundreds of lights then, thousands of them, all coming in as a continuous stream from the city and the surrounding towns, long, crawling streams of light that snaked their slow, determined way to the caves outside Croyes.

At first it was exciting, that the whole world seemed to have decided to follow Tethia's call. They had seen her baby, they had loved her baby, and they were willing to stand up and protect their own children. The feelings she had projected were universal and it seemed that every person in the Empire had heard her call.

The legions heard, too, as well as Special Services. Tethia saw more than one familiar face. The later Citizens brought news with them. There were riots in New Rome, they said. Great crowds were already gathered outside the Palatine.

Sorha had Tethia gather the newcomers together outside the caves. In the distance, a warning bell told them that the nebula would rise in an hour. Tethia felt like it was tolling the doom of Caesar. She climbed up onto a rocky promontory to address them.

'My daughter is dead,' she told them, raising her voice to make sure that they all heard her. 'But there are others, other daughters, other sons whom we may yet save.' She looked around and climbed up onto a rock so they could all see her. 'Today the world has learned of our Cause and today we must act. Today, we are not powerless individuals, unable to make a difference in the world. Today we stand together and we fight. We demand a new world. We demand a ruler who will obey our laws and respect our people. And when the nebula sets tomorrow morning, there will be a new world for every single one of us!'

The roar of approval was intoxicating. Tethia stood on the rock, dazed with the sudden swell of noise.

'But what if we die?' someone asked. He was shouting it, trying to be heard over the roar of the crowd.

Tethia raised her hand for silence. The whole world seemed to hold its breath at her command. 'You ask, what if we die!' she cried. 'I say to you, all of us, today, tomorrow or the next day, will surely die. None of us are immortal. But, even at the risk of my life I cannot tolerate such atrocities to continue. Yes, I may die and you may die, but I can never go back to a world that allows children to be destroyed. I may die, but I tell you that here, I am born again with you today. I will live with you. I will fight beside you. I will die among you. And because we have lived and fought and died, those who come after us will be free. I accept that; I glory in it and I run to my future. Will you run with me?'

After that there were no more questions and everything moved at a breakneck pace. The rebels armed themselves and prepared to storm New Rome. Sorha was in charge, moving from unit to unit, making plans and co-ordinating everyone's movements.

Tethia watched it all happen and felt very useless. It

all seemed futile. Even if they won, even if they deposed Caesar, it didn't mean that anything would be different. Her mind went around in circles. One person couldn't change the world, she thought, despite what she'd said to the crowd. Times may change, but people, never.

Then Merrim was before her. 'Stop brooding. It'll happen. Everyone has heard the news. We just have to put you up there in front of everyone and the whole world will march behind us.'

\#

Sitting together in the back of the skipper on the way to New Rome, Beris sought Tethia's hand.

'I know you're brave,' he whispered. 'But remember, you don't have anything to prove.'

She looked at him and thought that he was, hands down, the most handsome man she'd ever met. Every moment she'd known him, he'd grown greater in her estimation. She loved him. He was the best man she'd ever met and she knew she didn't deserve him.

'It's not about proving anything,' she said. 'Not now. We have a job to do. That's all.'

He gripped her hand tighter. 'I need you to be safe,

Lerina. I don't want you to be in the thick of it – but I know that's where you'll end up. Just promise me that you'll do your best to still be here with me when the last bell rings. You haven't lost *everything*, you know. I'll always be here for you.'

She put up her hand to touch his face, delighted when he pressed his cheek into her hand. 'We're fighting for a new day,' she whispered. 'Who knows what a new day will bring?'

Merrim looked back at her from the seats in front. 'You take care of yourself,' he said softly. 'You're the only sister I've got.'

Tethia turned her face away, too choked up to answer.

Once they were in New Rome, Tethia was surprised to see what they found there. Her news had hit its mark and the streets were thronging with people. Lightsticks bobbed above the crowd and here and there some had dared to waste resources by starting a fire. The light from the fires was eerily red, bathing the faces of the people around them with a crimson glow.

They had to leave the skipper behind not long after they entered New Rome. There were too many people in the streets to be able to manoeuvre the vehicle safely, so they continued on foot. They didn't have to fight the crowds – the vast throng of people was moving inexorably towards the Palatine Hill. There was no-one in charge anymore. The mob had made up its mind and the only thing that could be done was to go along with it.

The Palatine was lit up as though it was daytime. Every circle of it glowed, even the section that was thick with gardens. Even from a distance it was obvious, too, that the whole hill was crawling with soldiers. Lights glistened on breastplates, helmets and spearpoints, gleaming in the dark mass of men.

Tethia heard the first warnings in the distance. She heard the heavy march of the legions, the sound that had brought down whole civilisations. The people cried out in response, in defiance, and then in fear. Arrows rained down on the populace first, followed by spears and lastly a charge from the legions. Hundreds fell beneath the charge, but behind them were hundreds more. The bulk of Caesar's army were still in Bethillia, completing the Crush of Chiau. Even the Emperor couldn't bring the legions back from Bethillia so soon.

Tethia's hand went down to grip her sword – partly to be ready, and partly to make sure it wasn't taken from her. Most of the people around her were unarmed, or armed with things they found around them, carrying kitchen knives and wounding the people around them more often than they wounded soldiers, brandishing brooms and shovels and walking sticks.

Her breathing sped up as they neared the gates. Not far from them now was the mêlée, a writhing mass of soldiers and civilians, struggling and screaming, shouting and dying. Tethia nearly tripped over the first dead body, unbloody, lying prone in the street, arms outstretched in a final embrace of the earth.

'Come,' Ala whispered. She was directing them away from the mêlée and slightly off to the side. They had to fight the crowd to change direction, but the strongest rebels carved a path before them, Tethia and Ala following close in their wake, with the rest of the rebels trailing behind them.

Ala took them to a house. There was nothing to distinguish it from the houses around it, standing tall and unlit around them, their occupants either among the struggling crowd or hiding in fear. Ala opened the door, pressing her thumb to a subtle panel above the knob to unlock it.

They followed her into the dark house, through a trapdoor in the kitchen and into a series of tunnels. All of a sudden, the order of precedence changed. Ala moved confidently through the dark, guiding Merrim; then Tethia guiding Beris, her eyes trained on Ala, a pale shape in a darkness that was profound even for her eyes.

They walked through long, unlit tunnels, Ala insisting that any light they carried would only draw unwonted attention to them. They moved slowly, in a line where each person had to grasp the shoulder of the person in front of them. Of them all, only Ala and Tethia could see where they were going. Tethia didn't want to tell them that she couldn't see much more than they could – there was nothing but the long tunnel, stretching out to infinity in front of them.

It only took a few minutes of walking through the dark before Tethia began to wonder if they could really trust Ala, after all. It would only take a moment's misdirection in the dark and one sharp attack by a small company of Palatine Guards to destroy the leaders of the rebellion in one fell swoop. What the others were thinking, she could only guess, but Beris's hand was steady on her shoulder and in front of her Merrim never wavered, taking bold, broad steps as though he were walking along a well-lit path.

'This door leads to Caesar's private quarters,' Ala

whispered suddenly, stopping so quickly that they all bumped into one another and stumbled a step before coming to a halt. It was only a plain door, the same as dozens they'd passed along the way.

'Are you sure?' Tethia asked.

'I'm sure. Caesar might have spent most of his time with us in Capreae, but I lived in the Imperial Household long enough to know where I was going in the night.'

For a moment Tethia stared at the pale oval of Ala's face, nearly luminescent in the dark corridor. 'I heard rumours,' she began but Ala screwed up her face in distaste.

'Not that. And more than you could imagine. There is a sign,' she said, pointing to a symbol above the door. It was a triangle, nothing more, nothing to explicitly say that Caesar was beyond that door, but Tethia thought back to the pillar. Three points to a triangle, she thought. One people, one law, one goal. This symbol must go back to the very earliest days of the Empire, even, perhaps, to before the Empire.

There was a brief flurryof activity as the rebels prepared themselves for battle, drawing their swords and daggers and kitchen knives, preparing themselves for one last final push. Ala opened the door and they all rushed out.

#

The fight was brief. The Palatine Guards were well trained and prepared but there were simply too many rebels for them to fight. In moments, the Guards were surrounded and disarmed, watching as a corpulent man was dragged from his bed. Tethia saw him up close as he was pulled past her. She even saw the tiny gold studs embedded in the skin of his face to which his golden mask would attach. This was Caesar: a man designed for disguise.

The slaves were clustered in a corner, at least ten of them, all women, glued together by fear. Among them, Tethia saw a familiar face. The slaves cowering in the corner were all reasonably young women. They only wore the traditional chiton with the red belt of those who served Caesar and it exposed their muscular arms and toned legs through its gauzy panels.

These were not ordinary women. The only one among them not built like a Palatine Guard was a familiar face. A large woman, jowls rolling down from her chin to meet her chest, her white veil not hiding the pellucid-fair face within.

All of a sudden, everything became crystal clear for

Tethia and the idea that Caesar could have neither a name nor a face was preposterous. She went to the group of slaves and stood between them and the rebels.

'Have no fear,' she said, making sure the men around her could hear her. 'I will not allow you to be harmed.' Her gaze sought Mira's face. 'No innocent shall be harmed.'

Mira stared straight back. Tethia had been right the first time she'd met the woman. She was too brazen by half to be just a slave.

Tethia offered to guard the slaves. Ala said, casually, that she would stay with her, so naturally Merrim had to stay too. Tethia insisted on a few other men joining them. She'd been a soldier all her adult life and she had no plans on being a fool on the spur of the moment just because her tal, muscular, athletic prisoners were women.

The slaves were transferred to a truck and sent to the prison. Tethia watched them all climb into the truck and made sure herself that the count was correct before the truck was sealed and driven away.

Then there was Caesar to bring to justice. Beris had provided the documents yesterday for Caesar's Audit. This was all completely legal, just as it was completely barbaric. Tethia stood in the front row of seats in the arena amid a roaring crowd, every single one of them wildly waving their arms, their thumbs pointed at the ground, crying that the mock-court should execute him.

'Put him down like the dog he is!' Tethia heard one man scream and the chant was taken up by those around him. 'Put down the dog! Put down the dog!'

This is what we're fighting *against*, Tethia thought with sudden clarity: the idea that any person doesn't have the same rights as others.

She stood.

She didn't know what she would say, didn't know if she could even make herself heard in the tumult. She looked down into the arena and saw the man standing before her. She didn't even open her mouth before one of the jury ran forwards, arm raised, a dagger gleaming in his hand.

Before she could even speak, the man who wore the mask of Caesar crumpled on the sand. She sat back down. There was no point saying anything now. They wanted blood. And now they had it.

If the party after the ambush had been restrained by some kind of strange ambivalence, the feasting and revelry that followed the death of Caesar was unrestrained by any kind of boundary whatsoever. Fires burned throughout New

Rome for three days, regardless of wastage and conservation laws. There was music and dancing in the streets and parties in the squares. More laws were broken in those three days than had been broken by Caesar in the whole of his reign.

Tethia missed most of it. As soon as possible after the execution, she took her leave. She told Beris in strictest confidence where she was going and took a skipper, driving herself through the dark, deserted country streets. She had never gone this way before, despite travelling to every far-flung corner of the Empire in her service as a translator. It was amazing how rarely revolutions, she thought, happened by the seaside.

She parked the skipper near the beach and took the path that lead around the heads, the water dark, loud and enormous by her side. Mira was there, sitting on the sand, careless of her white chiton, gazing out at the water. She saw Tethia approach but didn't try to run.

'I thought I'd find your fierce maidens with you,' Tethia said.

'They're in prison,' Mira answered, 'and one of them is pretending to be me.' She smiled. 'As if any of them could! I'm twice the woman they are.'

'Twice the woman... and also a man, when it

pleases you, is that so?'

'I find so many things about the world interesting that are still closed to women. I wear clothes to suit the occasion, whatever that might be.'

'And wear a mask to suit the occasion, yes?'

Mira nodded, a little ruefully and lifted one of her artful white curls to show the golden studs where Caesar's mask would be attached to her face. 'There are places where even Caesar cannot go. Caesar could not possibly be a woman, therefore I must remain in secret.'

'Was it you who proclaimed the Edict of Caracalla or the man in the mask?'

Mira gave Tethia an arrogant tilt of her head for answer before deigning to say, 'I am Caesar. I rule the world.'

'You know you'll be found, don't you? If I could figure it out, someone else will. Ala probably knows.'

'Ala won't tell.'

'How can you be so sure?'

'I have ruled since I was a child. My father died when I was only fifteen, you remember. I know how people think. I know Ala and I understand her. She would never dare reveal me. I might make some revelations of my own.'

'I'm not here to reveal you.'

Tethia and Mira both turned at the sweet voice with its transient Caprese accent. Gold studs glittered near Ala's ears, ready to hold Caesar's mask to her face.

Mira didn't look surprised. 'I wondered how long it would take you to find me.' She turned back to look at the waves, washing black and white on the unlit shore. She stood up, brushing sand ineffectually from her chiton. Tethia stood with her.

Ala turned to Tethia. 'Mira and I have known one another all my life. Would you leave us alone, please, Tethia?'

Ala's pretty face was set, even hard. Mira stood proud and tall, a massive figure against the background of the wide sea. Tethia looked from one to the other, then nodded. She spent the whole of the drive back to New Rome wondering why she'd left them there.

#

Three days later, Ala, from her place on the golden throne and speaking from behind the golden mask, put an end to the revelry. The people had enjoyed their time of celebration, she said. Now it was time to create a new world, a better world. The people listened and calmed to her voice. It was time to put out the fires. They were against the law, after all, and the preservation of the planet and the population was now the concern of every person. The fires were doused. People went back to work. The trains started running again.

Tethia had gathered the few of her possessions she bothered to keep at the barracks and moved into the remains of the villa at Valdennes. Beris moved in with her, and to satisfy the new conventions that weren't really any different from the old conventions, married Tethia.

Merrim had stayed in New Rome – stayed on the Palatine Hill, in fact. In her more cynical moments, alone with Beris, Tethia complained that it seemed that the laws still didn't apply to Caesar, or to Caesar's lover, and Beris told her to shut up before she got them all into trouble.

The Starlight Project was officially disbanded. It was Ala's first official act. The members of the Starlight Council were brought to the Palatine in chains and Ala received them in the Ocean Court. Tethia didn't attend the trial. She saw the Lectors, Overseers and Researchers in their parade up the long avenue that led to the Ocean Court, from the quarters she shared with Beris.

Tethia watched as Rinn went past in the long line. No matter what he'd done, what he'd been to her in their youth would always remain. There would never be a reconciliation. He would never learn, never see what he'd done to her, never be again the boy whose smile had turned her heart on its end. But he would always be the first boy who'd smiled at her like that.

The parade of the damned returned down the avenue after the trial. There had never been any doubt about how the trial would end. The Council was taken to the arena for execution. When Rinn had passed beyond her sight, Tethia brought her hand up to her face to try and keep quiet. After all he'd done, she was ashamed to think that she could still cry for him.

#

Beris, with his usual sensitivity, had allowed her privacy to watch the parade. He remained inside the apartment and came to meet her when she came back inside.

'I have a gift for you, darling.' He rose from the couch, a light glinting in his eyes that made Tethia wonder what he was up to.

'I'm all ears.'

Beris grinned and pulled the bell for the slave. He

went back to the couch, inviting Tethia to recline next to him. He passed her a dish of wine and she managed not to make a fool of herself this time.

The slave that arrived… was very familiar. Tethia's eyes widened and she turned to stare at Beris behind her. That light in his eyes. He was happy and excited to give her a gift, but there was a nasty glint there, too, that she loved. She didn't want to be the only one with a mean streak, and this was the first time she'd seen Beris display one. 'I approve,' she murmured, and gave him a kiss.

'So, you're my new slave, are you?' Tethia looked him up and down. He looked like any other slave, dressed in a knee length white chiton and red belt. He was comparatively tall and heavy set, with dark eyes and a square jaw, something just past middle age.

'Yes, mistress. I am… I am so grateful. Until your kind husband employed me today, I was just an hourly slave, rented to anyone who wanted short-term help, no home, no security. I promise you I will be a faithful servant to you and your family all my life.'

He bowed and Tethia barely held in her nasty laughter. An hourly slave? The lowest of the low. Sometimes people hired hourly slaves just so they could have someone to beat when they'd had a bad day. Re-

Education had certainly done a number on him.

'Have you always been a slave?'

'No, Mistress. I was once a Citizen, and a Citizen's son, but I committed a crime when I was a young man and I have paid for that crime with a life of slavery.'

'Did you ever consider Service?'

Tethia felt Beris drop his head behind her and press his brow between her shoulder blades and she knew he was hiding a grin.

'No, Mistress.'

'No, it probably wouldn't suit you. You'll find we are a progressive household,' Tethia said. 'We allow our slaves to choose their own gender and use their own names. What is your name?'

'Tannep Baen, Mistress.'

#

Ala called for Beris and Tethia to attend her that evening. The banquet was sumptuous as ever. Wastage and conservation laws didn't apply to Caesar or his court. It was after the banquet that Ala and Merrim, Beris and Tethia managed to get a quiet moment alone. Ala kept her mask on until after the banquet. She watched the banquet but did not eat. Caesar only ate in private.

The small repast that awaited Ala in her private quarters was nowhere near as lavish as the banquet that had graced the tables in the public quarters. Merrim reclined next to her as she ate, balancing a dish of wine on his palm with as much elan as any of Ala's court. Tethia had no idea how many dishes of wine had preceded this one. Merrim was barely able to keep his eyes open.

'I've been learning a lot about the Empire,' Ala said. 'I had no idea it was so vast. There is a tribe that continually threatens the borders of the Empire – the Eridai, in the land of Eridea. Have you heard of them, Tethia?'

Tethia nodded. 'I had the opportunity of visiting Eridea once. It took weeks to get there, even travelling by skipper. So far away from civilisation, of course, there are no trains. We were trying to establish a treaty with the barbarians, but no one could make them see why being a part of the Empire would be only to their benefit.'

'And you went along, of course, to translate. How did you learn their language?'

'Their language is very similar to the ancient language of our own people,' Tethia explained. 'Their language hasn't evolved like ours has. They have a group of people – they call them bards – who keep their history and their language as close to their roots as possible.'

'What did you think of the Eridai? They are a unique people.'

'Unique is certainly the word. They live in small clans, and although they place a very high value on family, they don't protect their women the way the Empire does.' She shared a brief, sardonic smile with Beris. 'I know that the Empire has struggled in those provinces that border along the Eridai lands.'

'Was Kela with you when you went to Eridea?'

'No, that was many years ago. Kela wasn't my assistant, then.'

'How do you suppose she'd like life on the fringe of the Empire?'

'Ala, great Caesar, you know that to be in the heart of the Empire is the joy of every Citizen. Kela would grieve, as all of us would grieve, to be sent so even further away from New Rome.' Tethia had been unTied for more than a decade. She knew how to say the right things. 'Even in her new work, as a trainee translator in Bethillia working for the Imperial Special Services, Kela would still be grieved to be so far from New Rome.'

'Of course.' Ala popped another small pastry in her mouth. It burst, and the savoury filling stained her lips.

They chatted about mutual acquaintances, but Tethia had a feeling that Ala was very carefully guiding the conversation.

'So, what is your mother doing these days?' Ala asked, still picking delicately at the fine pastries.

'She has settled back into a quiet life in the villa at Valdennes,' Tethia said.

'Quite the firecracker, your mother,' Ala went on. 'She was a revolutionary for years and I had no idea. How do I know she'll be happy settling down to a quiet life in the country?'

Beris leaned forward. 'Shey-Leen only did what she did for her family, Ala.'

'Shey-Leen has done quite a bit for her family, Beris. Have you ever asked Tethia what happened to Meropius?'

Merrim roused somewhat and put his hand on Ala's arm. 'Honey, Mater only did what she had to do.'

Ala put down her fork and faced Merrim. 'Stay out of this – *darling*. Go back to our quarters and wait for me there.'

Blank eyed, Merrim got up from the couch and left the room at once, stumbling as he went.

Tethia stared. 'Ala, what did you do to him?'

Beris raised his voice. 'Ala, you swore you would never use that power!'

Ala just stared right back at the pair of them. 'I am Caesar, Beris. Telling people what to do is who I am. My voice, my power, that is the voice of Caesar.'

'You have a commanding voice,' Tethia whispered. 'Like Perry.'

'Yes, Tethia. Like Perry. Like your father, come to that. I have a task for you. Well, a task for Beris, of course. You're not unTied anymore. You don't need to worry yourself about work anymore.'

'Such a privilege,' Tethia muttered. She took Beris's hand and held it tightly. She was pretty sure that slapping Caesar would be considered some kind of crime and Ala was coasting dangerously close to the edge of Tethia's self-control.

'Why don't you just order me?' Beris asked, a sarcastic edge in his voice. 'If you're going to use your voice, anyway. I never thought you would abuse your power like that. And I've known you since you were a child.'

'Be careful, Beris.' Ala stood up. Standing up, she appeared even more small and slight than she did reclining on the dining couch. 'I don't want to have to command

you, but I will if I have to. I'm giving you a gift. I didn't
want you to be in a bad mood when I gave you a gift.' She
began to pace around the room, her hands fisting in the
purple robe that Caesar always wore on public occasions, to
keep from tripping on the hem. 'After all, you gave me a
gift. You helped me find someone we could use to tell a
sob story to the newsspeakers. You helped me become
Caesar. You made me free. I don't have to worry that I'll
be forced to carry a child at the will of Caesar anymore. I
don't have to worry that anyone will tell me what to do.
And that's why I'm giving you a gift.'

'I'm sure you really shouldn't have,' Beris replied.
Tethia had never heard him sound quite so sarcastic before.

'I'm going to make you a Consul. Like your father.
You won't have to worry about learning medicine
anymore. And Tethia, I'm giving you what you want, too.
You wanted to travel; I'm going to let you travel. You can
travel with Beris, all the way to Eridea.'

'Why?' Beris gritted.

'Because I can't afford for Tethia to have another
sob story to tell the newsspeakers. And I can't afford to
keep her here.' She turned to face Tethia directly, who sat
up straight on the couch to face Caesar.

'The Colonists hate you, Tethia. You destroyed

their Project. You destroyed their culture and their world. Now they're all through my society, spreading hate.' Ala smiled thinly. 'I would far rather they hate you than me.'

'So why not just get rid of me?'

'Tethia, don't say that,' Beris murmured, increasing his grip on her hand.

'I'm not going to kill her, Beris, don't worry. This is a very vulnerable time in our history. We can't afford another revolution right now. Your wife is a very public figure. Every person in the world right now knows her face. If she disappears, people will notice. If you and she announce that she needs to live a quiet life in another country to nurse her grief they will understand.'

When they arrived back in their quarters, Tethia turned to Beris.

'To be honest, I'm surprised we made it back here. I thought we were dead.'

A vein was pulsing in Beris's forehead. 'She wouldn't dare. She wasn't kidding when she said that the whole world is watching you right now. If you disappeared, her power as Caesar would crumble.' He picked up a vase and threw it at the wall. It smashed, pieces crumbling against the frescoes on the wall. 'I can't believe she's sending us into exile!'

'Ssshh.' Tethia put her arms around her husband. 'Did you really think we were going to get away with it? We changed the world, you and I. Even Caesar fears that. What if we decided the world needed changing again? No, we are safest, all of us, if we are far away from here.'

He sighed and put his arms around her. 'You're probably right. I've only ever heard of Eridea on the news. What's it like?'

'It's actually very beautiful. The whole of Eridea is a garden and the people there live among the natural world.' She laughed a little. 'The people are as wild and beautiful as the landscape. It's difficult to imagine a land so different from the Empire.'

Beris drew in a deep breath again, urged her face close against him and rested his cheek against her hair. 'I've never been anywhere except here and Capreae.'

'Then it will be an adventure, won't it?'

'Married to you, I was ready for adventure.'

Tethia pressed a kiss to his chest through his tunic.

'Tethia, what Ala said about your mother…'

She closed her eyes, dreading what he was going to say next.

'What happened to your father?'

Tethia drew out of his arms. She shrugged. 'What

happens in so many families, out in the country, isolated…? My sister, Proxima, bore our father a son even before she attained her majority. We all pretended Merrim was Mater's child. He is my nephew, and my brother, but he is not my mother's son. When I was seeing Rinn, Proxima was pregnant again. She died in childbirth. When Proxima was no longer available, Pater came to me.'

Tethia couldn't stand to look at his face anymore. She began to prowl around the room, examining every item in it as though she'd never been there before. She kept speaking, because if she was ever going to tell him the truth, it was now. 'Whatever Rinn's faults, he never revealed to the world that Sheya wasn't his daughter, but he knew as well as I did that she was Merrim's sister, as well as his niece.' She shrugged again, with a bitter smile. 'That's another good reason to leave. Merrim doesn't know. Proxima insisted that he never be told.'

Beris sank down onto the couch. 'Tethia… by all the gods…'

'Proxima told Mater. Mater didn't want to know, either. She refused to believe Proxima. Mater did nothing about it until Proxima was dead and I was pregnant. And then, well….' She went to stand at the closed glass door to the balcony. 'She dealt with the matter. But she was too late. Proxima was already dead and I would never forgive her for that.'

Beris's hands curved over her shoulders. She jumped, and hated herself for jumping. 'Tethia-'

'I'd really rather never speak of this again,' she said, looking out at the pink-washed sky through the protective glass. 'I want to look to the future. I'm glad we're going to Eridea. I want to get out of this stinking Empire. Do you want a baby, Beris?'

Behind her, his hands trembled on her shoulders and she told herself she could hear the hitch in his breathing. 'Tethia… my Lerina, my darling… after all you've been through… I couldn't ask it of you.'

She turned. 'Well, *I* want a baby, Beris. I want *your* baby. And it's just as well, because I'm having one.' She shocked both of them when she burst into tears and threw her arms around him.

They were ready to travel the next day, trunks packed, slaves lined up, the whole household prepared for the trip to Eridea. Tethia boasted that this was solely due to her. She didn't have enough personal possessions to even fill her old Service duffel bag. Perhaps, subconsciously, she'd been prepared to travel light. Maybe she'd even been hoping for it. All she knew was that she was happier about leaving New Rome than she had ever been to go anywhere.

They boarded a train bound for the coastal town of Galliae, from where would then sail to Ladena, at the north easternmost tip of the Empire. The final part of the journey would be on horseback.

Galliae was a large town, a transport hub, where goods and people came from every corner of the Empire to change trains. Most of them were apparently at the station that day, too, milling around and getting in one another's way. Tannep's large form proved useful in carving a path through the crowd so they could pass from the train station to the adjacent terminal.

Someone spat at Tethia as she passed and she glimpsed the shadow of Marks on the man's wrist. Ala had been right. The Colonists would never forgive her for what she'd done.

When they were finally settled in their suite, Tethia and Beris collapsed into the comfortable chairs provided and gratefully accepted the refreshments brought to them by one of the ship's stewards. After they'd drained their dishes dry, Beris went out again to look to the comfort of the rest of their household.

It was only after he'd gone that Tethia heard the noise. She put her dish down carefully and got out of her chair. She drew the sword that Beris was allowed to carry for ceremonial purposes.

There was another small thud. It was coming from the closet, where the steward had stored their trunks. Tethia approached carefully, then threw the door open.

Inside, standing defiant, if covered in stray pieces of clothing after having forced their way out of Tethia's trunk, were Perry and Dubhia.

Tethia just stared, the sword in her hand, and was unable to say a word.

Perry brushed a stocking from her shoulder while Dubhia surreptitiously removed a glove from her hair.

'We heard the newsspeakers,' Perry said, the voice still coming from Dubhia's lips. *'We've been asking questions. I spoke to Lector RS, before they took him to the Palatine. I believe that I am your daughter.'*

Tethia dropped the sword. With an incoherent cry, she gathered her daughter into her arms as though she would never let her go.

THE END

BONUS CHAPTER
AND
SNEAK PEEK!

Keep reading for an excerpt from my next novel, **Vengeance,** *the first book in* **The Umbra Chronicles,** *a new epic fantasy trilogy launching in December 2020!*

Cairnagorn used to be a city, but it was nothing but a network of caves now. Elisabeth and I sped through tunnels that used to be streets, caves that used to be ballrooms. I held Elisabeth's limp hand tightly. I was amazed she could still run. After the shock we'd had it was all she could do to put one foot in front of the other and follow my lead.

I kept glancing behind us. If I caught sight of him, if he came within arm's reach, I was going to bring the whole mountain down on top of us. My wand was in my hair, holding a bun in place as usual. If he caught us, I would kill us all. We would be better off dead.

'Come on, not far now,' I gasped. For all the difference it made I might as well not have bothered. She looked like she was still asleep. I began to breathe even faster. *Just let him catch up to us,* I thought. *Just let him catch up to* me, *and let him see what I can do.*

Oh, to laugh. *I'm so terribly, terribly brave in my imagination.* Not so much in real life. I glanced behind again and saw him round a corner past an old temple.

I was so brave in my imagination. Do you know what I did when I saw him?

I tripped. And I took Elisabeth down with me.

By the time I scrambled to my feet and dragged Elisabeth up with me, he'd caught up to us.

I ripped the wand out of my hair.

'Don't come any closer!' I waved the little silver stick that was no longer than my hand.

Maldwyn was faster than me. Even before my hair began to blow in the wind that is a side effect of magic, Maldwyn had thrown me backwards. He grabbed Elisabeth, his arm going around her neck as he held her upright, pulling her close against him. He held his other hand out towards me, keeping the tip of his wand pointed straight at me. He was faster, he was more ruthless. I had one vulnerability and he knew that he had his arm around her right now.

'Put the wand down, Emer,' Maldwyn's hand crept

across Elisabeth's chest, creeping towards her neck. Even in her passive state, her skin crawled. Her eyes met mine for a moment, dark and dull, before she closed them. She jumped when she heard the crack of lightning that came from Maldwyn's wand. I was barely able to jump out of the way in time. 'I said, put the wand down!' he shouted. His hand was under Elisabeth's chin now, fingers curling around her neck.

I opened my hand and dropped the wand. The little amethyst crystal at the end winked out. I kept my hands in the air. If he killed my sister, I would die. And, by God, so would Maldwyn.

'I'm your guardian again, Emer,' he said. 'I won the lottery, fair and square. You and Elisabeth are mine until next year, so you might as well stop fighting it. You know there's nowhere you can go. Make it easy on yourself and come with me quietly. Make it easy on Elisabeth.'

He tightened his hand for a moment, only a moment, but Elisabeth jerked like he'd stung her with lightning.

'All right!' The words burned like acid in my mouth. 'Stop it. Let her go. I'll come. I'm the one you enjoy anyway.'

Maldwyn loosened the hand around Elisabeth's

throat just long enough to crook his finger at me. When I was close enough, he let go of Elisabeth and grabbed me.

He pointed the wand into my neck, the point pressing into my skin. I was afraid he was going to stab me with it, push the slender stick clear through my throat. It wouldn't have surprised me. He'd always hated me the most. And Maldwyn was the type of man who got great pleasure out of my pain.

He bent his head and kissed me. He hadn't had his hands on me for four years, not since I was fourteen. It was even worse than I'd remembered. Because I wasn't a fool, because Elisabeth was still so close, because that wand still stuck tight against my throat, I just stood there and let it happen, when I'd sworn I would never let it happen again.

The ground rumbled beneath our feet. 'What the hell is that?' he muttered. There was a louder rumble and a light rain of dirt shaken free from the collapsed stones above that enclosed the remains of the city. Elisabeth sank to her knees and looked up at the ragged ceiling of the cavern, like a devout worshipper of an ancient stone god. When a third rumble knocked loose the smaller stones above us and opened up a crack wide enough to expose the sky, we all stared upwards.

Elisabeth started to laugh.

Above us, in that crack of light, a dragon appeared, its wings wide enough to block out the whole world. It swept its wings upwards and forced its feet against the crack, making more of the ceiling collapse. Maldwyn left us behind. He sprinted for cover deeper in the old temple. Elisabeth just knelt there, looking up at the falling rocks, laughing.

I flung myself over Elisabeth, clutching her with one hand while I raised the other above our heads like I was going to catch the falling rocks.

Maldwyn was faster with his wand, more ruthless, but I was more powerful. Even as a child I had been more powerful, but all he had to do was touch Elisabeth and I'd let him do anything he wanted to me. But Maldwyn needed a wand. He used the magic that was in the crystal at the base of the wand. I used the magic that was in my bone and blood. I held up my hand and the rocks fell all around us but not so much as the smallest stone grazed Elisabeth's cheek.

There was no silence to follow the cave in. People were shouting, their voices distant but determined beneath the roar of dragons that filled the air.

Elisabeth squeezed my hand. 'This is our chance,' she whispered. 'We need to go through the dark door now.'

447

I only hoped that Maldwyn's head was stoved in by a very large, very sharp rock, but it seemed too much to hope for. The only thing I would like better than his accidental death would be to kill him myself.

Elisabeth and I clambered over the rocks. Some of them were enormous, as large as horses, as large as houses. Somewhere under there was my wand. I longed to look for her. She had never spoken any other word than my name, whispered in my mind, but she had made her feelings clear on more than one occasion. I already felt lonely without her.\, but I had no time to stop and look for her. It was the wand or Elisabeth. Elisabeth was my twin. I didn't hesitate, but I still regretted leaving the wand behind.

Maldwyn must have seen us as we climbed over the top of the mound of rocks that had fallen around us. He shouted, 'Emer, you treacherous bitch, you come back here!'

This was not language likely to induce me to return. I took a moment to shout back, 'Not if it meant giving up the last breath in my body!'

'What about the last breath in Elisabeth's body?' Maldwyn shouted back. I glimpsed his wand still in his hand. He cast lightning towards me, but I had Elisabeth. He had no power over me now. I just flicked my finger towards him like I was getting dust off my tunic and he flew backwards the whole length of the street.

We ran. We didn't have the witch light of the wands to light the dark tunnels anymore, but the dragons had caved in the roof over such a large area that we could see for what seemed like miles.

We could see – and could be seen. There was still shouting from soldiers and roaring of dragons, but I heard a recurring sound in the soldiers' shouts. 'Emer!' and 'Elisabeth!' I didn't know if it made me feel better or worse to know that soldiers knew our names.

I'd heard about magi in ancient times, when magic was more plentiful – and not against the law. They'd been able to change themselves into birds. That kind of skill was lost long ago. Elisabeth and I had to try and clamber our way over the rocks and I just hoped like blazes that neither of us hurt ourselves because healing magic not only took a lot of energy but also took a lot of time.

We had an advantage over the soldiers and Maldwyn. We knew where we were going.

We'd been here before, the last time Maldwyn had won the draw and became our guardian for the year. He'd kept us inside Cairnagorn, so no one from the outside would know what he was doing to us. But we found a secret place. We planned to escape.

I terrified Elisabeth half out of her wits when I first took her there. We were still only fourteen, and Maldwyn had only been our guardian for a few weeks. Already it was obvious that this year was going to be a very bad year. It started bad, and it was going to get worse.

Every year, at the winter solstice, we'd go back to Caillen, the village that had sprung up when the city of Cairnagorn was destroyed a few months before Elisabeth and I were born. The person who looked after us in the preceding year took us to Caillen. I always described them as creepyguardians if I managed to say it before Elisabeth could stop me. She was always the mature one, not that I set a very high bar for maturity.

I found the secret place first. I was the one who explored. Elisabeth would follow, but only if I went first. It had been a Library, still famous the world over but no one dared venture into Cairnagorn for that kind of knowledge anymore. Magic was illegal, and the punishment for any man, woman or child found to be using it was being burned at the stake.

The Library was ruined now. Even before the avalanche that covered the city, the Library had been deep inside the mountain, accessible by tunnels that would open only if you knew the right words – or if you had enough magic in your bones. The gates would never open for Maldwyn.

Inside the Library was a series of large rooms, many with ceilings collapsed. The ornate stonework lay in crumbled piles among heaps of scrolls and books. I'd wandered along the piles and picked up a book or two on the first day. And then I'd come back the next day and read a bit more. I'd gone every day after that. I didn't tell Elisabeth about the Library until I found the Portal, nearly nine months into the year.

The room with the Portal was enormous and virtually untouched by the damage caused by the avalanche. The Portal was a large, upright circle of darkness that whirled with shadows deep within its surface. It didn't have a border or anything to make it stand up and when I walked around it, I saw it was a narrow slice of darkness, as thin as a sheet of paper. The back was the same as the front.

I stuck my arm into it, standing at the side, and watched my hand disappear into the surface of the dark… and not come out the other side. Feeling terribly brave, I stuck my face into it.

There was no more darkness. There were colours,

more colours than I'd ever seen before. They moved toward me, around me, engulfed me. I drew my head back smartly.

'Wow,' I said to the empty room. 'I've got to get Lynnevet to see this.'

Elisabeth's name that year was Lynnevet. Mine was Emer that year, too. Our creepyguardians chose our names. For whatever reasons, Maldwyn decided that I looked like an Emer and my sister looked like a Lynnevet.

I brought Lynnevet to the Library. She was strange when she saw the Portal. 'I know what this is.' She stood in front of the sheet of darkness and stared at shadows as they moved. 'These take you places – they take you to different times. Our last guardian mentioned it – she didn't know I was listening – when she was talking to the Master. No one has the power to make them anymore. We could leave. We could leave now.'

Before I could stop her, she stepped through the Portal. At the last moment, I managed to grab her wrist. I was left holding an arm unattached to anything else as Lynnevet vanished into the Portal. I pulled Lynnevet's arm with all my strength. I was afraid I was going to pull her arm off, or the Portal would close and I would be left holding an amputated arm. My feet skidded towards the Portal. I threw my weight backwards and fell to the stone floor. My momentum pulled Lynnevet back with me. She landed on top of me. I started shouting because Lynnevet was screaming.

When I got her calm enough to use words, she shouted at me about colours and dead people and three of me, and a magic wind so strong it created first one vortex then another until a dozen tornadoes were twisting around the room like mad dancers.

Lynnevet never went back to the Library. I did, though. I had more and more incentive to find something to help me use my magic against him. In the end he broke me. Then he took the most precious things I had away from me and broke them too.

As we ran deeper into the ruins, deeper into the mountain, I thought of how Elisabeth had described that other place. Colours and the dead and me, surrounded by tornadoes of magic wind. It wasn't the kind of place a sensible person would flee *to*, but we were out of options.

We came to the gates of the Library. I opened my arms and held my hands closed into fists, out towards the stone doors. They only opened for the right words, which I didn't know, or for magic in bone and blood. I opened my hands.

The gates slid open, rolling along a track on the

floor as they opened into the Library's entrance room. Elisabeth and I hurried through when they were open wide enough for us to slip through sideways. I turned, just beyond the doors, and closed my fists to them. They slid shut again.

That had to buy some time. The soldiers were the ones who would burn a child at the stake for having magic. They wouldn't be able to open the gates. Maldwyn had no magic in his bones and if he tried to open the gates with magic the soldiers would arrest him – maybe even kill him on the spot. I could but hope, anyway.

We were safe. Exhausted and gasping for breath, I sank to my hands and knees. Elisabeth folded up neatly into a cross-legged position on the floor, then bent in half at the waist until it looked like she was trying to tie herself into a knot.

Finally she raised her head.

'He can't get through the gates, can he?' she asked. She hadn't even caught her breath yet. I was a little better. Last year's creepyguardian did not encourage exercise, so naturally I was as fit as I had ever been in my life.

'He can't get through the gates,' I said. I bent over her, resting my head on her shoulder blade. We sat like that for long minutes. The soldiers shouted beyond the gates.

They couldn't get through. And with any luck they'd kill Maldwyn.

'We can't stay here forever,' Elisabeth said.

'Neither can they,' I said.

'Don't make me go back through that Portal, Emer.'

I didn't reply.

We caught our breath. There was a new voice beyond the gates. The soldiers had stopped shouting. It was a woman speaking, her voice low and confident. The soldiers cheered.

The gates began to open.

Elisabeth and I scrambled to our feet and ran for our lives. I didn't look back. The soldiers were close behind us. I could even hear them breathing.

As we gained the final chamber where the Portal stood, a streak of lightning sparked through the corridor and struck Elisabeth in the back. She arched and stopped like she'd been pulled backwards by a string, then she fell forward, her hands raised, like the string had been cut.

I turned to fling fire at Maldwyn. The fireball had already left my hand by the time I realised it wasn't Maldwyn who had sparked lightning at my sister. It was a woman, one who looked so much like me she might have been my own reflection in 20 years' time. But I had never looked like that.

Her white gown and silver cloak still swirled from the winds caused by magic. Red hair was piled into a roll on the top of her head surrounded by a silver crown that sparkled with diamonds. It could only be the White Queen.

We were dead, yeah. We were dead. The White Queen was the only person in the world allowed to use magic, and she was a very, very powerful mage. The whole country saved money on executioners when the Queen could incinerate the guilty with a wave of her hand. All we needed was a good dustpan and brush.

Elisabeth was flat on the floor and I'd just flung fire at the White Queen.

Yeah. Dead. Since I was probably dead anyway, I plucked another fireball and raised my hand ready to throw it.

'Get away from us!' I shouted. 'Or so help me I'll throw it!'

The Queen glared at me. 'You are always so *dramatic*, Emer,' she spat. 'Even now, you're being theatrical.'

The White Queen knew my name? I hardly had time to wonder before the Queen herself threw up her hands and arched backwards, just as Elisabeth had. Behind her, riding in a chariot drawn by a Pegasus, wand pointed at the falling woman still sparkling with lightning, was the Dark Queen. She was dressed all in black and her long red hair flew in the wind as her Pegasus sped closer.

Apparently, she knew me too. I'd spent my life in secrecy and seclusion, changing my name and my guardian every year to avoid detection. When did I get famous? And how did I not know that not only did the White Queen and the Dark Queen look identical, they each looked like they could be my mother?

'Emer!' the rebel Queen shouted, 'get to the Portal! I'll hold her back!' I scrambled to my feet in time to hear her to shout, 'And don't let go of Elisabeth!' just as I grabbed my sister's hand.

We ran towards the deepest part of the Library. A quick glance over my shoulder showed two small armies fighting and the Queens casting magic at one another so fast the air around them blurred with light and wind whipped their cloaks into a frenzy. And behind them, struggling to pass behind the mass of fighting soldiers, was Maldwyn.

I didn't look back again.

We reached the inner chamber. I didn't even slow down. I jumped over a fallen column and dragged Elisabeth with me. She barely made it without tripping. I heard her say my name, but it would have to wait until we were on the other side of the Portal. We ran up the stairs to the dais and I leapt into the Portal.

The colours overwhelmed me, colours and darkness and lightning, brief glimpses of faces and rooms. I pulled Elisabeth behind me, but a sudden jerk pulled her hand from mine. I twisted, even where I was suspended in the swirl of colours and only had time to catch sight of Elisabeth as she was pulled away from me. The White Queen had hold of Elisabeth's other hand and as I struggled to change direction, the two of them retreated out of my sight.

***An excerpt from my debut novel,*
Daughter of a Captive God, *the first
book in The Author's Daughter
Series. Set in the same universe as*
The Night Princess, *it follows Katie as
she learns that not everything is as it
seemed and the world was more
dangerous than she ever knew.***

<u>CHAPTER ONE</u>

When I was twenty-three, my Dad ran away from
home. Given that he was living with my mother I was
sympathetic. Still, I had to go home to help Mum, no matter
how I felt about it. That's what you do. I spent my first day
back home talking to the police and spending a terrible,
terrible time in the morgue identifying a body that looked
enough like my father to fool the casual observer.

That night I lay awake, upstairs in the guesthouse in my parents' backyard. I planned my Dad's funeral. While I was at it I planned my own funeral and listened to the house settle.

I'd never slept in the Guesthouse before. It was a very old building and to give my Dad credit, he'd renovated it thoroughly. It had a big bedroom upstairs with an en-suite with a lounge room and a kitchenette downstairs. They say old buildings make noises as they settle, though you'd think they had enough time to settle in the last century and a half.

There was another noise. That wasn't the house settling.

I swung my legs out of bed. Silly me, I'd packed clothes and soap and deodorant. I hadn't packed a weapon — not that it would do much good, since I didn't know how to use one. Mum had moved all my toys from my old room into the Guesthouse with me, so I picked out the one I could most easily use as a club.

A hobby horse, with a plush fake-fur horse's head on top of a stick might sound like something out of a horror novel, but it's an actual thing. When you're five and pretending you're a knight on horseback it serves well enough as a horse. Now it served well enough as a pointy stick.

I crept downstairs, quiet, quiet, the hobby horse raised in my hand.

There was nothing there. An empty room, kitchen benches clean and tidy, the bank of storage cupboards that lined the back wall… wait. One of the doors wasn't quite shut.

There was another thump. You couldn't miss it. It was inside the cupboard. I braced myself, hobby horse at the ready. The cupboard doors bumped slightly, hiccoughed almost. They burst open with a loud crash.

I took stumbling steps backwards as a slavering, bestial thing shouldered its way out of the splintered remains of the cupboard doors.

It was enormous, looming over me, a Thing of leathery skin and teeth and claws and its breath tasted of things long dead. It lunged towards me and knocked me to the ground, claws digging in to my arm and drawing blood. I screamed in pain and fear and rolled away, the force of my movement ripping my own flesh on the monster's claws.

It caught up to me, roaring in fury as I beat it around the head, swinging the hobby horse with more strength than I knew I possessed. I screamed again, this time in fury. I spun the hobby horse around and drove the sharp end into

the belly of the beast. As it fell it reached out a clawed hand
and dragged me down with it.

The Thing pinned me to the floor. I tried to roll and
scramble away but it drew me back to it. I gagged on the
smell of its breath and fought to free myself. The beast
lowered its head, its teeth ripping my shoulder. I screamed
in horror at the idea that it might torture me, play like a cat
before finally killing me. It lowered its head again and from
that bestial mouth came a sound, a word. My name.

'Katie,' it growled.

*   *   *

Three days before the only person I had to hide from
was the boss. I was gardening, gardening, I say, when the
boss called out from the verandah that there was a phone
call for me. I could have been gone into the bush and not
been found for… well, usually people who go into the bush
aren't found, so I answered the damn phone.

'Yes, Dad?' I said, cradling the phone next to my ear
while I picked dirt out from under my fingernails. It was
only just past sunrise but that's the best time to get started
on garden work. I had to be sure I worked hard and was
seen to work hard. It had been hard for me to get work and

I couldn't afford to lose this job. I had no ID. When I'd asked Mum for my birth certificate she told me that I didn't have one.

'Do I exist?' I'd joked.

'No,' she replied and kept a straight face. So when I ran away I disappeared into the Australian outback and did odd jobs on enormous stations for cash in hand, bed and board.

'Katie, it's Cecilia. I'm so sorry to call-'

'Silly?' I asked. It wasn't my fault I called her Silly. Her name was Cecilia Beally, what else did her mother expect? 'Silly.' I sat down. I sighed into the phone and she sighed on the other end of the line in response.

'I'm sorry, Katie.'

'Don't be sorry. It's just my family I ran away from, not you.'

'Katie, it's about your Dad.'

'Yeah, what?' I rubbed gingerly at my chest. The scars were still fresh and sore, so I poked at them five or six times an hour to see if they were any better yet.

'Katie, your Dad's gone missing.'

I stopped probing the sore spots. 'Missing? He hasn't left the house since I was sixteen. Has Mum checked behind the lounge?'

'Katie!'

'Sorry.' There weren't many people on earth I'd say that for, and even for Silly it was a recalcitrant mumble.

'Katie, your Mum needs help.'

'Can you stop saying my name like that? It's not Simon Says. Has Mum even *tried* to do anything or has she been too busy weeping into a lace hankie and complaining that Sherlock Holmes hasn't been any help at all.' I reached into my jeans pocket and pulled out a crumpled scrap of paper. It was my bucket list, treated with no more respect than it deserved.

'Katie, you know your Mum…'

'I know my Mum lost her grip long before she sent me away to that stupid boarding school.' *Go cross country walking (start with a small country).*

'Bunty sounded nice. You were always so mean about her in your letters.'

'I didn't want another best friend. And Mum didn't want me so I'm not going back and that's final.' *See a glacier before they all disappear.*

'Um, Katie…?'

Oh, God. 'Yes, Silly?'

'I've already driven up to get you. I'm in Collarenebri. I stayed at the pub last night. I just need directions to the property.' *To Do: Live longer.*

I pursed my lips. Now I was screwed, wasn't I? What else could I do? She'd already come eight hundred odd kays, she might as well come the last twenty kays from town. When I got off the phone I threw the bucket list away. There was no point, really.

It's not the number of breaths that you take, they say, but the number of moments that take your breath away. They say. Smug bastards. You don't say things like that when you've got cancer. It was only after the mastectomy they told me that I was doomed anyway. More important than that, I only had fifty bucks in my account. You can't get far on fifty bucks.

Silly had been my best friend since her parents moved in next door when we were three. By the time we'd driven through eight hundred kays of the picturesque Australian countryside, four hundred of which passed while I tried to wedge a towel in the window so I didn't burn to a crisp, I was ready to end our friendship in a number of creative ways. All methods were going to be permanent, but the hotter the sun got, the more reasonable they sounded.

'Why didn't you tell me your air-con was broken?' I asked, as we passed through Narromine.

Silly had her eyes fixed on the road. There were only two or three turns in the road between Sydney and Collarenebri so I understood why it took her full attention.

'Oh, um, you know…'

'Silly, it must be fifty degrees outside! And it's *hotter* in the car! We're going to die.' Or at least, one of us is going to die.

'I hate taking the car to a mechanic. They always overcharge me. They get this look in their eyes when they see me coming.'

'You could try standing up for yourself.'

'Oh, um… I know…'

Yes, I knew.

As we got to Come-by-Chance (and, as they say, went like blazes) I realised that the sun had shifted. I yanked the towel down from the window and wound it down. The sun was shining in Silly's window now. I was unforgivably smug all the way to Penrith.

When we pulled up outside the house I seriously considered not getting out of the car. I might have stayed there a lot longer if it hadn't been so ready to murder my best friend. Anyway, I felt disgusting, like a sweaty, smelly, dishevelled remnant of what had once been a woman and at the very least, if I got out of the car, I might be allowed to shower.

Mum met us at the door. Weeping. I said 'There, there, Mum,' and lugged my bags inside.

'I'll see you tomorrow, Katie,' Silly said from the doorway. 'Bye, Mrs Elliot.'

'Silly don't you dare leave me here-' but she was already halfway down the path.

I dumped my bags in the lounge room.

'Oh, Katie, darling,' Mum said damply, 'remember when you were a little girl? You used to play behind that lounge for ages.'

'Dad told me I'd be chased by an army of the undead if I came out.'

'Him and his silly stories.' She pressed the predictably lacy and realistically damp hankie to her breast.

'There's sure... *something*... to be said for being the daughter of a horror writer.'

'It was good practice, anyway,' she said. 'I'll put the kettle on.'

Good practice? It would be nice if she'd hold it together for just a few minutes until I caught my breath but I knew I was asking too much. That was why I was here, wasn't it? I sighed and followed her.

'Make the tea would you, darling?' Mum said when I

joined her in the kitchen. 'I've got Atahualpa and eighty thousand Mayan soldiers in the Guesthouse and I want to make sure that Mrs Danvers isn't feeling too overwhelmed.'

'Sure thing, Mum.' This wasn't the weirdest thing she'd ever said to me, so whatever, right? 'Are Jenny and Lance staying?' They were the only guests I'd ever seen in the Guesthouse. It's not like a business run by my mother would ever do a roaring trade.

'No, darling.' Mum came over and ruffled my hair, which I *despised*. 'They only come at Christmas. Open a packet of biscuits if you like. They're... well, they're somewhere.'

The biscuits were in the cutlery drawer, but they were chocolate coated, so I was OK with it.

I'd had my tea and biscuits and I was upstairs, unpacking, when the police officers knocked on the door.

Mum was downstairs so I let her answer the door but I stood near the top of the stairs so I could eavesdrop.

'Mrs Elliot, we've got some news about your husband,' a man said and I was down the stairs in time to see Mum's confused look.

'Do I know you?' she asked.

'He's a policeman, Mum,' I said. 'That's probably

as much as you need to know.'

There were two police officers, one male, one female. The man looked me up and down and so help me, I did the same to him. Tall and strong and handsome in his uniform, dark hair curling under his hat — but then, I was a wreck of a woman who didn't have breasts and couldn't have children thanks to the cancer treatment. It didn't stop his dark eyes from looking me up and down like I was his new best friend.

'Katie Elliot,' he drawled.

'Am I on a list somewhere?' I asked.

'No.' His face went very bland as he seemed to gather his thoughts. 'You're Mr and Mrs Elliot's daughter. Is your brother at home, too?' The other officer gave him a look and he said, almost as though he was explaining it to her, 'We have news for your whole family, Katie.'

'The whole family *is* right here,' I snapped

'My Ricky's away,' Mum said. She reached into her sleeve to draw out her lacy hankie and dabbed at her eyes. 'He's fighting for King Arthur.'

The officers looked at each other.

'Mrs Elliot,' the woman said, 'can we come in and sit down? We need to have a talk with you.'

'Oh dear!' Mum cried, the hankie still flailing. 'Oh,

dear, I just can't!'

I should probably say here that even though she was a nutter my Mum was still very beautiful. She was pale and lovely and the perfect foil to my dark, handsome father. Even with children old enough to have homes of their own she was still slim and her hair was still a shining blonde. Her eyes were wide and blue and even from behind I could see the officers turn to putty in her hands. The big one reached out a chivalrous arm for her to take.

'Mrs Elliot, let me help you to a chair.'

I rolled my eyes.

'Maybe *I* can help you, officers?' I felt that I should say something before Mum fluttered her eyelashes or fainted. She did both pretty often, but Dad was always there to deal with both. He always knew how to deal with Mum's histrionics and heaven help me, I had no idea. Both officers ignored me.

The officer steered Mum into the lounge room and towards a chair. I was annoyed that he was making himself so at home so I grabbed Mum's other arm just as she started to lower herself into the chair. She ended up being lowered by the policeman on one side and lifted by me on the other. I took a vicious pleasure in seeing a beautiful woman in such an ignominious position. She let out a little squawk.

'Mum, why don't you go lie down and I'll deal with the nice officers,' I said as though to a child. The policeman holding on to Mum gave me a sharp look. He examined my face as though he was making sure he could give a full description of me later. Terrific. They thought Mum was a wilting flower in need of care and protection and I was a suspicious character who should be watched closely.

'She doesn't cope,' I snapped, suddenly furious. I'd been pushed about as far as I could go. I'd run away from home, severed all connection with my family for this very reason. I was sick of always being the sensible one, the strong one, the one to guide my stupid mother through the complexities of the real world. I was sick and exhausted and I wished desperately that just once Mum could deal with this on her own.

'Mrs Elliot needs to be here,' the suspicious policeman said, still giving me that detailed stare.

'Fine!' I flung myself onto the chair next to Mum's. 'Don't blame me if she weeps or faints.' Seating themselves, the police officers regarded us sympathetically. Even the suspicious one looked compassionate. The fight went out of me when I realised what those sympathetic looks meant. Mum was going to faint for sure.

The female officer told us. 'Mrs Elliot, Katie, I'm sorry to have to inform you that we found Mr Elliot's body this morning.'

Body. Oh, God.

Mum went white, but she didn't faint. 'What happened?' she asked in a thin, reedy voice I didn't recognise.

'We found his body in the national park, ma'am,' the kindly officer said.

'What happened, she said,' I snapped.

The officer hesitated. 'It appeared that he was attacked by some kind of animal. We have to wait for the post — mortem to confirm the cause of death.'

If possible Mum went even whiter. She flicked a quick glance at me and up the stairs to Dad's study, as though she expected him to come down and deny the charges. I was too shaken to despise her for it.

Good Cop cleared her throat. 'Ma'am? We're going to need someone to identify the body.'

So help me, I couldn't say a word. Mum said, 'Katie — Katie.'

'Yes, Mum. I'll do it.'

After that the police didn't stay for long. Desperate

for comfort I went to sit next to Mum on the lounge. Despite my best efforts a few tears escaped and I was heartily ashamed of them. Mum cried a few pretty tears but held herself upright until the officers left, like a woman who has discovered her own inner strength for the first time. She closed the door behind them.

Then she fainted.

*　　　　*　　　　*

A morgue is not a nice place to be. Trust me, you only want to visit one once. And there are so *many* reasons why you don't want to be in a position to notice details. Everything was very clinical, sort of like a hospital. But you know how hospitals try and make themselves look cheerful and restful? The morgue doesn't have to impress anyone. The guy at the desk didn't make any effort, either.

'Jeez, we're really busy at the moment…'

I stared back at him as he sullenly rustled papers. I wanted to identify the body of my father, not get my hair done.

'Yeah, I can imagine that you would be. The dead can be so impatient.'

He looked up at me, trying to see if I was sympathetic and stupid or a smart arse and stupid enough to open my mouth. You pick which one I am.

The idiot wiped his greasy hair away from his face and pulled at his wilted collar. He looked me up and down. I wanted to kick him but the desk was in the way, so I tilted my head — just so — and smiled, just like Mum would have. He decided I was sympathetic and stupid and warmed up to me immediately. 'Yeah, things just have to get done and we're stretched real thin right now. Look, it's just me on, 'cos everyone else has gone home already, would you mind just coming into the cooling room?'

The cooling room. What was my father, preserved meat?

'No, I don't mind,' I lied, disgusted at the idea of my father being in a cooling room. 'I don't want to take up too much of your busy day.' The living can be impatient, too.

The guy led me down a corridor into a room clearly designed for ease of washing down. Linoleum curved up the walls for a few inches, so no… so nothing got caught in the skirting boards. A gurney covered with a cloth was in the middle of the room and I tried not to think what it had been used for. One wall was made up of stainless steel doors, like you see in movies. However, in movies they pull the bodies out of a drawer at a convenient height, which was not to be the case here.

Mr Slimeball checked his list. 'Body's in A7,' he said

to me, as though it meant something. He disengaged the wheel-locks on the gurney with a violent kick and pushed it close to the wall. He took off the cover, revealing a row of rollers, then cranked it up like a jack until the surface of it was higher than my head. Slimeball could barely reach up to open the door.

A small tug pulled out a board, bearing a corpse in a bag.

Air was forced out of my lungs by the grotesqueness of it all and I turned my head away. I couldn't bear it. My father — jerked out of a hole in the wall in a cooling room onto a table that looked like something out of the Inquisition. Slimeball didn't notice — he was lowering the gurney.

'Come have a look,' he said. He wiped his hands on the back of his trousers.

So I went to have a look. The body was badly ravaged. No wonder he was dead. Taking a step closer I looked at the face. It was my father's face, stripped of the soul that enlivened it. He looked different, but it was definitely his face. I stepped closer still and lay my hand on his. He was cold, but it was the last time I would ever touch his hand. 'Goodbye, Dad,' I whispered, the words too precious for Slimeball to hear.

I stroked my finger over the cold hand to find the webbing between thumb and forefinger as I had done so often before. When I was a little girl Dad and I had an accident. He was helping Mum wash up, elbow deep in dishwater while Mum swiped at the plates with a tea towel. I was in the kitchen, too, and reached up to grab a stack of saucepans. They all came clattering down around me. I screamed, and I still remember the crack as one of the saucepans fractured my skull. Dad cried out but I hardly heard anything through the pain in my head and the blood that ran into my eyes.

I passed out, waking up on the kitchen floor with Mum's fingernails digging into my tongue — she was afraid I would swallow it. Five minutes in front of a mirror was enough to teach me that my tongue was attached and could not be swallowed. I was spitting blood when the paramedics arrived. It was years later that I found out the reason behind the scar on my Dad's hand. He'd had a hand full of cutlery when I screamed and his sudden movement had driven a fork right through the webbing on his hand.

A prosaic injury, but a distinctive one. This hand, under my caressing fingers, had no scar. In fact, it was pristine. It might have been a baby's hand. I drew back my hand. This might look like my father, but it wasn't him. I looked closer. Now that I was suspicious I could see that it wasn't really my Dad. Tiny things were wrong — you don't realise how well you know the look of a person until you see those details missing. And yet it looked too much like my father for it to be anyone else.

Who would do this? Who *could* do this? Whoever it was and however it was done, they expected me to just identify the body and go home. They must have gone to a *lot* of effort to do this. They expected the story to end here.

No way was that going to happen. If someone had killed my Dad, then they were going to answer to me.

ABOUT THE AUTHOR

Grace Martin writes fantasy novels and loves to read. Her favourite authors are Sarah J. Maas, Anne McCaffrey and Suzanne Collins. She finds endless inspiration in the world around her and lives in Sydney with an obsessive, abusive and adoring mini cat. Connect with Grace via her website at www.gracemartinauthor.com where you can sign up for her newsletter for exclusive notifications about coming promotions and new releases, or you can follow her on Instagram at www.instagram.com/grace.martin.author or Facebook at www.facebook.com/GraceMartinAuthor/.

COMING SOON FROM GRACE MARTIN

❖ Vengeance: The Umbra Chronicles Book 1

OTHER WORKS BY GRACE MARTIN

❖ Daughter of a Captive God: Book 1 in The
   Author's Daughter Series
❖ The Night Princess

A Game of Starlight and Secrets

Printed in Great Britain
by Amazon